Fire!

Even as the dreaded word reared like a monster inside her head, a thin trickle of smoke crept out of the dark storage room. A deluge of terrifying images of flame, smoke and searing heat threatened to overwhelm her. For a nightmare second, she was back in the midst of scorching heat and roaring flames.

Using all her strength of will, she tore free of the chilling memories. Instead of fleeing, she placed one wobbly step in front of the other and inched toward the storage room. Her nostrils flared at the acrid tang of gasoline and smoke. With a shaking hand, she gripped the door handle and opened the door wider.

A figure burst out of the darkness, crashing into her, knocking her back.

She yelped at the pain of the blow and the shock of falling. A jolt of agony and blinding light as her head hit something hard.

Heavy boots pounded across the tile floor.

Cold air washed over her. And then, darkness.

BITTER LEGACY
is the third romantic suspense C.B. Clark has
published with The Wild Rose Press, Inc.
She has previously written *MY BROTHER'S SINS*
and *CHERISHED SECRETS*.

Bitter Legacy

by

C.B. Clark

Bitter Legacy

Cover Art by *Angela Anderson*

The Wild Rose Press, Inc.
PO Box 708
Adams Basin, NY 14410-0708
Visit us at www.thewildrosepress.com

Publishing History
First Crimson Rose Edition, 2017
Print ISBN 978-1-5092-1488-4
Digital ISBN 978-1-5092-1489-1

Published in the United States of America

Dedication

For Douglas,
my biggest supporter.
Many thanks as well to EL Felder,
my long-suffering editor.
A journey complete.

Chapter 1

Sharla-Jean Bromley had wanted only two things in life—a red dress and her father's death. She'd waited years. Hell, she'd prayed for this moment. Why then, wasn't this a celebration? Why was a ball of acid churning through her stomach? Taking a deep breath, she climbed out of the taxi and smoothed the skirt of her figure-hugging, red, silk dress over her hips.

The crowd of somber mourners stood in clusters on the sweeping steps outside the old stone church under the late-October, overcast sky. The damp air was ripe with the familiar sweet-sour smell of freshly cut Douglas fir. Over the hill behind the church, steam trailed in white plumes from the two lumber-drying kilns at the mill. A wind gusted, marshaling scattered piles of gold and red leaves into the gutter.

Goose bumps riddled her arms, and she fought back a shiver as she strode forward, knees quaking, jostling through the crowd on the wide sidewalk.

A collective gasp filled the air, and her name swept over the mourners in a rising crescendo. "It's her! Sharla-Jean. Big Jim's daughter."

"I can't believe she has the nerve to show up after all these years."

"My God, look what she's wearing!"

"She always was wild."

"Big Jim would roll over in his grave."

1

With each comment, each insult, each condemnation, the layer of ice encircling her heart thickened. The shock and disapproval didn't surprise her. There was no love lost between the people of Renton Falls and Sharla-Jean Bromley. Hadn't been for years. What did surprise her was how much their disapproval bothered her. Like a well-aimed arrow, each snide remark penetrated the armor of her daring red dress.

The lump in her throat thickened, threatening to choke her. She did an about-face and headed back toward the curb, but then she stopped. *What was she doing?* She'd waited too long for this moment to chicken out now. Turning, keeping her gaze fixed at a point in the distance, she ignored the disparaging stares and shouldered through the throng. Tears burned her eyes, but she blinked them back. She'd come here today to bury the past along with her father. Then maybe, just maybe, she could move on.

"She looks like a whore," hissed a piercing voice.

Sharla-Jean met the blazing gaze of a short, pudgy, blonde woman. Her heart lurched at the venom in the woman's stare. She sucked in a breath as a flash of memory washed over her. Betty Ann Jawarski. She'd been Sharla-Jean's best friend all through grade school, the two of them inseparable.

"Why did you come back, Sharla-Jean?" Betty Ann's frizzed hair bobbed in a mass of over-bleached curls around her fleshy face. "You killed your father. Do you know that? The poor man died of a broken heart because of you."

Sharla-Jean stared, immobilized by the woman's scorn.

Betty Ann's red, painted lips twisted into a thin, disapproving line. The furrow between her over-plucked brows deepened. "Well, what do you have to say for yourself?"

Sharla-Jean opened her mouth to finally tell Betty Ann and everyone else who listened with morbid curiosity, the truth about the nightmare seventeen years ago, but the secret was buried too deep, the years of silence too ingrained.

A tall, thin man, his balding head gleaming as the sun peeked from behind dark clouds, stepped forward and placed his arm around Betty Ann's shoulders as if protecting her from something vile. "I told you she was trouble." His mouth twisted in a sneer. "She always was. Seems she still is."

Betty Ann swung back to Sharla-Jean, her hands planted on her wide hips. "Why don't you go back where you came from, where you've been all these years? You don't belong here anymore."

Her words slammed into Sharla-Jean, and she stumbled back a step. *Betty Ann was right. She didn't belong here.* Once again, she wheeled around, desperate to escape the sea of disapproval surrounding her, wanting to run back to her apartment in Portland where no one knew her past, and no one cared.

But once again she recalled why she'd come today. Why she'd tossed everything aside to be here. She dug deep for strength, raised her head high, and climbed the steps of the church. Her legs trembled, and she prayed she wouldn't stumble.

Someone grabbed her arm, stopping her. She tensed, resigned to facing more of Betty Ann's animosity. But the woman holding her wasn't Betty

Ann.

Pauline Rafferty, a warm smile wreathing her lined face, her faded blue eyes filled with compassion, stood on the step below Sharla-Jean. "Hello, Sharla-Jean." Her quiet voice cut through the crowd's muttering. "It's been a long time."

Sharla-Jean's breath whooshed out. "Pauline." She wrapped her arms around the old woman, hugging her tight, and inhaled the familiar scent of lavender. A thousand bittersweet memories assailed her—Pauline teaching her to ride a bike, singing to her when she couldn't sleep, tending to her when she had chicken pox, making her favorite spaghetti and meatballs that time she broke her arm climbing the apple tree in the back yard. Pauline had always been there, through the good times and the bad.

Pauline drew back from the embrace and studied Sharla-Jean. Love shone in her eyes. "You look well, dear. Portland must agree with you."

A few more lines creased Pauline's forehead, and her hair was more gray than auburn, but she looked the same. Sharla-Jean blinked back tears. "You haven't changed a bit."

Pauline chuckled. "You never were a good liar." She pulled Sharla-Jean in for another quick hug. "Oh, it's wonderful to see you, dear. I'm just sorry it has to be under these sad circumstances." She clasped Sharla-Jean's hand. "I'm so sorry about your father."

Before Sharla-Jean could respond, a tall, skeletal man with thick, gray eyebrows shoved past them, knocking Sharla-Jean aside. She stumbled and would have fallen if she hadn't grabbed onto the metal railing. "What the hell?"

The man turned and glared, disapproval radiating off him in waves. "Now why aren't I surprised you're blaspheming in the Lord's House, Sharla-Jean Bromley?" He wrinkled his long, pointed nose and sniffed loudly.

Pauline stepped beside her and jammed her hands on her narrow hips. "Why, George Foster, I'm shocked. Where's your Christian spirit of forgiveness?"

His face paled under her censure, and he opened his mouth to say something, but Pauline, her voice rising over the hum of the crowd, cut him off. "This is Big Jim's daughter. You all know her."

People stopped talking and turned to watch the unfolding scene.

Sharla-Jean's face heated as a small space cleared around her and Pauline, and they became the center of attention. She didn't need Pauline to defend her, but the old woman looked so fierce, Sharla-Jean didn't have the heart to explain her real reason for being there.

Eyes blazing, Pauline stared at each person in the encircling crowd. She placed her arm around Sharla-Jean and drew her to her side. "This young woman was born and raised in this town. No matter what she did, that's in the past. Everyone deserves a second chance. What's important is she's here now to lay her father to rest."

The heavy silence continued, except for the sound of feet shuffling and a smattering of nervous coughs. No one met Pauline's gaze.

A lone male voice called out. "Where's she been all these years? Why didn't she come back when Big Jim needed her?"

A chorus of agreement rippled through the throng.

Pauline released Sharla-Jean and faced the heavyset, dark-haired man with the bushy black beard who'd spoken. Her slight body brimmed with indignation.

In spite of her discomfort, Sharla-Jean bit back a smile. Pauline was like a mother bear protecting her young. These people didn't stand a chance.

"You should be ashamed of yourself, Jim." Pauline shot him a scathing look, and then swung on a frowning woman standing at the front of the crowd. "You too, Mabel." She pinned each person with a stern gaze. "You all should be ashamed. We're here to honor a man we loved and respected. What would Big Jim think? Would he want his daughter treated this way?"

More nervous shuffling, more coughs. One or two people edged away, and then another and another, and the crowd thinned. Several mourners cast sidelong glances at Sharla-Jean, but no one said anything. One old, stooped-shouldered, gray-haired lady even smiled at her.

Sharla-Jean barely noticed. She was too caught up in Pauline's last words. *Would he want his daughter treated this way?* The ball of acid burned its way from her gut to her throat. Her father wouldn't give a shit how the townspeople treated her. You could take that to the bank. She startled when Pauline grasped her arm again.

The stern lines in the old woman's face softened, and tears shone in her eyes. "I'm sorry, dear. I know how hard this is for you."

Sharla-Jean blinked away her own tears. Pauline had always had her back, even when Sharla-Jean had acted out. But nothing Pauline said would change people's low opinions. She deserved their scorn, had expected to revel in it, to use the animosity to fuel her anger and add to her sense of righteous outrage.

Instead, she felt dirty, tawdry in the red dress she'd chosen with such care for today; even her attendance at the funeral was a ridiculous farce. She shouldn't be here. That was more than evident. But she was here now. There was no going back.

She placed her hand on Pauline's shoulder. "Look, I appreciate what you just did, but you don't have to defend me. These people are your friends. I don't want to make this more difficult for you."

Pauline's smile didn't falter, though the sheen of tears glistened in her eyes. "Nonsense. We've been through worse, my girl. Much worse. We'll do this together. Like always."

Sharla-Jean leaned down and hugged the old woman again, shocked at the fragility of her slender, stooped body. Fresh tears stung her eyes at this reminder of the years she'd been away. Her throat thickened. "I love you, Pauline."

Pauline beamed. "Right back at you, kiddo."

A giggle burst from between Sharla-Jean's sealed lips. "Let's do this, then." Clasping Pauline's hand in hers, they strode side by side up the final two steps, into the church, and along the carpeted aisle to her family's front pew.

****

Who dresses like a bombshell for a funeral? Josh Morgan craned his head to watch as the woman in the tight red dress strolled with feline grace through the throng of people. He gulped at the enticing swell of her hips and long, shapely legs ending in ridiculously high heels the same vibrant color as her dress. Thick waves of auburn hair curled over her shoulders, swinging with the seductive sway of her hips. His heart raced at the intriguing set of her shoulders, the graceful slip and slide of her body.

Who was she? He'd only glimpsed her from the back, but he knew with a visceral certainty he'd never seen her before. She wasn't from Renton Falls. He'd lived in town ten years, and he knew pretty much everyone. He'd remember if he'd seen her before.

He studied the tantalizing curve of her backside. Yes, he most certainly would have recalled her. The desire to see her face, to find out if her front matched the beauty promised by her rear view, overwhelmed him. He elbowed through the crowd, straining for another glimpse.

Some idiot grabbed his arm, yanking him to a stop right when he was so near to getting the up-close-and-personal view of her he wanted.

"Did you see her?"

Irritation flooded Josh. He was tempted to brush off the other man's grip, but past experience had taught him the futility of such an action. He blew out a breath and faced J.D. Webster's heavily jowled face. The agitation in the man's eyes surprised him.

James Daniel Webster, senior partner at Webster, McComber, & Friest Associates, the law firm started by the man's grandfather, was also a town councilman. He took his position of prominence in the town of three thousand very seriously. He was also the man responsible for the mill's legal matters. Over long years of practice, J.D. had schooled his face to be as unreadable as a champion poker player. Today his face was flushed, his well-upholstered body bristling with outrage.

Josh's curiosity was piqued, but then he caught a flash of red out of the corner of his eye. *Right. The woman in the red dress.*

"Josh?"

"Hey, J.D., give me a minute." He surveyed the throng of mourners where he'd last seen her. *Where is she?*

"That's her!"

J.D.'s deep baritone reached him through his distraction, but just then the crowd opened up, and there she was. Josh's heart beat faster. A group of four people moved in front of her and blocked his view. *Damn.*

"Josh, are you listening. I told you, that's her."

He frowned. "What? Who?" What was J.D. jabbering about? One more glimpse. That's all he needed, just one more look at the sexy lady in red.

J.D. stepped in front of him, blocking his view.

Josh peered over the shorter man's shoulder. There—a flash of red near the front pew.

J.D. jerked on his arm. "Josh, you're not listening. I tell you, that's her. Sharla-Jean Bromley."

The lawyer had his full attention. "She's here? Where?" He scanned the crowd searching for the woman he'd heard so much about.

J.D.'s body vibrated as he pointed. "There. In the ridiculous red dress. Can you believe her gall? Coming to her father's funeral looking like a floozy."

He heard no more than J.D.'s first words. The woman he'd seen and so admired wearing the exciting red dress was Sharla-Jean Bromley? Impossible. Sharla-Jean Bromley was built like her father—big-boned and stocky, with her father's wiry red hair. He'd seen the resemblance himself in the numerous photos Big Jim had shown him over the years.

The woman he'd been watching, the woman who'd set his senses on fire, was tall and slim, her hair a shimmering fall of curling auburn strands streaked with gold. She didn't look anything like James Bromley. He shot J.D. a quick, sidelong glance. "Are you sure it's her?"

"She's changed, but it's her all right. No mistaking the Bromley looks." J.D. frowned. "And that's Pauline Rafferty with her."

Josh almost laughed at the irony. Just his luck the most attractive woman he'd seen in years happened to be Sharla-Jean Bromley, the woman whom, sight unseen, he'd grown to despise.

"What are you going to do, Josh?" Salacious curiosity gleamed in the old lawyer's eyes.

Josh grimaced. The whole town would be asking themselves the same question by the time the sun set. What *was* he going to do?

No one knew what happened to Sharla-Jean Bromley after she'd run away at the age of sixteen. He'd heard the rumors. She'd been wild. Everyone in town had a story to tell of her escapades, each more shocking than the last. Hell, what could be worse than burning down the lumber mill and putting half the townsfolk out of work? Even so, people might have forgiven her if she hadn't done the unthinkable and broken her father's heart.

Josh's gut clenched. Now, like a bad dream, she'd appeared out of the blue in time to claim her inheritance and ruin all his plans.

A buzz settled over the room. People stood on tiptoe in an attempt to catch a glimpse of Big Jim's notorious daughter. The crowd shifted again, and there she was.

She sat in the front pew, one long, shapely leg crossed over the other, a red high heel dangling from her narrow foot, her face a mask of cool indifference.

A grim smile tightened his mouth. In spite of the complications her unexpected return would certainly cause, he couldn't help but admire her style. She'd made quite an entrance. People would be talking about her for months.

"Josh? Did you hear me? What are you going to do?"

He forced his attention back to J.D. "Do? Why I'm not going to do a thing." He hadn't missed the shocked comments and sneers following her like a pack of ravenous wolves. He chuckled, though the sound came out more hostile than he intended.

J.D.'s eyes widened. "What?"

"I don't have to do anything. Our little Miss Bromley will do it all for us." He patted J.D. on the back. "Nothing to worry about. We'll sit back and wait for her to shoot herself in the foot." He studied the woman in question.

She shifted and their gazes met—her eyes a cool, mysterious green framed by thick, dark lashes.

He sucked in a breath.

Her full lips, brilliantly red in her pale face, quirked in a knowing smile.

He couldn't help smiling back. Hell, he was only human, and she was one damn good-looking woman. But then he considered who she was, and his jaw tightened, his teeth clenching. He glared, not bothering to hide his anger and derision.

Her eyes widened, and her smile vanished. A furrow formed between her elegant brows. She stared for a second more, and then faced the front of the church, her posture stiff and unyielding.

He swallowed the sour taste of guilt. He hadn't done anything anyone else in town hadn't already done. Why wouldn't he be angry with her? She was Big Jim's daughter, and as such, now part owner of Bromley Forest Products.

He'd worked hard to get where he was, put in countless long days struggling to keep Bromley running at a profit even when the market took a dive last year. Harder still this past year when Big Jim was too ill to run the mill. It was now a state-of-the-art business running efficiently and smoothly, bringing in a tidy profit for the shareholders.

He gritted his teeth until his jaw ached. He'd be damned if he'd turn half of Bromley Forest Products over to this so-called daughter of Big Jim's. Who did she think she was, showing up after all these years? After all the hurt she'd caused her father? Did she honestly think she could waltz back into town and take over the company? Well, if she did, she had a fight ahead of her, one hell of a fight. He wasn't going to roll over and play dead.

No damn way.

Chapter 2

The large, executive office on the fourth floor of Webster, McComber, & Friest Associates was the last place Sharla-Jean wanted to be. Yet here she was. Her foot tapped on the glossy wood floor in time to the antique clock ticking on the cream-colored wall. A dull ache throbbed in her temple, threatening to turn into a full-blown migraine.

Attending the reading of her father's will hadn't been in her plans. She smoothed her snug-fitting dress over her hips. Showing up at his funeral wearing this wicked red dress should have been enough. But Pauline had insisted, and after the old woman's staunch defense at the funeral, Sharla-Jean couldn't refuse.

She wrinkled her brow. Nothing had changed. Even after all these years, the people in town didn't understand. Everyone revered her father as if he were some sort of saint. Somehow he'd managed to earn their undying loyalty. Her mouth tightened. If only they'd known the real man, the one beneath the guise of good-natured benevolence. The man she knew so well.

Muted footsteps sounded in the hall outside the office, and her fingers tightened on the arms of her chair, her nails digging into the soft, leather upholstery. She sat up straighter and pasted what she hoped was a confident smile on her face.

The door swung open, and the man who'd caught

her attention at the funeral stood framed in the open doorway.

Her heart skipped a beat. All too well she recalled how when their gazes locked across the sea of mourners in the church; she'd been struck lightheaded, pinned under the heat of his piercing gaze, and his slow, appreciative grin. But then the color of his eyes had changed in an instant from smoldering charcoal to icy black.

The same chilled black they now reflected as he examined her as if she were a particularly nasty specimen of bug who'd crawled out of his shower drain. Seconds ticked by before he closed the door behind him and stalked to a leather chair across from her and sat down.

Who was he? Why was he there? More to the point, why did his dislike of her feel so personal?

Each tick of the clock was louder than the previous one as his scrutiny continued unabated.

Did he ever blink? She fought the urge to tug her dress over her knees and tightened her lips. Damn it. She was not going to be the first to break the uneasy silence.

"Do you want something to drink? Coffee? Water?"

The unexpected sound of his voice, a rich, deep baritone, washed over her like a warm bath. "Uh, no, I'm good."

He arched an eyebrow.

She winced at her choice of words. No one in this town would ever say *she* was good.

"J.D. should be here any minute." He withdrew his cell phone and proceeded to ignore her as he texted a message.

Rude as his behavior was, his fixation on his phone allowed her to observe him. The light from the brass lamp on the nearby desk accented the stark planes of his face. Sharp cheekbones and a square jaw lent his face a handsome ruggedness. Even under his well-tailored, dark suit, his firmly muscled body looked hard and unyielding. His hands were broad, the backs tanned and sprinkled with fine dark hairs. His mop of unruly, dark-brown hair reached the collar of his pristine white shirt. A stray curl fell across his forehead. Although, his lips were sealed tight, a pulse throbbed in his jaw, belying his surface calm.

Good. He wasn't as unmoved by this situation as he appeared.

The silence between them thickened and coiled as if it were a living beast.

Who was he? Why was he here? She had to know. "Are you a lawyer? Are you working with Mr. Webster?" The even coolness of her voice surprised her.

He continued to type on his phone, his thick thumbs flying across the tiny keys.

She pursed her lips. "Well? Who are you?"

He stopped his incessant tapping and scorched her with a scathing look. The corners of his full mouth tightened and he leaned forward. "Does it matter? I know who you are. I know *all* about you, Sharla-Jean."

She stiffened at the venom in his voice. "Really? And what exactly do you think you know, because I don't know a damn thing about you." She drew a quick breath and continued. "Why are you here anyway? This is a private meeting. Who invited you?"

His dark eyes hardened, but incredibly, the corners of his mouth twitched, as if he fought back a smile.

What the hell? She hadn't said anything humorous. "Look, I'm sick to death of this whole macho thing you have going on. You don't like me. You couldn't be more obvious." She brushed her hair off her shoulders. "I don't really care what you think of me. But I'll ask you one more time. Who are you, and why are you at the reading of my father's will?"

His eyes blazed. "You're a piece of work, aren't you?" Twin patches of red blossomed on his rugged cheeks. "I can't believe your father had so much faith in you. Seems pretty obvious all the stories are true. You were a spoiled brat, desperate to do anything to get your father's attention. When smoking, drinking and running wild didn't do the job, you set fire to his lumber mill." His derisive gaze slid over her from head to toe, settling on the bodice of her dress where a considerable expanse of cleavage was exposed. "Looks to me like you haven't changed."

She winced as each barb struck home. She opened her mouth to defend herself, but no sound emerged, and she sat frozen beneath his onslaught.

"Tell me," he sneered, lowering his voice, enunciating each word as if he were speaking to a child, "before you set the fire, did you even consider how losing the mill would affect so many people's lives? How did you think the employees were going to feed their families?"

The unfairness of his accusation rocketed through her, and she shot to her feet. "You don't know anything, not a damn thing. Did you or anyone else in this town stop to ask why I would set fire to Bromley

Forest Products? What I would gain?" Unable to face the contempt on his face, she stormed across the room toward the door, determined to get out of the office and away from him.

"So tell me what really happened. I'm listening."

His quiet voice, filled not with his earlier anger, but a note of compassion, seeped through her turmoil. She removed her hand from the door handle and swung toward him. For a second—the briefest heartbeat—she wanted to tell him, to finally reveal the truth. But she shook her head. "You wouldn't understand. You're just like everyone else. You think my father was wonderful, and I'm the devil who burned down his mill, snuck away in the middle of the night, and broke his heart."

"I pictured you many ways, Sharla-Jean, but never as a coward." He arched a dark brow. "Anyone who'd wear that red dress to her father's funeral isn't frightened of anything."

She sagged against the door, her back pressed to the cool wood. "You don't know what my life was like. He wasn't the man you knew, not by a long shot."

"I know he was a good man. I know he loved you."

She laughed, the sound brittle. "If he loved me so much, why did he treat me the way he did? Why didn't he believe me when I told him what happened the night of the mill fire? Why didn't he help me? Did he tell you he was reeling drunk and driving the car when he killed my mother?" She jammed her fist in her mouth, stopping the flow of heated words. Tears stung her eyes, and she blinked them back. What the hell was she doing telling this stranger all her secrets?

"He hurt you. I understand. He never forgave himself for the accident."

The compassion in his voice was the last straw. She could either break down in tears or get angry. She chose the latter. Pushing off the door, she threw back her shoulders. "I don't need or want your damn pity." Again she grasped the door handle. "This was a mistake. I'm outta here."

And again, his words halted her escape. "What's the matter? Are you afraid to find out what your father left you? Are you afraid to find out the truth?"

She snorted.

"Isn't that why you're here? To claim your inheritance?"

Her mouth twisted in a bitter smile. "My inheritance? Not likely. My father didn't leave me a damn thing."

"What if you're wrong? What if he left you the mill? What would you do?"

She sucked in a steadying breath. "That won't be an issue."

"Are you sure?"

She frowned. Why was he grilling her? This wasn't any of his business. He wasn't a secretary or an assistant, and he certainly didn't look like any lawyer she'd ever seen. His tailored suit, starched white shirt, red power tie, and shiny black shoes were expensive, but at odds with his shaggy hair and large, rough hands. He sat stiff and tense as if he weren't used to wearing such formal attire.

"So, now you know why I'm here, what about you?" she asked. "What's your interest in my father's estate?"

Before he could answer, the door opened and J.D. Webster burst into the room.

"Sorry I'm late." The portly, middle-aged man hurried across the room and lowered himself with a heavy exhalation of breath onto the large, leather chair behind the mahogany desk. He studied her and the irritating stranger through the thick lenses of his gold-rimmed glasses. "I'm pleased you're both here. I apologize for my tardiness. Something arose at the last minute." He unlocked the snap of his leather briefcase and removed a sheaf of papers. He glanced at her. "Why don't you sit down, Sharla-Jean and we'll get right to the reading of the will?"

She didn't budge. "Why is *he* here?" She pointed toward the handsome stranger.

"Oh, I'm sorry. I assumed…" J.D. coughed. "Allow me to make introductions. Sharla-Jean Bromley meet Josh Morgan. Josh, this is Big Jim's daughter."

So the man did have a name. She fought back a shudder as his cold, dark gaze settled on her. "Look, I don't know what's going on." She faced J.D. "I'm here only because your secretary informed me I needed to sign some papers." Glancing significantly at the clock on the wall, she prompted him. "Let's get this over with." Retracing her steps to the chair she'd earlier vacated, she sat down, crossed her legs, and sat back in the chair as if her heart weren't threatening to explode out of her chest. Her fingers drummed a rapid tattoo on the chair arms.

"She's right, J.D. The sooner we get this over with, the better for everyone," said Morgan.

The lawyer tugged a white handkerchief from his pocket and mopped his gleaming brow. "I suppose you're right." He rustled through the papers he held and removed one. His gaze met hers. "As you know, I've been your father's lawyer since he started Bromley Forest Products."

A fresh burst of anger fired through her. J.D. Webster had often come to the house to discuss business with her father. He'd been there after her mother died. His efforts had allowed her father to escape unscathed from any criminal charges after the car crash that resulted in her mother's untimely death. An acrid taste filled her mouth. "I remember."

The lines etched on either side of his full mouth deepened, but he nodded and lowered his eyes and scanned the paper in front of him and began to read.

She forced herself to concentrate as he spoke the usual legalese lawyers are so comfortable with, but which was meaningless gibberish to the layman. In spite of Josh Morgan's relaxed posture, she wasn't fooled. A deep furrow carved between his brows, and the twitching in his jaw sped up. If he kept on grinding his teeth, he'd crack a few molars.

Their gazes met, and she choked as if the air had been sucked out of the room. His predatory gleam set her on edge. *Why the hell was he here?* She still didn't know. She bit down on her bottom lip, knowing she wasn't going to like the answer.

"And so, I leave the following bequests…"

Her teeth bit down harder, the pain helping her focus. *Here it comes*. In a few seconds everyone would finally know the truth. Everyone would know how her father cut his only child out of his life and his will. She blinked back the unexpected sting of tears and inhaled a deep, steadying breath, preparing for the lawyer's next words.

"To my daughter, Sharla-Jean Bromley, I leave the

house on Marwood Street and all the contents, all my investments and stocks, and one-half of the shares of Bromley Forest Products."

J.D. paused and studied her as if assessing the impact of his words.

Her eyes widened. "What? He...le...left me...everything?" Heat flared in her cheeks at the painful, halting words. *Not now. Not in front of* him. She'd worked too hard to overcome her childhood stuttering. She met Morgan's cold, unreadable expression and shivered. She opened her mouth to ask J.D. to repeat what he'd said, but her tongue refused to form anything but a painful, agonizing, "Bu...bu...bu..." *Turtle talk. Turtle talk.* Her speech therapist's mantra to stop her stuttering ran through her mind. *Slow down, take a breath. Turtle talk.* She tried again. "J...J...J.D., do...do you mean to tell me my father left everything to...to...me, the...the house, his investments and Bromley Forest Products?" This was too much to take in. She'd detested her father. Hell, she'd run away and hadn't contacted him again, nursing a hatred that ran deep and strong. She'd come here today just so she could prove to everyone what he was really like. But now—

The lawyer coughed and dabbed his brow. "Well, he didn't exactly leave you *everything*." He twisted toward the other man in the room and shrugged before he swung back.

"What...what do you mean?" she asked. "You said he left me the house and the mill. What else is there?"

The lawyer shifted in his seat, crossing and re-crossing his thick thighs. The papers he held rustled. He opened his mouth to reply, but was cut off when Josh

Morgan interrupted.

"I also own half the shares of Bromley Forest Products." His dark eyes pierced her, his mouth set in a firm, uncompromising line.

She furrowed her brow. "You own half the mill?"

"Big Jim left me half his shares in Bromley Forest Products."

He was a beneficiary? "Why would he leave you anything?" She shook her head. "He'd never leave his most-prized possession to a stranger."

His tanned skin tightened over prominent cheekbones. "Big Jim and I were friends, close friends." He smiled coldly, the light never extending to his eyes. "But you'd know how close we were if you'd ever bothered to visit him."

Once again, the need to defend herself flared to life, but she resisted. What did she care if her father left his precious mill to this arrogant lout? Hell, he could have her half, for all she cared. She wanted nothing to do with her father, the mill, or this damn town. "Well, lucky you, Mr. Morgan. My father made you a very wealthy man." She gathered her purse and rose to her feet.

"Er, Sharla-Jean, I'm afraid we're not finished," J.D. said.

"What do you mean, 'we're not finished'?" Her head started pounding.

J.D. eyed Morgan and then her. The papers in his hand rustled. He coughed into his handkerchief.

"Well?" she demanded, desperate for this to be over with so she could leave.

J.D. pushed to his feet with a grunt and strode over to the window and perused the scene outside as if he needed time to find the words for what he was going to say next.

"J.D.?" Morgan frowned. "What else is in Big Jim's will?"

"There's something you both need to know."

Her stomach twisted in knots, and her need to flee amped up a few dozen notches. "Come on, Mr. Webster, this has taken long enough."

J.D. wheeled around and faced them, his eyes wary behind his thick lenses. "The will states in order for the ownership of the mill to be finalized, certain conditions must be met."

"Conditions?" Morgan shook his head slowly. "What the hell are you talking about, J.D.? What sort of damned conditions?"

J.D. blew out a breath. "You, Sharla-Jean, and you, Josh, must work together to manage the mill for one full year."

"Together?" She fought to get the word out.

The lawyer nodded. "You must both work at Bromley Forest Products for twelve consecutive months. If, for whatever reason, one of you fails to do so, the company will be sold to Remington River Industries at fair market value. The money from the sale will be split between several of your mother's distant relations and a variety of charities Big Jim supported. Neither you, nor Josh, will receive a penny."

He paused and inhaled another deep breath. "On the other hand, if you successfully complete the year together, the shares in the company will be split equally between you. You may do as you wish with your own shares. You can sell them, keep them, whatever."

Silence filled the room.

"Let me get this straight." Her voice was halting. "My father left me half of Bromley Forest Products, but I have to stay here and manage the mill. I can't sell the business for a year."

J.D. nodded.

"And if I walk away, this"—she pointed at Morgan—"this *person* gets nothing?"

J.D. nodded again. "That about sums up the situation."

In spite of her shock, she almost smiled. How like her father to manipulate her from beyond the grave. He must be laughing his head off in whichever of the nine fiery circles of Hell he currently inhabited. She studied Morgan. He didn't look any happier than she was. At last, something they agreed on. But then he spoke, and her anger at her father found a new home.

"What the hell?" Morgan exploded, vaulting out of his chair, glaring at J.D. "This is insane. Big Jim would never sell the mill, especially to Remington River. They've been trying to buy our mill for years, but Big Jim knew they only want access to our timber licenses. Once they have those, they'll log all the trees and ship the logs to one of *their* mills to be processed. They'll shut down the mill here in Renton Falls."

"I'm sorry, Josh." J.D. spread his hands before him in a placating manner. "I tried to dissuade Big Jim from installing these stipulations in his will, but he was adamant. As his lawyer and his executor, my legal duty is to see his wishes are fulfilled accordingly." He heaved another heavy breath. "Of course, there is another option. You can choose to work with Ms. Bromley for the required year. After the year is up, the mill will be yours to do with as you will."

Josh stomped across the office, his hands clenched at his sides, his body vibrating beneath his form-fitting suit. He stopped mere inches from J.D. "Well you'd better remember who pays your bills and find a loophole. No way in hell I'm working with *her.* She doesn't give a damn about the mill or Renton Falls."

Fury burned low in her belly. What was his problem? Did he think she wanted this? He was right, though. She didn't give a damn about the mill. She didn't want any part of the company or anything else of her father's. She'd come back to Renton Falls for one reason and one reason only: to lay the ghosts to rest. Being saddled with a lumber mill was not her idea of freedom. The mill would be a constant reminder of her father.

She faced Morgan, a tight smile forming on her lips. "Well, Mr. Morgan, I'm going to make your day. You don't have to work with me." She whirled about to J.D. "Go ahead and sell the mill to Remington River."

"Don't be foolish, Sharla-Jean." J.D. furiously polished his glasses with a cloth he'd yanked from his suit pocket. "Think what you're saying. Bromley Forest Products is worth millions. Your shares alone will make you a very wealthy woman. You don't want to throw away that kind of money."

"Oh, but I do." She spun toward the door. "I most definitely do."

"This is fucking bullshit," Morgan shouted after her.

The force of his outrage staggered her, and she stumbled back a step.

He strode toward her until they were nose to nose and glared down at her. His cinnamon-scented breath fanned her face. "Because you're holding a childish grudge against your father, you're going to destroy this town. Do you have any idea what Bromley Forest Products means to Renton Falls? Do you know how many people count on the mill for their livelihood?" He wiped his mouth with the sleeve of his jacket, his eyes shooting venom. "You don't give a damn about this town. You never did."

She reeled back from his fury. Of course she knew what closing the mill would do to Renton Falls. Without its main employer, people would move away, and Renton Falls would become another ghost town. But was that her problem? This town had turned its back on her years ago. She didn't owe Renton Falls or any of its inhabitants a damn thing. "You're right, Morgan," she bit off. "You and this town can go to hell for all I care."

J.D. hurried to stand between them. "Easy now, you two." His voice was placating. "Let's not be hasty. This is a big decision. Both of you need to take some time to calm down and think about this. You're intelligent people. You'll work this out."

Josh snorted, his opinion of her intelligence clear.

She clenched her fists, her nails digging into her palms. Hatred for her father burned like a hot coal in her stomach. This debacle was his damn fault. He'd placed her in an impossible position. She'd spent the past seventeen years trying to forget Bromley Forest Products and Renton Falls and all the awful memories. This trip was supposed to end her acrimony, free her once and for all from the overriding anguish of an unceasing stream of all-too-vivid nightmares.

She didn't need time to think. She was leaving

town…today. Taking a deep breath, she faced J.D. "Send the details of the will to the house. I want to look them over before I decide anything." She covered her mouth with her hands to stop the words, but it was too late. They hovered in the air like condemning ghouls. *What the hell?*

The clock ticked, loud in the hushed silence.

"Does this mean you're going to stay and work with me at the mill?" Josh's mouth twisted as if he'd bitten into something sour. "Just so you know, I won't allow you to ruin the business. Your father and I worked too damn hard to make the mill a success."

She opened her mouth to tell him she had no intention of working with him, but once again some perverse devil had her saying words she never imagined she'd utter in a million years. "I had planned to leave today, but—" She paused, forcing a smile to her stiff lips. "I think I'll stick around. Things are starting to get interesting."

What the hell was she thinking? She'd spent the past ten years working as a preschool teacher. She didn't know anything about running a lumber mill. She hated this town and the narrow-minded bigots who lived here. Most importantly, staying and managing the mill would mean working with Morgan. But the shock on Josh Morgan's face more than made up for her unease. She grinned and swept out of the room, slamming the door behind her.

****

Josh stared at the closed door and waited for his heart to stop pounding. Acid churned in his gut. He clenched his hands at his sides, fighting the urge to slam his fist into the wall.

Sharla-Jean Bromley was one hell of a piece of work. Just because she had the face of an angel and a body a man dreamed about, she figured she could waltz back into town and act like she was better than everyone else. She hadn't blinked an eye when J.D. told her of her father's bequests. As if being half owner of a major lumber mill was no big deal.

What about the stipulation to remain in Renton Falls and run the mill? With him? For an entire year? Big Jim must have been flying high on his pain meds when he'd come up with that crazy idea. What the hell did she know about running a lumber operation, or any other sort of business?

The stories about her were true. She didn't give a damn about her father or the mill, and she sure as hell didn't care about this town. Oh, she was good, very good. She'd actually had him feeling sorry for her with her haunting, luminous eyes, delicate beauty, and oh-so-sad tale. He ground his teeth together until his jaw ached.

"Er, Josh? Are you all right?"

J.D.'s concerned voice cut through his outrage. "I'm fine," Josh ground out. "Just fucking dandy."

"At least she's thinking about remaining in Renton Falls." J.D. busied himself stuffing the legal papers in his briefcase. "I was sure once she heard the conditions of her father's will, she'd head back to Portland as soon as possible."

Josh's hands ached from being squeezed so tight. "You're not serious? Of course she's gonna stick around. There's no way she'd walk away and give up all that money. Why do you think she came back?" He inhaled a breath to expound further on his intense dislike of Big Jim's daughter, when the door swung open with a bang, and the object of his anger stood in the doorway. Her tight, red silk dress looked as if it had been painted on her shapely body. Beneath the short skirt, her legs were impossibly long. She was quite a package. Too bad a cold heart beat beneath the fancy wrapping.

She smiled coolly. "Sorry, to interrupt, gentlemen. Mr. Webster, I forgot to ask if there were any other bequests in my father's will."

J.D.'s mouth opened and closed like a fish out of water.

"What?" Josh snarled. "Your father didn't leave you enough? You're back looking for more?"

She ignored him. "J.D., did my father leave anything to his housekeeper, Pauline Rafferty?"

"Yes, yes, of course he did. He bequeathed her more than enough money to see her comfortably settled for the rest of her life."

"What about the mill employees?"

"Each employee will receive a settlement commensurate with their length of employment. Your father also left sizable donations to the town and various charities. The details are all in the report I'll send over."

She nodded as if satisfied with his answers, and without another word, she about-faced and stepped into the hall, and closed the door silently behind her.

The ticktock of the clock and the distant rumble of traffic four floors below filled the office.

"Well, that was interesting," J.D. said.

Josh nodded in agreement. Maybe there was a shred of decency in dear Ms. Bromley. He snorted.

Nah. She'd come back to town for one reason and one reason only: to get what she figured she had coming. He regarded J.D. "So, what's our next step?"

The lawyer shrugged. "I don't know. If she actually stays, you'll have to try your best to run the mill with her."

Josh spewed a stream of curses.

J.D. frowned but calmly continued polishing the lenses of his glasses. "There's no other option. If she leaves, you lose everything."

"But what if she does decide to stay? What will her decision mean to the mill?"

J.D. shook his head. "I don't know, Josh. As much as we don't like what's going on, she has every right to claim her half of the business." He eyed Josh, his brow furrowed. "I would have figured you'd be relieved she's considering staying. If she doesn't, you lose the mill."

"This is a game to her." Once again, Josh's hands curled into fists. "She wants to get back at her father. What better way than to destroy his life's work? She'll run the company into the ground." He rubbed his temples. "Do you think she'll let me buy her out? The bank might give me a loan, and I can—"

J.D. shook his head, cutting him off. "Won't work. The will clearly states the two of you have to work together for a full year before either of you can sell your half."

Josh threaded his fingers through his hair. He had to figure a way out of this mess. He'd worked too hard to roll over and play nice with the lady and watch her destroy everything he and Big Jim had worked for. He jolted upright as an idea popped into his head. "That's it!" For the first time since he'd noticed Sharla-Jean Bromley at Big Jim's funeral, hope filled his heart. He spun on his heels and strode toward the office door.

J.D. called after him. "Where are you going?"

"To convince the bitch to stay."

"Josh, be careful. Don't do anything you'll regret. If she agrees to remain in Renton Falls and manage the mill with you, you two will have to work together."

"Don't worry. I'll do what I have to do to save the mill." He swept out of the office and down the hall, anger fueling his steps.

Chapter 3

The rich, oaky smell of the cheerful, crackling fire in the marble-fronted fireplace permeated the room as Sharla-Jean removed another paper from the thick file on the coffee table. She rubbed her eyes and yawned. It had been a long day. First, confronting the townspeople's animosity and derision at the funeral, and then the reading of her father's will with all its shocking revelations.

The file J.D. Webster had promised arrived by messenger a few hours ago. She'd been busy ever since reading the thick stack of papers, sifting through the volumes of unintelligible legal jargon, but she was no closer to understanding why her father had included such ridiculous terms in his will, or why he'd left her anything at all. True, she was his only living blood relative, but after how things had ended between them, she'd assumed he'd written her off long ago. Her father had been a cold-hearted bastard who'd murdered his wife, ignored his only child when she'd needed him most, and betrayed her in the deepest, most painful way.

"Are you still reading those papers?" Pauline hovered in the doorway.

Sharla-Jean heaved a sigh and sagged back against the cushions. "There's a lot to go through."

"Your father's estate was vast. He invested in

numerous high-end stocks."

"All he cared about was making money." She tossed the paper aside.

Pauline crossed the room and sat on the couch beside her, pressing Sharla-Jean's cold hand between her warm ones. "After your mother died, your father's business was his life." She let out a breath. "In the end, he was a very lonely man."

"That was his choice."

Pauline's gaze met hers.

Sharla-Jean flinched at the sorrow in the faded depths of Pauline's eyes. Pauline had cared deeply for Big Jim and had stood by him all these years. "I'm sorry, Pauline. I don't mean to hurt you. I know you miss him. It's just…just…" her voice trailed off as she struggled to find the words to express her anger and resentment at the man who'd been her father.

Pauline patted her hand. "It's okay, love. This is a very trying time for you as well. You've just lost your father, and you have unsettled emotions to sort through." She rose and smiled gently. "You're like him, you know. You're strong and smart. You'll figure this out."

The tip of Sharla-Jean's tongue burned with the need to deny Pauline's claim. She was nothing like her father. Nothing at all. But she didn't want to cause the old woman any more pain. Besides, nothing she said would change Pauline's opinion of Big Jim Bromley. She cleared her throat. "What's the story on Josh Morgan?"

"What do you want to know?"

"Everything. Who is he? I mean, how did he come to inherit half the mill? If they were so close, why didn't my father leave him the entire mill? Why go through all this?" She pointed at the stack of papers.

"Josh arrived in town several years ago and started at the mill as a laborer on the green chain. He was a hard worker, and your father liked him. Soon Josh was his right-hand man."

"That's it? He's a good worker so my father decided to leave him so much?"

"Oh, there's more. Much more, but you'll have to ask Josh yourself." Pauline patted her hair and then fussed with collar of her white, silk blouse. "I have to get going, or I'm going to be late for the movie." She smoothed the wrinkles out of her wool skirt. "I'm meeting Doris McPhee. She'll be a mass of raw nerves if I keep her waiting in the lobby again."

"But—"

"I'm sorry, dear, I really do have to run. We'll talk later." She hurried toward the door, but then paused and called over her shoulder. "Some things are better if you find them out for yourself." With the enigmatic comment hanging in the air, she walked out of the room, leaving Sharla-Jean staring after her.

The doorbell pealed and voices sounded in the front hall. Glancing down at her baggy, gray sweat pants and comfortable sweatshirt, she winced. Over the course of the long afternoon, several strands of hair had escaped the loose ponytail. She hoped Pauline turned the visitor away. She wasn't dressed for company. A laugh escaped her lips. No need to worry. Whoever was at the front door wasn't here to see her. No one in this town would bother to visit her. Unless they had some rotten tomatoes they wanted to throw.

The front door banged shut, and the murmur of

voices silenced.

Good. Whoever the caller was, he or she had left with Pauline. She picked up the top sheet from the pile of papers on the table and settled in to fight her way through the confusing language of lawyers. Somewhere in this sheaf of legal documents was a clue as to why her father had made his astounding will.

"Those papers won't do you any good."

She jumped at the sound of the deep masculine voice, and leaped to her feet, the papers falling from her lap, scattering across the hardwood floor.

Josh Morgan's broad-shouldered frame filled the doorway. Dressed in snug, faded denim jeans and a dark T-shirt showing off an impressive set of pecs, he was the epitome of virile male. His dark hair was windblown, his cheeks ruddy. His mouth quirked in what could almost be called a smile, but when she peeked at his eyes, she shivered at the cool, assessing gleam in the dark-brown depths.

Her hands shook as she smoothed them over her hair in a futile attempt to control the wayward strands. Heat flared up her neck and onto her cheeks. Why hadn't she dressed in nicer clothes instead of her comfortable, but definitely shabby sweats? *Stop this nonsense. You don't give a damn what anyone in this town thinks, remember?* She straightened her shoulders. "What are you doing here?"

"The same thing you're doing. Trying to find a way out of this mess." He pointed to the papers strewn across the floor. "Reading through that crap's a waste of time. I had J.D. on it all afternoon, and he couldn't find a way to break the conditions of the will."

She tried not to flinch under the steel in his gaze. "I

haven't finished reading all the details yet." She stuck out her chin. "Maybe I'll find something your lawyer missed."

His dark brows quirked, but he didn't respond to her challenge. He strolled across the room to an antique oak cabinet against the far wall, opened a door, and withdrew a bottle of whiskey.

"Go ahead. Make yourself right at home." Her sarcastic comment was childish, but his easy familiarity with the room irritated her.

He poured a hefty portion of the amber liquid into a glass. Grabbing the drink, he gulped more than half, as if he needed the alcohol. He set the glass down and called over his shoulder. "Want one?"

She'd better have something stronger than the tea she'd been sipping if she were to endure this confrontation. "I'll have a vodka."

He withdrew a bottle of vodka from the cabinet, poured her drink, and strode to where she stood by the couch and handed her the glass. Raising his own drink, he clinked his glass against hers. "To partnership."

"Partnership?" She eyed him, noting the cold glint in his dark eyes. His assumption she'd placidly go along with the terms of her father's will irked her, but she gulped a mouthful of vodka. The potent liquor burned all the way down her throat, fingers of warmth easing the block of ice in her stomach.

There was no partnership, and they sure as hell weren't partners. She wasn't sticking around to work hand in hand with him. She was walking away as planned. He didn't like her. He'd made his opinion clear. But he needed her. If she left, he lost everything. If she stayed for the required year, he won. He'd sell his half of the mill and be rich.

His lips twisted in a parody of a confident grin, though his eyes remained shuttered. He strolled across the room and stretched out in the padded leather chair in front of the fireplace. He sipped his drink, swallowed, drank again, and gestured for her to sit.

She gritted her teeth. This was *her* house. *He* was the guest, not she. She opened her mouth to tell him, but once again, held back. He'd come here tonight with a purpose in mind. Better to find out his intentions before she attacked. Swallowing the sour taste of anger along with another sip of vodka, she perched on the edge of the couch. "Why are you really here?"

"I want to make a deal."

"A deal?" She gulped a mouthful of her drink, choking as the alcohol forged a fiery path down her throat. Her eyes watered, but she managed to sputter, "What sort of deal?"

His smile didn't slip. "As I see it, you don't have many options. According to your father's will, we both hold equal shares in the lumber mill. You have to stay in Renton Falls and manage the company with me if you wish to retain your shares." He took another drink. "I know you don't want to stay here. Why would you give up your life in Portland to return to a town you detest and try and run a lumber mill? If the mill's sold and operations are shut down, you won't care. Hell, you'll probably be ecstatic. You'll have taken your revenge on those who done you wrong."

Anger at his smug assumptions built in her until she was surprised steam wasn't pouring out of her ears. "Why you—"

He held up his hand. "Don't say anything yet. Hear

me out. When I'm done, you can tell me exactly how much you despise me. Okay?"

Her outrage was a living, breathing entity. Her nails dug into the soft fabric as she gripped the couch cushions and fought for control. "I'm listening," she bit off through clenched teeth.

"As I said, you're free to walk away and never look back." His eyes narrowed, their dark irises pinning her to the couch. "But you won't."

"I won't?"

He shook his head. "Even I can see you're too intelligent to do something so idiotic. You'll stay and do as your father's will dictates. We'll manage the mill together." He made a face, not bothering to hide his feelings about working alongside her.

She banged her glass on the coffee table, not caring that vodka slopped onto the gleaming wood. Springing to her feet, she jammed her hands on her hips. "This is ridiculous. Do you actually think I want to work with you? No way in hell, buddy. I—"

His hand shot up, palm out as he cut off her tirade. "Hear me out."

She shook her head, her chest heaving.

"Please." His dark eyes softened to a warm chocolate brown. "What can it hurt?" He shrugged. "Who knows, you might even like my plan." His lips quirked in a smile, and a dimple made an appearance in his rugged cheek.

She gulped, dazzled under the power of his boyish grin. But then she reflected on who he was and why he was here and sanity returned. "You've got five minutes and then you're leaving. I've got packing to do."

His smile faltered. "J.D. tells me at the end of a

year's time, I can buy your half of the mill from you. You'll have enough money to do whatever you want. The mill will continue to employ the people in this town, and I'll be the sole owner of Bromley Forest Products." His grin returned. "Everyone wins." He sat back in his chair, one hand holding his drink, the other resting on the arm of the chair, calm and relaxed, except for the muscle twitching like a metronome in his rigid jaw.

"You have everything figured out, don't you?" She tossed her head, setting the ponytail swinging. "Except for one thing. And it's a big one. I have no desire to work with you. A year's a long time, and as you said, I have a life in Portland, a life I enjoy."

To her surprise, he smiled. "Believe me, I understand. I have no wish to work with you either, but…" He shrugged and grinned that boyish smile again.

Again she was distracted, intrigued by the tightening of his shirt as the thin, black cotton strained over his muscular chest. He lifted his glass to his mouth and his biceps bulged. His forearms were lean, tendons strong. *Did he work out, or were his toned muscles a result of hard physical labor?*

"…and so you see there really isn't a choice. Unless—" he broke off. "Are you listening?"

She blinked. Heat burned her face. "Um, yeah. Unless what?"

"Unless you agree to co-manage the mill with me, but we handle this a different way." He leaned forward. "On paper, you'll be a mill manager; in reality, you'll leave the day-to-day running of the mill to me. I'll look after all the business transactions, payroll, employee relations, everything."

"And what will I be doing all this time?"

He grinned, showing an expanse of even, white teeth. "You'll be in Portland. Oh, you'll have to make an appearance in town every few months. You know, publicity stuff…meet with the public, act as hostess when our buyers come to town, arrange events…that sort of thing."

A chill settled over her. "I'd arrange the sandwiches and coffee at meetings, you mean? Those sorts of *feminine* chores?"

He sat back and beamed. "Exactly."

A snort of laughter exploded out of her. "Are you serious? You really expect me to sit back and leave you to manage the mill while I smile and look pretty?"

The edges of his mouth tightened, and his smile slipped a notch. "Think about this before you say no. You don't want to run the mill. Hell, you don't know anything about the lumber business." He pointed his thumb at his chest. "I do. I've been managing Bromley on my own for the past year, ever since your father grew ill."

He set his glass on the maple table beside his chair and rose. "You wouldn't have to stay in town. You could go back to Portland, do your thing, whatever. All you'd have to do is show up here once in a while and sign a few papers. When the year's up, I'll buy you out, and we'll both be happy." He crossed his arms over his chest. "Don't you see? This is win-win."

"You want me to leave the responsibility of running the mill to you while I live in Portland?" She wanted to make sure she'd heard him right.

"Why not? This is what you want, isn't it?" He

moved a step closer. "As I see things, you came home after all these years to bury your father. You assumed, since you're his only child, you'd inherit everything. You probably figured you'd sell the mill and return to Portland, a much richer woman. I can imagine your outrage when you found out a virtual stranger had inherited half of the mill, and you have to actually stay and run the company if you want any money."

She studied his dark, penetrating eyes. He was very persuasive, and he wasn't saying anything she hadn't already envisioned. Except for the fact she hadn't come back to town to reap any benefit from her father's estate. Her reasons for being here were revenge and closure, as simple and as complicated as that. His plan, crazy as it was, offered her an out. She wouldn't have to stay. She could return to her job in Portland and get on with her life. And she wouldn't have to live with the guilt of the mill closing.

"Anyway," he continued, "I'm sure you're anxious to return to Portland. The last thing you want to be bothered with is a lumber mill. You have other plans for your life. My proposal gives you the freedom to do what you want. Think of the benefits. In twelve months, you'll walk away a wealthy woman. The beauty of my plan is you won't have the hassle of having to remain here trying to run a lumber mill"—he grinned sheepishly—"with someone you don't like." He heaved a deep breath and crossed to the liquor cabinet, and poured himself another drink.

Anger from deep within her arose, filling every cell until she feared she'd explode. "You overbearing, arrogant…" She spluttered, struggling to come up with suitable invectives to describe him and what she thought of his so-called generous offer.

His dark brows dew together, and a wary expression crossed his rugged features. "So. Do we have a deal?"

She stormed across the room, halting when her sock-clad toes butted against the front of his black, scuffed boots. "You must really think I'm a fool. Do you honestly believe I'd walk away and let you run the mill? My *father's* company?"

He shrugged. "Of course."

She leaned closer. "Look here, Morgan, I don't know you, and I don't know what your game is." Her finger poked his chest, punctuating each word. "I don't care what you're scheming. The bottom line is Bromley Forest Products was my father's mill. He built the business from nothing. I don't intend to give the place away to you or to anyone else. I'm staying. I'm going to run the damn mill whether you want me to, or not. And I sure as hell am not serving coffee." She reeled back a step, stunned. *Had she just told him she'd stay and manage the mill?*

Josh's mouth tightened to a thin line.

Tension built until the air in the room was thick and viscous.

He lifted her finger from his chest and placed his hand over hers, pressing her palm flat against his chest. He shifted his big body until his hips nudged hers.

Shock waves ricocheted through her as his warmth engulfed her. The pounding of his heart pulsed strong and steady beneath her palm. She inhaled his scent, a mixture of fresh autumn air, sweat, and something spicy.

He laughed a harsh, bitter sound and abruptly

released her hand and stepped back. "Well, then, my earlier toast still holds." He held up his glass. "We're partners, at least until one of us decides to murder the other."

She started, a chill rippling through her as she met the frost in his gaze. He couldn't be serious, though at this moment, she was tempted to kill him in an especially painful and agonizing manner. She'd have to check with J.D. Webster and see what would happen to the terms of the will if Morgan were to unexpectedly die. She met the challenge in his eyes. "I'm going to run this company. I'll find out what needs to be done, and I'll do it, and do it well."

"I didn't imagine you'd do anything less." His gaze drilled into hers, the dark irises glowing with something she couldn't read. The air throbbed with expectation. He stepped closer.

She read his intent a heartbeat before he lowered his head, and the warmth of his mouth settled over hers. Sensation swamped her as their lips fused. Closing her eyes, she gave in to the moment.

The kiss deepened, but when his tongue brushed hers, he cursed and jerked away.

Still caught up in the magic of the kiss, she raised a finger to her mouth where her lips tingled and burned. She opened her eyes.

He watched her with narrowed eyes, sipping from his drink as if nothing had happened.

"Wha…what was th…that?" Her voice was a rasping croak as she struggled to breathe.

He quirked an eyebrow. "That? You mean the kiss?" His eyes reflected his anger. "That, my dear, was the equivalent of a glove in the face."

"What?"

"Surely you've heard of the practice." He smirked. "Years ago, when a man challenged another man to a duel, he slapped him across the face with a glove."

She gaped, struggling to think over her rioting senses. "What are you talking about?"

"Don't be obtuse, Sharla-Jean. Surely you're aware I'm not pleased with your decision to reject my proposal. You really can't expect me to take this lying down." He laughed a harsh laugh.

A shiver rippled along her spine.

"The kiss, my dear, Miss Bromley, was merely my way of letting you know the battle is on."

"Battle?" Her anger, too long held at bay, exploded. "You haven't seen anything yet, Morgan. If you want a battle, you're on."

His gaze, filled with challenge, bore into hers. He drained his drink in a gulp, slammed his glass on the coffee table, and strode across the room toward the door. "So be it." At the doorway, he scorched her with one last, long look. "Don't bother to see me out, *partner*." And then he was gone.

Her knees gave way, and she collapsed on the couch, and stared at the flickering flames in the fireplace. *What the hell?* What was all that nonsense about battles and duels? She ran her fingers through her hair, tugging the long strands free of the elastic holding her hair off her face. He wasn't happy she hadn't agreed to his ridiculous, chauvinistic plan. Her blood heated as she recalled his smug face as he'd laid out his scheme. Had he really believed she'd agree to be a figurehead while he ran the business?

But you were prepared to walk away from the mill.

She flinched at the blatant truth in the insidious notion. Before Josh Morgan sauntered into the room, she'd had every intention of returning to Portland, but his arrogant assumption she'd agree to his inane plan sent her over the edge.

She rubbed the back of her neck, trying to ease the growing knot tightening her muscles in a painful vise. *What the hell have I done?* She'd committed to spending an entire year of her life in this damn town. She groaned and fell back onto the couch. Indeed, what the hell had she done?

She jammed her hands over her ears and closed her eyes and willed herself to vanish into the soft cushions of the couch, into silence, some place where she'd never heard of Renton Falls, Bromley Forest Products, or Josh Morgan. The fateful refrain continued unabated. *What the hell have I done?*

Chapter 4

Josh yawned and rubbed his hands over his face, frowning at the loud rasp of beard. He hadn't shaved this morning. He glanced ruefully down at his grease-smeared jeans, the same ones he'd worn yesterday. His shirt was streaked with dust, and tiny motes of sawdust clung to the black cotton.

He eyed the clock on the wall and yawned again. Not even eight o'clock in the morning, and he was exhausted. Grabbing his mug from the desk, he gulped coffee, frowning at the bitter, cold brew. He longed for a fresh cup, but Audrey wouldn't be in for another half hour, and he was too exhausted to make another pot himself.

He'd been at the mill since before dawn when Bob Friesen, the night foreman, called to tell him one of the circular saws used to cut the logs when they first passed into the mill, had jammed. Normally, a saw fitter was on call, whose job was to see to such problems, but the man had phoned in sick, and so Josh was nominated to undertake the repairs.

He didn't mind. Truth be told, he enjoyed the opportunity to get his hands dirty working with big machinery. Repairing machines and servicing motors amidst the sweet smell of oil and acrid tang of grease and lube, relaxed him and took his mind off the often-challenging work of managing a large lumber company in the current tough market.

The problem was, this sort of thing had been happening too often. Over the past two months, he'd been called in to repair equipment twelve times. Each time it was something simple—a loose gear, a bent sprocket, a chain off its guides, a broken saw blade, a burned-out motor—all common occurrences in a lumber mill. But not usually so many incidents, nor with such frequency. The equipment failures, though easily repaired, bothered him, and he couldn't help thinking he was missing something, something important, something right in front of his face.

He didn't mind helping in the mill, but last night hadn't been a normal night. Last night he'd made the mistake of going to see *her*. Scowling, he ran his fingers through his tangled hair. Damn, he needed a haircut. He should have known Sharla-Jean Bromley wouldn't be reasonable. She'd done her damnedest to make this snafu difficult. Hell, she'd made it damn near impossible.

His gut churned when he recalled his ridiculous words last night. Had he really threatened her with duels and battles? He lurched from his chair and paced the perimeter of the spacious office. That was the problem. He hadn't been thinking. Not with his brain at any rate.

The damn kiss was his downfall.

Until then he'd been doing fine. He'd laid out his idea and shown her he was a reasonable man; explained all the advantages of his proposal. But then he'd ruined everything and kissed her, and all his carefully laid plans took a nosedive straight into the toilet. From the moment he'd set eyes on her wearing that skin-tight red dress and matching, sky-high, fuck-me heels at Big Jim's funeral, he'd dreamed of kissing her, fantasized about melding his lips with hers. Even the baggy sweat pants and loose-fitting top she'd worn last night hadn't cooled his desire.

Fantasizing about tasting her lips was one thing; actually kissing her was another. But when her breasts grazed his chest, and her alluring scent surrounded him, he'd done the unforgivable.

One little kiss, a quick peck on those soft, pink lips. That's all. At least, that's how it had started. He wasn't prepared for what happened once his lips stroked hers. Even now, hours later, he relished her warm sweetness. He rubbed his hands over his face, scrubbing hard to erase the memory.

Things had gone south after the kiss. He'd been so shaken by his reaction to kissing her he'd lost what little sense he had. He winced as he thought of his ridiculous challenge. All he'd succeeded in doing was antagonizing her. No different than flashing a red flag in front of an angry bull.

He'd fled her house, jumped in his truck, and driven like an idiot, desperate to reach the peace and serenity of the cabin. He needed time to figure a way out of the mess he'd created. Peace and quiet awaited him at the cabin. No radio, no television, and most importantly, no Sharla-Jean Bromley.

Situated at the end of a rough gravel road on the shores of a spring-fed lake, with a view of distant, snow-capped mountains, the cabin was a paradise. Big Jim had transferred ownership of the rustic log cabin to Josh when Big Jim's sickness first appeared. No matter how much Josh protested, Big Jim had been adamant.

He knew how much Josh loved the place.

Rather than providing the refuge he'd so desperately wanted, the cabin's stillness and silence only amplified the thoughts racing through his mind. He couldn't get the memory of that damn kiss out of his head.

Tormented by a thousand conflicting thoughts, he'd lain in bed, tossing and turning, listening to the unceasing serenade of frogs and crickets until he gave up all pretense of sleep. Stumbling through the small cabin in the dark, he'd grabbed the bottle of whiskey he kept in the kitchen cupboard and drained one glass after another, staring out the window at the darkness, waiting for the alcohol to numb his brain.

He squeezed his eyes shut in a vain attempt to ease the hammering in his aching head. When whiskey didn't work, he crossed to the tiny kitchen and splashed cold water on his face. A quick glance in the mirror above the sink confirmed his eyes were laced with myriad red lines and rimmed with dark circles. He resembled a man tormented by demons. In spite of his aching head, he almost smiled. He was tormented all right. Not by demons, but by a green-eyed, auburn-haired woman with a body to die for.

He stomped back to the chair behind his desk and flopped down. The springs in the soft leather chair squealed in protest. Rubbing his aching temples, he blew out a deep breath. He didn't need this shit today. He'd been up half the night downing the better part of a bottle of whiskey, and the other half up to his elbows in grease.

The buzz of raised voices in the lobby outside his office door broke through his dark thoughts. What the hell was going on? He stormed across the room, flung open the door, and gaped at the scene before him.

Six or seven secretaries, as well as George Swanson, the company's labor-relations manager, milled around the floor-to-ceiling window in the small lobby outside Josh's office, heads craning as they peered outside.

Their high-pitched, excited voices drilled into his brain, and the pounding in his head skyrocketed into the stratosphere. What the hell were they all looking at? And where was Audrey? He stormed over to the window, shoved George aside, and scowled outside.

Sharla-Jean Bromley, long, auburn hair gleaming under the morning sun, full hips swaying, strolled across the parking lot toward the office.

His gut clenched. Damn. He should have known she'd show up here today. Turning to the crowd of employees, he snapped, "What the hell are you all gawking at?" His voice came out harsher than he intended, but he couldn't stop. "Get back to work." He glared at them. "All of you."

They scurried away, their faces pale, casting puzzled glances at him over their shoulders.

Shit. Now look what she'd made him do. He prided himself on treating his employees with fairness and respect. He stepped back into his office and slammed the door. Hard.

****

Sharla-Jean had driven Pauline's small, blue car into the crowded mill parking lot and parked between two mud-spattered four-by-four pickups. She'd peered through her windshield at the bustling lumberyard. A small, yellow forklift had buzzed back and forth shifting stacks of lumber from one location to another. Another forklift loaded slings of paper-wrapped lumber onto an open rail car.

Across the yard, two massive semi-truck trailers, their diesel motors rumbling, spewing plumes of black smoke into the clear blue autumn sky, waited in line. Another truck idled under a gaping spout, as a thick stream of wood shavings poured into the open trailer, raising a roiling cloud of dust. She'd unrolled her window and breathed in the familiar smells as the stench of diesel and sawdust filled the interior of her car.

An air horn blared and a dust-covered logging truck, the trailer piled high with freshly cut Douglas fir logs, had driven into the yard. Amidst all this activity, workers clad in yellow hard hats, wearing ear protectors and fluorescent yellow safety vests, hustled over the ground like an army of ants.

With shaking hands, she'd opened her car door and stepped out. As she made her way across the busy lumberyard, she studied her surroundings. The mill was noisy. Busy. Profitable. A far cry from the mill she'd burned to the ground so many years ago. Two low-lying, aluminum-roofed buildings dominated the yard. These would be the new sawmill and planer mill. The roar of machinery and the high-pitched whine emanating from somewhere inside the two large mill buildings added to the frenetic scene.

A flicker of unease settled over her as she took in the bustling scene. She swallowed, her mouth and throat desert dry. The last time she'd been here, it had been nighttime, and the yard had been deserted, the machinery still and quiet. Her breath hitched in her throat as she fought back the rush of painful memories.

Don't do this. Not here. Not now. Not in front of everyone. With what seemed like a superhuman effort, she shut off the threatening stream of terrifying images and turned toward the mill office.

The main mill office was adjacent to the parking area. The attractive, cedar-sided two-story building, surrounded by a patch of lush green grass and pruned shrubs, hadn't changed. Brilliant-colored flowers in a variety of containers hung from the building's rafters. The words "*Bromley Forest Products*" were printed in large polished-brass letters on a sign over the smoked-glass entry doors.

She knew the second her presence was noted.

As if they'd rehearsed before her arrival, every employee within sight stopped what they were doing and stared. An angry hum of voices rose over the incessant thunder of machinery.

A shudder ran through her and her steps slowed. She was desperate to jump back in her car and escape. But she dug deep and found her backbone. If she was going to do this, she couldn't be cowed by a few disparaging comments and dirty looks. Pasting a bright smile on her face, she threw her shoulders back, and with her head held high, continued on shaking legs to the main office building.

The hair on the back of her neck prickled, and she glanced up at the wall of windows.

A sea of faces stared down at her, watching her approach.

Did one of those faces belong to Josh Morgan? Was he observing her?

She flung open the glass doors and passed into the

cool air-conditioned lobby. The doors swung closed behind her, shutting off the riot of outside noise. Closing her eyes, she reveled in the temporary respite. *So far, so good.* Smoothing her jeans over her hips, she nodded. *Now for the lion's den.*

Business hours had begun, and employees were settling down to their desks as she crossed the lobby and took the stairs to the executive offices on the second floor. Word must have spread she was in the building because an inordinate number of people milled in the hallway, watching her with stiff expressions as she strode past.

Her cheeks flamed under their silent censure, but she kept moving, one step after another, until she reached the end of the hall and the office where her father used to work.

Audrey Longsworth, her father's long-time secretary, sat behind the same scarred walnut desk she'd occupied seventeen years ago when Sharla-Jean had last visited these offices. Other than her once-rich-red hair having turned a soft gray, and a few more lines crinkling the outer corners of her eyes, Audrey hadn't changed. Her small form was still slim and lithe, her movements quick and efficient.

Audrey's eyes widened when she caught sight of her.

Sharla-Jean steeled herself for a repeat of the unpleasant, muttered comments she'd been the brunt of since she'd stepped out of her car.

The older woman's mouth curved in a wide, welcoming smile. "Sharla-Jean! Hello." She rushed over and clasped Sharla-Jean's hands. "How long has it been, dear?" Before Sharla-Jean could answer, she continued. "Look at you. You're all grown up. Why, the last time I saw you, you were no bigger than a flea." Audrey huffed out a breath. "I caught a glimpse of you at the funeral, of course, but I couldn't find you after the service." Her face fell. "I'm so sorry about your father." She dabbed at her eyes with a tissue she'd pulled from her sleeve. "We all miss him. Let me tell you. He was a wonderful man."

Sharla-Jean's pleasure at seeing Audrey faded at the loyal secretary's praise of her father. Before she could say anything, Audrey drew her along the hall.

"Come on. You must meet everyone. So much has changed since you were last here. The mill's a going concern, let me tell you. Why, ever since Josh Morgan took over, the business is booming."

Audrey's gushing praise of Josh Morgan fueled Sharla-Jean's anger, but she kept silent. No point upsetting Audrey. In the coming weeks and months, she was going to need the woman's help. She allowed herself to be dragged across the room and down the hall where she was introduced to several employees.

Before she knew what happened, she was the center of attention. Negative attention. Lots of negative attention.

A restless group of six or seven people faced her, arms crossed over their chests, their faces set in stern lines of disapproval.

Sharla-Jean swallowed over the lump in her throat. They obviously knew the terms of her father's will. They'd heard she was staying and had every intention of managing the mill for one year, and they weren't pleased. That was putting it mildly. She wanted to run, cower in a hole somewhere, and hide, but Audrey kept a firm grasp on her arm.

Audrey nodded at her, as if encouraging her to face the rising swell of animosity head-on.

Sharla-Jean opened her mouth, but nothing came out. She inhaled and tried again. "You know the terms of my father's will." She waited, but no one spoke. Wiping a damp palm on her jeans, she tried again. "I plan to stay and manage the mill." Still no one said anything. "I promise to do my best and keep Bromley Forest Products at the forefront of this industry."

Someone snorted.

A tall, thin woman at the back of the group nudged the woman beside her and muttered something under her breath. Both women snuck a peek at Sharla-Jean and smirked.

A middle-aged man shook his head. "You'll help Bromley, all right. You'll set fire to the damn thing just like you did before, and then we'll be done."

There was a chorus of agreement and more angry comments.

Sharla-Jean sucked in a breath, reeling from the anger in their faces. She knew coming here today wouldn't be easy, but she hadn't expected such outright animosity.

Audrey's authoritative voice rose over the angry muttering, and the crowd quieted. "I think you're forgetting who you're talking to." Her eyes flashed. "This is Big Jim's daughter." She studied each person for a heartbeat, and moved on to the next. "Big Jim wanted her to run this place when he was gone. You all know he did." She heaved a breath. "So whatever beef you have with her, get over it, and get on with what you do every day, what you've been doing for the past year when Big Jim was ill. Work your tails off to make Bromley Forest Products the number one lumber company in North America."

Audrey's calm voice gave Sharla-Jean the strength to face the brunt of the crowd's all-too-obvious disdain. She straightened her shoulders, preparing to make another statement.

The door to Josh's office opened, and he appeared in the doorway.

Their eyes met.

She staggered back a step at the furious outrage in his torrid gaze, feeling as if he'd struck her.

The employees noticed him, and a heavy silence descended as they shifted restlessly and looked anywhere but at him. One person after another edged away, but not before casting final sneers of distrust and suspicion at Sharla-Jean.

Morgan scowled, his dark brows lowering in a deep vee. "Audrey, come in here." He spun on his heels and stomped back into his office.

With a reassuring smile and a quick squeeze of Sharla-Jean's arm, Audrey bustled into Morgan's office, closing the door behind her.

Sharla-Jean wiped her damp palms on the denim of her jeans and blew out an unsteady breath.

A door down the hall opened, and a tall, well-built man with long, dark-blond hair and a handsome, boyish face stepped out of an office. His tanned face and supple body were indications of the time he probably spent on the tennis courts or golf links.

He swaggered toward her with a cocky strut, surveying her from head to toe, lingering for an inordinate amount of time over her breasts and hips before glancing at her face.

Uncomfortable with his too-enthusiastic examination of her body, she edged away, intending to slip into Audrey's office and avoid another unpleasant confrontation.

He sidled in front of her, blocking her escape. Holding out his hand, he grinned. "Kevin Nelson. I'm an executive here at Bromley. How do you do?"

After a second's hesitation, she shook his hand. "Sharla-Jean Bromley."

He held onto her hand a heartbeat too long before releasing his grip.

She resisted the urge to wipe her hand on her jeans.

His icy blue eyes studied her, and his gaze once again slipped below her neck.

She resisted the urge to follow his gaze and check to ensure she hadn't spilled coffee on her blouse.

"I know who you are." His smarmy grin widened. "You've made quite a stir around this place. You're all anyone's talking about."

Her back stiffened. She'd met men like him before; sure of themselves, certain women would fall all over them after one lazy, sultry smile. She crossed her arms over her chest, blocking his view. "Please move out of my way, Mr. Nelson. I'm leaving."

His eyes widened. "Leaving? Already? You just got here." His smile never wavered, his gaze sweeping her body as if memorizing every inch. "I bet no one's offered to give you a tour of the place." He chuckled. "The mill's changed since you were last here. Let me show you around."

She hesitated. She was anxious to see the changes since her father had rebuilt after the fire, but she wasn't comfortable going anywhere with this man. But if she intended to see this through, she needed to understand the workings of the mill. A tour of the operation would be a first step.

"I'll be your personal escort." Nelson's grin inched up a notch. "What do you say?"

She glanced around the deserted hallway. "Sure, why not?" No one else was lining up to offer to help her. "Let's go."

Chapter 5

Audrey bustled into the office, her face flushed with excitement. "Did you see her?"

Josh didn't have to ask Audrey whom she was talking about. He had only to close his eyes and the image of Sharla-Jean Bromley's auburn hair gleaming under the bright fluorescent lights of the outer office blazed before him. Her snug-fitting jeans and simple, cotton blouse, did nothing to hide her ample curves, or the sleek lines of her long legs. He'd somehow dragged his inspection up to her face. The unnatural paleness of her cheeks and her large, wounded eyes had floored him.

His first reaction was to help her. Even though she was the last person he wanted to see in the office, he wouldn't stand by and watch her be attacked. But then her gaze met his, and he read the challenge in her emerald depths. His anger returned full force and he'd bellowed at Audrey.

Not his finest moment. Audrey had been Big Jim's secretary for years. Once he was no longer healthy enough to come into the mill, Audrey took over as Josh's assistant, helping him understand a million little details over those first, few, difficult months. He didn't know how he would have survived if she hadn't guided him. And how did he repay her? He yelled at her like an overbearing, arrogant boor. He opened his mouth to apologize, but her next words dried the apology on his tongue.

"Isn't she lovely?" Audrey busied herself filling the coffeepot on the side table with water and making coffee. "Why, I haven't seen her since she was a child. My, how she's grown. Big Jim would have been so proud."

Josh glowered.

She ignored his sour mood as she tidied his desktop and continued singing the praises of the Bromley woman. "She certainly has turned into a beauty. I hardly recognized her. Mind you, she does have the look of her father about her, don't you think? All that red hair? Just like Big Jim's."

Josh wanted to cover his ears to shut out her endless chatter. A sudden craving for a stiff drink hit him, and his mouth watered. He wanted alcohol and he wanted it now. Anything to deaden the incessant throbbing behind his eyes.

Audrey poured him a cup of coffee, added a spoonful of sugar, and set the cup before him on his desk. Her sharp gaze raked over him and she tsked. "Rough night, last night?"

He bit back a groan. "You don't know the half of it."

"I think I do." She patted him on the shoulder. "It's going to be all right. Everything's going to work out just fine."

He snorted. "Yeah, right." He reached for his cup, hoping she didn't notice the tremble in his hand.

"Big Jim was a smart man. He knew what he was doing when he made his will." She smiled and with a final pat, left him alone in peace.

His respite didn't last.

No sooner had she closed the door behind her than a light tap sounded on the door. It opened before he could tell the unwelcome visitor to go away, and George Swanson strode into the room.

Isn't anyone working today? "What is it?" Josh snapped, and was immediately contrite. He'd had a hell of a night and an even worse morning, but he shouldn't take out his irritation on George. "Sorry, George. What can I help you with?" He rubbed his temples, trying to ease the vise-like pain.

"Did you see her?" George's voice was breathless with excitement.

Josh bit back a groan. *Here we go again.*

George's thinning gray hair stood out in wild wisps as if he'd been running his fingers through it. "I almost passed out when I stepped out of my office and saw her standing in the hall bold as brass. I can't believe she has the nerve to come here." He wiped his gleaming forehead with his shirtsleeve. "I have to admit, she's a looker. That red dress she wore to Big Jim's funeral was something else. I'm not saying I approve of her outfit. I mean, it was her father's funeral and all, but man, oh man." He fanned his hand before his flushed face.

Josh wished all sorts of excruciating torture on the man, anything to stop his blathering, but George prattled on.

"I tell you, Josh. I was shocked. I mean, after all the atrocious stuff she's done, I expected her to be different. But, she seems okay. I mean, if Audrey's willing to vouch for her, maybe we've misjudged her. I mean, she was a kid when she left. Maybe she's changed." He paused and studied Josh through the lenses of his smudged glasses. "You've met her, haven't you? At the reading of the will, I mean. I heard her old man left her pretty much the whole shot. Well, except for your half of the mill. She said she's staying to take over the business. Is that true?"

Josh slammed his palm down on his desk. His cup wobbled, and coffee spilled onto the old oak surface. "I'm part owner of this mill." Each word fell from his mouth like a shard of ice. "Last I checked I'm still the manager. I run this place, always have, always will. Best you remember that, George."

George paled and backed toward the door. "Er, I didn't mean…Josh…um…er…I uh…"

George's nervousness fueled Josh's fury, and he leaped to his feet. "Where is she now?"

"Um…er…she's over at the planer mill. Kevin Nelson offered to give her a tour." He smirked. "Lucky Kevin."

Josh's long legs carried him across the room in two quick strides. He ignored George, who'd backed into the corner as Josh stormed out of the office. Every step intensified the pounding in his head. Who the hell did she think she was? Showing up out of the blue after all these years? Thinking she could take over?

Where was she when he'd worked his ass off the past five years to make this place a success? He'd stayed by Big Jim's side even when the old man was so sick he couldn't get out of bed. He'd wiped the vomit off Jim's face, helped him to the toilet, and listened to his drug-induced ravings. He'd watched the man he loved like a son loves his father endure unspeakable pain as the disease ate away at him. Hell, he'd even arranged Big Jim's funeral and the old man's burial.

This mill was his, all his, no matter what the damn will stated. No way would he let some heartless, conniving bitch waltz in here and steal his dream. If anyone was to give her a tour of the mill site, he would. He'd start with making sure she knew where all the exits were so she wouldn't have any problem leaving when she slunk out with her tail between her legs.

Grabbing a hard hat and safety goggles from the storage locker, he yanked open the heavy metal door and burst into the dusty gloom of the planer mill. He spotted her over by the number-four conveyor belt surrounded by a crowd of at least a dozen mill workers. *His* mill workers.

He stormed toward the group, fire boiling in his belly. The besotted expressions on the faces of his men increased his ire. They were drooling over her as if she were the last piece of prime rib on the buffet. And it wasn't just her gorgeous green eyes they were staring at. "Nelson," he barked.

All gazes swung toward him. Without a word, the group of men dispersed, returning to their stations, until only one man remained by her side.

Glowering at Nelson, Josh was inordinately pleased when the man's cheeks flushed, and he stumbled back a faltering step.

Big Jim had hired Kevin Nelson six months prior, just before Big Jim's illness hit hard and caused him to stop coming into work every day. Nelson was the company's comptroller. He'd come with first-rate references, but something about the man bothered Josh. Maybe it was his movie star looks or his overly unctuous manner. Whatever the reason, the man wore on his nerves.

Like now, when he hovered over Sharla-Jean, his body brushing against hers, his hand resting on her arm in a proprietary manner. Josh didn't pause to wonder why the sight of the two of them together bothered him so much. "What are you doing?" His question was directed at Nelson, but he glared at the woman standing beside the man. In spite of his fury, he couldn't help admiring the way her tight denim jeans fit her narrow waist and curving hips. Even wearing a hard hat, ear protectors, and plastic, protective goggles the woman was a sight to behold.

"I was giving Ms. Bromley a tour," Nelson said.

Before Josh could snarl at him again, Sharla-Jean interrupted. "I asked Mr. Nelson to show me around the mill."

"Why?"

Her green eyes widened, the challenge in them unmistakable. Her full mouth, the one he'd kissed yesterday, pursed. "I would think my reason's obvious. I'm part owner. I intend to learn whatever I need to about this operation."

Their gazes locked, and the atmosphere changed, charged with an indefinable excitement and hyperawareness.

His heart raced, blood heated and surged through his veins.

Her pupils dilated, and the clear green of her eyes darkened to the color of a deep, glacial lake.

Nelson's harsh cough broke through his daze, and Josh planted his hands on his hips, irritation flaring. He raked the other man with a hard look. "Don't you have work to do, Nelson? Those purchase orders for Japan need to be completed by the end of the day."

"Don't worry. I'll get them done." Nelson stuck out his chest. "I figured Ms. Bromley would enjoy a tour of the place."

"Last time I checked, I'm still the boss," Josh said. "Go back to your office. I'll show her around." He wheeled toward Sharla-Jean and glared, daring her to protest.

Nelson hesitated, but he smiled tightly at Sharla-Jean. "I guess I'd better go. Good luck, Ms. Bromley. I wish you all the best here at Bromley. If you need anything, don't hesitate to ask. I'll be more than happy to help."

Josh bit his tongue to stop a harsh rebuke. *I'll be more than happy to help.* Could the man be any more obvious? His pique increased when Sharla-Jean beamed a mega-watt smile at Nelson and clasped his hand in hers.

"Thank you so much, Kevin, for your warm welcome. I may take you up on your offer." She batted her ridiculously long eyelashes. "Lord knows, I'm going to need some help; at least, until I get my feet under me."

Nelson's cheeks flushed, and he grinned like a besotted schoolboy. "Okay, then." He backed away, still smiling an idiotic smirk. "Good-bye."

Josh struggled not to throw up. As Nelson retreated, he inhaled several lungsful of air, fighting to cool his temper. What the hell was wrong with him? He wasn't usually like this. What did he care if Nelson helped her? Hell, what did he care if the two of them hooked up? So long as they didn't do their screwing on company time.

When he turned back, he was unnerved to find her watching him with a cool, assessing scrutiny. Could she read his mind? Did she know what he'd been thinking? He sure as hell hoped not. Because no two ways around this, he'd acted like a jealous ass. *Time to admit the truth, buddy boy. You want her.* So what? What man wouldn't? She was a damn fine-looking woman. Nelson's reaction was normal. A lot of guys working here were going to react the same way. He'd better get used to the spike in male testosterone.

A deep furrow formed between his brows. He didn't need this shit. It added one more complication to an already complex situation. If he had any sense, he'd kick her shapely ass off the premises and deal with the lawyers later. Surely he could figure a way to circumvent the ridiculous terms of Big Jim's will. He blew out a breath. No hope there. The will was solid. If J.D. couldn't find a loophole, no one could. If Josh chased Sharla-Jean away, the mill would be sold and shut down, and the town he'd grown to love, would be destroyed.

He rubbed the back of his neck and forced a smile to his stiff lips. "Well, shall we continue the tour?"

****

Sharla-Jean studied the scowling man towering over her and shook her head. What was it about sweaty men in grease-streaked jeans and hard hats? Even the safety goggles and ear coverings he wore added to his rugged good looks. If his face weren't fixed in his habitual frown, he'd be downright handsome.

"Well. Shall we proceed with the tour?" Josh asked again, bending from his waist in a half bow before her.

She blinked, drawn out of her thoughts and

66

nodded.

He led the way through the noisy, dusty mill, past men and women working at a variety of tasks.

The skin on the back of her neck prickled from the weight of censorious eyes watching her. Once or twice, she spun around, but she never caught anyone looking at her. The workers were focused on the job at hand.

Josh halted beside a wide conveyor belt that extended into the dim reaches of the mill. Boards of various lengths rumbled past on the conveyor. A red, laser light marked a line across each piece of wood. Two employees stood before the belt, inspecting the steady procession of boards, flipping and straightening them, at times hitting a large red button and slowing the speed of the belt in order to examine a particular board.

Josh spoke to the two employees watching the lumber file by on the large belt, but she couldn't hear his words over the raucous screech of machinery.

The workers chuckled, and one of them said something to Josh.

He threw his head back, guffawing and slapping the man on the shoulder.

She'd never seen Josh smile, let alone laugh. He should laugh more often. When he laughed, the dark charcoal of his eyes lightened, and the lines on his rugged face softened. He caught her staring, and she gulped, waves of warmth washing over her.

He leaned closer and shouted, "This is the grading station." He pointed to the conveyor belt. "Those men determine the market quality of each board. The red laser light determines the best length of wood for each piece of lumber, to prevent waste."

She nodded, though she didn't really understand.

The deafening noise and massive moving machinery surrounding her was overwhelming. Her stomach plummeted. She had so much to learn. How was she ever going to understand enough to run the company?

"Come on." Josh gripped her arm, guiding her across the floor littered with sawdust and chunks of bark and wood. "Watch your step."

They made their way from one section of the building to another. Much to her surprise, she found herself enjoying the tour. Josh explained the intricacies of the planer mill workings. His love for the mill and respect for the employees shone in his face and was reflected in his encouraging words to the workers, and expert adjustments on a finicky piece of equipment. She could learn a great deal from him if he'd let her.

They finished the tour of the planer mill, and she followed him out the door and across the covered breezeway to the sawmill. The ever-present dust and clamor of big machinery was the same here as it had been in the planer. Her head throbbed. What exactly happened in a planer anyway? It was all so confusing.

He stopped before a giant dark-green machine towering over them. Sharp, claw-like metal spikes grabbed huge, raw logs and dragged them along a conveyor belt into a tunnel where lethal-looking, jagged saw blades scraped along the sides of the log and removed the bark. As each log entered the tunnel and the saw blades attacked, a high-pitched grinding scream like a wild beast suffering in agony, filled the air.

Josh leaned toward her and shouted something, but his words were lost in the racket.

She shook her head and motioned she hadn't heard.

He stepped closer, his shoulder brushing hers, his

arm around her waist drawing her near. His warm breath fanned her face as he lifted her ear protector and placed his lips against her ear.

A myriad of sensations rocketed through her, every cell in her body acutely aware of his big, muscular body wedged against hers, the weight of his arm across her back, his hand at her waist, his face mere inches from hers. Her mouth lost all moisture and she fought to swallow.

His lips brushed her ear.

She shivered.

"This is the debarker," he shouted over the din, and then he replaced her ear protector.

She shivered again. Was she imagining his fingers lingering on her skin?

His eyes narrowed as he studied the massive machine growling overhead, and he mouthed a swear word. He marched across the floor to where a man sat on a stool before a lighted panel below the debarker. He spoke to the operator and the man pressed a large red button. The clunking roar ceased as the machine ground to a halt.

As soon as the metal cylinder stopped spinning, Josh leaped over the wooden barrier and climbed onto the gigantic contraption. He slid under the sharp-toothed saw blades with a lithe, athletic grace. Bits of bark clung to his hair and grease streaked his shirt and pants as he reached deep into the inner workings of the debarker and fiddled with gears and chains, adjusting the machine.

His hair fell across his forehead, and he brushed back the stray lock, leaving a dark smudge on his broad brow. His jeans tightened as he bent over the machine.

The faded denim molded to his lean hips, outlining the hard muscles in his thighs.

He glanced down, and she flushed, realizing she'd been caught staring. Again.

He grinned, displaying startling white teeth. A dimple danced in his stubbled cheek.

Once again his smile transformed his face, and her breath caught in her throat. He'd been good-looking before, but now…now he was trouble.

His gaze bore into hers.

She gulped, transfixed.

A crease formed between his dark brows, and he jerked away, severing the connection. He jumped down from the debarker, wiped his hands on his dirty jeans, and pressed the red button to restart the machine.

Her knees wobbled, and she leaned against a rusty metal railing for support. Praying he hadn't noticed how he'd unsettled her, she gulped several deep, steadying breaths, breathing in the dust-laden air.

He made a thumbs-up sign and slapped the debarker operator on the shoulder.

"Thank you for the tour," she hollered. "I have to go." She ran off before he could stop her; desperate to escape, terrified of what would happen if she stayed.

Chapter 6

Sharla-Jean stepped into the office Audrey had arranged for her to use, closed the door behind her, and slumped against the cool wood door. She pressed a hand on her chest to slow the furious beating of her heart. *What the hell just happened?* She didn't need this complication. Josh Morgan wasn't her friend. He wanted the mill, and he'd stop at nothing to ensure he got what he wanted. Even if it meant pretending he was attracted to her.

He wasn't her only problem. She blew out a ragged breath. Pauline had warned her of the townspeople's animosity. After all, Sharla-Jean had done a great deal to deserve their acrimony. In her childish attempts to get her father's attention, she'd done her level best to cause him grief and embarrassment. The bigger the trouble and the more upset her father, the better, as far as she'd been concerned.

She'd driven dangerously fast, committed countless traffic violations and caused two spectacular crashes, each time totaling her father's cars. If she wasn't roaring around town terrifying everyone on the roads, she found trouble other ways. Her teenage rebellion had earned her the derision of the townspeople, but not their acrimony. No, she'd done something far worse to cause their intense dislike.

She jammed her fist against her stomach in a futile

attempt to forestall the rush of terrifying memories threatening to overwhelm her. With a groan, she sank to her knees as the room around her dissolved, and the biting stench of smoke and the crackle of flames filled the air.

She froze, her mind blank with rising horror. Clouds of black smoke stung her nostrils and burned her eyes. A towering wall of flame hungrily devoured the neatly stacked piles of kiln-dried lumber. Unbearable heat seared the skin on her arms, blistering her face.

Wind gusted and the fire leaped to the sawmill's cedar shake roof. In seconds, the conflagration soared to the heavens, sparks shooting through the night air like tiny, heat-seeking missiles. A fiery ember landed on her arm, and the sharp pain jerked her out of her trance. She gagged at the stench of seared flesh. "No!" She choked on acrid fumes. "No!

She flew across the rough ground as she raced toward the blazing building. Grabbing a canvas tarp draped over a pile of lumber, she swatted at the flames crawling up the walls of the sawmill. The heat suffocated. Her lungs burned, her face hot, lips cracking.

The tarp smoldered and burst into flames. Yelping, her hands stinging, she dropped the red-hot sheet. Tears streamed down her cheeks, mixing with soot and ash. The fire was everywhere. Where was the night watchman? Where were the fire trucks? Why hadn't someone reported the fire?

A loud animal-like groan rent the air. She squinted through the thick veil of smoke. Metal saws and conveyor belts buckled under the blistering heat. A visceral sickness struck her with rising horror. The entire building was engulfed. Soon the walls would collapse.

In the distance, the wail of sirens filled the night as the town's two fire trucks raced to the scene. A flood of relief washed over her, easing her panic. Help was on the way.

In the next breath, reality struck, and her dread returned. She'd done this. She was responsible for the terrible devastation surrounding her. Tears stung her eyes as an oppressive weight settled over her. Coughing and choking, she struggled to breathe in the cloying layer of ash and smoke. An image of her father rose before her. She moaned. He'd never forgive her. She'd destroyed the one thing he cared about. Everyone would blame her.

No one would ask why she'd commit such a horrific act. She'd done the unforgivable, and so they'd condemn her. Her actions this night would earn her the anger of every man, woman, and child in Renton Falls. She'd be found guilty in the court of public opinion without the benefit of a trial.

She swiped her hand over her streaming eyes and stared at the hell before her. Every muscle in her body tensed to flee, to escape the anger and hatred. But she couldn't. Not without giving her father a chance. She'd go to him and explain what happened. Maybe he'd understand. Maybe he'd help her. And so, instead of disappearing into the night, she spun on her heels and ran home.

When home hadn't worked out, she'd taken what money she'd saved and snuck out of town, hitchhiking until she reached Portland and anonymity. Sitting on the carpet of her new office, her back against the closed door, she wiped the tears on her face and sucked in deep breaths.

The *Renton Falls Observer* had run several articles in the aftermath of the fire. Bromley Forest Products had been fully covered by insurance, and her father rebuilt the mill within a matter of months. Everyone returned to work in a newer, more modern mill. Knowing this didn't assuage her guilt.

She raised a shaking hand and brushed a strand of hair off her face. She wasn't an angry, frightened girl anymore. What happened so long ago wasn't entirely her fault. She'd earned her share of the blame, but she hadn't been alone. She bit her lip and moaned as once again she succumbed to the horror of that fearsome night.

"Hey, Sharla-Jean. What's up?" Tyler Maddox leaned out the open window of his black, shiny, four-wheel drive pickup truck, a grin on his handsome face. A wisp of smoke trailed from the cigarette stuck in the corner of his mouth.

She gulped, thrilled, yet terrified he knew her name. Tyler was trouble. Big trouble. Everyone in Renton Falls knew the hell he caused. He was also the best-looking boy in town and could have any girl he wanted. He was nineteen, and if the rumors were true, he'd spent time last winter in a jail cell somewhere out East for stealing cars.

"Cat got your tongue, little girl?" he teased.

Her heart raced. Tyler was bad news. She should tell him to leave her alone, but a vision of her father's outrage when he learned she'd spent time with the local punk, had her answering, "I'm looking for something to do. Any suggestions?"

He chuckled deep and low in his chest and jerked his thumb toward the dark interior of the truck cab. "Me and Jack here are headin' over to Poulson Point." He grinned. "We've scored some great weed. Why don't you come along? We'll have a party." His grin widened, a matching set of dimples dancing in his chiseled cheeks.

She chewed on her bottom lip. She was no angel, but for all her antics she'd never used drugs. A voice deep inside urged her to walk away, cautioned her that Tyler Maddox was too much trouble, even for her. Getting back at her father was one thing; risking her life, another.

As if reading her mind, he taunted, "Afraid, little girl? Afraid what your daddy will think?"

His goading words carried over the idling truck motor and circled around her like a bear trap. Her father would freak if he knew she was anywhere near Tyler Maddox, let alone contemplating going to Poulson's Point, the local make-out spot, with him. She wiped damp palms on her jeans and studied him. Even in the dim light the challenge in Tyler's brilliant blue eyes was clear.

Her father would be furious. Perfect. Before she changed her mind, she grinned back at Tyler. "Sure. That sounds like fun." The passenger door opened, and she ran around the hood of the truck and climbed inside.

She didn't smoke any of the marijuana Tyler and Jack offered, but she chugged three bottles of warm beer as she fought to overcome her nervousness at being alone with the much older boys. Something about the way they stared, their hot gazes sliding over her again and again, chilled her. As she drained her beer and accepted the new one offered by Tyler, she giggled and staggered against the truck.

"Hey, I got an idea." Tyler's red-veined eyes pierced hers with an unsettling intensity.

"Wha...what?" She struggled to form the single word, her tongue thick, her mouth parched in spite of the beer.

"Let's head on over to the lumber yard." He sucked in a deep drag of the joint.

"The lumber yard?" She blinked, her voice slurring. The ground heaved up and down in waves.

Jack giggled. "Yeah, let's go have a look. My old man's worked at the mill for years. He's always naggin' me to get a job there. Let's go see what the place looks like at night when no one's around."

"No." She rubbed her eyes trying to clear the fog. The mill was the last place she wanted to go. It was her father's domain. "We can't get in. The gate's locked, and a night watchman's always on duty."

Jack snickered. "Are you kidding me? I heard that old geezer sleeps all night. He'll never know we're there." He staggered toward Tyler's truck. "Come on, Tyler, let's go. It'll be rad. I've always wanted to ride on one of them conveyor belts."

"What's wrong, little girl?" Tyler grabbed her arms and pulled her against his chest. "Don't tell me you're afraid." His hot breath washed over her. "Come on, babe. We'll have a gas. You can give us our own private tour." He leaned down and kissed her. His mouth expertly parted her lips, his tongue probing.

She staggered and clung to him, overwhelmed by

the sensation of his mouth on hers. Her first real kiss. Part of her wanted to wipe his saliva from her mouth. Another part trembled and ached for more.

Tyler broke away and stared at her, his pupils dilated, his eyes scalding. "Whoohee! You're somethin' else, little girl." He grabbed her hand and towed her toward the truck. "We're gonna have us a grand old time tonight."

She stumbled along behind him. Don't go with him. *The warning rang through her beer-fogged brain.* Don't go. *She opened her mouth to tell him she'd changed her mind and didn't want to go to the mill, but before her numb lips formed the words, he lifted her in his strong arms and heaved her onto the front seat of the truck.*

Jack scrambled in beside her and slammed the door.

Tyler settled behind the steering wheel, and with a roar of the engine, and the squeal of tires on the cracked blacktop, they thundered into the night.

She barely noticed when the truck stopped. Groggy from alcohol coursing through her veins, she allowed Jack to help her from the vehicle. She stumbled after Tyler's tall, lean form to the yellow barrier gate blocking the entrance to Bromley Forest Products.

Ignoring the large white sign with big red block letters warning this was private property and no trespassing was allowed, he ducked under the barricade. "Come on. Let's go."

Butterflies danced in her stomach, and she balked. Her inner voice screamed an endless warning.

"What's wrong? You chicken?" The corners of his mouth tightened, and his eyes narrowed.

"We shoulda left her behind. I told you she wouldn't be no fun. Too much daddy's little girl." Jack smirked, his acne-riddled face inches from hers, his beer-laced breath sour.

She bit back a heated retort. She was nobody's little girl. Besides, what was the big deal if they were caught? Her father owned the whole damn place. She could be here if she wanted. "What are we waiting for?" She crouched down and crawled under the barrier.

Giggling and stumbling in the dark, she welcomed the clasp of Tyler's warm hand as he guided her across the deserted lumberyard between the endless piles of cut and stacked lumber. They halted in a small alcove between a stack of wood scraps and a massive heap of shavings swept into a neat mound.

Jack staggered as he weaved toward the pile of lumber and sagged against the wood. He tugged a book of matches from his front jeans' pocket, and fished a small plastic bag filled with two rolled joints from his back pocket. With fumbling fingers, he tore off a match and flicked the end with his thumbnail. A tiny flame flared, growing in the night breeze. "Shit." He cursed as the flame singed his skin and dropped the match, blowing on his burned finger. "That fucking hurt." Reeling, his legs unsteady, he flicked another match and held the wavering flame to the rolled joint.

Sharla's mouth dried. "What…what are you…you doing? You can't smoke here. It's too dangerous." The danger an open flame posed to a lumber mill had been drilled into her since she was a toddler. Signs prohibiting smoking were posted throughout the mill. For good reason. Stacks of kiln-dried lumber were piled in the yard. Mounds of bone-dry sawdust were swept up every day, and the mill buildings were made of wood. Even the roofs were covered with tinder-dry cedar shakes.

Jack giggled, his narrow shoulders heaving with mirth. "Too dangerous." He flicked the ash from his joint onto a pile of wood shavings. "Oops." He cackled. The smoldering ash glowed, igniting a few flakes of dry wood before fading to black.

Her breath whooshed out in relief.

He lit another match. Weaving drunkenly, he held the flame to the end of a two-by-four. "We'll be careful, won't we, Tyler? Fire's dangerous." His high falsetto voice mocked her. His eyes gleamed with a maniacal light as the flame scorched the pine a dark brown. He waited until all the matches in the book ignited and then he threw the flaming matches onto a pile of wood chips and sawdust.

Her blood chilled. Suddenly she was stone cold sober. "Let's...let's g...go. This isn't any fu...fu...fun." She rushed over to the smoldering pile of shavings and stomped on the hot coals.

"Whoooeee! You got some moves, girl." Jack laughed and fished in his jacket pocket and yanked out another book of matches. Giggling, he tore off a match, struck it against the cover, and flicked the flaming stick into the dark. "Come on, little girl. Let's see you dance some more." He lit another match, and then another and another. His crazed cackle echoed in the night.

"St...stoooop!" She charged, knocking the flaming matchbook from his hand. It flew out into the night, a small, fiery torch. "This...this is stu...stupid. I...I...I'm go...going home."

Tyler chortled. "You really are a baby, aren't you, little girl? You can't even talk right." His eyes narrowed. "But you're right. This isn't much fun." His gaze roamed over her, lingering on her breasts. He licked his lips and grinned. "Maybe you're not such a baby, after all. You look all grown up to me."

She shuddered and stumbled back from the cold, assessing gleam in his blood-shot eyes.

"I'll bet I can think of something a lot more fun. Can't you, Jack?"

Her stomach lurched and bile filled her throat. Mistake! This is a mistake. *The words blazed through her in an unending refrain.*

Tyler yanked her toward him. His fingers dug into her waist, forcing her hips against the growing bulge in his pants.

"Wha...wha...are...are...you...do...doing?" She forced the words over her tongue, struggling to form each syllable. "Le...let...m...m...me...g...g...go!" She twisted her face away from his searching mouth and shoved him with all her might.

He didn't budge.

She might as well have pushed against a brick wall. Goose bumps prickled along her arms.

"What's the matter, Sharla-Jean? Scared?" He smirked. "Nothin' to be afraid of. Jack and me are gonna teach you a few lessons, is all. Fun lessons. Lessons you're gonna love."

"N...n...no! Sto...stop! Le...l...et me g...go!" She fought against him, twisting and heaving, kicking his shins, stomping on his boots.

"Hey!" He fended off her blows. "What's all this? I thought you liked me." His grip on her tightened, and

his fingers dug into her flesh. His hot breath, heavy with the rancid stench of marijuana and beer, fanned her face.

"No!" Her anguished cry split the quiet of the office, and she shuddered and swallowed hard. Her hands fisted and her fingernails dug into her palms. Her body was strung tight, her muscles rigid, as she fought against the onslaught of the long ago nightmare. She bit off another keening wail.

Not now. Please, not now. Not here in her office at the mill with people just outside the door. Her hand covered her mouth, pressing hard, silencing the shuddering sobs.

How many nights had she awakened, tears streaming down her face, terror chilling her blood, as she relived the cruel attack? How many days had she been driven to her knees by the brutal memories?

Wiping her damp forehead, she sucked in one cleansing breath after another, easing the stranglehold of the mind-numbing fear. She was a fool. This was a mistake. A bad one. She shouldn't have returned to the mill. How could she have thought the years had distanced her from the harsh reality of the rape? Nothing, no amount of time, nor space, would erase the fear that laced the very air in this place.

Uncurling, she pushed off the floor, sat up, and leaned back against the cold, hard door and drew her knees up. The nightmare hadn't ended there. No, it only got worse. She moaned as once again the pull of the past overwhelmed, drawing her in as a new monster reared its head and the heavy stench of that long ago smoke stung her nostrils.

"Come on, Tyler. Let's get the hell outta here."

The brutal hands pawing her stilled. "Holy Hell." The weight squashing her chest eased.

"How the hell did the fire start?" demanded Tyler.

"Who gives a shit? The cops'll be here any minute. Let's go." Jack's voice cracked with fear.

Through the rising cloud of smoke, the man who'd raped her rose to his feet, adjusted his clothing, and strode away.

"Wait," Jack called. "We can't leave her."

"No piece of ass is worth going to jail again. I'm gettin' the hell out of here before we get blamed for this damn fire."

The sound of retreating footsteps echoed in the night.

Her chest heaved, her body ached; her mind was numb. She drew her knees to her chest and wrapped her arms tight. The demonic crackle of fire, the acrid sulfur sting of smoke, searing heat. This was Hell.

She opened her eyes, but the sight of flames flaring to life remained imbedded on her retinas. Even though she was safe in the office, and the events of that terrible night were in the past, the image of the pile of shavings consumed by fingers of hot flame seared into her brain.

Chapter 7

The files lay scattered across her desk in loose piles. More were stacked on the floor at her feet. Sharla-Jean stretched her aching back and rubbed her grit-filled eyes. Two weeks had passed since the reading of her father's will. Two weeks of working harder than she ever had in her life, and she was no closer to understanding the intricate workings of a lumber mill than when she started.

She rested the back of her head against the cool leather of her chair and closed her eyes, enjoying the quiet. The continuous ringing of phones had ceased; the chatter of a dozen people silenced. Work hours were long over, and all the employees had gone home to their families. She was alone.

Doubt assailed her as it had so many times these past weeks. How could working as an instructor with small children in an inner-city preschool prepare her in any way to run Bromley Forest Products? Bad enough she had to deal with her own employees' reservations and even outright hostility, but she also had to handle the chauvinistic attitude of the men who ran the large corporations that purchased lumber from Bromley Forest Products. Their condescending manner drove her crazy.

Their attitudes stemmed not so much from the fact she was Big Jim Bromley's daughter, but more from the reality of a male-dominated lumber industry. Very few women held positions of authority in the major lumber companies; a fact made more than clear to her on numerous occasions.

These past weeks she'd been lucky to get three hours of sleep a night. There was so much to learn. It would be far easier to quit. No one would be surprised. A lot of people waited for her to fail. Josh Morgan, in particular, hovered like a predatory hawk, watching everything she did. He'd like nothing better than for her to agree to his plan for her to act as a figurehead and not take any real role in the business of the mill.

His ridiculous scheme tempted her. To return to Portland and her cozy apartment, see her friends, and live the life she'd worked so hard to build…Heaven. She missed the kids in her class at school. Missed their laughter, their no-holds-barred affection, and their unflagging enthusiasm for life.

After taking her on the tour of the sawmill her first day, Josh had avoided her. He stayed in his office, and she remained in hers. The few times their paths crossed, they'd passed each other in tight-lipped silence, neither meeting the other's gaze.

She rubbed her eyes again, fighting back a yawn. What had her father been thinking when he made up his will? A loud thump in the hallway outside her door cut off a yawn. She froze, staring at her closed door.

Another thud, louder this time.

Had she locked the door?

Thump.

Over an hour ago, Charlie, the head custodian, had stuck his head in her office and asked if she wanted her office cleaned. She told him not to bother, and he'd nodded and told her the cleaners were finished for the night, and they were leaving. There'd been silence. Until now.

Clunk, thump, clunk, thump.

She gulped. Something heavy was being dragged down the stairs. She reached for her phone to call security, but hesitated. What if it was nothing? What if the cleaners weren't finished after all? All too easily she pictured the derisive looks and snide comments she'd face tomorrow if she called for help and nothing was wrong.

A door slammed.

Her heart stuttered. She tiptoed across the office and eased open the door. Audrey's workstation was dark, but the light from Sharla-Jean's office flooded across Audrey's desk and computer, illuminating the small space. Everything looked the same as it had when the secretary left hours ago.

She stepped into the hall and peered up and down the corridor. The red exit sign provided enough ambient light to see the hall was deserted. She exhaled a shaky laugh. *Look at you. Jumping like a mouse at the slightest noise.* This was Renton Falls. Criminal types didn't lurk in deserted office buildings waiting to attack. A shudder ran through her, chilling her blood. Violent crime did happen in this town. Who better than she to know?

She ran her hands up and down her arms, trying to erase the goose bumps. Exhaustion was getting the better of her. The building was old. Old buildings creaked and groaned in the night as the outside air cooled, and the timbers settled. She studied the empty hallway one more time, blew out a ragged breath, and swung back to her office.

The squeal of a door opening in the main lobby below echoed from the stairwell at the end of the hall.

She pressed her hand against her chest to slow her heart's frantic racing. Tensing, she waited, but no other sound broke the building's grave-like silence. She edged back into the safety of her well-lit office, but halted before she closed the door. What if someone was stealing the computers or the petty cash kept in the locked safe in the main lobby? She couldn't just hide up here in her office and lock the door and pretend she hadn't heard anything.

She should call mill security and have the night watchman come over and investigate. An image of Josh Morgan, a smug smirk on his all-too-handsome face rose before her. Inhaling a deep breath, she checked her pocket for her cell phone. If she heard so much as a mouse squeak, she'd call for help. Shuffling one careful step after another, she headed down the corridor toward the stairs and pushed open the door.

Security lights flickered to life and lit the narrow stairwell, and she moved onto the landing. The door slammed shut behind her, and she jumped, her hand going to her throat. Her heart threatened to beat out of her chest. She waited, inhaling several deep, lungfuls of air. Silence surrounded her.

The clunk of her shoes on the tiled stairs echoed in the enclosed stairwell. She tugged open the door at the bottom and peeked into the lobby. Light from the outside yard lights streamed through the large windows, creating ribbons of shadow and light between the reception desk and visitors' couches.

Opening the door wider, she stepped into the dim

lobby. Nothing seemed out of place. Thank goodness she hadn't called the night watchman. A cool breeze wafted over her, and the leaves of a large dieffenbachia plant in a brass pot on the floor beside one of the leather visitors' couches swayed. She glanced toward the main entry door, and her breath caught in her throat. The door was open.

What the hell? A rock the size of a baseball was jammed in the opening, preventing the door from closing. The thud of her heart amped up until all she heard was its frantic pounding. She fumbled in her pocket for her cell phone, drew it out, but dropped it. The tiny phone clattered across the tile floor and slid under the reception desk. She scrambled after it, but spotted the storage room door and froze. The door was half open, the tiny room beyond a dark void.

The cleaning staff stored their supplies in the closet, and the office manager ensured the door was closed and locked. She studied the gaping door. The wooden frame was gouged. Small chunks of wood lay scattered on the floor below as if someone had pried open the lock. Why would anyone break into the storage room? Who'd steal paper towels and liquid soap?

She dropped to her knees and scrambled under the desk for her phone. Where was the damn thing?

A whisper of sound leaked from the storage room. A small pop, followed by crackling.

Heart hammering, she rose to her feet and backed toward the front doors, never taking her eyes off the dark storage room. A familiar odor stung her nostrils, and she halted.

Fire!

Even as the dreaded word reared like a monster inside her head, a thin trickle of smoke crept out of the room. Terrifying images of flame, smoke and searing heat threatened to overwhelm her. For a nightmare second, she was back in the midst of scorching heat and roaring flames.

Using all her strength of will, she tore free of the chilling memories. Instead of fleeing, she placed one wobbly step in front of the other and inched toward the storage room. Her nostrils flared at the acrid tang of gasoline and smoke. With a shaking hand, she gripped the door handle and opened the door wider.

A figure burst out of the darkness, crashing into her, knocking her back.

She yelped at the pain of the blow and the shock of falling. A jolt of agony and blinding light as her head hit something hard.

Heavy boots pounded across the tile floor.

Cold air washed over her. And then, darkness.

****

Josh rubbed the dull ache in the back of his neck as he watched the paramedics strap Sharla-Jean onto a wheeled gurney, cover her with a thin, gray blanket, and wheel the stretcher through the office doors to the waiting ambulance.

They loaded the stretcher into the back of the vehicle with calm precision. One ambulance attendant climbed into the back with Sharla-Jean. The other slammed the door shut and hurried around to the driver's seat. The engine rumbled to life, and with a burst of siren and the flash of lights, the ambulance pulled away from the mill office and crossed the lumberyard to the road beyond.

Josh's heart pounded in his chest, a holdover from the rush of adrenaline that had coursed through his body when he'd opened the stairwell door and spied Sharla-Jean lying unconscious on the floor in the lobby, blood pooling on the floor by her head. Each stride seemed to take forever as he'd rushed to her side. Her face was pale, her lips bloodless. For a heartbeat, a terrible nanosecond of dread, he'd feared she was dead.

With fumbling fingers, he'd grabbed her wrist and felt for a pulse. It was thin and thready. He called for the ambulance and waited, holding her cold, limp hand in his. What the hell had happened? He'd believed the building deserted, as it was every night while he toiled in his office until the wee hours of the morning. He hadn't heard a sound until her cry of alarm.

The siren faded in the distance.

"There's something you oughta see, Boss."

Josh met Fred Kowalski's anxious gaze. Fred was the mill's night security guard. He worked the late shift from eight in the evening until eight in the morning. Fred had worked at Bromley Forest Products since Big Jim started the company. With the buttons on his uniform shirt gaping as they strained over his impressive belly, his three chins, and thunder thighs, he cut a substantial figure. He was in his late sixties, but had a sharp mind and kept a close eye on the mill. At least, he did when he was awake.

Josh had found the security guard asleep on the job on numerous occasions, but he didn't have the heart to fire him. You couldn't put a price on loyalty. And Fred was as loyal as a Saint Bernard. He was also good-natured and quick with a joke, but not now. His bushy brows were furrowed and his mouth turned down.

Josh braced himself. "What is it, Fred? What did you find?"

Fred ran his hand over his thinning, gray hair. "Better see for yourself, Boss." He led the way back inside the office building, limping slightly, favoring his bum hip.

Josh winced at the streak of blood on the gleaming tile floor.

"Boss?"

Josh tore his gaze from the blood. "Show me what you found."

Fred pointed to the gouges in the wood on the doorframe beside the door handle on the storage room door. "Looks like someone broke in." He pulled the door open, reached inside and flicked on a light and pointed.

A wave of gas fumes stung Josh's nostrils. *What the hell?* A frisson of unease trilled along his spine, and he elbowed Fred aside and bulldozed into the room. The stench of gas and smoke was overpowering in the small, confined space. His eyes watered from the pungent fumes, but his tears did nothing to hide the shocking sight before him.

"I haven't touched anything." Fred's voice was all business. No joking this time. "I figured you'd want to see this before I called the police."

A red, plastic, five-gallon gas container lay on its side on the floor in the middle of the small room. Gasoline leaked from the gas can's plastic spout and pooled on the tile floor. Beside the can, were several scrunched up cleaning rags, their edges charred. File folders lay scattered across the floor, their covers damp from spilled gasoline. Josh's gut lurched. "What the hell?"

"Looks to me like someone wanted to burn the place down." Fred wiped his streaming eyes with a red plaid handkerchief. "Lucky for us those rags didn't burn worth shit."

The ache in Josh's neck throbbed with increased intensity. "All this stuff was here, just like this?"

Fred nodded. "Want me to call the cops?"

Josh crouched before the can of gas and picked up a file folder and lifted the cover. *What the hell?* The file was one of the accounts Audrey had told him Sharla-Jean had requested. The next file was the same. And the next. All the files were from Sharla-Jean's office.

Sinking back on his heels, he rubbed the pounding ache in the back of his neck. Why the hell were the files here? Had Sharla-Jean dropped them before she fell and hit her head in the lobby? He shook his head. That didn't make sense. There was no reason for her to be in here. Not in the middle of the night. Besides, she had a key. She wouldn't have to jimmy the door to gain access.

He studied the storage closet. Nothing of value was kept here. Cleaning supplies, plus packages of toilet paper and paper towels were neatly stacked on the metal shelves. An industrial-sized vacuum cleaner sat in the corner. Several mops stood in a large, blue, plastic, wheeled pail. A wide-brush push broom leaned against the shelf. Everything was as it should be…except—

A small metal file cabinet was almost hidden behind the mop bucket. He shoved the bucket aside. A chill settled over him as he recognized the deep gouge on the top of the three-drawer file cabinet and the large rust stain on the bottom corner. The file cabinet was from Sharla-Jean's office. He'd wanted to replace the old cabinet years ago, but Audrey had refused. The cabinet had been in the office since Big Jim started the company. She'd wanted Sharla-Jean to have it as a memento of her father.

So what was it doing down here? The ache in his neck sharpened. What the hell was going on? Was this someone's idea of a joke? He wasn't laughing. If the fire had taken hold, the entire office could have burned.

As if reading his mind, Fred said, "Damn good thing the fire petered out. If it had taken off, no telling the damage it a done." He mopped his brow.

Josh focused on the strange assortment of materials before him. The entire setup stunk to high heaven. It was as if it had been staged. There was no way the gas-soaked rags and files would have resulted in a fire big enough to do any real damage. Before the flames reached a dangerous level, the smoke detectors would have sounded, and the state-of-the-art sprinkler system he'd convinced Big Jim to install all over the mill five years ago would have sprayed a stream of fire retardant over everything, dousing the flames.

The tightening in his gut knotted. Whoever did this hadn't planned to burn the building down. This was something else. A warning? The more he studied the arrangement of the gas container, rags, and file folders, the more he was certain he was right. Whoever did this wanted the fire to be discovered before any real damage occurred. That's why no effort had been made to hide the broken lock. But why place the file cabinet from Sharla-Jean's office and the files she'd requested here?

"Um, Boss?"

Josh glanced over his shoulder at Fred. "What is

it?"

Fred scratched the back of his neck. His gaze skittered around the room, not settling anywhere. "You don't suppose Miss Bromley had something to do with this, do you?" He flushed, shifting from one foot to the other, still not meeting Josh's gaze. "It's no secret she wasn't happy with the terms of Big Jim's will."

Josh didn't even have to think about Fred's suggestion. "She didn't do this."

"How can you be so sure? Everyone knows what she done before."

Josh shook his head. "That's just it. Everyone knows. She's too smart to do something this obvious. Besides, how do you suppose she fell and hit her head?" The knot in his gut fisted. "Someone else did this. When Sharla-Jean came to investigate, that same someone attacked her and escaped."

This was another of the acts of vandalism that had plagued the mill these past two months. So far, he'd been able to keep everything quiet. He hoped the creep would make a mistake, and then Josh would nail his balls to the wall.

"Should I call the police, Boss?"

Josh got to his feet and shook his head. "Don't call them."

"What?" Fred's brows arched. "Someone tried to burn down the building and hurt Miss Bromley. We have to call the cops."

Again Josh shook his head. "No police. I'll deal with this."

"But—"

"I said, I'll handle it, Fred."

A long silence ensued, and Fred blew out a breath.

"Okay. You're the boss."

"Good job tonight, Fred." Josh patted him on the shoulder. "Finding this was smart."

Fred's swarthy face flushed red. "Wish I'd been here sooner, then maybe Miss Bromley wouldn't have been hurt. Never figured I'd say this, but good thing Big Jim's not alive. He'd rip me a new one if he thought I'd let someone hurt his daughter." He mopped his gleaming brow. "Speaking of which, I should get back to my rounds. If you don't need me no more."

"No, that's fine, Fred. Thanks."

"Sure." He nodded and lumbered away.

"Oh, and Fred." Josh called after him. "Don't tell anyone what you found. Okay?"

Fred stopped, his brow furrowed. "Are you sure, Boss?"

"I'm sure."

"All right, then." He gestured a small salute and strode off into the dark.

The burn of anger flooding through Josh's veins transformed into icy determination. The carefully staged scene was arranged to make it appear as if Sharla-Jean had tried to set fire to the office complex. Hell, he wanted the woman gone and out of his life more than pretty much anything, but even he could see this was a setup.

No point calling the police. All a police investigation would do was succeed in frightening everyone. Production would slow, and the bastard would win. If someone wanted his attention, he'd sure as hell succeeded. Hurting Sharla-Jean was the end of the line. He'd find the person responsible. He wouldn't sleep until he did. Josh would be watching. And waiting. No one messed with his mill.

He strode out of the lobby, locked the door behind him, and loped across the yard to his truck

Chapter 8

Sharla-Jean fought her way through thick layers of cloying fog toward the light. The second she opened her eyes she moaned at the stabbing brightness and squeezed her lids closed. The distant murmur of voices and the squeak of rubber-soled shoes on tile floors crept through the haze. An acrid medicinal smell stung her nostrils. She licked her lips. They were cracked, her mouth dry, her tongue thick.

"Here, dear, drink some water."

She pried open her heavy lids. Pauline's face wavered above her. She blinked, fighting to clear her vision.

Pauline held out a plastic glass with a bendable straw. "Come on, drink. It'll do you good." She pressed the straw between Sharla-Jean's lips.

The first mouthful of tepid water tasted like fine wine, and Sharla-Jean sucked down the entire glass. She laid her head back against the pillow and tried to think through the waves of pain. Why was she in the hospital?

Pauline seemed to read her mind. "The doctor says you have a concussion."

"Concussion?" Sharla-Jean's voice was a croak. "What happened?"

"You don't remember?"

She shook her head and grimaced as a wave of

agony rocketed through her. A myriad of disjointed images flickered before her—smoke, the crackle and pop of fire, pain and darkness. "Josh?" His name slipped from her lips. Had she heard his voice? Was the memory real? Or had she imagined he was there?

"He's on his way." Pauline patted her arm. "He called me from the mill. He's very worried about you."

Sharla-Jean struggled to compute Pauline's words with the reality of her relationship with Josh. He hated her. He wanted her out of his life and out of the mill.

Pauline prattled on. "He was the one who found you and called for help. I swear, I've never heard that boy so upset. Not even when Big Jim was ailing."

Before Sharla-Jean could digest this surprising news, the door swung open, and Josh strode into the room.

His hair was rumpled as if he'd run his fingers through the ebony curls. His clothes were wrinkled, and a black streak marred the front of his shirt. His gaze met hers, and he smiled. "You're awake."

She blinked, stunned by the power of that hundred-watt grin. His normally harsh features softened, and golden flecks danced in his dark brown eyes. Her heartbeat kicked up a notch. His smile was a deadly weapon, one she seemed defenseless against. Good thing he didn't use it often around her.

He stepped closer to her bed and grasped her hand. His warm, callused palm rested against hers as his long, tanned fingers interlaced with hers. "How are you doing?"

"Good." She couldn't stop what must surely be a foolish grin spreading across her face.

He chuckled. "I don't believe you. You took a hard

blow to the head. I imagine your head's throbbing right now." A dimple danced in one rugged cheek, and he leaned closer. His warm breath washed over her. "So, tell me the truth. How are you really feeling?"

Gaping like a schoolgirl, she fought to push out the words stuck in her throat.

Pauline jumped in. "She has a minor concussion. The doctor told me the CAT scan showed some brain swelling, but if she takes things easy for a few days, she should be as good as new." She squeezed Sharla-Jean's other hand. "Thank the Lord."

"Did she tell you what happened?" He directed his question at Pauline.

"Not yet. She just opened her eyes a few minutes ago." Pauline blew out a breath. "I can't tell you how worried I was when you called telling me she was on her way to the hospital in an ambulance. I about had a heart attack."

"I figured you'd want to be here with her."

"I sure did. Thank you for calling."

"I'd have been here sooner"—his face darkened— "but there were a few things I had to do."

"Hey, you two," Sharla-Jean said. "I'm right here. I can hear what you're saying."

Pauline patted Sharla-Jean's arm. "I know, dear. I'm so relieved you're okay."

Josh grabbed a chair and sat beside Pauline. His gaze pinned Sharla-Jean to the bed. "Can you tell me what happened?"

She started to shake her head, but froze at the stab of pain. Tears stung her eyes, and she blinked them back. Careful to keep her head still, she tried again. "Everything's kind of a blur. I was working in my office and I heard noises. It sounded like someone hauling something heavy down the hall."

Josh frowned. "What were you doing at the office so late? I didn't know you were there."

"She's there every night," said Pauline. "I tell her she works too hard, but she doesn't listen." Her mouth tightened into a moue of disapproval.

Josh's eyes narrowed. "Okay, so you heard a noise. What happened next?"

"I checked the hall to see what was going on, and a door slammed somewhere downstairs."

He jerked upright with such force, the chair skidded back. His dark eyes flashed fire. "Let me get this straight. You heard a noise, and as far as you knew, you were all alone in the building, and the first thing you do is investigate? You don't call for help?" His upper lip curled in a sneer. "Have you never watched a slasher movie in your life?"

"I didn't want to bother anyone." Even to her own ears, her reasoning sounded feeble. She'd been more concerned about making a fool of herself than calling for help. She licked her dry lips, wishing she had more water to moisten her parched throat.

He cursed under his breath and stormed across the room to the window and stared outside.

"Are you still thirsty, dear?" Pauline's voice broke the strained silence. "Do you want another drink?"

"I'll get it." Josh turned from the window and removed a small plastic water glass from a stack, and filled it with water from the pitcher on the rolling cart beside Sharla-Jean's bed. He added a bendable plastic straw to the glass. Leaning close, he eased the straw between her lips.

Sharla-Jean inhaled his scent, a mixture of smoke, sweat, and man. A flood of warmth washed over her.

"Look"—he set the empty glass on the bedside tray—"I'm sorry. I didn't mean to bite your head off." He blew out a breath. "It's just, I feel this is my fault."

"Your fault?" She blinked. "How could this be your fault?"

He ran his fingers through his hair. "I was in my office."

The movement distracted her, and her heart fluttered. Was his hair as soft as it looked? But then his words sank in, and she jerked, setting off a fresh wave of agony. She pressed her hand to her head and breathed deep until the pain eased. He'd been working in his office just down the hall from hers? She'd assumed she was alone in the building. "You were there? Why didn't you hear that thudding in the hall? The noises were really loud."

He jiggled the change in his pockets as he rocked back and forth on the balls of his feet. His face reddened. "I guess I fell asleep. I didn't hear a damn thing until you called out. I'm sorry."

"Both of you have been working far too hard lately." Pauline stood and placed her hands on her narrow hips. "It's time you stop this silly feud and work together. That's what Big Jim would have wanted."

Josh's eyebrow arched a fraction of an inch higher.

Sharla-Jean gulped, reading the challenge in his dark irises. Work together? The two of them? Not likely. This was a temporary truce. Once she was better, their animosity toward one another would resume.

"Sharla-Jean? Tell us what you remember. We need to know what happened." Pauline's no-nonsense voice broke through her thoughts.

Sharla-Jean dragged her gaze from Josh. "I went down to the lobby to check on the noise. I thought maybe one of the janitors was working late, or an employee had come back for something he'd forgotten." She rubbed her head, willing the unceasing ache to ease. "The front door was open. A rock blocked it from closing. The storage room door was open as well. It looked like someone had broken the lock."

Josh's mouth tightened. "What happened next?"

She squeezed her eyes shut and remembered the crackle of fire...the stench of something burning...smoke...panic...and... Her eyes flew open. "Someone hit me."

Pauline caught her breath.

Josh's eyes darkened. "Are you sure?"

"Someone shoved past me. I fell and must have smashed my head on something." She shrugged and met his gaze. "That's all I remember."

The muscles in his jaw clenched. "Did you see who pushed you?"

"Everything happened so fast. I smelled smoke." Her eyes widened and she struggled to sit. "Was there a fire? Is the mill all right?"

He gripped her shoulders with both hands and eased her back on the bed. "The mill's fine. The fire didn't take." Dark shadows filled his eyes. "We were lucky."

A wave of relief washed over her, but then she saw his frown. "What is it? What aren't you telling me?"

"Where do you store the files you request from Audrey when you're not using them?"

"Files?" She rubbed her temples. "In my office.

Why?"

His sharp gaze fixed on her. "Several of your files were on the floor in the storeroom."

She blinked. "That's impossible."

He arched a brow. "Is it?"

"They're in my office," she insisted. "I stuck them in that old filing cabinet Audrey gave me. It's the ugliest thing I've ever seen, but it belonged to my father, and she was determined I have it." The breath whooshed out of her. "That's right. I forgot. I asked Kevin Nelson yesterday to put the cabinet in that alcove in the hall when Audrey was off on lunch. I didn't want a constant reminder of my father in my office. Kevin must have forgotten to take out the files before he moved the cabinet." She rubbed her temples. "Why does this matter right now? What do you care about that old cabinet?"

"Someone hauled the filing cabinet down to the janitor's storage room and tossed your files on the floor."

A chill settled over her. "Someone wanted everyone to think I started the fire, didn't they?"

"Looks that way."

Pauline's gasp filled the shocked silence.

Sharla-Jean placed a hand over her chest to stop the furious pounding of her heart. "So that's the noise I heard. Someone dragged the cabinet down the hall and downstairs to the storeroom."

"I don't understand." Pauline sank onto a chair. "Why would someone go to all that trouble? Why would they want Sharla-Jean blamed for a fire?"

Sharla-Jean spoke first. "I'm not the most popular person at the mill. Lots of people would be happy if I were charged with arson." She narrowed her eyes and pinned Josh with a hard look. "Do you think I did this? You do, don't you? You believe I set fire to the office and tried to burn down the building." Her stomach twisted. His suspicion felt like a betrayal. Why did it hurt so much? He'd never hidden the fact he wanted her to leave.

"I don't think you did it."

She stared. *I don't think you did it.* His words acted as a soothing balm on her ravaged soul. "You don't?"

He shook his head. "You wouldn't have left your files and the cabinet in the storage room. You're too smart for that."

Her relief faded at his halfhearted support, and in its place arose a deep-seated anger. "I get it. You think if I wanted to set fire to the office, I'd do a better job. Isn't that right? After all, I've had experience. I mean, I did a damn good job of torching the old mill, didn't I?" She collapsed back on the bed, her head pounding from her outburst.

"I didn't say that." His face was hard, his mouth a tight line, his jaw rigid.

"But that's what you meant."

Pauline put up her hand, stopping his retort. "Enough, you two." Her stern voice brooked no argument. "This isn't helping. Someone hurt Sharla-Jean tonight. She could have been killed." She gripped Sharla-Jean's hand, her fingers squeezing until it hurt.

"I was afraid something like this would happen. That's why I wanted her to stay in Portland and leave the running of the mill to me." Josh shoved a lock of hair off his forehead. His fervid gaze settled on Sharla-Jean. "You were too damn stubborn to do what was best. Now look what's happened."

And just like that, the truce was over. Fire boiled her blood. "Are you blaming me for what happened?"

Pauline spun to Josh. "This isn't Sharla-Jean's fault."

"Isn't it?" he asked. "Plenty of people in this town hold a grudge against her for the way she treated Big Jim. Hell, no one wanted her to come back, let alone try and take over the mill."

"Ridiculous," Pauline scoffed. "No one would set out to deliberately hurt her. They had too much respect for Big Jim. They might be irritated at Sharla-Jean, but they wouldn't lay a hand on her."

Josh stared pointedly at the white gauze bandage wrapped around Sharla-Jean's forehead. "Sure as hell doesn't look that way from where I'm standing."

Sharla-Jean found her voice. "This attack wasn't personal."

"Really?" His brows arched. "How do you know?"

"Because anyone, the security guard, one of the cleaners, or even you could have heard the noise and gone to check. No one could have counted on me going downstairs on my own."

He blew out a breath. "Okay, you tell me what you think happened."

She rubbed her temples in a vain attempt to ease the furious pounding. "Some kid probably broke into the office looking to steal cash or computer equipment."

He snorted. "The lock on the front door wasn't broken. How would some punk get in?"

She shrugged, and then winced as a wave of pain washed over her. "The cleaners must have left the door unlocked. Why are you so certain someone was out to get me?"

He shook his head, his frustration with her more than clear. "I'm not doing this with you. Not here. Not now." He paced to the window, his shoulders tight, the muscles in his arms rigid, his hands bunched into fists. "You're not to be alone in the office anymore. No more working late. You'll leave when everyone else leaves."

Her breath hissed out. "You're telling me what to do?"

He spun around. "Yep."

She laughed, a harsh, rough sound. The movement sent a shard of agony through her throbbing head, and she closed her eyes for a minute and breathed. The pain ebbed, and she pried her eyes open again. "I don't need you or anyone else telling me what to do. I'll do what I want, when I want. I own half of the mill. Don't ever forget I'm also the boss around here." She fell back panting, her head throbbing, drained.

His eyes narrowed to slits. "Oh, believe me, lady, I'm perfectly aware of who you are, and what you are."

"Josh," Pauline said, "enough. It's time you left."

He shook his head and stormed out of the room. The door swung closed behind him.

"Well, I never." Pauline's lined face was a study in outrage. "That young man has a thing or two to learn about manners. I can't begin to imagine what's gotten into him."

Through numbing exhaustion and throbbing pain, Sharla-Jean wondered the same thing.

****

His anger propelled him out of Sharla-Jean's hospital room and down the hall. He seethed as he stormed across the dimly lit parking lot to where he'd parked his truck. Leaning against the hood, he withdrew a crumpled pack of cigarettes. He removed one and jammed the cigarette between his lips, savoring the sweet tang of tobacco.

In the next breath, he cursed and yanked the cigarette out of his mouth, tossed it on the pavement, and ground it beneath his boot. The cigarette package followed. He raised his foot to crush the package and the remaining cigarettes, but stopped. Cursing again, he bent and retrieved the package and tugged out a cigarette. He searched in his pocket for his lighter, flicked it, and set the tiny flame to the tip of the cigarette.

Inhaling deeply, he dragged in the sharp bite of smoldering tobacco, drawing the smoke deep into his lungs. As the rush of nicotine attacked his bloodstream, he swore. *Damn that woman.* She'd be to blame if he ended up with lung cancer.

The moon's cold light shone across the almost-deserted parking lot. He massaged the back of his neck as he puffed on the cigarette. The image of Sharla-Jean laying pale and injured in the hospital bed was burned into his retinas. She'd been in pain. He hadn't missed the way she'd flinched at the slightest jarring.

He'd acted like an ass. He hadn't meant to take his fear and guilt out on her. But if he hadn't fallen asleep at his desk, he'd have heard the same noises she had, and he'd have been the one to investigate. She wouldn't be in the hospital.

Had she been the target? Or was she right, and it was just rotten luck she'd been the one to catch the jerk in the act? He tore the smoldering cigarette from his mouth and tossed the butt on the ground, grinding the glowing ash beneath his boot.

Someone broke into the office; someone intent on causing trouble. That same someone had a key to the front door. He didn't believe Sharla-Jean's theory the cleaning staff had left the door unlocked. The janitors hadn't broken into the storage room. They hadn't placed the gas and rags. They certainly hadn't hauled the old filing cabinet down there and scattered the file folders all over the floor.

Someone was out to cause trouble, and the creep had just upped the ante. Josh spit out a thread of tobacco and ran his fingers through his hair. How the hell was he supposed to protect the mill and keep Sharla-Jean safe?

Chapter 9

Pauline's endless fussing was driving Sharla-Jean nuts. If she ate one more bowl of chicken soup, or drank one more cup of ginger tea, she'd murder someone. She adored Pauline and appreciated all she did, but Sharla-Jean needed to get back to the mill. Over the past three days, the painful ache in her head had lessened to a dull throb, and the cut on the back of her head was almost healed.

And what was up with Josh? When he'd arrived at the hospital, she'd been stunned at the concern in his dark eyes. He'd acted like he cared. She'd almost believed him, but then in a heartbeat, his warm kindness had morphed into outrage, and he'd blamed her for the attack.

She grimaced. Why waste the effort to try and figure him out? Her job at the mill would end in eleven-and-a-half more months. After that, she'd return to Portland and never see him again. In the meantime, she had more important issues to worry about.

Managing a mill was challenging. Foolish to think she could do this on her own. She needed a mentor. Someone to teach her what she needed to know.

Under normal circumstances, Josh would be the obvious choice. The mill employees respected him. How many times over the past weeks had someone told her how Josh had singlehandedly transformed the mill from a small lumber company with a regional base to one of the biggest in the Northwest? All the upper management employees were loyal to Josh. Like him, they bided their time, watching like starving hyenas waiting until she gave up and returned to Portland.

Josh wouldn't help her. She needed someone who didn't hold any loyalty to him, someone willing, even eager to help, if for no reason other than to spite Josh. One name came to mind: Kevin Nelson. He'd taken her on a tour of the planer mill her first day. She hadn't liked him, but he seemed knowledgeable; at least, he had until Josh appeared and chased him away. She recalled the flash of anger that had hardened Kevin's boyishly handsome face when Josh ordered him back to work. He just might be the one.

Later that day, after she'd promised Pauline she'd take it easy and be home for supper, Sharla-Jean headed to the mill determined to put her plan into action.

She hadn't been in her office ten minutes before Kevin appeared at her door sporting a wide, toothy grin. "Audrey tells me you need some help." He lounged in a chair uninvited and crossed his long legs. His blue-eyed gaze slid over her, lingering on her breasts, before checking out her mouth. With his slicked-back, blond hair, cocky grin, and roving eyes, he was a playboy, far too aware of his attractiveness to women.

She stiffened, resisting the urge to cross her arms over her chest. Maybe asking him for help wasn't such a smart idea. But who else was there?

He ogled her breasts, a faint smile on his lips.

Her irritation flared. "Are they big enough for you? Or do you prefer larger breasts?" Her voice was cold.

A wash of red flared along his neck and over his

face, settling on his ears, which she was pleased to note were large and stuck out from his head.

"I…I…" he sputtered, stumbling over the words.

She almost smiled at his discomfort, but kept her face stern and her voice hard. "I need someone who knows the ins and outs of this company. Audrey tells me you do."

He opened his mouth to speak.

She held up her hand, forestalling him. "If we're going to work together, we need to get a few issues straight." She leaned forward her gaze connecting with his. "First, this is strictly a business relationship. I'm your boss; you're my assistant. Nothing more. You will treat me with respect, and that means keeping your eyes on work and your hands off me. If you can't handle my conditions, you'd better leave."

A new flush of red coursed over his face, but this time the heat wasn't from embarrassment. Anger tightened his mouth and narrowed his eyes.

She waited, heart pounding, as he fought for control. Would anyone hear her if she called for help?

He blew out a breath and nodded. "I'm sorry if I gave you the wrong impression, *Miss* Bromley. I'd like to help you if you're willing." His words were clipped, his smile forced.

A wave of victory washed over her. *Score one for feminism.* She nodded. "Okay, let's get to work. I need to know how this place runs, and I need to know now."

"Where do you want to start?"

****

She peered through the windshield at the clear blue sky and rolled down the car window, breathing in the sharp, peppery scent of decaying leaves. She'd promised Pauline she'd forget work and relax, at least, for today, but her mind kept returning to the past days at the mill.

In spite of her initial trepidation, Kevin Nelson was proving to be an invaluable help. He demonstrated surprising patience, never complaining about the long hours spent closeted in her office going over financial statements, or wandering around in the lumberyard explaining the mill process. His behavior was above reproach, but once or twice she'd glanced up from a document she was studying and found him watching her, a predatory gleam in his pale-blue eyes. As soon as he noticed she was looking at him, the gleam vanished, leaving her to wonder if she'd imagined the look.

Because of his assistance, she had a better grasp of the complicated workings of Bromley Forest Products. She was learning the diverse aspects of the company from the licensed forestlands with their stands of mature coniferous trees, to the sawmill, the planer, and the markets throughout the States and Japan where they shipped their products.

She steered the car around a curve and squinted against the bright sunshine streaming through the windshield. The day was one of those rare fall days. Brilliant robin's-egg blue skies gave the appearance of warmth, but the air was cool with a hint of frost. The leaves on the trees were resplendent in their golden glory.

She hadn't been to the lake in years, but her memories of the place were crystal clear. Her father had built the cabin when he was a young man, and he'd often taken his wife and small daughter to enjoy the peace and silence of the little log cottage in the woods.

Life changed after her mother died, and for years, no one used the cabin, but then Sharla-Jean rediscovered the place. The cabin in its remote wilderness setting provided the perfect refuge for a troubled teenager and an escape from the unbearable tensions at home.

A sense of anticipation filled her, as she swerved off the highway onto the rutted, winding gravel lane. She steered the car into a tiny clearing and stopped before a modest log cabin surrounded by thick stands of old growth forest.

A host of memories surrounded her, and once again she was an angry, young girl furious with her father and determined to cause him as much grief as possible. She'd driven too fast, smoked cigarettes, drank alcohol, and hung around with the bad crowd. Anything to antagonize and embarrass him. Each time the sheriff had hauled her into his office and called her father to come and get her was a victory.

Only here, at this isolated cabin in the woods, surrounded by four sturdy log walls had she let down her barriers. Here she'd given vent to her grief, both over the senseless passing of her mother, and the subsequent loss of her father as he shut himself off from her, turning into a cold, soulless, angry, bitter man. Without a doubt, the night her mother died, she'd lost both parents.

Inhaling a deep breath, she thrust the past away. She'd come here to escape her problems, not relive them. She studied the rustic cabin. The log walls had faded to a soft gray, and the small front porch sagged crookedly, but the cabin was as she remembered.

The slanting rays of the late afternoon sun streaked

across the moss-covered, cedar-shingled roof. A thin stream of smoke puffed out of the stone chimney. The evidence of a fire unsettled her for a moment, but Pauline had mentioned a caretaker was looking after the place. He must have started a fire to warm up the cabin in preparation of her arrival.

Climbing out of the car, she contemplated the lake. The emerald-green waters rippled in the breeze. The sloping banks were thick with red willows and birch trees. The old, lopsided wooden dock extended ten feet into the small bay. A fish jumped with a splash near shore, and a loon's haunting cry echoed across the lake. The sun caressed her back. She breathed in deep gulps of fresh air.

She opened the back door of her car and hefted her overnight bag, purse, and paper bag of groceries, and packed them across the clearing. The warped, planked boards creaked under her weight as she crossed the porch to the door. Juggling her bags, she fumbled in her jeans' pocket for the key Pauline had given her and unlocked the door.

Pushing open the door, she stepped inside. A fire blazed in the old, river stone fireplace, and the cabin was warm and cozy, the air redolent with the scent of smoldering fir. She stood in the middle of the small room, pleased nothing had changed. A large picture window looked out over the lake. On the opposite wall, wooden shelves sagged under the weight of dozens of dog-eared pocket books, countless board games, puzzles, and stacks of magazines, their yellowed pages rippled from damp, the corners curled.

The same overstuffed couch with the faded floral print sat facing the fireplace. Two sagging, well-worn chairs, one matching the fabric on the couch, the other covered in butter-soft, cracked leather filled the space. A single kerosene lantern sat atop a battered pine end table.

Behind the couch, was the tiny kitchen with the propane stove and fridge. An oval oak table with four mismatched chairs was shoved against the log wall. To her left was the short hallway leading to the cabin's sole bedroom. The outhouse was outside around the back of the cabin.

Pauline was right. This was what she needed. By tomorrow morning she'd be rested and ready to face another grueling week jousting with Josh. With light steps, she walked into the bedroom and set her overnight bag on the double bed in the center of the tiny room. A faded patchwork quilt covered the bed. An old wooden bureau stood against one wall, a chipped, white enamel washbasin and matching pitcher on top.

A framed watercolor of the lake was on the wall above the bed. She studied the picture, and tears stung her eyes at the artist's signature. Joanna Bromley. Her mother. For the first time, she wondered what had happened to the other paintings her mother had done. None of her artwork was hanging in the house. She'd have to ask Pauline.

The crunch of gravel on the lane outside drew her out of her memories. She peered out the window, but couldn't see who'd arrived. No one but Pauline knew she was here. The caretaker must have come by to say hello. She headed into the main room and opened the cabin door and stepped outside. The welcoming smile froze on her lips.

Kevin Nelson climbed out of a shiny, blue sports

car, a wide grin wreathing his handsome face. "Hello."

She scowled.

He bounded toward her and enfolded her in his arms.

She stiffened and shoved against his hard chest.

Unfazed, he kissed her on the cheek before he released her. "Surprised to see me?"

Surprise was not how she'd describe her reaction. She swiped her cheek with her sleeve, trying to erase all trace of his stolen kiss. "What are you doing here?"

"I had a devil of a time finding this place." He grinned boyishly. "You really should put up some road signs."

"Why are you here?" Her voice was tight with anger.

His smile didn't falter. "I thought we could review last year's budget. It's pretty dry reading, but there aren't any distractions out here. We might be able to get through it without falling asleep." He retraced his steps to his car and withdrew two bottles of red wine. He held the bottles aloft like prizes. "You know what they say…all work and no play." He loped up the steps to the porch and marched into the cabin as if she'd invited him in.

She gritted her teeth and stormed after him, leaving the door open, prepared to blast him for his unwelcome interruption. Instead, she stared dumbfounded.

He'd found a corkscrew and two wine glasses somewhere and had opened one bottle and poured wine into the wine glasses. He grinned, his gaze sweeping over her, lingering a nanosecond too long on her breasts. "Come on, let's have a toast."

Fire burned in her belly. "A toast?"

"To us. You've been working at the mill for four weeks. High time we celebrated the new, and may I say, much prettier management of Bromley Forest Products." He held out a glass.

"Go home, Kevin."

He sipped some wine. "Come on, try the wine. This stuff isn't half bad."

Crossing her arms over her chest, she glared. "Leave. Now."

He guzzled the entire contents of his glass in one long gulp. Downing the second glass even faster, he set the empty glasses on the counter.

A ripple of unease crept up her spine, all the old fears crowding in. She rubbed her damp palms on her pants and edged toward the couch, putting its solid bulk between them.

His gaze never left her face as he stalked across the room toward her.

She backed away.

He was quicker. The toes of his boots bumped against her sneakers. Heat from his body seared her. His sour, liquor-filled breath assaulted her as he leaned close and brushed a lock of hair off her forehead.

She flinched as his fingers lingered, caressing her cheek. A thousand thoughts raced through her, a thousand actions to take, but she remained frozen. *Not again!*

"You don't have to play coy with me, Sharla-Jean. We're not at the office." He smirked. "We can do whatever we want. No one will know."

His words, so utterly ridiculous, broke through her panic. Outrage fueled her fury, and she raised her hands to shove him away.

He stopped her, grabbing her arms, holding them in a vise-like grip. Leaning close, he lowered his head, and his mouth mashed against hers.

"Well, well, well. Isn't this cozy?"

Kevin released her and sprang back as if he'd been burned. "What the hell are you doing here, Morgan?"

She spun at the sound of Josh's voice, relief washing over her like a cooling balm.

Josh's mouth tightened, and a deep vee formed between his dark brows. "I could ask the same of you." He shot her a hard look. "But it's pretty obvious."

She stumbled away from Kevin and collapsed on the couch.

"This is none of your business, Morgan," Kevin said. "I'm not on the clock now."

Josh's eyes were steely. "Why don't you take your"—his lip curled in a sneer—"girlfriend and get the hell out of here, before I do something I won't regret?"

Sharla-Jean blushed under his censure. "This isn't what you think, Josh. I'm not—"

He held up his hand stopping her and pointed to the two empty glasses and the open bottle of wine. His face was livid. "Save it. I don't give a damn what you do, as long as you don't do it on my property."

She stiffened, his words sinking in, dissipating her earlier embarrassment. *His* property? Who did he think he was? Coming uninvited to her cabin and passing judgment on her. "I'd like you to leave." She glared at Kevin, and then at Josh. "Both of you."

"Hey, what did I do?" Kevin waved his hands in the air. "Come on, Sharla-Jean. Don't listen to him. We were just starting to have a good time."

His words, so at odds with reality, infuriated her,

but the condemnation in Josh's dark eyes made her anger explode. "Get out! Now."

Josh shook his head. "I don't think so." He crossed his arms over his chest and leaned against the log wall.

Suddenly she was exhausted, as if in the space of a few minutes, all her energy had drained out of her. She rubbed her hands over her face. "Why won't you go? Why are you pushing this?"

"I'm not leaving because this cabin is mine. Your father gave the place to me before he passed away."

My father gave him the cabin? Impossible. But the truth gleamed in his eyes, his certainty he was right. All her fight vanished, and she sagged against the cushions. Her father gave him the cabin. Why was she surprised? Her father had always taken away the most important things in her life. Why would the cabin be any different?

Chapter 10

"Big Jim signed over ownership of the cabin to me before he died." Josh studied her huddled figure on the couch. "Ask J.D. if you don't believe me. He has a copy of the deed." A brief spurt of guilt washed over him as he realized she hadn't known Big Jim had given him this place. But why would she know? She hadn't poked her nose around here for years.

She regained some of her fire, and thrust to her feet, and jammed her hands on her slim hips. "Look, I don't know what game you're playing, but what you're saying is ridiculous. You were at the reading of my father's will. He left everything to me, the house, his assets, everything."

"Not quite *everything.*" He meant his comment to be smug, but the flash of disappointment on her expressive face hit him like a slap. But he couldn't seem to stop. "He left you the house, *half* the mill, and his money. Wasn't that enough? Why do you care so much about this old cabin?"

She tightened her lips, but instead of attacking, she stormed out of the room into the bedroom, slamming the door behind her.

He pushed away from the wall and followed her to explain somehow, to tell her he was sorry, anything to erase the dull defeat in her vivid green eyes.

"Well, that didn't go very well." Nelson sniggered.

Josh stopped. He'd forgotten the other man. He'd been standing here the whole time, watching, listening, enjoying every tense second of the argument between Josh and Sharla-Jean. Josh wheeled around and faced the cretin, stuffing all his anger into his gaze. "Why the hell are you still here, Nelson? She told you to leave."

Nelson's grin widened, exposing a row of too-white, too-perfect teeth. He leaned against the counter and poured some wine into a glass and raised it to his lips and sipped. "Just enjoying the show." His grin widened. "I think she really cares for this old pile of rotten logs and mouse shit." He raised his glass in a toast. "Good on you to convince her old man to give the place to you. Between this cabin and the mill, you're batting a thousand."

"Get the hell out of here." Josh clenched his fists, fighting for control, resisting the urge to crush Nelson's smirk off his face.

"And now you're screwing Big Jim's daughter." Nelson arched his eyebrows. "From what I hear, she always was an easy lay." He sipped more wine and winked lewdly. "Tell me, is she as hot in bed as she looks?"

Josh's fury boiled over. He leaped across the room, grabbed Nelson by the shirtfront and twisted. The wine glass flew out of Nelson's hand, shattering on the scuffed wooden floor, red wine spraying across the room.

He held the squirming man with one hand and drew back his arm, his fingers clenched in a tight fist. Before he let fly and smacked the bastard in the face, he paused for a breath, enjoying the way Nelson's face paled, and his eyes dilated with fear.

"This is crazy," Nelson sputtered. "You don't want to do this."

"Oh, but I do. I most definitely do." He drove his fist into the other man's face, smiling at the crunch of cartilage and spurt of blood erupting from Nelson's nose. "Time you left, asshole."

Nelson sagged to his knees. Blood dripped on the floor, mixing with the red wine. "What the hell, Morgan?" He cupped his nose with his hands. "I think you broke my nose."

"I sure as hell hope so." Josh grabbed him by the arms and dragged him across the room, ignoring his futile attempts to break free. Josh freed one hand and twisted the door handle, kicking the door open. He shoved Nelson through the door.

The other man landed in a heap on the porch. He glared at Josh, his eyes filled with hatred. "You're going to regret this, Morgan. I'll sue your ass."

Josh swiped at the sweat streaming into his eyes. "Go ahead and try."

Nelson struggled to his feet, one hand pressed to his nose in a vain attempt to stop the bleeding. His eyes flashed fire. "I'll get you for this. You'll pay for what you've done." He staggered across the porch and stumbled to his flashy car.

"Oh, and by the way, Nelson," Josh called. "You're fired."

Nelson shot him the finger and climbed into his car, started the engine with a roar and skidded onto the lane, spraying gravel in his wake.

Josh's gut tightened, knowing he'd made an enemy. He rubbed his bruised knuckles. They'd be even sorer in the morning, but man, he felt good. Pummeling

Nelson had felt damn good.

"Did you hit him?"

He pivoted back to the cabin, letting the door swing closed behind him.

Sharla-Jean stood in the middle of the room, her face pale. She had her coat on and held a small canvas bag in her hand. Her purse was slung over one shoulder. "You attacked him." Her gaze settled on his cut knuckles, and then shifted to the floor. "Is that blood?"

"Some of it's wine."

"How badly is he hurt?"

He shrugged. "He'll survive."

"There's a lot of blood. Are you sure he's okay?"

Her concern for Nelson pissed him off, and he lashed out. "Why do you care? Are the two of you having an affair? Is that what this was? A lover's tryst? Are you screwing him at the office too? Is that why you were *working* late the other night? Was Nelson with you?"

Her face drained of color.

His stomach clenched. He knew in his gut his accusations were groundless, but he couldn't stop attacking. "Well, are you? Are you sleeping with the bastard?" His breath huffed in and out of his chest as if he'd run a marathon.

The bag in her hand dropped to the floor with a thud. She stood unmoving, her eyes dark hollows, tears glistening in the emerald depths.

A heavy silence filled the cabin, broken by a log shifting in the coals of the glowing fire.

He crossed to the kitchen counter and emptied the remaining wine into a clean glass. His hand shook as he raised the glass to his lips and tossed back the drink. He swiped his hand over his mouth. The alcohol settled him. "Look, I'm sorry. I shouldn't have said what I did. What you do with your personal life is none of my business."

She didn't move, didn't speak; didn't look at him.

He set his glass down and moved toward her. "Sharla-Jean?"

She stared at the flickering fire, her breathing ragged.

"Look, I'm sorry." He edged closer, wanting to comfort her, to ease the pain of his harsh words. He grazed her arm, a brief brush of his hand against her warm, soft skin.

Her wild-eyed gaze fastened on him, and she shuffled back several steps. Fear radiated off her in palpable waves.

He didn't move, giving her the space she so obviously needed and gentled his voice. "I'm sorry for what I said. I didn't mean to frighten you."

Her eyes remained dark hollows, the pupils dilated.

Why was she so afraid? Minutes ago she'd been a tigress arguing with him over ownership of the cabin. And now, she quaked with fear.

She shivered, and his gut tightened. He ached to comfort her, but was afraid if he touched her, he'd frighten her even more. "Look, I'm sorry I punched your boyfriend, but other than a broken nose and a bruised ego, he's fine."

"He's not my boyfriend." Her voice was a raw whisper.

Guilt flooded his mouth like a bad taste. "I know." Of course he knew. She and Nelson hadn't been embracing when he walked in on them. She'd been fighting the bastard off. "I'm sorry."

She picked up her bag and headed to the door.

"Where are you going?" Lame, but the best he could come up with.

"Home." She flung open the door, and it smashed into the wall and bounced back, almost striking her.

A blast of wind and rain gusted into the room through the open door. A blinding flash lit the late afternoon sky followed by a tremendous boom. The tiny cabin shuddered under the onslaught of the sudden storm.

Her auburn hair blew back from her pale face, darkening as rain drenched her.

"You can't leave in this storm," he shouted over the roar of the wind. "You know what the road will be like. Stay until this blows over."

Rain poured in. The wind howled. Another flash, this one almost directly overhead, followed immediately by a rolling wave of thunderous sound.

"Let's call a truce." He pointed to the unopened bottle of wine. "Okay? Let's have a glass of the wine Nelson so kindly provided and forget Bromley Forest Products, forget Kevin Nelson, and forget your father's will. Just for tonight." He held his breath, not knowing why he so desperately wanted her to stay, but he sure as hell didn't want her to leave. Not like this. And not before he figured out why she was so spooked. "Please."

She tossed her bag on the floor and used both hands to slam the door closed, shutting out the raging tempest. "Okay."

His breath whooshed out in a burst. "Okay?"

"Okay."

Yes. He stopped short of fist pumping the air.

****

The soft light glowing in the depths of his eyes unsettled her. Why was she still here? She'd had every intention of leaving, but then he apologized, and just like that, her defenses crumbled, and she'd agreed to his offer of a truce.

Truth be told, she was exhausted. The confrontation with Kevin had drained her. She didn't have the energy to fight anymore. Besides, Josh was right. The storm would make the road to the highway impassable. She'd stay until the rain stopped and the road dried enough to navigate in her small car. What would a few hours hurt?

Josh yanked open a drawer in the kitchen, grabbed a small towel, and handed her the cloth. "Better dry your hair." Tugging another cloth from the drawer, he knelt down and wiped the smears of Kevin's blood and spilled wine from the floor. He picked up the shards of the broken wine glass and tossed them in the garbage.

Then he squatted before the fire and stirred the coals with a poker. Picking up a few pieces of wood from a box beside the fireplace, he set the wood in the grate and blew on the glowing coals until flames flared to life.

She rubbed her hair, never taking her gaze off him. The flickering light created intriguing shadows across the planes of his rugged face, softening the sharp angles. His jeans tightened around his firm haunches as he crouched, emphasizing his lean hardness.

He sat back and shoved the sleeves of his flannel shirt up over his tanned, muscular forearms. "How about we try some more of this wine?" The skin at the corners of his eyes crinkled. A single dimple danced in his cheek as his smile grew.

"Okay." She frowned. Was that the only word she knew?

He used the corkscrew to open the second bottle of wine and poured two glasses and handed her one.

She sucked in a breath at the sight of his injured knuckles. "Your hand."

He glanced at his wounds. "They're a little scraped, is all." His grin widened. "You should see the other guy."

"Let me see." She set her glass on the counter, lifted his hand, and examined the wound. The skin around his knuckles was swollen and beginning to bruise. A cut ran across one knuckle. "This must hurt."

"Not too bad, but it'll sting like a mother in the morning."

"Let me get some ice."

"It's okay." He tugged his hand away. "I'll be fine. I don't need any ice."

She ignored his protests and crossed to the fridge and opened the small icebox, removing the plastic tray of ice cubes. She emptied the cubes into the towel she'd used to dry her hair. Taking his hand once again, she gently pressed the cloth over his wound.

He flinched, but kept his hand in hers.

"Sorry." The moisture dried in her mouth. He was close. Too close, but she remained still, inhaling the scent of wood smoke, autumn leaves, and man. Her body swayed toward him as if drawn to a flame.

A piercing flash of lightning lit the dark outside the large picture window, and the cabin shook with the rumble of thunder.

She jerked back, but didn't release her hold on him.

His hand rested in hers. Fine, dark hairs sprinkled the tanned skin. His nails were cut short and square. The thin, jagged line of a faded scar stretched across the web of his thumb.

She turned his hand over and her fingers grazed his callused palm. His hand bore the marks of a man who built and repaired, a man capable of accomplishing anything. It was a warm, comforting hand that she wanted to hold and never let go.

He tugged free. "Um, I think that's good enough." Grabbing a full glass of wine, he drained it in a single gulp. "So," he said brightly, "what are we going to eat?"

Her heart pounded. "E…eat?" She stumbled over the word. "I should go." She searched for her bag. Where was the damn thing?

"The storm's picking up. You can't leave yet." As if to prove the truth to his words, a sudden kaboom cracked in the skies over the cabin, followed by the drumming of rain on the shake roof. The old windows in their warped frames rattled and creaked under a blast of wind. "Come on. Have a drink." He held out the other glass of wine. An enticing grin wreathed his rugged face. "This stuff ain't half bad."

She hesitated. He wasn't her friend. They were enemies, opponents in a battle. Hadn't he told her that very thing weeks ago when he'd kissed her? But he'd declared a truce…at least for tonight. And there was a storm raging outside. Blowing out a resigned breath, she accepted the glass of wine. The liquor slid down her throat like silk, tasting of sun-ripened blackberries with a hint of vanilla. "This is good."

His smile grew, the dimple in his cheek dancing. "Told you." He opened the fridge. "Now, let's see what we can find to eat."

"I'm not hungry." Being alone with him in the cabin was one thing; sitting down to a meal was another thing entirely. "I don't want anything to eat." No sooner were the words out of her mouth than her stomach rumbled. She winced. Face flaming, she braved a glance at him. In spite of her chagrin, she burst out laughing at the expression on his face.

His dark brows were raised in comic disbelief. "Come on, let's stow the knives for now. I don't know about you, but I'm starving."

"I guess I am a little hungry."

"You think?" He chuckled.

She couldn't help giggling, but then their gazes met, and her laughter stilled.

Rain pounded a steady beat on the roof, wind howled, lightning crackled, thunder rumbled. Inside the cozy log cabin, the air was warm, scented with wood smoke and wine. The single propane light and the flickering flames lent an intimate glow to the room, as if they were cocooned within a secret refuge.

His muscular throat worked as he swallowed.

She tore her gaze from his. Her heart thudded, and her legs shook as she drifted to the fridge and stood beside him, her shoulder brushing his as she peered inside. "Let's see what's in here." Her voice breathless. "Pauline told me the caretaker stocked a few supplies, and I brought some groceries." She jerked her thumb over her shoulder at the paper bag she'd set on the table by the couch when she'd confronted Kevin and his unwelcome advances.

128

Chapter 11

They worked side by side in the small kitchen in companionable silence.

He chopped onions and green peppers.

She beat the eggs in the glass bowl and added milk, keeping her eyes downcast, afraid what would happen if she looked at him. The unnerving awareness sizzled between them. The kitchen was tiny, and shoulders, arms, and hips grazed against each other in unsettling caresses that set her heart stuttering. She lifted her glass and sipped a mouthful of wine, hoping he wouldn't notice the way her hand shook.

By the time the eggs were cooked to a rich golden color, her body thrummed, every nerve buzzing as a hunger of a different kind filled her.

He heaped a steaming mound of fluffy eggs dotted with melting cheddar cheese and chopped green onions onto a plate and held it out. "Here you go."

"Looks good." She sniffed, inhaling the savory aroma. "Smells even better."

Filling another plate of food, he held out a chair and indicated she should sit. "Come on. Let's eat." He refilled both wine glasses and sat across from her.

The smell of the scrambled eggs made her mouth water, and she scooped up a mouthful and chewed. "This is really good."

"We make a good team." His mouth twisted. "At

least in the kitchen."

"I thought we weren't going to talk about work."

"You're right." His eyes twinkled. "So, how about those Knicks?"

She chuckled, and once again, the tension eased.

Over the next two hours their conversation flowed from one topic to another. He had an unexpected, quirky sense of humor, and she smiled until her cheeks ached. He was easy to be with…too easy.

He drew her like a kitten to a patch of catnip, and she couldn't take her eyes off him. His dark curls gleamed in the flickering firelight. The dips and hollows of his cheeks and strong jaw fascinated her, and she studied every line, every crease in his rugged face. Her gaze kept catching his, and each time, her breath hitched in her throat before she glanced away.

Later, they sat by the fire sipping cognac. She sat cross-legged on a large cushion she'd dragged from the couch onto the floor. He rested beside her, his back against the couch, long legs stretched before him, crossed at the ankles. His scent surrounded her, and every cell in her body was acutely aware of him as a man.

His muscled thigh grazed her knee.

She flinched as if she'd been branded, the room suddenly too warm, the air too close. A trickle of unease flickered low in her belly.

"Everything okay?" His voice was a rumble from deep within his broad chest.

"Of course." She fought to steady her breathing, pushing back the rising panic. *Relax. He's not going to hurt you.* The words ran like a mantra through her. *He's not going to hurt you.*

He studied her through narrowed, assessing eyes. "You're as nervous as a prize turkey in November."

The corners of her mouth twitched, and just like that, her tension eased. "A turkey in November? Really?" She chuckled.

He shrugged and his eyes crinkled. "My grandfather used to say that." He shifted closer and placed his hand over her knee.

She flinched, but didn't pull away. He wasn't doing anything wrong. She wanted him close, wanted to see where the disconcerting attraction between them would lead. Closing her eyes, she inhaled several deep breaths, breathing in through her nose, exhaling through her mouth. When she opened her eyes, the tautness of her muscles had relaxed and her heart had slowed its frantic racing. She lifted her glass and sipped some cognac and smiled. "So where were we?"

"Right here." With infinite slowness, his gaze never leaving hers, he lowered his head. His warm breath fanned her face. One hand gripped her hip and slid her closer. His other hand cupped the back of her head. "Okay if I kiss you?"

She sucked in a gulp of air and nodded. Oh, she wanted this. Even as her heart threatened to leap out of her chest, she wanted his kiss more than her next breath.

The first brush of his lips was electric, the kiss soft and gentle as if he were giving her time to know his touch and taste. His lips were warm as they molded to hers.

A flicker of excitement warmed her blood, and her breath hitched in her throat.

With a groan, he deepened the kiss, urging her

mouth open.

And just like that, the old fears rushed back, swamping her with panic. She tensed, every fiber of her being vibrating on alert. *He won't hurt you. He won't hurt you.* The mantra repeated again and again, but her heart was beating too fast and too loud, and the calming words were lost in the clamor.

Seeming unaware of her rising panic, he pulled her closer and traced her lips with the tip of his tongue.

He won't hurt you. Tendrils of fear trickled through her, interlacing with the seductive whispers of rising excitement. She shuddered.

He drew back. "You're trembling." His brow furrowed as he studied her. "You're afraid." He sat back on his heels. "That's what this is, isn't it? You're afraid."

She sat frozen, immobilized with shame. Heat enveloped her face. She couldn't look. Couldn't bear to face his disgust, his outrage, his anger. He was right. She was afraid. Terrified of a man's touch, petrified of being brutalized again.

The debilitating fear was her constant companion, and the reason she'd never had an intimate relationship with a man. Her life had changed the night of the attack in the lumberyard. Scarred? Hell, yeah. She was traumatized, wounded to the depths of her soul by the brutality of the rape. The experts were wrong. Time didn't heal all wounds. The terror of that night seventeen years ago was as fresh in her mind as if it had happened yesterday. No amount of therapy or self-coaching would change that.

Josh's deep voice broke through the maelstrom raging in her head. She risked a glance.

The hard planes of his face had softened. "What are you're afraid of, Sharla-Jean?" His throat worked as he swallowed. "Believe me, I'd never hurt you."

Her mouth tingled where he'd kissed her. She wanted to trust him, ached to feel the press of his lips once more. But—

He placed his hand on her arm, his fingers caressing her skin in soft brushstrokes.

Her heart lurched, and she scrambled to her feet.

He stood and held his hands out to his sides, palms up. "I'm not going to hurt you. I promise." He ran his long fingers through his hair. "Jesus Christ, you're shaking like a leaf."

Was she? She clenched her hands to stop their trembling, but she couldn't stop her knees from quaking, or her breath from rasping in and out in frantic pants.

He edged nearer. "I don't know why you're so frightened, but I do know what it's like to be hurt by something, something so raw, the very thought of it coming to light rips you in two." His gaze drilled into hers. "I also know keeping the pain inside will eat at you, erode everything that's good until it destroys you. Then they win. Do you understand? The people who did this to you win." He moved closer still. "I want to help you, Sharla-Jean. Will you let me?" He held out his hands.

The compassion and understanding in his dark gaze melted her resolve, and she reached for him, but before their fingers touched, she snatched back her hand. Stumbling, she backpedalled away from him. "I…I can't. I'm sorry."

"Okay." He backed up a step. "No problem."

His concerned gaze pierced the armor she'd built around her soul, and she pressed a hand to her throat in a futile effort to slow her breathing. Now he'd reveal his anger, his fury, his outrage. She'd led him on, and then spurned him. She braced, prepared to defend against his touch when he forced himself on her and wrested what he wanted.

He didn't move. His eyes blazed, but he remained where he was. "I'll tell you one thing. I'm going to find out what happened to you, and when I do, the bastard who hurt you will wish he'd never been born." He spun around and strode across the room to the small kitchen and slammed cupboards and banged dishes as he cleared away the remnants of their meal.

She stared after him for a heartbeat, and then escaped into the bedroom, closing the door and sinking on the bed. Her chest heaved, and she sobbed, her tears dampening the old, musty comforter.

****

The first faint streaks of pink lightened the sky outside the bedroom window when she crawled out of the warm bed, shivering in the frigid air, and struggled into her jacket. She gathered her overnight bag and purse, and crept out of the bedroom and tiptoed across the main room of the cabin past the couch where Josh slept.

The fire had gone out long ago, and the cabin was cold in the early morning chill. She gulped as she stared at his strong, almost-naked body.

He sprawled on his back, the quilted blanket bunched around his waist, his chest bare. Long, dark eyelashes caressed cheeks flushed from sleep. His jeans and T-shirt were crumpled on the floor beside the couch.

In spite of the cabin's frigid air, she was suddenly much too warm. Her heart pounded as she knelt and rummaged through his clothes, searching the pockets of his jeans.

He shifted onto his side, the rustle of the quilt loud in the morning quiet.

She froze, but after a heartbeat, his breathing deepened, and he began to snore. She rose to her feet, a small ring of keys clutched in her hand.

Unable to resist, she once again gave in to the luxury of studying him without his knowing. His hair-roughened chest rose and fell, the muscles well-defined even at rest. His stomach was a flat plane with an intriguing trail of dark hair arrowing under the quilt. He was built like a Greek god, with a face destined to break a woman's heart.

A log shifted amid the ashes of the fireplace, sounding like a gunshot.

She sprang for the exit and flung open the heavy wooden door, fleeing before he awakened and caught her drooling over him. She ran to his truck, crouched by the right rear tire, and using the edge of her car key, squeezed the needle in the middle of the valve stem. Air hissed out as the tire lost pressure. She'd learned this little trick when she was a teenager and had flattened many a tire on her father's vehicles. Nothing pissed her father off more than setting out for work in the morning and finding a flat tire. And she did like to piss off the old man.

She held the needle steady until the tire was flat and rested on the rim. Panting as if she'd completed a circuit at the gym, she hurried to her car, climbed inside, inserted the key in the ignition, and started the engine. The motor coughed and sputtered and rumbled to life. She rammed her foot on the gas, and the car shot forward, spraying mud and gravel in an arc behind.

Sweat dampened her palms as she steered around mud puddles and fallen branches. Josh was handsome, and he had an athlete's well-toned body. He could be incredibly charming when he wanted. But, and it was a big but, he was the one man with whom she couldn't risk becoming involved. *I'm going to find out what happened.* His words, almost a threat, chilled her to the bone. He couldn't find out the truth. No one could.

Last night he'd kissed her, and just like that, her old fears returned, and she'd become a blubbering, frightened idiot. In front of him. She imagined all too well what he thought of her. *Cock tease. Slut. Whore.* She'd heard all the ugly slurs.

It would have been better if he'd gotten angry. But what he'd done was worse: instead of anger, his dark eyes had filled with pity. Her stomach churned. Pity! She didn't want his sympathy. And she sure as hell didn't want him snooping around in her past.

No matter how kind and understanding he'd seemed last night, he didn't fool her. They weren't friends. With his compelling words, and dark, compassionate eyes, he'd almost convinced her to reveal her darkest secret, but at the last moment, she'd resisted and kept her mouth shut.

He'd let slip he was hiding something from his past. She needed to find out his big secret. Knowledge would give her leverage. He spent most of his time in his office. She'd start her search there.

An hour later, she steered her car into Bromley

Forest Products' nearly empty parking lot and parked in a slot away from the main parking area, behind a row of tall, cedar bushes. Sunday morning at this god-awful hour, the last shift of the week had ended and everyone, except the individuals necessary for security, was gone.

She climbed out of her car and eased the door closed. She didn't have to answer to anyone as to why she was here at the crack of dawn on a Sunday morning; after all, she owned the place. But, she didn't want to draw undue attention and have someone tell Josh she'd been snooping around.

Breathing hard from her sprint across the lumberyard, she hurried up the steps to the front door of the office complex. After the break-in, Josh had installed an alarm system and new locks on the front door. Only a few people had access to the security code or the keys. Luckily, she was one of those people.

She inserted her key in the lock and opened the front door. Once inside the foyer, she punched in the security code to turn off the alarm system. Studying the storage room door, she blew out a shaky breath. The door was closed. No intruder lurked within the storage room waiting to attack.

Her steps echoed hollowly in the empty building as she headed across the lobby to the stairs leading to the executive offices on the second floor. She shot a glance over her shoulder. This was the first time since the attack she'd been alone in the building. Not wanting to attract the notice of the weekend security guards, she didn't turn on any lights, and the hallway was gloomy and filled with deep shadows.

Once in the reception area outside Josh's office, she halted and removed the key ring she'd taken from his pants' pocket. She inserted a key in the lock, and unlocked Josh's office door. With a final, furtive glance up and down the corridor, she slipped inside the dark office.

She paused a minute to steady her breathing. The office smelled like Josh, and her mind flashed to images of cooking beside him, the warmth of his thigh as he'd brushed his leg against hers, the press of his hand in hers, and the taste of his kiss. She bit hard on her bottom lip, hoping the sharp stab of pain would focus her on why she was here and what she was about to do.

Josh wouldn't be here for hours. His truck's tire was flat. Once he woke up and left the cabin, he'd have to change the tire. Since he couldn't drive far on his spare, he'd be forced to stop and have the tire filled with air before he drove back to town. He'd be furious when he realized what she'd done, but she hadn't caused any real damage. All she'd done was ensure he'd be delayed a few hours, hours she intended to put to good use.

The office blinds were closed, but enough early morning light seeped around the edges she could make out the darker shapes of the furniture. She crossed to the desk and switched on the desk lamp. A small pool of soft yellow light spilled over the desk, dark-brown leather office chair, and six-drawer, oak filing cabinet.

Everyone had something shameful in their past. If she could find Josh's skeleton in the closet, she'd have a hold over him and could use her knowledge to convince him to stop probing into her own past.

The first place she searched was his filing cabinet, sliding open each drawer and skimming through the rows of alphabetized files. Finding nothing of interest, she shifted her search to his desk.

A cordless phone sat on the top of the expansive, polished oak desk. Nothing else. No framed photographs of family, no laptop computer, nothing but the phone. She slid open the top drawer. The usual assortment of pens and pencils, paper clips, staples, a stapler, and a blank writing pad littered the drawer. The next drawer contained several thick file folders. She flipped through them, but they all related to business. No secrets here.

The bottom drawer was locked. Once again she drew out the stolen ring of keys, trying first one key and then another before she found the one that opened the drawer. Under a stack of pricing sheets, purchase orders, a crumpled tie, a package of miniature chocolate bars, and a small vial of prescription pills, she hit pay dirt. Her hands shook as she removed the small black book. *Caught you!* She hadn't expected her search to be this easy.

Sharla-Jean ran her fingers over the finely tooled leather cover. The letters JCM were etched in flaking, gold paint across the cover in a swirl of elaborate filigree. Josh C. Morgan. What did the C stand for? Charles, Carl, Christopher? Con man? She opened the front cover.

A door slammed in the distance.

Her breath caught in her throat. While she was confident she could explain her presence in the office building, being in Josh's office with the door shut and the blinds closed was another matter.

Heart pounding, she closed and relocked the desk drawer and placed the ring of keys beside the phone. Maybe Josh would think he'd left his keys at the office.

She switched off the desk lamp and crept across the room to the door. Opening the door a few inches, she peered into the dim corridor.

A light down the hall flickered to life, and footsteps echoed on the hardwood floor. She closed the door behind her, eased into the reception area, and raced down the hall away from the approaching footsteps. As she fled down the back stairs, she slipped the book she'd taken from Josh's office into her sweater pocket and continued down the stairs toward the exit.

Taking the book was a mistake, but all she'd had time to see was pages filled with closely written words, penned in Josh's neat script. The book was important. Why else would he keep it in a locked drawer? She'd return the book where she found it once she'd had a chance to read what he'd written. With any luck, Josh wouldn't notice its absence.

The book bumped against her side as she hurried across the parking lot to her car. Guilt weighed her down, slowing her steps. The contents of the book were private. Josh wouldn't want anyone, least of all her, reading his inner thoughts.

She slowed to a stop. What was she doing? She wasn't a thief, and she didn't pry into people's private business. Dragging out the small book, she examined the cracked leather cover. Remorse twisted her stomach in knots. She couldn't read his journal. His secrets would remain secret. Josh never had to know she'd taken the book. She spun around and started back toward the office, but froze at the loud blast of a horn.

Josh's dark blue truck raced across the asphalt and skidded to a stop beside her.

Heart pounding, she stuffed the black book back in

her pocket.

He set the brake, flung open the door, and leaped out of the truck. The powerful engine rumbled behind him. "What the hell did you think you were doing?" His eyes shot darts. "Why did you let the air out of my tire?"

Her mouth lost all moisture.

"Well?" he demanded.

She shook her head. How could she tell him she'd flattened his tire so she could snoop into his private life?

He blew out a breath. "What the hell's going on, Sharla-Jean?"

"I...I..." She bit her lip in frustration, struggling to get the words out to defend herself, to somehow explain. *Explain what? That she was a thief?* And so she remained, head bowed, tears stinging her eyes.

"You're planning something, aren't you? Nothing's changed, has it? You still want to destroy this place. Just like you did years ago when you set fire to the old mill."

"What?" Her head popped up, and she blinked.

Matching patches of red flamed on his cheeks, and his nostrils flared. "You heard me."

She gaped at him and opened her mouth to protest his unfair accusation.

He shook his head, cutting her off. "And to think I felt sorry for you." His lip curled in a sneer. "It's a damn good thing your father never lived to see how his precious daughter turned out."

"No. You're wrong. You don't understand. I—"

He waved his hand in the air, brushing off her words. "I understand too damn well. Don't think I'm going to stand by and let you ruin everything I've worked for. No damn way, lady. No damn way." He stormed back to his truck, jumped in, and slammed the door with an explosive bang. The big truck's motor roared, and he sped off in a cloud of dust and diesel exhaust.

Air rushed out of her chest, and she sagged, her knees weak, almost falling. Somehow she managed to stagger to her car, open the door, and collapse on the driver's seat, her head in her hands. Sobs tore at her throat.

Chapter 12

Sharla-Jean ran her fingers over the finely tooled leather cover of Josh's journal. Closing her eyes, she imagined what secrets he'd detailed on the pages between the leather-bound covers. Ignoring the voice deep inside telling her what she was about to do was wrong; she wiped her damp palms on her pants and opened the front cover. Any guilt she felt about invading his privacy had vanished when he accused her of planning to ruin the company.

Pauline bustled into the room. "Mary Beth Ashbury wants me to help with the upcoming church bazaar and…" Pauline's voice trailed off as she eyed the book in Sharla-Jean's hand. "What's that you're reading?"

Sharla-Jean slammed the book closed. "No…nothing." She winced at her stumbling answer. She'd never been a proficient liar. Whenever she'd tried to tell a fib as a child, the words stuck in her throat. Pauline always knew when she wasn't telling the truth.

"Sharla-Jean? What is that?"

She turned away from Pauline's probing scrutiny.

With a quickness belying her advanced age, Pauline hustled across the room and snatched the book. "JCM?" Her brow furrowed, and her eyes flashed. "This is Josh's journal, isn't it? How in Heaven's name did you get it?"

Guilt flushed Sharla-Jean's cheeks.

"Are you willing to sink to any depth to get what you want?" Pauline's voice was laced with disappointment.

"This isn't what you think," Sharla-Jean protested, knowing her words were a lie. What she'd done was exactly what Pauline envisaged.

"Josh doesn't deserve this. He's a good man." Pauline pursed her lips. "When your father was alive, Josh was here all the time. The two of them played cards for hours. If they weren't here at the house, they were at the cabin fishing. When your father grew ill, Josh came by just to talk to him, to take his mind off the pain."

A slow burn of anger flowed through Sharla-Jean's veins with each glowing description. "Interesting how dear old Dad found time for a stranger, but not for his own daughter."

"That's not fair. Your father was lonely after you left. Josh helped fill the void. He was like a son to Big Jim."

Sharla-Jean snorted. "He was certainly well paid for his time. My father left him half of a multimillion dollar company."

"Josh earned every penny. He worked hard, sometimes too hard. If not for him, the mill wouldn't be such a success." A veil of sadness settled over Pauline's lined face. "Your father changed when you left. He stopped drinking, but he lost interest in the mill. Oh, he showed up at the office every day, but more often than not, he just went through the motions. His heart wasn't in his work anymore."

Sharla-Jean opened her mouth to protest, but

Pauline held up her hand. "No, let me finish. Past time you heard the truth." Her rheumy eyes fixed on Sharla-Jean. "I've said this before and I'll say it again. Your father loved you. He made terrible mistakes, but he more than paid for his sins. Your mother's death nearly destroyed him. He lived with the guilt of what he'd done until he drew his last breath. Your leaving was the final thrust." She swiped at tear-filled eyes. "What your father did to you was wrong. I know. I was there. I watched the way his indifference affected you. But he hurt too."

Sharla-Jean smirked. "Poor Big Jim Bromley lost his wife, blah, blah, blah. I'm sick to death of hearing how brokenhearted he was."

Pauline shook her head sadly. "You've never forgiven him, have you? After all these years, and even though he's dead and buried, you're still mad at him."

Tears filmed Sharla-Jean's eyes, and she swiped them away with her sleeve. "You have no idea what he did to me."

Pauline shuffled to the couch, sat beside her, and grasped Sharla-Jean's hand. "Does this have something to do with the night of the mill fire, the night you left town?"

A fresh spate of tears filled Sharla-Jean's eyes.

"What happened?" Pauline squeezed Sharla-Jean's hand. "Will you finally tell me?"

Nightmare images of leering faces, rough hands ripping her clothes, tearing pain deep inside, choking smoke, and the searing heat of fire engulfed her. Sharla-Jean hunched into the soft cushions as sobs tore at her throat.

"Here."

A white, lace-edged handkerchief was stuffed into her hand. Sharla-Jean pressed the cloth against her eyes in a futile attempt to staunch the flood of tears.

"Telling someone often helps ease the burden." Tears flowed down Pauline's lined cheeks.

Sharla-Jean gulped. Josh had said the same thing the previous night. Maybe they were right. Maybe telling Pauline would help. *But she had told someone.* The night of the mill fire she'd run home to her father and told him of the brutal attack, hoping that for once he'd help her. She squeezed her eyes shut, trying to block the image of her father's harsh face as she'd sobbed on the floor at his feet and told him she'd been raped.

He sat behind his desk, slumped in his big leather chair, staring out the dark window. The sickly sweet stench of stale alcohol and rank body odor lay heavy in the air. An empty whiskey bottle sat on the desk, the glass beside it, half-full.

He turned when she entered the den and frowned. The furrow between his brows formed a deep vee over his aquiline nose. His eyes were sunken hollows. Tiny red lines streaked the corneas. His thick, red hair was a wild tangle around his flushed face. "What the hell do you want?" His voice was rough, the words slurred.

Her stomach plummeted, and she almost wheeled around and fled. He was a mean drunk. He hid his anger and callousness from other people, but not from her. He'd never smacked her, never laid a hand on her, but his biting, cruel words cut deeper and left more scars than any blows.

The faint peal of sirens penetrated the double-glazed French doors with their view of manicured lawn

146

and trimmed shrubs.

His lips curled in a sneer as his gaze raked her torn and dirty clothes. "What the hell have you done now?"

She bit her bottom lip, fighting back a fresh torrent of tears. "I...I...I..." The words stuck in her throat.

He lifted his glass and swigged a gulp of whiskey. "Your mother wasted a shit load of good money on all those speech therapists. You still can't speak worth a damn."

Familiar scorching shame filled her. "I...the...the fire...mill."

"Yeah the mill's on fire. I heard." His bleary gaze settled on her. Spittle flecked the corners of his mouth. His nostrils flared as he sniffed the air. "Jesus, you stink. Is that smoke I smell?" He lifted his glass and guzzled more whiskey. Wiping his mouth with the back of his hand, he slammed the glass on his desk. "You did it, didn't you?" He nodded toward the windows where the wail of sirens grew louder. "I'm not gonna protect you, you know. Not this time. By morning, the whole town's gonna know what you did." He sat back, a smug look on his sweaty face.

"I...I was...raped." Her voice was a hoarse whisper. "A man raped me tonight...at the mill."

A flicker of what could have been compassion lit his bloodshot, green eyes, and for a brief moment, a single heartbeat, a seed of hope unfurled inside her. He'd help. He wouldn't blame her for the fire. He'd understand.

His crowing laughter was a bellow. "You sure as spit are something, girl. You really are. Do you expect me to believe your bullshit story?"

"But it's true. I was raped." She lifted her face to his and pointed to her swollen mouth and scratched cheeks. "See what he did? He…he hurt me. Bad." A fresh wave of tears engulfed her.

His voice acquired a mocking tone. "Yeah, right. You think anyone will forget you set the fire just because you make up some story about being raped?" He smashed his fist on the desk, knocking over the glass. Whiskey spilled onto the shiny surface and dripped on the floor. "No one's gonna believe you. They know the trouble you are. This is just another one of your little shit-ass escapades."

His words struck like blows. Her knees buckled, and she fell on the floor sobbing. "It's…it's true. I'm telling the truth. I…I thought…I hoped…you'd…you'd help me." Tears dripped off her chin onto the burnished hardwood floor.

Sirens wailed in the distance. The clock on the far wall ticked, each tick signaling the death of another piece of her soul.

"Aww, shit!" He slammed his hand on the desktop, shoved his chair back, and lurched to his feet. Stumbling across the room, he knelt beside her. His sour, whiskey-laced breath washed over her.

She braced for a blow.

"Shit, girl." His voice cracked. An animal-like howl filled the room.

She jerked up, wiping her face with her sleeve.

He buried his face in his hands, and his shoulders shook while the ungodly keening reverberated through the room.

"Dad?" Her voice was a thin whisper.

The wailing continued as she stared, frozen in

place, unable to look away.

As quickly as it started, the crying ended. He raised his head, his eyes red and swollen, his face blotchy. "I shouldn't a said those things." He wiped his face, smearing snot and tears. "It's the damn booze. The shit makes me crazy. Ever since your mom passed, I—" He reached out a trembling hand.

She drew back. "Don't you dare touch me, you bastard!"

He reeled as if she'd struck him and fell on his back, and lay looking up at her with big, wounded eyes.

"You're drunk." Her voice was rough with years of anger and resentment. "You're always drunk."

"I'm sorry, so sorry. Forgive me. I...I didn't mean to hurt your mother. It wasn't my fault. The deer jumped out of the bush, and I couldn't, I couldn't..." He shook his head and pushed up onto his knees, and once again reached for her. "Let me help you."

Let me help you. *The words she'd desperately wanted to hear echoed like gunfire through the den and filled her throat with bile. Help her? He didn't give a shit about her. He didn't care she'd been violated. This was all about him. He could go to hell. She leaped to her feet and bolted across the room, flung open the door, and ran down the hall and out of the house, fleeing into the night.*

"Sharla-Jean." His voice bellowed after her, broken by wrenching sobs. "I'm sorry. Forgive me. Please. Come back."

She hadn't stopped running until she'd hit the highway out of town where she'd raised her thumb in the air and taken the first ride that stopped.

"What happened? I want to help you." Pauline's

soft voice broke through the painful memories.

Sharla-Jean shook her head. "I can't. I'm sorry. I just can't." What if Pauline didn't believe her? What if she too thought the story of her rape had been made up?

A heavy silence settled between them, thickening and growing with each second.

Pauline inhaled a deep breath. "Okay, but I'm here when you decide you want to tell someone."

Sharla-Jean peered through a tangle of hair.

Pauline's face was pale, and deep lines furrowed her brow. She patted the journal she held. "Don't take your anger at your father out on Josh. None of this is his fault." She struggled to her feet. "Think carefully before you do something you'll regret." She set the journal on the table beside the couch and left the room.

The journal glowed as if a nimbus of light emanated from the black leather cover. Sharla-Jean picked it up and studied the initials on the cover. The confrontation with Josh in the mill parking lot ran through her mind. Each word he'd hurled had drawn blood.

Her hand shook as she opened the book to the first page. The words swam in front of her, and she slammed the book shut. *What was she doing?* Pauline was right. This wasn't worth losing a piece of her soul.

With a heavy tread, she crossed the room to the tall teak china cabinet, slid open the bottom drawer, and laid the journal inside, covering it with a pile of folded cloth napkins. She'd return the book as soon as she could. Josh would never know how close she came to discovering his secrets.

****

Josh spun in his chair and leaned back against the

cool leather. He stared through the large window at the view of the bustling lumberyard with its piles of stacked and wrapped lumber ready for shipment. The forklifts worked at a frenetic pace as they maneuvered back and forth loading lumber onto the open rail cars.

He had reports to write, calls to make, people to see, but he couldn't concentrate. His mind kept returning to the events of the past two days. When he needed an escape from the stress of work, the cabin was the logical choice. If any place could help him forget the frustration of dealing with Sharla-Jean Bromley's stubborn refusal to go back to Portland and leave him to run the mill, the isolated log cottage in the middle of the forest was the place.

And so he'd gone there, but his plan for peace and relaxation went south the second he drove into the tiny clearing and spotted the two vehicles parked beside the cabin. He'd recognized Kevin Nelson's sports car and Sharla-Jean's rental. Audrey had informed him Nelson was helping Sharla-Jean learn the workings of the mill, but what the hell had the two of them been doing at his cabin?

Frowning, he rubbed the back of his bruised right hand. He should have spun his car around and driven away, but instead he'd stormed into the cabin and caught the bastard with his hands all over Sharla-Jean. Without thinking, without wondering why he was so enraged, he'd punched Nelson in the face and tossed his sorry ass out the door.

He didn't regret hitting Nelson, or firing him, but he did regret convincing Sharla-Jean to stay and have dinner. What the hell had he been thinking? He should have known he was opening himself up to trouble, but all he'd been able to think of was her luminous green eyes and her shiny fall of auburn hair. He'd ached to run his fingers through the silken strands.

The inevitable happened, and he kissed her. He couldn't have stopped himself if he tried. Even now, hours later, his lips tingled from the sweet taste of her. But then she stiffened like a board and jerked away as if she'd been burned. When he recovered his senses enough to think straight, she'd stood frozen, her face white and drawn, eyes wide, looking at him as if he were Jack the Ripper.

Her fear had struck him like a blow, and he clenched his fist, ignoring the pain of his scraped knuckles. His fingernails dug deep into his palms. Some animal had hurt her; hurt her bad. Before he had a chance to find out what had happened, she'd fled to the bedroom and hidden there the rest of the night.

After polishing off whatever liquor he found in the cupboards, he'd passed out on the couch and awakened to find her gone. His truck's flat had hit him like a fresh blow, and his irritation flared to a fever pitch. He'd changed the tire in record time and broken every speeding law in the county driving like a madman to the mill.

He figured she'd be in her office. Hell, wasn't everybody talking about the long hours she worked? She was always at the mill, shut in her damn office with Kevin Nelson. The two of them conspiring together to do God knows what.

He'd run into her in the parking lot. He shouldn't have gone after her. But, hell, a man could only take so much. Her shenanigans with his tire, and the guilty look on her face propelled him over the edge.

He rubbed his temples as he relived the stormy confrontation. Had he really brought up the old fire? *Good one, bucko. Why not kick her and be done with it?* Did he really think she was out to destroy the mill? He knew the long hours she put in. On the surface, she seemed to be trying to make this difficult situation work. But then he recalled the guilty flush on her face, and the way she averted her eyes and wouldn't look at him. She was up to something, all right.

Sharla-Jean bore a lot of anger toward her father. Why? Plenty of children grew up with parents who had problems with alcohol. Her mother's death was a terrible tragedy, and her father was responsible. The loss of her mother must have been hard on a young child. But there had to be more behind her hatred. Something else had happened, something bad enough to drive a sixteen-year-old out of her home and keep her away for seventeen years.

Whatever it was, her fear was real. He'd witnessed firsthand her distress when he kissed her. The terror trembling through her slim body had staggered him. At that moment, he'd have done anything—slay dragons, fight foes to the death, anything—to erase the stain of fear from her face.

He gripped the leather armrests. They had to share the management of Bromley for another eleven months. They wouldn't make it another week if they continued the way they were. He had to get to the bottom of her fear and figure out what she was up to. He snatched up the phone. "Audrey," he barked, "tell Ms. Bromley I want to see her. Right away. In my office."

"I'm afraid that won't be possible, Josh. She's not in her office."

"What? Where is she?"

"The sawmill."

"The sawmill? What the hell's she doing there?"

"Ace McGuff called. There's a problem."

"What sort of problem? Why didn't Ace call me?"

A short silence ensued, and Josh pictured Audrey's hard-done-by expression. "I don't know. You'll have to ask him." Her heavy sigh echoed through the phone line. "I wish he hadn't called on her to help. That poor girl works too hard. She's here every morning at the crack of dawn. Lord knows what time she leaves at night."

Josh tuned out his secretary's long-winded praise and glanced at the clock. The office would soon be closing for the day. A stirring of unease settled low in his gut. Why had Ace called Sharla-Jean instead of him? He was the one who dealt with problems in the mill.

"I'm heading over to the sawmill, Audrey. You may as well call it quits for the day. I don't know when I'll be back in the office." Without waiting for her reply, he slammed the phone on the desk, shoved back his chair, and vaulted to his feet. Grabbing his hard hat and safety glasses from the shelf by the door, he opened the door and strode out of the office.

He heaved open the heavy metal door, stepped inside the sawmill, and breathed in the familiar odors of sawdust and heavy-duty machine lube. With the dayshift finished, and the nightshift cancelled tonight, the cavernous building was eerily silent. Banks of blinding fluorescent lights blazed down on the cement floor from high above.

His footsteps echoed hollowly as he hurried past

the main conveyor. The thick belt was motionless and empty of boards. He strode past the giant-sized, metal air compressor, and alongside the band saw with its razor-sharp, jagged metal teeth.

A loud whump resounded through the building, and the overhead blowers kicked in, their motors whirring as the filters fought to cleanse the air of residual dust. A sharp clang of metal against metal resonated from the far end of the building. Hurrying his steps, he ducked under the safety chain and stepped onto the corrugated metal boardwalk, cutting through the maze of machinery to the debarker.

Ace crouched below the hulking machine in front of the operator's panel. He held a heavy wrench in one hand, a flashlight in the other.

Sharla-Jean hovered over his shoulder, her attention fixed on whatever Ace was doing.

Neither heard him approach, and he coughed loudly to draw their attention.

Sharla-Jean spun to face him. Her face paled. "Josh."

Ace glanced over his shoulder. "Hey, Boss. What are you doing here?" He returned to examining the open panel before him.

Josh's mouth tightened. "I could ask the same of you, Ace." He shifted closer; not missing how Sharla-Jean flinched and edged away from him. "What's up?"

Ace sat back on his heels, removed his hard hat, and ran his hands, black with heavy grease, through his thinning red hair. "This here machine's broken, but I'll be damned if I can figure out how it happened. Ms. Bromley and I been here a good hour tryin' to git to the bottom of this, but so far, we ain't made no headway."

"You and *Ms. Bromley*?" Josh slid a glance at Sharla-Jean. Her tight designer jeans and tailored white blouse were in pristine condition. Silken strands of perfectly coifed auburn hair gleamed under the lights. Her creamy complexion and soft red lips were hard to miss. No grease stains or dust marred her perfection. He snorted. "Yeah, right. I'm sure she's been a big help."

She exhaled loudly, but he didn't look at her. He didn't have to. All too well he pictured her eyes flashing green fire. "You haven't answered my question, Ace. Why didn't you call me?"

Sharla-Jean cut in. "I told Ace to call me if he had any problems. Time I accepted more responsibility. After all, I'm running the mill now."

He guffawed, the harsh sound reverberating off the surrounding metal walls. "You mean you're *helping* me run the mill. Last I checked, you didn't know the difference between the canter and the band saw." He was wrong. Her eyes weren't flashing green fire, they were cold and hard like emeralds, shining bright in her flushed face.

She opened her gorgeous mouth to say something, but then tightened her lips as if thinking better of what she was about to say. "This isn't getting us anywhere." She gave a dismissive wave of her hand. "You need to hear what Ace has to say."

For some perverse reason, he wanted to continue bickering with her, but she was right. The mill was the priority. Their petty differences would have to wait. "What's going on, Ace?" he demanded. "What's wrong with this machine?"

Ace pushed to his feet and shoved his hard hat back off his forehead. "I don't rightly know, Boss. If I didn't know better, I'd think someone deliberately bent the head."

A chill rippled along Josh's spine. "The head's bent? But it's carbide-tipped. We replaced the head during our last shutdown. It's not supposed to break."

Ace nodded. "Damned straight."

Josh ran his hand over his jaw, the rasp of a day's beard growth loud in the quiet mill. "How bad is it?"

"Bad." Ace shifted from one foot to the other. "The day shift boys ran the debarker until ten minutes before the end of shift when they noticed she was runnin' rough. When they called me in, I took one look and shut 'er down." He shook his head. "Looks like we're gonna have to replace the whole damn thing."

Josh swore. Debarkers were expensive. How the hell could he afford to replace the main debarker? He cursed again. A big shipment of raw logs was due in next week.

"Sorry, Boss. I know this ain't what you wanna hear."

"It sure as hell isn't." He moved over beside Ace and crouched before the open panel. "Hand me your flashlight." Josh peered into the guts of the machine, studying the bent head. The metal head was coated in grease. Miniscule chunks of bark and clumps of damp sawdust covered the sharp, curved end. He leaned closer and wiped off a blob of greasy wood chips. His stomach plummeted. Tiny scratches marred the smooth surface where someone had used some sort of tool to bend the head, and then covered the evidence with wood chips and grease.

Whoever had done this was familiar with the machine and knew the debarker would run for several hours before the damage was detected. The bent head would have played havoc with the feed roll and shaft, eventually destroying the machine.

"What do you see?" Sharla-Jean hovered over his shoulder.

He shook his head, too angry to speak.

"We're gonna need a new debarker, ain't we, Boss?" Ace asked.

A sudden wave of fury thundered through Josh. Someone was out to destroy his mill.

"Boss?"

"Go on home now, Ace." Josh bit the words out through his clenched teeth.

Ace's brow furrowed. "You sure?"

Josh nodded. "I'll deal with this."

Ace hesitated, but strode away, his footsteps loud in the silent mill.

Josh bent down once again and studied the damaged head. Cursing, he picked up the wrench and threw the heavy tool across the room where it clanged against the wall.

"What's going on, Josh?" Unease filtered through Sharla-Jean's normally soft tones. "What aren't you telling me?"

"Nothing," he muttered. The less people knew of the acts of vandalism, the better. If word got out someone was trying to destroy the mill, the company shares would drop in value, and the shit would hit the fan.

"I don't believe you." She faced him, her hands planted on her shapely hips. "You wouldn't be this upset over a bent head. Something else is going on."

He jumped up and moved toward her, not stopping

until inches separated them. Her perfume, something floral yet woodsy, reminding him of a meadow in early spring, surrounded him. He leaned closer, forcing her backward. "Do you want to know what's bothering me? Do you really want to know?"

Her face paled, and the green lights in her eyes dulled with fear, but she held her place and nodded.

His anger evaporated. *What the hell was he doing?* None of this was her fault. He backed up a step, giving her the space she so obviously needed. "This wasn't an accident, or normal wear and tear. The head was deliberately bent."

She inhaled sharply. "Someone did this on purpose? Why?"

He shrugged. "No clue. But willful damage like this has been happening all over the mill for the past three months."

"Why haven't I heard anything about it? Ace didn't mention this."

"He doesn't know. No one does."

"So why are you telling me?"

All sorts of responses came to mind, but he went with the truth. "Damned if I know. Maybe because you care for this place almost as much as I do."

The corners of her mouth twitched. "Well, thanks, I guess."

He scowled. "What's so funny?"

"I guess this means you trust me. Good to know." She smiled, the light in her eyes once more turning them a brilliant, emerald green. "Who do you think did this?"

"I don't know. After the first few incidents, I had security cameras installed throughout the sawmill and planer mill, but the bastard seems to know where they're mounted and manages to avoid being caught on camera." He pointed to the ceiling where a diminutive surveillance camera was mounted, a red light flashing. "The camera up there covers most of the area around the debarker, but not the front of the control panel. There's too much shadow. Easy for someone to slip in during the shift, bend the head, and be off before anyone knew any better."

"You must have some idea who's doing these things? I mean, from what you're saying, the person responsible must be someone who works here. He'd have to be. An outsider wouldn't know the security system."

What she said made sense. When the incidents first started, he'd considered the possibility of an employee being responsible, but he hadn't wanted to go there. He liked to think the workers at Bromley were loyal. But now that she'd voiced the same suspicions, he realized he couldn't trust anyone. He started walking away, his mind whirling, his one focus to search the employee files and ferret out the bastard who was trying to ruin him.

"Where are you going?" she asked.

"I have work to do," he called over his shoulder.

"Josh?"

He paused and glanced back. She was a dream amidst the grit and grime of the massive machinery looming over her, out of place, but beautiful…so damn beautiful. "Look, you've been a great help, but you should go on home. Pauline will be worried. I'll see you tomorrow. We'll talk then."

Without waiting for her reply, he loped across the

floor, flung open the door, and burst into the fresh evening air.

Chapter 13

The doorbell rang, the strident peal echoing through the house. Sharla-Jean opened her eyes and blinked in the late afternoon light streaming through the large living room window. A stack of papers slipped off the couch onto the floor when she sat up. She'd nodded off reading the reports on the Federal government softwood lumber-cutting agreements. No wonder. The stilted, formal, bureaucratic language used in the documents was a better sleep aid than a sleeping pill.

The doorbell sounded again, louder, more demanding, as if the caller had his or her finger jammed on the ringer.

Her irritation inched up another notch. Smoothing a hand over her rumpled hair and tugging down her wrinkled blouse, she stormed out of the room and flung open the front door. She glared at the person standing on the step, his finger pressed to the doorbell. "What are you doing here?"

Kevin Nelson affected an offended expression. He placed his hand over his heart. "Ouch. If I didn't know better, I'd think you weren't glad to see me."

"You'd be right." She studied his battered face. Josh had done a number on him. One eye was swollen shut. His bottom lip sported a cut that had to hurt when he smiled. A wide, flesh-colored bandage covered the bridge of his nose. He wasn't looking near as pretty as usual.

He stepped forward as if to move past her into the house.

Her anger flared hotter, and she blocked the opening with her body. "Look, Kevin, I'm busy." After what had happened at the cabin, she wanted nothing more to do with him. She grasped the door handle and yanked the door closed, but not before he jammed his foot in the doorway, stopping the door from closing all the way.

"Sharla-Jean, please, listen to me. I have something important to tell you, something you need to know." He spoke through the crack in the doorway. "What happened the other day at the cabin was a mistake. I handled the situation all wrong. I'm sorry."

"You shouldn't have been there. You weren't invited and you weren't welcome. Just like you're not welcome here now." Her heart raced, but she held her fear at bay. He'd frightened her once; she wasn't about to let him do it again. She glared at his foot planted in the doorway. "Move your foot, and get out of here, or I'll call the police."

"Okay, okay. But please, will you hear what I have to say? It'll only take a minute." He lifted his foot out of the way and stepped back.

She slammed the door and twisted the security lock.

His muffled voice reached her through the thick wood. "Sharla-Jean, open the door, please. It's about the mill and Morgan. He's been stealing from the company."

Unable to stop herself, she flung open the door. "What are you talking about?"

"It's true. Morgan's been stealing money for months."

She studied his bruised face. He was lying. He had to be. This was an attempt to get back at Josh for punching him and then firing him. Josh was many things, but she didn't see him as a thief.

He moved a step closer. "I can see you don't believe me. It must be hard to hear the man you're sleeping with is a crook."

She gaped. "What are you talking about?"

"Look, you don't owe me an explanation. Whom you sleep with is your business." He jammed his hands in the front pockets of his pants. "Can I come in? We need to talk."

"Josh fired you. The mill is no longer your concern."

"That's where you're wrong." His pale blue eyes shone with earnestness. "Come on, I promise I won't touch you."

She eyed him. He'd acted like a jerk at the cabin, but he had helped her these past weeks. Without him, she wouldn't have learned so much about the mill. Hoping she wouldn't regret it, she opened the door the rest of the way, and with a crook of her finger indicated he should follow her as she led him to the living room.

He sat on the couch and studied the room. "The place hasn't changed."

She perched on the arm of a chair on the far side of the room. "You've been here before?" It was hard to imagine her father inviting Kevin over for a social visit.

He pierced her with a sharp stare. "I've been here many times. Big Jim didn't want anyone to know about our meetings. That's why we didn't meet at the office."

Butterflies fluttered deep in her gut as the first pangs of unease settled over her. "Why would my father want your meetings kept a secret? What was going on between you two?"

"Before I tell you what I know, I want to apologize again for my behavior the other day." He exhaled a deep breath. "Believe it or not, I'm not usually so clumsy around women." He examined his hands, and chewed on a cuticle. After a minute, he met her gaze. "Anyway, I'm sorry."

"Moving on." She brushed off his apology. She'd never forgive him for his attempted forced seduction, but there was no point dwelling on the incident. The sooner he said what he'd come here to say, the sooner he'd leave.

All trace of remorse vanished, and he flashed his hundred-watt smile. "I knew you'd understand." He leaned forward, his hands on his knees. "What I told you before is true. Josh Morgan is stealing from the company."

A shaky laugh burst out of her. "Come on, Kevin. Josh wouldn't steal from the mill. You're just trying to get back at him because he fired you."

"This has nothing to do with that. I've been suspicious of Morgan for awhile, but now I'm certain."

She studied him. Gone was the habitual sardonic twist to his mouth, and for once his gaze didn't stray from her face. "You're serious, aren't you?"

"I've never been more serious in my life."

A chill settled over her. "Tell me what you know."

"Six months ago, your father hired me to investigate irregularities in the company's finances. The thefts have been going on for the past year, beginning when Big Jim first grew ill. Even though his illness kept him at home for days at a time, he noticed the discrepancies in the accounts."

"And he hired you to find this thief?" She rubbed the back of her neck, fighting off the rising certainty he was telling the truth. "What do you know about investigating a crime? You're our comptroller. Or, at least you were until Josh sacked you."

A small smile played about his lips. "I'm not who you think I am. I own a private investigation firm, Nelson Investigations. Our specialty is ferreting out fraud and embezzlement in the corporate world."

Her mind whirled. Fraud? Embezzlement? "*You're* a private investigator?"

He smiled smugly. "One of the best."

"Let me get this straight. My father hired you because he suspected someone was stealing from the company?" Hearing the words again didn't make them any more real.

"Big Jim hated that one of his employees was stealing from him. He liked to think everyone at the mill was one big, happy family." He jerked his chin up a notch. "I was to come in under cover, keep a low profile, and see if I could discover the thief."

A band of steel tightened around her forehead. "What sort of money are we talking? Hundreds of dollars? Thousands?"

"Over five hundred thousand dollars is unaccounted for."

"That much?" She sank back on the chair.

"You can see why it was important to find the culprit."

The band tightened and she rubbed her temples.

"And you say you've found proof Josh is the thief?"

He nodded. "The investigation took me longer than anticipated. Usually, employees looking to make a quick buck, but lacking any real expertise, commit these sorts of thefts. They're easy to find." He blew out a breath. "This case was different. This thief knew what he was doing and hid his actions well. It's a fluke your father discovered the thefts in the first place."

"How could that be? All that money."

"In a big company like Bromley Forest Products, the profit margin is high. The company accountants place money in several different accounts. The money's used for maintenance and equipment upgrades, employee wages, benefits, and the pension fund, taxes, timber licensing fees, unforeseen expenditures…" He shrugged. "There are dozens of different accounts. The money we're talking about was siphoned over a period of months from these accounts."

His words flowed more quickly as he warmed to his topic. "Morgan was smart. He didn't steal the money all at one time. Such a discrepancy would have been detected right away. He pilfered small amounts out of each account over a long period so anyone looking would think the errors were minor bookkeeping ones. Half a million dollars missing and no one aware of the theft." He sat back on the couch and crossed his long legs. "The perfect crime."

"My father noticed the money was missing."

He nodded. "This was his company. He knew the mill inside and out. Even as ill as he was, he caught the discrepancies."

She massaged the back of her neck, hoping that would help ease the increasing pressure. "How can you be certain Josh stole the money?"

"I haven't found direct proof…yet. That's why I haven't gone to the police, but there's no question in my mind he did it."

"Why? Why would he? He was my father's right hand man. He stood to gain half the mill upon my father's death. Why would he risk all his hard work for a few hundred thousand dollars when it would all be his in a matter of months?"

"J.D. Webster and Morgan are pretty tight. I wouldn't be surprised if that pompous ass of a lawyer told Morgan the details of your father's will. Morgan knew that in order for him to gain control of the mill, you and he had to work together for a year. Given the way you've been absent for the past seventeen years, there was a good chance that wasn't going to happen." He stood, his hands out to his sides. "Think about it. He'd worked for ten years to get to where he was. If you'd refused to stay and help manage the mill, he'd have lost everything." He shrugged. "He couldn't risk walking away with nothing."

The band in her forehead tightened even more, and her stomach knotted. Bile filled the back of her throat. Josh had seemed as shocked as she was when he'd learned the details of her father's will. Could it have been an act? Had he known what was in the will all along? That would explain his anger in J.D.'s office before the will was even read. But to steal from the company? The very thought made her ill.

Kevin crossed the room until he stood over her. "All the evidence points to Morgan. He had direct access to the funds, and he was working alone late at night at the mill each time money was taken from the accounts." His gaze pierced hers. "I know this is hard for you. I mean, what with you and Morgan being so close, but he's guilty. Take my word. Josh Morgan's a thief."

She opened her mouth to tell him she and Josh weren't lovers, but stopped. What difference did it make? If Kevin was right, Josh was stealing from the company. All the years he'd befriended her father, acting like a long lost son, he'd been stealing the old man blind. A tingle of doubt lingered, and she couldn't help asking, "Are you certain Josh took the money?"

"I wouldn't make the accusation if I weren't hundred per cent sure."

"But you don't have any proof. Everything you've told me is circumstantial."

"I don't have enough evidence for the police to charge him, but believe me, the clues all point to Morgan." He narrowed his eyes. "Set your hormones aside for a minute and think. The man had motive, access, and opportunity. He's guilty. We just have to prove he did it."

"*We*?"

He nodded. "I can't do this on my own. I need your help. Since your boyfriend fired me, I no longer have access to the mill."

She gritted her teeth. "I told you, he's not my boyfriend."

He waved her words away. "And I told you I don't care. That's not what's important here."

The ache in her head rose to a crescendo. "If what you say is true, why are you telling me this now? You should have told me when I first arrived in town."

"Your father wanted the investigation discreet.

After he died, I wanted to respect his wishes, but then Fred Kowalski, the night watchman told me what happened at the mill the other night when you were attacked, and I realized I had to tell you. That's why I went to the cabin." He touched his hand to his nose and winced. "Before I could say anything, Morgan showed up."

She kneaded her temples and then rubbed the back of her neck, feeling as if she were Alice and had fallen through the rabbit hole. "You still should have told me."

"That's why I'm here today." He studied her. "Morgan's getting desperate. He'll stop at nothing to keep his thievery secret."

"What are you talking about? What else has Josh done?"

He strode to the fireplace and stared at the empty grate, hands clasped behind his back.

The butterflies in her stomach thrashed. "Come on, Kevin, you've gone too far to be coy now."

He turned and faced her. "Fred told me files from your office were scattered around the storage room and a fire was set. Even your father's old filing cabinet was placed there." His lips curled in a sneer. "Morgan's amateur attempt to point the finger of blame at you."

She stared at Kevin slack-mouthed. "Are you telling me Josh"—she shook her head—"Josh wanted to burn down the office and make it seem like I did it?"

"That was his plan."

"You actually think Josh set fire to the mill office?" Even as she said the damning words, they didn't make sense. "Come on, Kevin. That's ridiculous."

He arched a sly brow. "Is it?"

"Why? What would he gain?"

"If the office burned down and you were the prime suspect, you'd be disgraced. Even if they couldn't prove you were responsible, you'd be shamed into leaving. Josh would be in sole control of Bromley. After the year was up, he'd get the mill. Just like he's always wanted."

She chewed her bottom lip. His theory that Josh had orchestrated the setup in the storage room was crazy, but Kevin was right about one thing. If the fire had burned out of control, she'd be the prime suspect. Who more likely to want to burn down the mill than the person responsible for the same act years earlier? "But his plan didn't work. The fire didn't take hold, and the police weren't called. No one knows about the arson attempt. So, what was the point?"

He met her gaze. "Fred Kowalski knows, and he's the biggest gossip at the mill."

Struggling to think through the riot of conflicting thoughts, she recalled Josh's outrage over the willful damage to the debarker. "I don't believe it. Josh would never risk a fire. He cares too much for the mill."

"True, and that's why he set the fire in the office building. A fire there wouldn't reach the mill itself." Kevin's eyes narrowed. "Think about it. Why were you the only one who heard the noises in the offices that night? The thumping must have been pretty loud. Why didn't Morgan hear? He was there. His office is right down the hall from yours."

"He said he fell asleep and woke up when he heard me scream."

Kevin nodded. "Pretty convenient, don't you

think?"

"Do you really believe Josh did this?"

"I do. He hoped you'd investigate the strange sounds you heard. When you did, he shoved you hard enough to knock you out."

A chill hurtled through her. "I…I can't believe this. He wanted to harm me?"

"He hoped you'd be frightened enough to go back to Portland, or you'd be accused of trying to burn down the mill." He shrugged. "Either way, he'd win."

Her hands were icy cold, and she rubbed them on her thighs in an attempt to ease their numbness. Was Kevin right? Was Josh really so devious?

"There's more."

She flinched as if he'd struck her as the deep timbre of his voice broke through her thoughts. "What more could there possibly be?"

"Are you aware of the vandalism that's been happening lately?"

"Josh told me about it last night. Someone bent the debarker blade. He said things like that have been happening for the past few months." She sucked in a gulp of air. "You don't think Josh is responsible, do you?"

He didn't answer, just watched her with an unnerving gaze.

She wrapped her arms around her stomach and rocked in her chair. "But why? Why would he want to wreck the equipment?"

Kevin shrugged. "I don't know. I haven't figured that out yet. Maybe he's hoping word gets out, and the price of Bromley shares drop. That'd make it far cheaper for him to buy your half of the mill."

Her mind whirled. Had Josh fooled her father and everyone else all these years? The mill was worth millions. Greed made people commit atrocious acts. She read about it in the newspapers every day. Why would Josh be any different? Anger began a slow burn deep in her belly, and her hands fisted into tight balls. He'd played her for a fool.

"Sharla-Jean? Are you okay?"

She started at the sound of Kevin's voice. She'd forgotten he was there, watching with his sharp, almost feral gaze.

"I'm sorry I had to tell you this, but I wanted you to know before you get too involved with Josh." His gloating smirk belied his words.

Disgust filled her. He was enjoying this. She refused to give him the pleasure of seeing how upset she was. She pasted a bland expression on her face. "Thank you for telling me. I'll take what you said under consideration. But right now, I'd like to be alone."

"I understand. This is a lot to take in." He rose to his feet and headed out of the room, but paused before he reached the door, and whirled around to face her. "Will you help me?"

She rubbed her aching temples. "I don't know. We can't involve the police. Not yet. You don't have any proof Josh did any of these things."

His mouth tightened. "Trust me. He's guilty as hell, and with your help, I'm going to prove it."

Trust him? That was the clincher. She'd sooner trust a coyote in a henhouse. But she had to find out the truth. If Josh was responsible for these underhanded acts, he needed to be punished. She met Kevin's gaze. "What do you need me to do?"

"Give me access to the offices."

She shook her head. "I can't do that. Josh fired you."

His mouth quirked. "So rehire me. You're the manager as well. Overrule Morgan."

"All right. I'll do it."

His grin widened.

She held up her hand and stopped him before he could speak. "But if you step out of line even an inch, I'll fire your ass. And this time it'll be for keeps." Her gaze drilled into his. "There'll be no repeat of what happened at the cabin."

His smile faded, and the light left his eyes, but he nodded and saluted her with three fingers in the air. "Scout's honor." He spun and strode from the room. His footsteps echoed on the hall's hardwood floor. The front door closed with a thud as he let himself out.

For some inexplicable reason, tears filled her eyes and spilled onto her cheeks. Her legs gave out, and she collapsed onto the chair. One thought filled her mind— Josh had kissed her…not once, but twice. How could a man who kissed like he did be capable of such cunning?

Chapter 14

Sharla-Jean sank lower into the warm, soapy water and reveled in the soothing heat. The floral scent of bubble bath filled the steamy bathroom. She rested her head against the back of the tub and closed her eyes. Kevin's shocking accusations had rattled her. Was Josh a thief? Had he planned the elaborate setup in the storage room? Was he prepared to go to any lengths to get what he wanted? Even harm her?

She lifted the glass from the edge of the tub and sipped. The chilled white wine eased the thickness blocking her throat and warmed her body from within. The house was silent. Shortly after Kevin left, Pauline had returned, only to rush out a few minutes later on yet another mission of charity.

Sharla-Jean was torn. Her first reaction on hearing Kevin's suspicions had been to leave Renton Falls. The terms of the will would be broken, and Josh wouldn't get anything. But he had half a million dollars of stolen funds. He deserved to go to jail for theft.

She couldn't suppress the niggle of doubt making her stomach knot and her head ache. Kevin made no secret of the fact he despised Josh. Was this Kevin's way of getting back at the man who'd fired him?

She and Josh had shared such easy-flowing conversation during their cozy meal at the cabin. And his kiss, gentle, comforting, and reassuring;

transforming in a heartbeat to passion. She pressed her lips together as she conjured up his taste, the intimate caress of his tongue as he urged her to open for him. She'd lost herself in the riot of sensations heating her blood and speeding her heart. But then her old fears had reared their heads, and she'd stiffened and backed away from his touch.

His chocolate-brown eyes hadn't been cold with anger at her sudden withdrawal, but cloudy with confusion. She'd wanted to tell him why she'd frozen him out, but how could she, when the secret was buried so deep? How could she explain the terror of the worst night of her life, when she hadn't shared the details of the attack with anyone other than her father?

How could Josh be responsible for the crimes Kevin accused him of? She sipped more wine. The full-bodied, fruity liquid slid down her throat and washed away the foul taste in her mouth. The only way she could be certain he was innocent was by examining the evidence Kevin had uncovered and confronting Josh.

She refused to hand over her father's company to a thief and a liar. If Josh was guilty, she'd make damn sure he paid for his crimes. She'd call in the police and watch as they dragged him away to jail.

Condensation clouded the outside of the crystal wine glass, and she pressed it against her forehead, enjoying the icy sensation on her hot skin. Time to retrieve Josh's journal from its hiding place in the china cabinet and read what secrets he'd written. If he was responsible for the theft of hundreds of thousands of dollars and was scheming to drive her away, he may have written his plans in his private journal.

Climbing out of the bathtub, she grabbed a towel

from the rack and wrapped the soft cotton around her dripping body. She opened the bathroom door and shivered in the frigid air of the hallway. The furnace was on the fritz again. Pauline had called a repairman, but he wasn't able to come until the end of the week. Hot baths and bulky sweaters would have to suffice until then.

Shivering, she scurried down the hall to the stairs. If she was quick, she'd retrieve the journal from the cabinet and be back in the warm bath with the scented bubbles before the water cooled.

She was midway down the staircase when the doorbell pealed. Clutching the towel to her chest, she froze. Two long windows lined either side of the oak entry door, but no one standing on the front steps outside the door could see through the frosted glass.

The bell rang again, followed by a lengthy silence. Obviously, whoever had been at the door had figured no one was home and left. She released the breath she'd been holding and continued down the stairs. The foyer's tile floor was cold on her bare feet.

A key scraped in the lock, the lock clicked, and the front door swung open.

She spun around and yelped. And yelped again, when as if in slow motion, the damp towel wrapped around her naked body slipped. She grabbed for the towel, but missed. A sudden chill blasted her as the towel slid to the floor.

Josh Morgan, eyes wide, and his dark brows raised almost to his hairline, stood in the open doorway, his tall, muscular body outlined by the porch light.

Heat flared along her neck and engulfed her cheeks in fire. She slammed her eyes shut, as she tried to cover herself with her hands.

"I believe you dropped this."

She pried her eyes open.

Amusement twinkled in his eyes. His teeth gleamed as his grin widened. He held out the damp towel.

Flushing hotter, she snatched the treacherous towel out of his hand, and held it in front of her like a shield. "Wha…what are you doing here?"

He kept his gaze fixed on her face, but the damage was done. He'd seen it all, every naked inch of her. "When you didn't answer the doorbell, I assumed no one was home."

She gaped in disbelief. "And so you what…broke in? There aren't any valuables here. Nothing worth stealing."

He studied her nearly naked body, his gaze roaming slowly over her expanse of exposed legs and the all-too-revealing towel. Sparks of gold danced in his dark eyes. "I wouldn't say that."

She gripped the towel tighter, wishing the damp fabric didn't cling so tightly to her curves. Warmth infused her at the same time goose bumps rose on her arms. She longed to cross her arms over her chest but was prevented from doing so by the necessity of holding the towel.

Embarrassment transformed to anger. This was *her* house. She had every right to wander around naked if she chose. He was the one who'd broken in. "How did you get in?" Kevin's accusations rang through her head, and she shuddered. Was he here to harm her?

He held up a key. "Your father gave me a key years ago. He said I was to treat this place as if it was my home; to come and go as I pleased." His dark eyes bore into hers. "Pauline never minds."

"Pauline's not here." As soon as the words were out of her mouth, she bit her bottom lip. If Kevin was right, Josh had already tried to harm her once. What was to stop him from trying again? "But, I…I'm ex…expect…expecting her…her b…b…back any min…minute." She ground her teeth together, hating the painful, stuttering sounds emerging from her lips.

He watched her for a long, drawn-out minute, and then turned so his back was to her. "Go ahead and cover up. You must be cold."

She seized advantage of the scant privacy and wrapped the towel around her, snugging the ends between her breasts. "I'm going upstairs to get dressed. Don't go anywhere. I'll be back." She ran for the stairs and leaped the steps two at a time.

"Don't bother to dress on my account. You look fine the way you are."

His laughter followed her up the stairs as she fled to her bedroom. Hands shaking, she tugged on a pair of crumpled jeans and yanked a sweatshirt over her head. She ran her fingers through her wet, tangled mass of hair.

Fully clothed, dignity restored, her anger grew. Why was he here? What did he want? Kevin's words of warning replayed through her mind. Was she in danger? Should she call the police? Her heartbeat quickened. Had he found out she'd taken his journal? Fear congealed in her throat.

Reason reasserted itself, and she steadied her frantic breathing. Even if Josh had noticed the absence of his journal, he had no reason to suspect she was responsible. The journal had been in his desk drawer. Any number of people at the mill had the opportunity to take his book.

She twisted her mouth. Well, maybe she was the logical person to have taken the journal, but he had no way of knowing for sure. At least she'd had the foresight to hide the black book. She couldn't begin to imagine how she'd explain his private diary being in her house.

Besides, she wasn't the one who'd stolen money from the mill. And she wasn't the one conniving to take her share of the mill. Maybe this was the time to confront him, to find out if Kevin's accusations had any basis in reality. Squaring her shoulders, she inhaled a deep breath, opened the bedroom door, and stepped into the hall, prepared for battle.

He wasn't at the bottom of the stairs. Nor was he in the living room, or the kitchen. She searched the house, room by room, and found him kneeling on the floor at the bottom of the narrow steps leading to the dimly lit cellar. He held a massive hammer above his head in one hand, ready to strike at something hidden in the shadows on the hard-packed, dirt floor.

"What are you doing?" Her voice, rife with accusation, echoed within the tight confines of the old dugout cellar.

His shoulders tensed, and the tendons in his arms bulged as he smashed down the hammer with a mighty blow. Instead of striking hard-packed dirt and breaking through to a secret hideaway, a loud clang reverberated throughout the dimly lit room as the hammer struck metal.

Her confusion deepened when he raised the

hammer again and pounded another vicious blow. The sharp bang of metal resounded hollowly in the low-ceilinged space. She inched down one step and then another.

He set the hammer on the ground and knelt beside an antiquated metal furnace. Grasping a rust-encrusted spigot in one hand, he grunted as he strained to turn the tap. With a loud, wrenching screech, the handle twisted. The hiss of steam filled the room. He sat back on his haunches and wiped his brow with the sleeve of his plaid flannel shirt and shot a glance at her standing above him. "Did you say something?"

"What are you doing down here?"

He fished a greasy rag from the back pocket of his faded jeans and wiped his face, leaving black streaks on his lean cheeks. "Pauline asked me to see if I could do something about this old furnace. I guess the usual repair guy's tied up. Anyway, I had some free time tonight, and figured I'd stop by and fix this beast." He patted the rusted metal tank almost fondly. "She acts up every few months. I've done my level best to convince Pauline to buy a new one, but she says you don't get rid of something just because it's old."

A loud bang rang out, the furnace gurgled, and the loud hissing quieted to a smooth rumble. Heat blasted out of an open furnace duct above her head.

He chuckled. "I guess she's right."

Sharla-Jean was nonplused. "You're here to repair the furnace?"

"Disappointed?" He grinned, a boyish gleam in his dark eyes. "Believe me, if I'd known you'd greet me at the door buck naked, I'd have been over sooner...a lot sooner."

A heated flush crept up her neck onto her cheeks.

His hair was tousled as if he'd run his fingers through the dark strands, a habit she noticed he did when he was stressed. A stray lock fell over his broad forehead. The smudges on his cheeks added to his masculine appeal. The world narrowed to the tunnel of light shining from the single, dim light bulb above his head, silhouetting him in a warm glow.

Awareness arced between them, searing and heady.

Her heart raced.

His gaze drilled into hers. He swallowed, the muscles in his throat working.

She gulped and licked suddenly dry lips.

Rising to his feet, he advanced one slow step, and then another until he stood at the bottom of the stairs, the desire in his smoldering eyes blatant.

The intriguing scent of his aftershave floated up the stairs. Seconds ticked by. Her breath rose in short, tortured pants, leaving her dizzy. She wanted him. Every female part of her cried out in need. His name formed on her lips, part plea, part groan. "Josh."

His mouth curved in a smile full of promise, and the dimple in his cheek danced. But he didn't budge.

He wouldn't. She read that in his eyes. It was up to her to close the distance between them. Up to her to make the first move. As if in a trance, she lowered her foot and descended the stairs, one step at a time, until they stood face-to-face.

He reached for her, but out of nowhere, Kevin's accusations clamored through her mind. *Josh is a thief. He tried to hurt you.* She stiffened as if doused by a bucket of ice water. A chill trembled through her. Shaking her head, she backed away.

"What are you so frightened of, Sharla-Jean?" The furrow between his brows deepened. "Is it me? Jesus, is that it? Are you afraid of me?"

Afraid? She was terrified, but not of him. Surrounded by the sight, the smell, the promise of him, her body craved to be wrapped in his muscular arms. At the same time, just the thought of being that close to his large, male body terrified her. The physical injuries from the long ago attack had healed, but the wounds to her soul were raw and bleeding. And then there were all the shocking claims Kevin had made. What if they were true? "Did you steal the money?" The second she blurted the words she clapped her hand over her mouth.

"What money?" He stepped toward her, his eyes fierce. "What the hell are you talking about?"

Fear ricocheted through her, and her legs sagged, and she wobbled on the step. She grabbed for the railing, missed, and yelped as she fell.

He lunged forward and grasped her arm, holding her steady. "Christ! Take it easy. You don't want to break your neck."

The skin on her arm burned under his grip, and she tugged to break free, but he held her tight. "Please, let me go." Her voice was a thin squeak. What had she been thinking? Confronting him in this dark and gloomy basement was reckless. They were alone. No one would hear her screams.

He loosened his grip, but drew her toward him until the heat radiating from his body simmered between them. "Answer my question. What money do you think I stole?"

Overwhelmed by blinding fear, the adrenaline pumped, firing her blood as a thousand nightmare images rose before her. *No! Not again.* Sweat beaded under her arms and dampened her upper lip. "Let me go, please. Don't hurt me." The long strands of her wet hair slapped across her face as she twisted and yanked her arm from his grasp. She stumbled back, her chest heaving, struggling to breathe.

He backed away, his hands raised in front of him, palms out. "Hey, take it easy. I won't hurt you. I promise." He shoved his hands in the pockets of his jeans. "I mean that. You're safe with me."

The soft rumble of his voice was a soothing balm to her shattered nerves. Her breathing steadied, and she swiped her damp forehead with her arm. She studied him.

His brow was furrowed, and his mouth was turned down at the corners, but his eyes were soft, filled with concern rather than anger.

Her fear vanished at the visceral certainty she had nothing to fear. He wouldn't hurt her. Not now. Not ever. "I…I'm sorry." The apology was a mere breath of sound. Tears stung her eyes, but she blinked them back. Now wasn't the time for crying.

He studied her for several, long heartbeats. "Sorry?" His lip curled in a sneer. "You're *sorry*. You accuse me of stealing money from God knows where and now you're sorry?" He shook his head. "You're a real piece of work, lady. You know that?"

She opened her mouth to speak, to say something, anything, but her throat clogged and words failed.

"I don't know what your problem is, and right now, I don't give a damn." He rolled his shoulders. "Just get your shit together so we can finish out this year from Hell without you looking at me as if I'm going to attack you every time we're alone." He brushed past her and stormed up the narrow stairs.

"Josh, wait." Her voice was a thin squeak.

He stopped and turned and looked down at her. An unreadable expression filmed his dark eyes.

"I really am sorry."

He watched her for a long minute. "What did you mean about the money?"

Fighting to swallow over the thickening lump in her throat, she attempted a casual shrug. "Nothing. It was a mistake. I shouldn't have said anything."

His eyes narrowed, his gaze piercing.

She grasped her hands behind her back, hoping to hide their trembling.

He exhaled a loud breath. "You look tired. You'd better get some sleep. I'll see you in the office in the morning. We'll talk about this then." Shaking his head and muttering under his breath, he turned and strode into the kitchen and through to the hall. The front door slammed closed and then there was silence. Except for the steady hiss and rumble of the old furnace and the creak of expanding pipes.

Chapter 15

Josh ignored Audrey's cheerful greeting. "No interruptions this morning, Audrey." He strode into the quiet confines of his office and slammed the door behind him. Sinking onto his chair, he leaned his head back against the cool leather and closed his eyes.

Images of Sharla-Jean Bromley's exquisite face, shining fall of auburn hair, and brilliant green eyes filled his mind. He clenched his jaw and ground his teeth. *Think of something else, Aunt Mabel's pot roast, last night's Knicks' game, the price of rice in China…anything but her.* He rubbed his eyes with the heel of his hands. He couldn't get the damn woman out of his thoughts. Since the first moment he'd seen her, he'd been in the same crazy tailspin, as if she'd cast some sort of spell over him.

His mouth twisted as he recalled his confident words to J.D. at Big Jim's funeral when he'd first discovered the attractive woman in the dazzling red dress was Big Jim Bromley's daughter. How could he have thought he'd get rid of her so easily? He'd been the worst kind of fool.

But how was he to know she'd turn his world upside down? Sure, she had curves to die for, and she oozed sex, but he'd been around plenty of good-looking women. They'd never affected him this way. She sure as hell wasn't what he'd expected, which was part of the problem. Instead of the hard-nosed, cold-blooded bitch he'd prepared for, she'd thrown him for a loop with her wounded green eyes filled with shifting shadows.

A loud rapping broke the tomb-like silence. Before he could yell at his visitor to go away, the door opened and J.D. Webster bustled into the room. Josh grimaced. "So much for telling Audrey I didn't want to be disturbed."

The lawyer lowered himself into a chair and set his ever-present, black, leather briefcase on the floor beside him. A sheen of perspiration glistened on his brow. His eyes, behind thick lenses, were bright with excitement. "Don't blame Audrey. I told her this was important." He slid a red silk handkerchief out of his suit coat pocket and dabbed his brow.

Josh glared in rising irritation. "Is the mill on fire?" Everything was crucial to J.D. The man possessed an inflated sense of his own importance.

J.D. shook his head.

"Have terrorists taken over our offices?"

The lawyer's brow furrowed. "Of course not."

"Then get the hell out of here."

"Josh, this is important." J.D. remained seated and picked up his briefcase, set it on his lap, and flipped open the shiny brass locks.

A thousand forms of torture, each more excruciating than the previous one ran through Josh's mind. But he recognized the stubborn set of J.D.'s mouth, and he puffed out his cheeks in resignation. Past experience had taught him the old lawyer could be as obstinate as a hungry bear in the fall. He wouldn't leave Josh in peace until he said what he'd come to say. "All right." Josh blew out a breath. "Tell me what's so important. Then you can get the hell out of my office and leave me alone."

The stiffening of J.D.'s shoulders was the sole indication he was offended by Josh's rudeness. He removed several sheets of paper from the briefcase and set the case back on the floor by his feet. Sitting back in his chair, he crossed his hands over his straining paunch. "How's your relationship with the Bromley woman these days?"

"*That's* what's so important? You want an update?"

J.D.'s full lips tightened. "I wondered what you thought of her now you've had a chance to get to know her better."

Josh pinned the other man with an intent look. "Why?"

"People are talking. They're saying she's doing a decent job. She works late every night, weekends too, from what I hear. She's making a real effort to learn about the company."

Josh grunted in response.

"Looks like she has more depth of character than we anticipated."

A vision of Sharla-Jean naked in the front entryway when he'd opened the door to her house last night flashed before him. Even before the towel fell, the scrap of damp fabric did little to hide her curves. When the towel dropped to the floor, his heart had stopped beating. He'd looked his fill for those few seconds before he caught himself and forced his gaze away. Too late. He'd seen a sight guaranteed to keep him awake at night for the rest of his life.

"Josh?"

J.D.'s voice cut into his musings. "What?" he snapped, his voice harsher than he'd intended.

"I see you're distracted. Who can blame you? You have a great deal on your mind right now, but"—J.D. mopped his brow again—"we have something to discuss."

The lawyer's words were an unintelligible buzz as once again Josh's mind wandered to the events of the previous evening. Sharla-Jean looking at him, her impossibly large eyes filled with desire, her body soft and responsive under his touch, her heady scent surrounding him. She'd taken his breath away. But then desire had turned to fear, and instead of returning his kiss she struggled to get away.

Her fear of him pushed him over the edge, and he wanted to strike out, to wound her as she'd wounded him. What was her problem? Why was she so frightened? What the hell had happened to her to cause such fear at a man's touch?

"Are you listening, Josh?"

Leaping up from his chair, Josh strode across the room. His body demanded action, anything to force all thoughts of *her* out of his mind. He had a business to run, for God's sakes, and he still hadn't figured out who was sabotaging the company. He rolled his shoulders and rubbed the rising throb in his temples. "Yeah, I'm listening."

The lawyer harrumphed as if he didn't believe him. "As I was saying, rumors are going around about discrepancies in our books."

Josh halted his pacing and spun to face J.D. "What?"

J.D. nodded. "Nothing definite. Just vague talk of missing funds and falsified documents." He cleared his throat. "I don't have to tell you what this could mean to the company."

Josh's mind raced. Rumors of irregularities, no matter how unfounded, could destroy a business. If word leaked out, investor confidence would be shaken, and the mill would suffer irreparable losses. Many a successful company had been brought to its knees by rumors. "Any possibility there's truth to these stories?"

J.D. shrugged. "I don't see how. We'd know if something was going on."

"Not good enough." Josh punched his fist into the palm of his other hand. "We need to be sure. If these rumors aren't squelched, we could be in big trouble."

J.D. held out the sheaf of papers. "These are copies of our financial statements for the past year. I'm sure you'll want to examine them yourself."

"Why haven't we heard anything about this before now?" Josh ground his back molars until they ached. He'd always prided himself on having his ear to the ground, of knowing every detail of what happened in the mill. But that was before. He'd been distracted these past few weeks. First Big Jim's death, and then the appearance of Big Jim's long-lost daughter had flipped his world upside down. To say nothing of the fact he'd been so tied up in knots over the damn woman, he hadn't thought of anything else.

Were the rumors true? Was someone stealing from the mill? He'd stake his life on the loyalty of his employees. They were honest people, grateful for the opportunity to work in well-paid jobs with full benefits, a rarity in this part of Oregon where the average wage was below the poverty line. Big Jim had treated his workers fairly, and Josh continued the same tradition. But Bromley Forest Products was a large, growing company, and in a company this size, anything was possible.

Not everyone was pleased, he reminded himself. Someone had deliberately damaged thousands of dollars worth of equipment, and someone had placed the container of gas in the storage room the other night and lit the rags on fire. That same someone was out to harm the company.

If the scuttlebutt was true and someone was stealing from the mill, he had to figure out who the thief was before all hell broke loose and everything he'd worked for crumbled to ruins. One thing was damn sure, he'd find out what the hell was going on and who was the bastard responsible.

Sharla-Jean's words from last night flashed before him. His breathing quickened. *Why did you take the money?* Was this what she was talking about? Did she think he stole money from the mill? Had she heard the rumors, or did she know something he didn't? His head throbbed as the questions, one after the other, tumbled through him.

He jammed his hands on his hips and faced J.D. "Get our best financial people on this. I want every penny accounted for. Find out if there's any truth to these stories." He strode over to his desk. For the first time in days his mind was clear and focused. "Oh, and J.D.?"

The lawyer paused in collecting his briefcase. His heavy gray eyebrows rose in question.

"Keep this matter between us. The fewer people

who know, the better. Stick with people you know we can trust." His gut twisted. "And that isn't Sharla-Jean Bromley."

J.D. nodded. "Of course."

Josh snatched up the phone, but hesitated. J.D. hadn't yet left the office.

The lawyer hovered by the door as if reluctant to leave.

"What is it?" Josh asked.

"You don't suppose Sharla-Jean has something to do with this, do you?"

Josh opened his mouth to refute the lawyer's suspicion, but frowned. Creating a sense of instability would be an effective ploy if she was intent on getting back at her father by destroying his company. If the rumors of financial impropriety continued, the stockholders would lose confidence in the mill, and shares would lose their value. He would be held responsible for the entire debacle. Sharla-Jean could swoop in like a knight in shining armor and take over the company and return the mill to its former glory.

Was she so underhanded? She had a reputation for getting into trouble as a teenager, and he had no idea what she'd been doing in Portland all these years. He rubbed his aching temples. Until he found the true culprit, he'd maintain an open mind. But he wasn't a fool. He'd keep a wary eye on her. If she was involved in this, he'd find out, and then he'd deal with the lady. "Find out who's responsible, J.D. Find out now."

J.D. nodded and hurried out the door.

The door hadn't closed behind the lawyer before a light tap sounded on the doorframe, and the door swung open again. "What now, J.D.?" Josh snapped.

"Hello, Morgan."

Josh swung his head around with a snap and pinned Kevin Nelson with a withering glare. "What the hell are you doing here? I kicked your ass out. Remember?" He pointed at the door. "Get out, or do I have to toss you out of here on your ass like I did at the cabin?" What was the point of a secretary if she ignored his orders and let in any fool? One of these days he'd fire Audrey. Bad enough she'd let in J.D.; Kevin Nelson was another matter.

Nelson settled himself on the chair recently vacated by J.D. and crossed one long leg over the other. "I thought you heard." He smirked. "Sharla-Jean rehired me. It seems she values my work here more than you do." He examined his perfectly buffed fingernails. "I'm here until I decide to quit."

"Sharla-Jean rehired you? Why the hell would she do that?" Josh bunched his hands into fists. Nelson was a lunatic. No way would Sharla-Jean hire him back, not after what happened at the cabin.

Nelson's smirk grew. "I think she likes me." He winked lewdly. "If you know what I mean."

Josh's anger redlined, and it was all he could do to remain in his seat and not throttle the guy. But what if he was telling the truth? What if Sharla-Jean had rehired him? "I don't give a damn what Sharla-Jean did, as far as I'm concerned you're fired. You have no right to be here." His turn to smile. "Before I'm finished with you, you'll slink out of here with your tail between your legs. No reputable company will hire you to scrub the piss off their toilets."

Nelson waved his hands as if brushing off Josh's threats. "We need to talk."

Josh ground his teeth. He could follow through on his threat and toss Nelson's sorry ass out of here, but it might be wiser to hear what he had to say. He could always throw him out later. He made a point of looking at his watch. "I'm busy. Make it quick."

Nelson's thin lips cracked in a smug smile.

Josh ached to smash the jerk's teeth in, but he held back. Instead, he stomped around his desk and plopped down in his big leather chair. He leaned back and placed his hands behind his neck, affecting a calmness he was far from feeling. Again he studied his watch. "You have five seconds, Nelson."

"The whole office is talking about you and Sharla-Jean."

Anger burned, scalding and heady, in Josh's belly. "What about me and Ms. Bromley?"

Nelson shrugged his shoulders. "You don't have to pretend with me. I see the way you two look at each other." He licked the tip of his forefinger, raised it in the air and made a hissing sound. "You're so hot for each other, I'm surprised flames don't ignite when you're in the same room."

Josh glared with such ferocity at the arrogant bastard he was surprised Nelson didn't burst into flames. He breathed in several steadying breaths, forcing an outward, icy calm. "Why don't you tell me why this is any of your business?" He bared his teeth in a snarl.

Nelson smoothed an imaginary wrinkle from his pressed slacks. "I don't think the shareholders would be impressed to hear the *co-presidents* of this company are involved in an affair. I mean, how much time are you two focusing on running the mill if you're busy screwing each other, especially with certain *financial* improprieties going on?"

Josh's hatred for this worm of a man filled him to bursting. His hands clenched into fists ready to strike. He wanted to beat the smirk off the bastard's ferret-like face. "You have any proof?"

In spite of Nelson's relaxed posture, a gleam of moisture shone on his forehead, and the fingers of one hand drummed on his thigh. "Well, no, but—"

"Exactly." Josh cut him off. "You have no proof. And the reason you have no proof is because your allegations are baseless. Ms. Bromley and I are *not* having an affair. Even if we were, I see no reason why this is any of your business."

"You're wrong, Morgan. If your actions harm the mill, it's my business."

Josh leaped to his feet, lunged across his desk, grabbed the other man by the collar of his expensive suit and dragged him half out of his chair. His face was mere inches from Nelson's. "Who the hell do you think you are, you sniveling little worm?"

Nelson's face paled.

Josh released him and stepped back, resisting the urge to plow a fist into his arrogant face. Kevin Nelson wasn't worth the trouble. "If I hear any more of these baseless rumors, I'll sue your ass for slander. Now get the hell out of here."

Nelson adjusted his suit coat and smoothed his rumpled hair. His pale blue eyes blazed with fury. "You have no idea who you're dealing with, Morgan. You've sounded the death knell for this company." With those cryptic words, he stormed out of the office, leaving the door gaping open.

Josh's brow furrowed. A sudden chill assailed him. Was Nelson the one spreading the rumors about missing money? Was he working alone, or was he in cahoots with someone? With Sharla-Jean? They spent a great deal of time together in her office. And, if Nelson was telling the truth, she'd rehired him, even after what had happened at the cabin. A fierce throbbing started behind his eyes.

Striding to his desk, he unlocked the bottom drawer and rifled through the pile of file folders and half-empty bag of chocolates searching for his bottle of painkillers. Grabbing the small vial, he twisted off the lid, tapped out two small white pills and then stopped and stared at the jumble in the drawer.

His heart raced as he emptied the drawer, piling chocolate bars, pens, paperclips, and all the other accumulated junk on the top of the desk. He stared at the empty drawer. The black, leather-covered journal was gone.

Maybe he'd hidden it somewhere else. Heart racing, he searched through the other drawers in the desk. When had he last seen the journal? Weeks ago, after the reading of Big Jim's will, he'd written his reactions to the stunning developments in its pages. He'd returned the journal to the bottom drawer in his desk like he always did.

He kept this desk drawer locked. Always. Not even Audrey had the key. He hadn't taken the diary anywhere, which left one possibility. Someone had found the journal and taken it from his office. His blood chilled at the repercussions if the information he'd recorded in the book ever came to light.

He stumbled over to his chair, slumped into the

soft leather, and rubbed his hands over his face. This was turning out to be one hell of a day. In the next breath, he shot out of the chair and strode across the office and out the door. He ignored Audrey's anxious look and probing questions as he raced down the hall. Taking the stairs two at a time, he thrust open the door and burst out of the office building.

He jogged through the lumberyard to the parking lot. Unlocking his truck, he opened the door and climbed in. The powerful vehicle's motor surged as he mashed the accelerator, spraying gravel as he sped out of the parking lot.

Chapter 16

Visions of penetrating brown eyes and soft male lips paraded before her as Sharla-Jean steered her car down the road toward the mill. Josh. It was always Josh. At least he'd been her sole focus since she returned to Renton Falls. His image was what she'd conjured during the many long, sleepless nights. Josh and his deep, rumbling voice. Josh with his firm muscles and cap of thick, tousled, chestnut hair.

A dark blue truck appeared in the road in front of her and barreled past, heading in the opposite direction, Josh behind the wheel.

She clutched the steering wheel. Even though she'd caught only the briefest glimpse as he roared past, his face had been a white blur, his gaze fixed ahead as if he was unaware another car was on the road.

Glancing in her rearview mirror, she watched as his red taillights disappeared around the bend. Where was he going in such a hurry? The mill and his house were in the opposite direction. She hesitated only a heartbeat before she spun the car around in the middle of the road. Pressing her foot on the accelerator, she roared around the corner after him.

She'd only gone a few miles when she spotted his blue truck parked in a small parking lot along the side of the road used by people visiting the town cemetery. She parked beside his truck and switched off her car's engine.

Josh's truck and her car were the only vehicles in the parking lot. The gray, freezing, fall day didn't lend itself to visiting mourners. Dead grass covered the ground between evenly spaced rows of granite headstones stretching over a hill, backing against the dark wall of the forest. A few deciduous trees, their branches bare of leaves, stood like sentinels amongst the graves. Cement benches lined a gravel walkway leading into the desolate cemetery.

Her heart lodged in her throat. This was one place she'd been determined not to visit while she was in town. Yet, here she was.

The cemetery was new since she'd last been in town. For the past five years, she'd subscribed to the *Renton Falls Review,* and once a week the newspaper was mailed to her home in Portland. The newspaper was filled with more advertising than news content, but it was a way for her to keep her eye on what her father was up to. That was where she'd read of his death.

The newspaper was also where she'd learned how the small pioneer cemetery on a sloping hillside overlooking the town, had been taken over by a developer who wanted the land for a hotel complex. The town elders had agreed, amidst a great deal of controversy, to sell the land to the developer and move the cemetery. They'd dug up the graves, and with great ceremony, reinterred the dearly departed in their rotting coffins in a new plot of land outside the city limits. Judging by the vitriol in the letters to the editor column, people were not happy with the decision.

Her stomach clamped tight as she climbed out of her car. The cemetery was bleak and cold, but in spite of the chill in the air, her palms were clammy and sweat dampened her forehead

The graveyard was bordered on three sides by thick forests of mature evergreen trees. Snow-covered mountains loomed in the distance. She shivered and huddled into her coat. The frigid wind seemed more forceful than in town; its howl more ominous as it whistled through the rows of headstones.

A thick lump filled her throat. Her mother was buried somewhere in this cemetery. Her father too, she supposed. After the funeral in the church, she'd had enough of the townspeople's resentment and had avoided the interment.

A fresh shudder ran through her. She tried to swallow, but her mouth was too dry. The leaden, gray sky matched her dark mood. The heavy weight of clouds hung over the thick stands of evergreen trees ringing the cemetery. Her breath frosted in the freezing air, and a bone-deep chill enveloped her.

Taking a deep breath, she started forward. Josh was here somewhere and she was determined to see what he was up to. She quickened her steps. Opening the wrought iron gate, she grimaced at the squeal of unoiled metal, and stepped inside the cemetery. A crow flew low overhead, its raucous call echoing against the tall spires of the pines, adding to the melancholy atmosphere. If a movie producer wanted to make a horror movie, this was the perfect place.

Jamming her hands in her pockets to keep them from freezing, she followed the gravel path meandering between the grave markers, circling the outer perimeter of the cemetery. Her footsteps sounded loud in the heavy silence. Her gaze skittered from gravestone to gravestone, refusing to dwell too long on any one edifice as she searched for some sign of Josh.

Heart pounding, she passed one grave after another. Which one was her mother's? Her father's? Her breath hitched in and out, and a dull headache threatened. She stopped, her body rigid, her spine stiff with tension. She couldn't do this. No matter what Josh was up to, no matter what secrets his presence here revealed, she couldn't stay a minute longer. Too many painful memories were buried here.

A flash of color, so at odds with the prevailing monochrome of gray and black, flickered in the distance. Josh. She hurried toward him, her unease forgotten. Rounding a grove of rosebushes, their blossoms dried husks, she halted, frozen in her tracks.

Josh knelt on the grass before an ornate gravestone.

Her stomach somersaulted at the familiar width of his shoulders and his dark swath of curly hair.

His shoulders were slumped, his dark head bent as if in prayer. His lips moved, though she couldn't hear what he was saying in the cold, still air.

Even at this distance the ornate gravestone stood out. The shiny black granite block rose at least five feet. Vases filled with flowers, some dried and withered, some fresh and wilting in the frosty air, and some plastic, their colors garish, littered the ground around the base of the grave. The grave was recent. Grass hadn't grown over the fresh mound of dirt.

Heart thrumming, she edged closer, anxious to see the name on the grave marker. Her boot kicked a pebble, and the rock skittered across the path, sounding like a gunshot in the heavy silence of the cemetery.

Josh jerked to his feet and spun to face her.

A crow cawed from within the dark line of trees, a lone vehicle passed on the road, a branch creaked in the wind, and the dry rattle of yellow leaves sounded like old bones.

Finally, he spoke. "Why are you here?"

A thousand answers roared through her, but none seemed sufficient. Deciding the best defense was an offense, she asked, "Why are *you* here?"

"Did you follow me?"

"I was on my way to the mill when you almost ran me off the road." She shrugged. "I wanted to see why you were in such a rush."

The corners of his mouth quirked. "So you did follow me."

Her face heated, and she avoided his penetrating stare.

"Do you want to know why I'm here?"

She bit her lip, but she couldn't deny her curiosity, and so she nodded.

He pointed toward the grave in front of him. "About time you showed up here. Come and have a look."

She gulped, swallowed, and gulped again, but read the challenge in his eyes, and shuffled a tentative step toward him.

He backed up and allowed her a clear view of the inscription on the granite stone in front of him.

The name inscribed on the smooth, black headstone rushed up at her. Her first impulse was to turn away, and she jammed her hand over her mouth, blocking a moan as her legs wobbled. The headstone was cold to the touch as she ran her shaking fingers over the indentations and traced the carved letters.

James 'Big Jim' Bromley.

Reeling under the revelation the very grave she dreaded seeing was right in front of her, she staggered back and would have collapsed if a strong hand hadn't gripped her arm and held her steady. Her vision swam and blurred with tears as she was pressed against a warm body and enveloped in muscular arms. She breathed in Josh's familiar scent and clasped his body, clinging to his reassuring presence.

"Easy, Sharla-Jean. Easy." His deep voice resonated through his chest, rumbling beneath her ear.

"This…this is my…my…father's grave." She shoved against him, backing away from his comforting warmth. "You…you…wha…what were…you…?" She groaned in frustration at the tortuous sounds. Taking a deep breath, she tried again. "Wha…what are you doing here?"

"I'm visiting his grave. Paying my respects." His face was unreadable. "Big Jim was my friend, the best friend I ever had."

Tears filled her eyes. She swiped at them. "You…you really cared for him, didn't you?"

The furrow deepened between his dark brows. He stared off into the distance as if seeing something other than the endless rows of gray headstones. "Big Jim was like a father to me." His voice roughened with emotion. "I miss him. I miss him a lot."

Sincerity was written across the rugged planes of his face. Josh had cared for her father. Along with this realization was the certainty he wouldn't have stolen from someone for whom he cared so much. A flood of relief washed over her. Josh Morgan wasn't the thief Kevin claimed he was.

His voice drew her out of her thoughts. "I have to get back to the mill."

"No, wait," she blurted, and her face flamed as he regarded her, his dark brows raised in query. "I mean, please stay. Tell me what he was like." The play of emotions crossing his rugged features entranced her. "Please."

"Do you really want to know?"

She nodded. Who was Big Jim Bromley? What sort of a man had he really been? Had she been wrong about him? Had he changed after she left, like Pauline told her? Was he more than the drunken, detached father she remembered? Who better to tell her about him than the man who'd been like his son?

"Okay." Josh nodded. "I'll tell you, but not here. Not now." He nodded again as if he'd reached a decision. "Come to my place for supper tonight. We'll talk. I'll tell you what I know."

She hesitated, uncertain. He exuded a powerful magnetism, one she couldn't resist. Alone with him for any length of time and no telling what would happen. She couldn't afford a repeat of the fiasco at the cabin.

"What are you afraid of, Sharla-Jean?" He cocked his head and arched one brow a fraction of an inch higher. "It's only dinner."

She read the challenge in his handsome face. "Fine. I'll be there."

He grinned as if he'd known what her answer would be before she spoke, but all he said was, "See you then." He strode away, his long legs eating up the ground. In minutes he disappeared from sight.

She stared after him as embers of excitement flickered and flared to life. A smile teased along her lips. *Dinner tonight. Oh, my.* Catching sight of her father's gravestone, her heart lurched, and she recalled where she was.

Edging nearer the grave, she examined the headstone, noting the ornate carvings incised lengthwise into one half of the massive stone. One scene depicted a thick forest of evergreen trees flanked by towering mountains. A replica of the original lumber mill was etched beneath the forest engraving. She leaned closer and read the inscription on the base of the monument.

James "Big Jim" Bromley
followed by the dates of his birth and death
Loving husband, father, and friend.
Caretaker of the sick,
defender of the weak,
beloved by all.

Words were also carved into the other half of the gravestone. As she read, tears blurred the faded epitaph.

Clarice Augusta Bromley
1951-1985
Beloved wife, devoted mother, angel on Earth.
Until we meet again.

Something else was etched into the granite, and she leaned closer and traced the worn grooves with the tip of one finger. As she rubbed away years-old grime, the full beauty of a delicate flower emerged.

Transported back in her memories to a happier time when her mother was alive, she gulped as the image before her shimmered. Her mother, holding a small, gold locket in her hand. Sharla-Jean, a child of five, grabbing the locket with her chubby fingers and studying the shiny trinket. Engraved into the locket was a gardenia, so detailed in design, she'd lifted the locket to her nose to smell the sweet nectar of the blossom.

Her mother, a true daughter of the South, was never without her locket. She'd told Sharla-Jean her own mother had given her the piece of jewelry, and one day the heirloom would belong to Sharla-Jean. Her mother had explained the gardenia was a symbol of the land where she'd spent her childhood, the place she loved and so desperately missed after she'd fallen in love with a handsome northerner and followed him to the rugged Cascade Mountains.

Tears stung Sharla-Jean's eyes as she tugged the thin gold chain free from under her blouse where it hung around her neck, revealing the burnished gold locket. Her fingers caressed the warm metal, tracing the familiar design etched into the worn surface. A tear slipped down her cheek.

Her mother never had the chance to pass on the family heirloom to her daughter. Instead, Pauline had given Sharla-Jean the locket the day of her mother's funeral. Sharla-Jean had worn the tiny locket ever since. The golden gardenia represented the painful loss of her mother and her anger at the man who'd taken her mother from her.

But now, on this dreary, damp day, standing before her parents' graves, the locket no longer filled her with anger and bitterness. She studied the linked graves with new insight. The two graves shared a single marker like so many other loving couples who'd passed on. She'd never imagined her father cared enough for her mother to wish to lie beside her for eternity.

Maybe she'd misjudged him and his depth of devotion to the woman he'd married. Maybe their relationship was deeper than she realized. Perhaps Pauline was right, and her father had suffered from the loss of the woman he adored.

A bouquet of fresh flowers in a plastic vase sat before the graves. The exotic, large white flowers were starting to droop from the cold. Had Josh left them? How had he known to leave gardenias? She knelt on the dirt and caressed a velvety white petal, crushing it between her fingers. The exotic scent of heavy, thick cream, orange blossom, honey, and earthy loam filled the freezing air. A thousand memories flooded her, and her shoulders shook with sobs.

The sun had set, and the air was getting colder by the minute when she finally wiped her face and stood on stiff legs. The plastic paper wrapped around the bouquet of gardenias fluttered in the rising wind with a dry, rattling sound. She shivered and tugged the collar of her coat closer and jammed her hands in her pockets. With a last glance at the two graves before her, she headed along the path to her car, knowing she'd return.

Chapter 17

"There you are." Pauline shuffled down the hallway toward her. "I was beginning to worry."

Sharla-Jean stepped across the threshold and closed the door behind her. "What's going on?"

"Audrey called looking for you. You didn't show up for work this morning."

Sharla-Jean was chastened by the concern in the old woman's voice. "I'm sorry, Pauline. Of course you were worried." She hugged the older woman, surprised again at how frail and thin she was. The housekeeper was over seventy, and in the past few months she'd faced her long-time employer's death, and the sudden arrival of his wayward daughter. Her entire world had been upended.

A wave of emotion washed over her. "I love you, Pauline. I don't know what I would have done if you hadn't been in my life."

Pauline's faded blue eyes shone with unshed tears. "You were my girl, my special girl." She patted Sharla-Jean's cheek. "You still are."

Matching tears welled in Sharla-Jean's eyes. "I'm sorry I treated you the way I did when I was young." She swiped at her wet cheeks. "You shouldn't have had to deal with all the mess I made."

Pauline extracted a tissue from the sleeve of her dress and dabbed at her eyes. "You were angry at the world, and you blamed your father for what happened to your mother. It wasn't easy for you to lose your mother when you were so young. I understood."

"The night I left...I...I'm sorry I didn't say goodbye or tell you where I was going."

Pauline raised a trembling hand and smoothed the damp hair off Sharla-Jean's forehead. "You have nothing to apologize for, child. I know why you left town."

A frisson of unease rippled along Sharla-Jean's spine. "You...you do?"

Pauline nodded. "Your father told me what happened the night of the mill fire. He confessed how you'd come to him and told him you'd been raped." She wiped her damp eyes. "He never forgave himself for how he treated you." She sniffled. "He stopped drinking the day you left and never drank a drop of alcohol again."

Sharla-Jean blinked through her tears, trying to reconcile her memories of a cold-hearted, cruel father with the tormented, remorseful man Pauline described. "He blamed me for the fire at the mill, but it was an accident. I never meant to—"

Pauline placed a gentle finger over Sharla-Jean's mouth silencing her. "I know, child. He knew too. You were headstrong and wild, but you'd never have done something so terrible. Your father knew the truth." Pauline sniffed again and blew her nose. "He hired private investigators to try and find the man who raped you. He vowed he'd kill him if he ever found the attacker." Fresh tears filmed Pauline's eyes. "He never did. He regretted his failure until his dying day."

"If he was so sorry, why didn't he try and find me?

209

If he had, maybe we could have worked through our anger and things between us would have been different."

"He wanted to, but he was ashamed of what he'd done, how he treated you. And he had the mill to rebuild. All those employees and their families were depending on him…" Pauline's voice trailed off.

Sharla-Jean blew out a breath. "I knew it. The damn mill was more important to him than his own daughter."

"Not true." Pauline's eyes blazed. "Not true at all. He loved you."

Sharla-Jean snorted. "He showed how much he cared, didn't he? Leaving his raped, sixteen-year-old daughter to fend for herself in a strange city."

"He didn't leave you alone."

"What do you mean?"

Pauline pursed her mouth. "You never understood your father. He wasn't always the cold, angry man you knew. He changed after your mother died. He loved her more than anything in this world, and she loved him."

Sharla-Jean balled her hands into fists and thrust out her chest. "That's why he killed her? Because he loved her so much?"

Shadows darkened Pauline's eyes. "The accident was a terrible mistake, but it was a mistake. Your father paid for his culpability in your mother's unfortunate death every second of every day for the rest of his life." She shook her head. "At first he tried to drink himself to death."

Sharla-Jean fought the image Pauline's words evoked of a broken, lonely, guilt-ridden man, but she refused to give up her deep-seated anger. "The crash was his fault. He shouldn't have driven home that night. He'd had too much to drink."

"He paid a high price for his mistake."

"So he should have. I lost my mother."

Pauline pinned her with a penetrating gaze. "Have you never made a mistake, Sharla-Jean? One so bad you had to live with the guilt of your actions the rest of your life?"

A lump in her throat threatened to choke her. Tears filled her eyes and overflowed, streaming down her cheeks, dripping onto her coat. The knowledge of what she'd done so many years ago when she'd been responsible for setting fire to the mill overwhelmed her.

For the first time in her life she had an insight into the terrible guilt her father had lived with every day, knowing his lapse in judgment resulted in the death of the woman he loved. No wonder he'd retreated into a vicious, hard shell. Hadn't she done the same? Like her father, she'd hidden from the world, paying daily penance for her mistake.

"If you want to find out more, I stored some boxes of your father's papers in the attic." Pauline's voice broke through her thoughts. "We can't change the past. What matters is what we do today. You'd do well to remember that, dear. Don't repeat your father's mistakes. Don't live your life in anger and resentment and regret."

Sharla-Jean brushed her lips over the old woman's damp cheek. "I love you, Pauline."

Pauline dabbed at her eyes with a tissue and stepped away. "Well, some of us have more important work to do than stand around crying all day." She hurried off toward the kitchen, her steps quick and light.

Sharla-Jean hung her coat in the hall closet. She wasn't due at Josh's house for a few more hours, and she had the sudden urge to examine the boxes of her father's papers Pauline said were stored in the attic.

Hours later, dust streaking her now-rumpled clothing, knees aching from kneeling on the bare, wooden floor as she searched through one dusty box after another, she sat back and suppressed a sneeze. She surveyed the piles of yellowed newspapers, mildewed, old-fashioned clothing, faded photographs of long-dead, forgotten ancestors strewn across the cramped attic.

She lifted the edge of an old canvas tarp and peered beneath. Musty stale air wafted over her, and she wrinkled her nose and sneezed again. Tugging off the tarp, she sighed as cardboard boxes filled with old, broken toys, a pile of record albums from the sixties, and photo albums, their cardboard covers warped from years of damp, were revealed. A neat stack of rectangular objects of varying sizes, covered in brown paper, caught her eye. She lifted one and felt the hard edge of a picture frame.

Swiping at a loose strand of hair caught in her dusty eyelashes, she tore the brown paper and tossed it aside. A detailed beach scene, the vibrant colors undiminished by the passage of time, covered the canvas. Her heart hammered in her chest as she ripped the paper covering from the next painting, and the next, until all six paintings were revealed.

She sat back on her heels and wiped the sweat on her brow with her sleeve as she studied her mother's oil paintings. So this was where they'd ended up, stuffed away in the attic, out of sight.

A photo album rested on the floor beside one painting, a corner of its yellowed cover ragged as if chewed by a mouse. She opened the cover, revealing a faded photograph of her parents on their wedding day. A lump filled her throat. They were so young, and their faces glowed with love and happiness.

Sniffing, she swiped her eyes again and turned the page. More photographs taken at different times and in different locations, filled the page. In each photograph, her parents smiled, their gazes locked on each other, their hands touching. She'd forgotten this was what it was like between them. Even as a young child she'd felt their deep love for each other.

Her hand shook as she flipped the pages. There were photos of her as a baby, then a toddler, and then a young girl heading off to school, grinning a gap-toothed smile. Page after page was filled with photos of happy scenes…Christmases, birthdays, and a family camping trip to a national park. Tears leaked down her face as she studied each picture and the wide smiles on her parents' and her faces. Had she ever been that happy? Had her father?

Beneath each picture, someone had written in precise script, the year and a brief description of the occasion. She recognized her father's handwriting.

Unable to bear the weight of bittersweet memories, she tossed the album aside. A stained manila envelope fell out of the back of the photo album and fluttered to the floor. Smoothing the crumpled envelope over her lap, she squinted in the late afternoon light streaming through the dusty dormer window and examined the typewritten words on the cover.

The envelope was addressed to her father. The return address was a dark smudge and the words were illegible. Butterflies danced in her stomach as she slid her nail under the flap, opened the envelope, and removed two pieces of paper.

The letterhead on the first sheet of paper was that of a private investigation firm with a head office in Portland. The papers were a summary of an investigation the company had been hired to undertake by James Bromley. She scanned the closely typed words, and her breath hitched in her throat when she read the name of the person whom the company had investigated. Sharla-Jean Bromley. Slumping against the wall, she struggled to make sense of what she'd read.

The date on the papers indicated the investigation began not long after she fled Renton Falls and had continued for ten years. Every detail of her life during those turbulent times was reported in these pages. She dropped the papers and clasped her arms over her stomach, rocking back and forth. Her head pounded as she stared, unseeing, into the distance.

Was it true? Had her father really hired this private investigation firm to check up on her? Had they watched her and reported to him all the ups and downs of her life? How had she not known? Tears filmed her eyes and streamed down her cheeks. If the words on these two pages were to be believed, he'd done more than just observe her from a distance.

She squeezed her eyes closed as memories of those first years in Portland swirled around her. Even staying in homeless shelters and sleeping in doorways, she'd soon run out of money. Without a high school diploma or any marketable skills, and reeling from her brutal attack, despair had set in. Then incredibly, she'd been offered a job at a nursing home as a care aide; a job that paid enough to cover her expenses with enough left over to pay her tuition at the local community college.

These reports—she picked up the papers, her hands shaking so much she could barely read the words—indicated her father was responsible for the job. She'd never questioned why the Glenn Oaks Nursing Home had agreed to hire an uneducated, inexperienced, sulky teenager and paid such high wages. This whole time she'd believed she'd escaped her father's overbearing presence, and he'd been the one who'd helped her when she needed help the most.

Rubbing her scratchy, tear-swollen eyes, she steadied her breathing as the stark reality of what she'd read sank in. All those years she'd held one fact to be true: her father hadn't loved her. Nothing he'd said or done had convinced her otherwise. The final straw had come when he hadn't believed her the night she'd told him she'd been raped, and had blamed her for starting the fire at the mill.

She swiped at her face, wiping away tears, and glanced at her watch. With a startled exclamation, she leaped to her feet. If she didn't hurry, she'd be late for her meeting with Josh. After what she'd just discovered, she was anxious to hear what he had to say about her father. What if she'd misjudged him? She'd spent so many years hating her father and blaming him for everything that had gone wrong with her life. Could she finally forgive him?

Hands shaking, she stuffed the papers into the envelope and placed the envelope back in the photo album and tucked it under her arm. She'd come back later for the paintings.

An hour later, a much different looking Sharla-Jean stood on the street before Josh Morgan's house. Dressed in slim-fitting, black wool slacks, offset by a green silk blouse, and her favorite, multi-colored silk scarf tied in a loose knot around her neck, she was ready to face whatever Josh had to tell her. Nothing he said could be as punch-in-the-gut shocking as what she'd read in those papers in the attic.

She tugged at the delicate gold chain around her neck and freed the gold gardenia locket from under her blouse. Caressing the warm metal, she traced the familiar incised markings of the gardenia design. She needed all the courage she had to face the upcoming meeting.

She grimaced when she recalled the hope lighting Pauline's faded blue eyes when Sharla-Jean had appeared downstairs and informed the old woman she was going to Josh's house for supper.

"A date? You two have a date? How wonderful."

Sharla-Jean frowned. "It's not a date. We're just meeting to talk about a few things."

"Of course, dear. You two have a lot to discuss." Pauline grinned. "I'm sure it doesn't hurt he's the best-looking man in town."

"Is he?" Sharla-Jean's heart fluttered. "I hadn't noticed." She held her breath, waiting for lightning to strike her for her blatant lie.

Pauline's smile didn't slip a notch. "That's a pretty blouse you're wearing. The green sets off the color of your eyes." She leaned closer and sniffed. "Is that gardenia perfume? Your mother used to wear gardenia." She fussed with the collar of Sharla-Jean's blouse. "Josh will love the scent."

Sharla-Jean rolled her eyes. "I told you, this isn't a date. It's business."

"Is that what you young folks call it today?"

"It's not a date."

"Whatever you say, dear. Have fun. I won't wait up for you." Pauline, still grinning a goofy grin, fairly skipped out of the room.

A car honked, startling her, and Sharla-Jean hurried over to the sidewalk. Pauline was wrong. This most definitely wasn't a date. She was here to learn the truth about her father. That's all. Nothing more.

She studied the well-tended houses surrounding her, a vastly different scene from the last time she'd been in this neighborhood. Seventeen years ago, the area had been filled with drunks, drug addicts, and a motley assortment of down-and-outers who frequented the many run-down bars and strip joints lining the road.

She'd snuck into a sleazy, smoke-filled bar and joined a table with a group of her friends. Soon she'd had a cigarette in one hand and a bottle of beer in the other. She was the height of cool until the door burst open and four police officers raided the place. Knowing she was under the legal age to be drinking in a bar, they'd hauled her down to the police station.

She'd waited hours in the freezing, dank cell for her father to retrieve her. Her friends' parents had taken them home long ago. She alone remained in the sour-smelling cell. Hours later, Pauline had appeared, and Sharla-Jean had finally been released. Her father was apparently too busy, or too drunk to come. She'd taken his absence as another sign of his disdain.

The events of the past weeks revealed the incident in a new light. She understood now that he might have been trying to teach her a lesson by showing her how awful jail was. Was he making sure she never broke the law again? Or had he been too drunk? Or had he just not given a shit?

She shook off her conflicting thoughts and focused on her surroundings. The neighborhood had undergone major changes. Gone were the sleazy drinking establishments and deserted, run-down buildings. In their place stood a row of immaculate houses, sitting well back from the curb, surrounded by lush, manicured, green lawns and colorful, fall flowers.

Josh's cedar-and-brick rancher was situated on a large, corner lot. As she ambled up the flagstone path, she admired the way the wine-red shutters and matching front door added a splash of cheerful color. She pictured Josh, after a hard day's work at the mill, sitting in one of the cane chairs on the wide, covered porch, sipping a cold drink, enjoying the view of the sun setting on the distant, snow-covered mountains.

Before she could knock, the door opened and the man himself, in faded denim jeans and a burgundy shirt, stood framed in the doorway.

She gulped, her hand at her throat, gripping the gardenia locket. Even so, her legs softened to rubber at the smile wreathing his rugged face and the dimple dancing in his cheek.

His dark hair was mussed and a streak of something white dusted one lean cheek. His smile widened. "I wasn't sure you'd come."

Her tongue was thick and unwieldy, and the words stuck in her throat. What must surely be a foolish grin adorned her face.

He grasped her arm and guided her up the steps to the porch and into the house. "You're fortunate. Only a select few are invited to my sacred abode." His tone was teasing and light.

She struggled to swallow. "I…I'm…honored." Her skin tingled under the press of his warm hand. She'd forgotten how tall he was, and tilted her head back to see his face.

He grinned, exposing even white teeth.

Her breath caught in her throat.

His dark eyes sparked with heated interest.

An answering excitement swirled low in her belly. He was different tonight; more relaxed, boyish, almost. She inhaled a deep, steadying breath. This wasn't a date. *Remember. You're here to learn about your father. That's all this is—an information-seeking mission.* The memory of Josh's searing kisses flashed before her, and she prayed he couldn't read her mind. She stole a glance at him and flushed.

His stare was fixed on her, a knowing smile tweaking the corners of his mouth.

The heat from where his hand rested on her arm penetrated her thin coat, and her nerves tingled, her senses vibrating.

"Let me help you with your coat." As he slid her coat over her shoulders, his fingers brushed her upper arm. He leaned closer and sniffed. "Mmmm. You smell good. What's that perfume you're wearing?"

Her breath hitched in her throat. "Gardenia."

"Your mother's favorite scent."

She gaped. "How…how do you know?"

"Your father told me."

"My father?" she parroted.

"Your mother adored gardenias. That's why Big Jim placed a fresh bouquet of gardenias on her grave every Sunday."

"He did?" She frowned. Her father had cared enough about his deceased wife to place flowers on her grave every week?

He nodded. "He had the local flower shop order them in special."

She recalled the fresh bouquet of fragrant white flowers she'd seen on her mother's grave this afternoon. "You placed the gardenias on my mother's grave today."

He shrugged. "Big Jim would have wanted me to." He hung her coat in the hall closet. "Come on, I'll give you the fifty-cent tour."

She followed him down a short hallway into the living room, her mind whirling. Josh had placed flowers on her mother's grave to honor her father's memory. That showed how wrong Kevin Nelson was. No one would do what Josh had done, and then steal from the mill.

He motioned for her to sit on a soft, nut-brown leather sofa situated before a brick fireplace where a crackling fire blazed. Dark oak, hardwood floors and rich, maroon walls gleamed in the soft light from a single brass lamp set on a white pine end table. Soft rock music played in the background. The scents of burning wood, floor wax, garlic, and tomato sauce filled the air in an enticing blend.

Perching on the edge of the couch, she folded her hands on her lap, leery of succumbing to the warm ambiance of the comfortable room. She wasn't about to repeat the events at the cabin. "This is nice."

"You sound surprised."

Heat seared her cheeks. "No…er…I…er. It's just—"

"You were expecting something different." He finished her sentence and chuckled, deep in his chest. "I don't deserve credit for any of this." He waved his hand at the room. "Your father's the one responsible."

Her gaze flew to meet his. "My father?"

"He felt the executive of an up-and-coming lumber company should entertain clients in his home. I couldn't very well invite buyers over the way this place used to look." He grinned. "My idea of decorating is a weight bench, a reclining lounger, and a giant, flat screen TV with a basketball game playing. Hell, I didn't know the difference between hardwood and laminate flooring, let alone care, until Big Jim sicced his decorator on me."

Her father had cared enough to find Josh a decorator? She struggled with this anomaly. It was another piece of the puzzle that had been her father.

"Can I get you a drink?"

"Yes…I mean, no."

His eyes twinkled. "Which is it? Yes or no?"

Embarrassed at her inability to talk in coherent sentences when he was so close she could touch his muscular thighs, she bit down on her bottom lip in an attempt to regain control of her spiraling senses. "Coffee would be great, thanks."

He nodded and strode out of the room.

She sagged against the cushions, finally able to inhale a full breath. Alcohol was the last thing she needed. She was reeling already. Glancing around the room, she noted the walls, furniture, and designer paintings were all color coordinated, designed for maximum appeal.

Two framed photographs stood out, set on the gleaming surface of an antique mahogany table in the corner beside the fireplace, at odds with the room's carefully orchestrated decor. Even from where she sat, it was obvious the frames were cheap, probably from a discount store. Definitely not something an interior decorator would suggest for this elegant room.

Giving in to her curiosity, she checked that Josh was still out of the room, and rose from the couch, and crossed to the table. The first photograph showed a young girl, not much older than twelve, sitting on a wooden fence. Behind her, cows grazed in a daisy-filled field. The girl's long, braided, dark hair gleamed in the sunlight as she grinned impishly at the camera.

She picked up the second photograph and caught her breath. Josh and her father posed, arms draped around each other's shoulders, grinning. She studied her father's beaming face, and her hand trembled as she gripped the cheap, plastic frame. His hair was a vibrant red unmarked by gray, but his face was thin and gaunt, the lines on his forehead carved deep into his leathery skin. Had she ever seen him smile with such obvious pleasure and joy at being with the person beside him? Josh's handsome face bore a similar expression of happiness.

The background was blurred, but she made out a dense forest of tall fir trees and the shoreline of a sparkling lake. Directly behind the men was a familiar log structure.

She flinched as gentle hands cupped her shoulders.

"Everything okay?" Josh asked.

She turned and held the photograph out before her. "This is a picture of you and my father at the cabin."

He nodded. "We went there a lot, especially during the last year when Big Jim was sick." His face softened. "He liked it there. The cabin seemed to give him some peace."

Glancing once again at the photo, she blinked back the sting of tears. The bond between the two men was unmistakable. "You were telling the truth. He gave you the cabin, didn't he?"

"Your father was sick. He knew he was dying." His voice caught and he coughed. "All he talked about was you. His one wish was to see you again before he died."

She thought of the private investigator's report she'd found in the attic. "Why didn't he contact me? He knew where I was."

Josh shrugged. "Maybe he was afraid you'd refuse to see him."

Sniffling back tears, she finally acknowledged her own role in their estrangement. Her father was right to fear she'd turn him away. If he'd shown up at her front door, she'd have slammed the door in his face.

"I had no idea how important the cabin was to you." He plucked the picture from her and set it on the table. "You can have the cabin if you'd like. I'll sign the deed over to you."

She shook her head. "I…I can't do that. He wanted you to have it. You love the place."

"True, but maybe we can share it."

She blinked. "What do you mean?"

"We can both use the cabin. We'll set out a schedule. You know, you use it in June, I'll go there in

July." He shrugged. "That sort of thing."

A fresh spate of tears erupted and flowed hot and steady. "You'd do that?"

He nodded and stepped closer, a smile forming on his lips. "If that's what you want."

She leaned into him, wrapped her arms around his neck, and hugged his strong body. "Thank you, Josh. This means a lot to me."

Chuckling, he tightened his arms until she melded into his warm embrace. "Hey, if I'd known I'd get this response, I'd have offered the cabin to you weeks ago."

Her tears came harder, her shoulders shaking with their force. Enfolded in Josh's embrace, hearing the rumble of his laughter and the steady, reassuring beat of his heart, she gave in to her sorrow for all the lost opportunities, past hurts, and misunderstandings. She cried for the forlorn, lonely child she'd been and the broken woman she was.

As her tears flowed, soaking the soft cotton of his shirt, a sense of lightness filled her. Soon her tears were not of sorrow and grief, but of healing; it was a catharsis of sorts. Eventually her sobs eased, and her breathing slowed.

The embrace transformed into something visceral. The rapid beating of his heart beneath her cheek indicated he, too, was aware of the change. The soothing touch of his hands on her back altered to an exploration of soft curves and sensitive skin.

Her breathing quickened as she ran her hands over the dips and hollows of his hard muscles and toyed with the silken, curling strands of hair brushing the back of his neck.

He moaned low and deep and drew her closer,

aligning his hips to hers, stomach against stomach; his firm chest against her soft breasts.

"Love me, please." Her voice was a thin husk of sound. Alarm bells rang through her, but their strident clang was muted by rising desire. Not this time. This time she was too needy, too hungry.

Stroking her neck, his callused fingers trailed a path of fire along the responsive skin. He anchored his hands on her hips. His eyes cloudy with desire, the irises the color of rich mahogany, he studied her mouth.

Her breath hitched in her throat when he lowered his head. *He was going to kiss her.* Tendrils of panic seeped through her blood, cooling her heated senses. *No!* She pushed the fear away and reached for him. *Not this time.*

The first touch of his lips was light, a mere whisper of air. He waited, his warm breath fanning her face, his body still as if awaiting her permission to deepen the kiss.

She grasped the back of his neck and drew him close. "Kiss me, Josh. Kiss me now."

His mouth slid over hers. His tongue danced along her lips, delved deeper and tangled with her tongue.

She caressed the smooth planes of his back, reveling in the play of hard muscle in his shoulders and arms. Lowering her hands, she smoothed her palms along his narrow hips and up along the ridges of his back until her fingers once more tangled in his hair.

The kiss deepened, and in their hunger for each other, his teeth scraped against hers.

The world swirled, the floor beneath her dipping and swaying, as her senses heated and flared to life.

He cupped her hips, shifting her against his rising

hardness. Abandoning her swollen mouth, he laved a trail of molten kisses along the tender skin exposed through the opening in her silk blouse. His scorching breath seared her to her soul, and she shivered and arched her neck, her breath huffing in and out in breathless pants.

His roving hands stilled. "Is this what you want, Sharla-Jean?" His voice was a husky rumble against her ear. "Do you want me to love you?"

His words were lost in her rising ardor. Her body cried out, aching for more, and she lifted on her toes and kissed his cheek, fascinated by the rasp of beard as she licked a trail along the hard line of his jaw.

His hands on her upper arms tightened, holding her away from him. "Sharla-Jean?"

She blinked through passion-glazed eyes.

"You know what's going on here, don't you? Once we start this, there's no going back. Not now, not ever. Are you sure this is what you want?"

She didn't want to talk, didn't want to think, and definitely didn't want to worry about tomorrow. The roller coaster of sensations rioting through her was spinning out of control, and she wanted him with a driving need that frightened her.

He shook her gently. "Sharla-Jean, I need an answer."

She drew him down for another soul-stirring kiss, answering him the only way she could. Her heart sang. *Yes, oh, yes.*

Chapter 18

Josh studied the desire blazing across Sharla-Jean's expressive face and bit back a groan. He ached with the need to feel her soft curves against him, to breathe in her sighs, touch every inch of her silken skin and smell the womanly scent of her arousal. Most of all he wanted to plunge into her moist warmth, and fill her until she screamed with pleasure.

He wanted her now, this very second. Hell, he'd desired her from the moment he saw her at Big Jim's funeral. He couldn't stop kissing her, couldn't keep his hands off her. But he hadn't forgotten her fear that had left her cringing the last times he'd kissed her. His arms shook where they clasped her and held her away. "Before this goes any further, I need to know you're not going to have any regrets."

She peered at him from under her long eyelashes, her green eyes luminous with passion.

All he could think of was kissing away the furrow between her shapely brows. He held his body rigid, his muscles taut, afraid what he'd do if he gave in to the rampaging hunger searing through him. His fingers dug into the soft skin of her arms as he fought with his desire.

"Will you?" A smile of womanly promise lifted her rosy, kiss-swollen lips.

"Will I what?"

She tugged an arm free and ran a slender finger along his chin and over his mouth. "Will you regret loving me?"

He sucked in a breath. "Making love will certainly complicate our situation." He almost smiled at the understatement. Complicate? Hell, if they made love tonight, complicated wouldn't begin to describe their relationship.

Her eyes cleared, the green depths turning the color of an alpine lake. "I don't know what this is between us or what the future holds."

Her husky voice washed over him and he shivered.

She licked her lips. "But right now, at this minute, I want you. I want your touch, and I want your taste." She scorched him with a heated look. "I want you, Josh."

He trembled at her brave words and with a groan, lifted her in his arms and strode toward the bedroom.

The room was deep with shadows, but he didn't pause to turn on the bedside table lamp, afraid she'd change her mind. He needed her far too much to stop. He lowered her on the bed.

Her hair was a dark cloud against the pillow. Moonlight streaming through the window gilded her face with an ethereal glow. She raised her arms toward him, her lips curving in a smile filled with promise. "Love me, Josh."

The muscles in his belly tightened. His hands flew, fingers fumbling as he tore at the buttons on his shirt. Swearing, he gave up on the buttons and raked the shirt over his head and tossed it on the floor. With a quick tug, he jerked down his zipper, and his pants and underwear followed suit. He stood before her naked, his need all too obvious. He waited, his breath scorching in his lungs until she met his gaze.

She lifted her hand and crooked a finger, beckoning. "Come here."

The last remnants of reserve crumbled, and with a deep moan, he climbed onto the bed and lowered himself beside her. With aching slowness, he ran his hands along her ribs, over the swell of her hips and along her thighs. The heat of her body burned him even through her clothes. The tips of her breasts hardened and poked through the silky fabric of her blouse.

His hands were all thumbs as he struggled with the buttons of her silk blouse, undoing one tiny pearl button and then another until her blouse gaped open, revealing the soft, creamy mounds of her breasts beneath the gauzy wisp of a white, lace bra.

His fingers trembled as he undid the front clasp. He kissed the gentle swell of her breasts, and with agonizing slowness, slipped the straps of her bra off her shoulders until the garment slid from her body. He covered one mound with the palm of his hand, molding the soft flesh beneath his touch, while his fingers toyed with the hardened tip of her other breast.

When the moist heat of his mouth engulfed her nipple, she mewed and writhed beneath him. He suckled, tasting her sweetness. *Still not enough, not nearly enough.* He unzipped her pants and slid them over her hips and down her long, slim legs. Her white lace panties soon followed.

****

She trembled as he smoothed his callused palm over her stomach and along her hips, then swept up the inside of her thighs. His mouth claimed hers at the same instant his fingers slid through the heated moisture at her core. She arched as his probing fingers danced across her sensitive flesh. Her body bucked and her breathing was ragged, every nerve screaming.

He rose over her and entered her in one long, smooth stroke.

His turgid length filled her, adding to the vibrations already rocketing through her. She grasped his hips and drew him closer, closing her eyes, reveling in the waves of passion spiraling through her.

His hips moved, slowly at first, increasing in urgency as he thrust deeper and deeper still. "Open your eyes, Sharla-Jean." His voice was a hoarse rasp. "Open your eyes and look at me."

She fought to focus.

Their gazes met.

Fire blazed in his dark eyes.

A shudder rippled through her, and a fresh wave of excitement swelled and crested.

His body stiffened, and with one last, deep penetrating thrust, he groaned and arched above her.

At the same instant, she succumbed to the unbearable tension and cried out, her cries mingling with his, as waves of pleasure overtook her, crashing one after another. She slumped against the pillows, gasping for breath, her body sated.

He drew her close, pressing her against the firmness of his damp chest. His heart pounded beneath her ear. "You're beautiful, so goddamn beautiful."

She snuggled closer to his warm bulk and ran her fingers over the sprinkling of soft, dark hair on his chest.

"So, what do you want to know?" His voice

rumbled through his chest.

Lost in her contemplation of his well-developed pectoral muscles, it was a minute before she answered. "About what?" *He must work out. How else could he have such fine pecs?*

"Your father. You came here tonight to find out more about him, remember?"

Her lethargy vanished like he'd doused her with icy water. She grabbed for the covers, all too aware of her nudity. "Well yes, I did, but—"

"We got sidetracked, I know." He leaned closer, and his thumb tilted her chin so she couldn't look away from his probing gaze. "Don't regret what just happened. We needed this. We both did."

"I have many feelings right now; regret isn't one of them."

His gaze bore into hers as if searching for some truth. He grinned, slow and easy, and released his hold on her chin. His mouth covered hers.

She moaned as the kiss deepened. Need flared, blistering and urgent.

This time their lovemaking was frantic as each sought and demanded more of the other until once again their cries echoed in the dim bedroom.

Gasping for air, her skin slick with perspiration, muscles leaden, she stopped thinking.

Laughter rumbled in his chest.

She opened her eyes. "What's so funny?"

"You. Me. Us." He pointed at her naked body, and then his. "This." He chuckled. "J.D. Webster would have an apoplectic fit."

"He wouldn't be the only one." Her stomach rumbled, and she grimaced.

"You're hungry." He grinned. "No wonder. We worked up quite an appetite." The white flash of his teeth provided a sharp contrast in his sun-bronzed face. "Why don't you hop in the shower while I see if our supper can be salvaged?" He leaned down and kissed her, his hand smoothing her tangled hair off her damp forehead. He rose from the bed, seemingly unfazed by his nudity as he yanked on his pants and socks, tugged his shirt over his head, and disappeared into the hall.

She listened to the distant sounds of pots banging and water running and stared at the ceiling. What the heck had just happened? She was in Josh Morgan's bedroom, naked on his bed, the musty smell of love heavy in the air.

She blushed as she recalled her bold words and blatant invitation. Images of Josh's dark eyes transformed to liquid chocolate, of him touching her, driving her into a frenzy of want and need, kissing her, loving her, ran like an old movie reel through her mind. No, no regrets. She raised her arms above her head and stretched. In fact, she felt pretty damn good.

Grinning like a fool, she climbed off the bed, tugged a sheet around her, and crossed to the adjoining bathroom and stepped into the shower. She was half-hoping, half-terrified he'd join her under the steamy spray. When he didn't appear, she shut off the tap and dressed and went in search of him.

He was in the kitchen, a floral-patterned apron tied around his narrow waist. His hair was rumpled, and he whistled an off-key tune as he stirred a steaming pot on the stove. Mouthwatering aromas of tomatoes, basil, garlic, and oregano filled the small state-of-the-art kitchen.

"Smells delicious." She swallowed the saliva pooling in her mouth.

He studied her and a slow grin bloomed. "*You* look delicious."

Her breath caught in her throat, and her knees wobbled as her body liquefied. She clung to the counter. "Wha…what are you cooking?"

"Spaghetti." He shrugged. "My go-to dish and pretty much all I know how to cook. I went all out. The sauce is from a jar, not a can."

She grinned. "Classy."

They laughed and their gazes met. The laughter stilled. He set the spoon on the stovetop, and stalked closer.

She gulped and moistened her dry lips as she waited, her body warming, blood thickening and pooling in her core.

His sock-covered toes brushed against her shoes, and his musky scent surrounded her. Heat from his body sizzled in the air between them. He anchored his hands on her waist and lowered his head, and his mouth slid over hers in a searing kiss.

She mewed and tangled her arms around his neck, drawing him closer.

He resisted her tug and backed away, his eyes heavy lidded with passion. "Let's eat." His voice was a husky rasp. "Something tells me you're going to need the energy."

They sat at the small kitchen table under the fluorescent light. He served spaghetti heaped with the tomato sauce from a jar, and a simple green salad. They sipped delicious red wine from stemless glasses. A comfortable silence settled between them, broken by the clink of a fork against a plate and the distant notes of an old country western song playing on the TV in the living room.

She focused on the food on her plate, twirling several strands of spaghetti around her fork, her appetite gone. Being with him in this cozy kitchen and sharing a meal left her shaken and confused. She didn't regret making love. She'd wanted him, needed him. God help her, she still did. But she wasn't naïve. There'd be complications. Big ones. Especially once they returned to work at the mill, and the continuing repercussions of her father's will impacted them.

"Finished?" His deep voice broke into her muddled thoughts.

She pushed away her plate. "Thanks. The meal was delicious."

He eyed her almost-full plate. "You didn't eat much."

"I guess I wasn't hungry after all, but the spaghetti was yummy." Her cheeks flared when his dark brows quirked in disbelief. "Really, it was."

"Let's talk." He stood up from the table and gestured toward the adjacent living room. "Time I told you about your father."

She perched on the couch while he chose a facing chair. The flickering firelight cast intriguing light and shadows across his rugged face. Her stomach knotted and she studied her glass, noting the way the wine reflected the flames of the fire in its crimson depths. What was she doing here? Did she really want to hear what he had to say about her father? Was she ready for it?

"Sharla-Jean?"

She roused herself from her thoughts. "I should go."

"I thought you wanted to hear about your father."

She set her wine on the end table and stood. "Maybe another time." She forced an immense yawn. "It's been a long day."

He studied her face and nodded. "You're afraid. I understand."

"I'm not afraid."

"Yes, you are. You're terrified you'll hear something that doesn't fit with your distorted memory of your father, that you'll find out you've been wrong about him for all these years."

She set her hands on her hips and glared. "That's bullshit. I'm not afraid of anything you have to say about my father."

His eyes narrowed. "Prove me wrong, then. Stay."

She threw up her hands. "Fine." Plopping back down on the couch, she crossed her arms over her chest. "Go ahead. I'm listening."

The corners of his mouth twitched. He crossed one leg over the other. "I met your father ten years ago on my first day in Renton Falls."

She would *not* get distracted by the intriguing play of muscles in his forearms.

"I was looking for a job and heard the mill was hiring. Somehow I managed to get an interview with Big Jim." His voice cracked, but he smiled. "I think Audrey felt sorry for me and pulled a few strings. Your father hired me even though I didn't have any experience or references. I started work on the green chain the next day." He shrugged. "The rest is history. Big Jim and I grew close. Over the years, he taught me everything he knew. I can never thank him enough for what he did for me. He was a wonderful man."

She gulped wine, trying to erase the sour taste in her mouth. "I certainly never experienced that side of him."

"Jim was kind to everyone. He was busy, but he was always available if someone needed help." Josh rose from his chair and strode into the kitchen. He returned with the bottle of wine in his hand and poured some into her glass and refilled his. "Big Jim was tough. If you didn't pull your weight, he let you know." He chuckled. "Man, did he let you know."

Tears burned her eyes, but she blinked them back, refusing to cry one more time over the man who'd deserted her when she'd needed him the most. "The man you're describing was not the one I knew. Not even close."

"Your father loved you."

"Yeah, right."

"It's true. He did. He kept your picture on his desk at the office, and he told me countless times he wished you'd come back so he could beg your forgiveness."

A mouthful of wine caught in her throat, and she coughed and sputtered. She wiped her streaming eyes with the back of her hand.

Josh rose from his chair and sat beside her on the couch, his thigh brushing hers. He clasped her hand in his and rubbed her cold fingers. "It's okay. You don't have to fight your past anymore. You loved your father. You always did. You still do. Why else would you be mad at him so long?" He cocked an eyebrow. When she didn't respond, he answered his own question. "Because he always mattered. That's why."

She wanted to believe him, but years of hurt and pain and anger held her back. No longer was she the lonely child desperate for her emotionless and distant father to show her love, to protect her, to believe her, to stand up for her. Her father had made mistakes. He hadn't been perfect. He'd committed many wrongs, but he was her father. Josh was right. She had loved him. His refusal to believe her the night she told him she'd been raped had devastated her, but it hadn't destroyed her love for him.

Admitting she loved her father made her feel as if a burden lifted from her shoulders, as years of grief and anger dissolved. The overriding thirst for revenge was over. In time, she might forgive her father, or maybe not. But she was finally free.

Her newfound peace of mind was all thanks to Josh. And how was she going to repay him? By reading his innermost secrets in the journal she'd taken from his office. Her face flamed at how she'd sneaked into his office and stolen the black leather journal. The fact she hadn't read it didn't excuse her actions; stealing the book was bad enough.

She peeked at Josh.

His head rested against the back of the couch, his eyes closed. The hand holding hers was relaxed, his grip loose.

She studied his rugged features, and a frisson of unease rippled up her spine. How could she confess she'd taken his journal? He'd be furious. She grimaced. Furious? He'd go ballistic. And rightly so. She deserved his anger and outrage. Maybe she didn't need to tell him. She hadn't read the journal. Maybe he hadn't discovered it was missing, and she could sneak the journal back into his desk drawer. He'd never have to know what she'd done.

But she'd know. She gulped wine, hoping the liquor would give her the courage to confess the truth. Fearing she'd chicken out if she waited another second, she set the glass on the table and licked her lips. "I…I borrowed your journal from your office." She held her breath, her heart hammering.

Seconds ticked by. The silence lengthened. She couldn't look at him, couldn't bear to see the disgust on his face. Still, he said nothing. Maybe he hadn't heard her.

She tried again, her voice louder. "I took your journal. I'm sorry, but I didn't read anything. I don't know what's in it. I have no idea. Really, I don't." The confession spilled from her, the words running together in a stream, leaving her breathless. "I opened the first page, but that's all I did. I closed the book right away, and I hid the journal in the cabinet in the living room at my father's house. I'm sorry. I don't know what I was thinking." She wiped damp palms on her slacks and waited.

Silence.

Her heart skipped a beat. "Josh?"

A snore greeted her.

"Josh?" She spun toward him, noting the steady rise and fall of his chest. "Are you asleep?" *Of course he is, you ninny. He's snoring.* Relief washed over her. He hadn't heard her confession. She should wake him and tell him the truth, but he looked so peaceful. She could come clean later. Plenty of time to confess her guilty secret tomorrow. What difference would a few hours make?

Freeing her hand from his, she smoothed a stray lock of hair from his broad forehead and rose to her feet. She tugged the throw from the back of the couch and covered him with the soft, wool blanket.

A gentle snore broke free from his parted lips, and he shifted, sinking deeper into the softness of the couch.

Part of her yearned to lie beside him and burrow into his warmth; spend the night wrapped in his arms. But he wouldn't sleep forever, and when he awoke, she'd have to tell him of her deception and face his anger and disappointment. She shuddered. Call her a coward, but she wasn't doing this now.

She tiptoed across the room, and with a last lingering glance, headed for the front door and retrieved her coat. She'd tell him she'd taken the journal in the morning, when they both were rested.

Chapter 19

Josh opened his eyes, blinking in the glare of lamplight. He sat up, shrugging off the blanket, and rubbed the stiffness in his neck. What the hell? He'd fallen asleep on the couch. Memories of Sharla-Jean slammed into him like a splash of icy water, and just like that, he was wide-awake.

He took in the living room's stark emptiness. Where was she? The fire had gone out, and coals smoldered in the grate. Had it all been a dream? Two empty glasses and an almost-empty bottle of wine sat on the coffee table. The tantalizing scent of gardenias lingered in the air.

"Sharla-Jean?" His voice was rough with sleep. "Sharla-Jean?" No answer. *Damn.* Why had he fallen asleep?

A piercing sound rent the stillness of the house with an urgent ringing. He lurched to his feet, knocking over the bottle of wine. Red liquid spilled out of the bottle onto the gleaming hardwood floor. Cursing, he righted the bottle, ripping off his sock, and using the dark cotton to wipe the sticky spill.

The phone rang again, the peal louder and more insistent with each ring. He glanced at his watch. Who the hell would be calling at this time of night? Tossing the sodden sock onto the floor, he stretched his aching back. Her scarf lay on the arm of the sofa. Ignoring the persistent ringing, he sank onto the couch and lifted the fragile wisp of silk to his nose and inhaled the heady scent of gardenias. A swirl of poignant memories surrounded him.

She'd come to hear stories of her father. One thing led to another, and before he had time to think, he'd carted her off to his bed. A vision of her alabaster skin glowing against the black satin quilt rose before him. Her skin was even softer than he'd imagined. And like a dream, she'd responded to his touch, her body arching against his as he sank deep inside her, and—

The phone stopped ringing, but the furious pounding of his heart broke the sudden silence. They'd made love, not once, but twice, and each time she'd scorched deeper into his soul. He cursed himself again for falling asleep like a boor and allowing her to leave without telling her how much she meant to him, and how he wanted so much more from her.

The strident clanging of the phone split the air. He jumped up. Maybe it was her. Maybe she was calling to tell him how wonderful the evening had been. He lunged for the receiver. "Sharla-Jean?"

"Josh? Thank God you're home. I'm at the mill. You'd better get your ass here right away."

His breath froze in his throat at the frantic voice. "What is it, Ace? What's going on?"

"The mill, it's—" Ace's words were lost in the background clamor of sirens and shouting.

"I'm on my way." Josh didn't wait for Ace to answer as he slammed down the receiver. Not stopping to put on a jacket, he ran through the dark house and out the door.

The second he stepped outside, his heart sank

further. The acrid stench of smoke filled the pre-dawn air. An unnatural red glimmer lit the horizon. Sirens blared and broke the silence of the night. He leaped into his truck and peeled away from the curb, scowling at the fiery glow in the distance.

An eternity later, he skidded into the parking lot at the lumber mill, his truck's wheels spewing gravel. He slewed to a stop and stared with unbelieving eyes through the dusty windshield.

The lumberyard was a scene from Hell. Shooting flames lit the mill site with an unearthly glow. The town's two fire trucks were parked in the yard, their emergency lights flashing. Firemen holding thick canvas hoses sprayed great bursts of water at the fiery inferno. Both the sawmill and the planer mill were engulfed in fire. Black clouds of smoke billowed as the fire blazed, devouring everything in its path. The sprays of water did little to quench the ravenous flames.

As if in a daze, he opened the door of the truck and climbed out. The full horror of the hellish scene rose before him. On wooden legs, he stumbled toward the chaos. Acrid smoke filled his lungs and stung his eyes. Coughing, tears streaming down his cheeks, he trudged onward.

A loud, piercing scream of protesting metal rent the air. He stared in morbid fascination as the metal roof of the sawmill buckled and collapsed in a monstrous roar that shook the ground. Showers of searing sparks swirled in the air, stinging as they landed on his arms, his neck, scorching his face.

One plodding step at a time, he drew nearer to the roaring flames. His skin prickled and tightened with the searing heat. A heavy cloak of thick, black smoke filled the air, burning deep into his lungs.

Another roar, like that of a ravenous beast, shattered the air, and the roof of the planer mill collapsed, leaving a blackened skeleton in its wake. Glowing hot ash burst into the air, lighting on the orderly piles of kiln-dried lumber, setting them ablaze. A coal landed on his arm stinging and singeing. He brushed off the burning ember, transfixed by the conflagration before him.

"Hey you, get back!" A hand grabbed his arm and jerked hard.

He resisted, yanking free, lurching another step closer to the fiery beast destroying the dream he'd worked for these past ten years. Hands grabbed him again, and in spite of his struggles, he was dragged away from the sweltering heat. He moaned as a storage shed succumbed to the voracious flames and collapsed in a tumultuous heap. Sagging, his muscles slack, he allowed the men grabbing at him to drag him to safety, unable to stop staring at the raging fire.

"What in the hell do you think you're doing? You could have been killed. More importantly, one of my men could have been killed trying to save your sorry ass." Ken Ralston, the fire chief, glared. His bushy gray eyebrows and craggy face bristled with anger.

"How the hell did this happen?" Josh demanded.

Ralston shrugged. Lines of exhaustion deepened in his soot-blackened face. "We don't know yet. She's burnin' way too hot. We'll have to wait until the situation cools down. Then we'll get the investigators on this."

Nausea roiled as Josh stared at the crackling flames and the piles of smoldering rubble. He swallowed back bile and gritted his teeth, grinding until his jaw ached.

"I'm sorry, Josh. We got here as quick as we could, but there wasn't much we could do. The bitch had too good a foothold." Ralston wiped his forehead with the sleeve of his yellow protective suit, smearing soot. "Looks like she's all gone."

Josh ignored the sympathy in the man's voice. "Find who the hell did this. Find the bastard responsible for burning down my mill."

"Now, Josh, don't go flyin' off the handle. We don't know the cause. The fire could have started any number of ways, faulty wiring, a cigarette left smoldering, anything."

"I want a name," Josh bit off through his clenched teeth.

A firefighter running the water hose shouted, and the chief said, "I'll keep you informed." He hurried off, leaving Josh glowering at the destruction before him.

Josh rubbed his eyes, but the nightmare vision didn't vanish. The mill he'd helped build into one of the premier lumber companies in the Northwest was now a pile of blackened rubble. Two tool sheds and the office complex were untouched. All the other buildings, all the inventory of raw logs and processed lumber were destroyed.

How would the mill survive? A dozen orders for lumber were sitting on his desk waiting to be filled. He glanced behind him at the crowd of onlookers gawking at the fire, and his gut knotted. He recognized most of the faces. What was going to happen to all the people who counted on Bromley Forest Products for their livelihood?

Kevin Nelson stepped forward from the crowd and

sidled up to Josh. "What a mess."

Josh twisted away, ignoring the unwelcome intrusion.

"Exactly like what happened the last time the mill burned, isn't it?" The flickering flames lit Nelson's face, revealing the gloating gleam in his pale blue eyes.

The bastard's enjoying this. Josh balled his hands, resisting the urge to drive his fist into the man's smug face. "What the hell do you want, Nelson?"

"Just saying, this has happened before. Surely you've heard. I mean, Sharla-Jean's reckless past isn't a secret or anything. The whole town knows what she did."

"Get to the point, Nelson. What are you so damn eager to tell me?"

Nelson's mouth tightened, turning down at the corners, but he suppressed his obvious irritation. "Bromley Forest Products burned to the ground seventeen years ago. What are the odds a lumber mill burns down twice in less than twenty years?"

Josh stared hard at him. In spite of his innate distrust of the man, Nelson's words echoed his own thoughts. "Not good, I'd say."

A long, tense silence stretched between them. The excited murmurs of the onlookers, Ken Ralston barking orders to his crew, and the roar of the rush of flames as the fire devoured the last of the available fuel filled the early morning chaos.

"You know who people say started the first fire." Nelson's voice cut through the uproar.

A chill trickled through Josh. He knew only too well what Nelson was talking about. People said Sharla-Jean started the fire years ago in the previous mill. Big Jim never believed she was responsible. He'd always told Josh his daughter would never do something so destructive. The townsfolk didn't see the situation the same way. To listen to them, she'd set fire to the mill, and then fled town like a thief in the night.

"Odd, don't you think?" Nelson grinned like a wolf. "Another fire at the mill the second Sharla-Jean returns to town?"

Josh lunged, grabbing him by the collar and tossing him to the ground, uncaring who witnessed his attack. "You fucking bastard!" Fury raged through him. How dare Nelson accuse Sharla-Jean of setting fire to the mill?

Nelson clambered to his feet and brushed off the seat of his pants. The collar of his fancy linen shirt was torn, and two buttons were missing. His cold blue eyes shot darts of venom at Josh. "You're a jerk, Morgan, a foolish, stupid jackass. You'll pay for this, you asshole. You'll pay big time."

Josh lashed out, kicking him hard in the gut, relishing Nelson's grunt of pain as he collapsed on the muddy ground. "Bring it on." He braced, fists up, daring the other man to come at him, wanting him to strike back so he could pound him to a bloody pulp.

Once again, Nelson staggered to his feet. Swaying and wheezing, fighting to breathe, he swiped a shaking hand across his mouth and glared daggers at Josh. "Why don't you ask your girlfriend where she was earlier tonight?" He swiped snot from his nose with his shirtsleeve. "Or are you too chicken to find out the piece of ass you've been screwing is trying to destroy you?"

All the blood drained from Josh's face, and he

swayed as if he'd been struck. How the hell did Nelson know he and Sharla-Jean had made love? And what the hell was he talking about? Had she started the fire? She'd been with him early in the evening, but when he woke later, she was gone. As the first stirrings of suspicion transformed his blood to ice, Nelson's smirk sent him over the edge, and he drew back his fist, ready to strike, determined to wipe the sneer off his face. He slid a glance at the watching throng.

No one spoke, all eyes trained on him and Nelson, watching, listening.

He grimaced. Within the hour, his confrontation with Nelson would be all over town. This was what Nelson wanted. Lowering his arm, he relaxed his fist. "Get the hell off my mill site." His voice was too low to carry to the bystanders. "I'll kill you if I see you here again."

Nelson's face blanched, and his pupils dilated, but he smirked at the gaping crowd and strode off, a swagger in his step.

Josh rubbed his burning, grit-filled eyes. He was bushed. His shoulders sagged. It was all he could do not to sink to the ground. Nelson's sly insinuations played through his head, his mind too exhausted to fight them.

Did Sharla-Jean have something to do with this fire? His immediate reaction was a resounding no, but he recalled her fury at her father, and her outrage at the terms of the will. Would she destroy the mill to get revenge on her dead father?

And what of him? Did their lovemaking mean nothing? His head pounded, and his gut clenched as he stood amidst the shattered ruins of what a few, short hours prior had been a thriving business. He had to know if Nelson was right. No matter the cost, he had to find the truth.

With a heavy tread, he strode across the now-crowded parking lot to his truck. Icy cold settled over him like a shroud, sinking through to his core, and he shivered. By doing what he was about to do, what he had to do, he was sounding a death knell on any chance of a relationship between him and Sharla-Jean. Once he asked her what he had to ask, any feelings she had for him would wither and die.

He swiped at the sting of tears. Ignoring the protesting voice deep in his gut, he started the truck and sped out of the parking lot.

Chapter 20

Loud pounding, and the persistent ringing of the doorbell woke her out of a deep sleep. Groaning, Sharla-Jean jammed the pillow over her head, fighting to hold on to the wisps of her dream. "Go away," she muttered into the pillow.

The pounding grew louder and more insistent.

She sat up and smoothed her tangled hair off her face. The room was dark, but the faint grayish-pink light of dawn leaked through a gap in the curtains drawn across the bedroom window. Who would be pounding on the door at this hour?

The doorbell pealed again, this time without letup.

She climbed out of bed and grabbed her robe. Whoever was at the door was not going to be satisfied until everyone in the house was up. The hallway was dark, the house still and silent except for the persistent ringing of the bell. She wasn't surprised Pauline hadn't awakened. The old woman removed her hearing aids when she slept. A bomb exploding in the living room wouldn't wake her.

Muttering, cursing the unknown visitor, she hurried down the stairs, shivering in the early dawn chill. Crossing the foyer, she flung open the door ready to blast whoever was on the other side. Her mouth gaped. Josh, his hair in wild disarray, his face streaked with black smudges, stood on the stoop. "Josh! What—"

He elbowed past her into the house. "About time you answered the damn door."

She trailed behind him as he strode with purposeful steps into the living room and over to the credenza. He snatched a bottle of whiskey out of the cupboard, and with shaking hands filled a glass and guzzled the contents in one gulp. Coughing, he swiped at his streaming eyes and refilled the glass. He drained the second drink and pinned her with steel-filled eyes.

She sank onto a chair, her heart racing. "What is it? What's wrong?" Her voice faded at the grim resolve on his chiseled face. She'd seen him this angry before. Her mind flashed to her first meeting with him when J.D. Webster had revealed the astounding conditions of her father's will. Josh had been enraged. Judging by the thunderous expression on his face, he was furious now. Why? What had happened since she'd left him mere hours ago?

The stench of smoke surrounded him like a pall. His clothes were streaked with dirt, and several, tiny, singed holes peppered his shirt. "What is it? Are you hurt?" She jumped up. Her first instinct was to offer comfort, but the cold, forbidding chill in his eyes stopped her.

"Tell me what happened seventeen years ago."

She blinked. "Seventeen years ago?"

"Everyone in town says you started the fire at the mill. Is that true?"

She gaped, fighting for words, but they stuck in her throat. "I…I don't understand."

"Answer me."

The fiery intensity in his dark eyes unsettled her. Was this the same man who'd kissed and caressed her, and made love to her with such passion?

He drained his drink. "Did you set fire to your father's mill?"

Blood drained from her face, and she sank back onto the chair. "The…the fire?"

He scowled, the lines on his face harsh and forbidding. "Why?" His eyes narrowed, the irises black. "Why did you do it?"

"It happened a long time ago. I was just a kid. I…I made a mistake."

"What happened to you the night of the mill fire has everything to do with what's happening now." His gaze delved into hers. "Answer my question."

She chewed on her bottom lip. "I think I'll have a drink too." Her mouth was bone dry, swallowing impossible.

His brow furrowed, but he spun toward the credenza and poured her a drink.

She blew out a breath, relieved for the reprieve from his unrelenting scowl. She used the brief respite to prepare for the impending ordeal.

"Here."

She seized the glass he offered, taking a hasty sip to steady her nerves.

He towered over her, tension bristling off him in palpable waves.

"Yes, I…I started the fire." Her voice was halting. She sipped again from her drink and coughed as the heady liquor burned a fiery path down her throat and pooled in her belly. "I'm responsible for the mill burning to the ground. It was my fault." Her heart pounded as she uttered the incriminating words. She flinched at the fury blazing in his dark eyes.

"*You* started the fire." His voice was unrecognizable, each word sounding as if chipped from a block of ice.

"Yes, but the fire was an accident. I—"

"Stop." He held up his hand and cut her off before she could explain how Tyler Maddox's friend had dropped the burning matchbooks onto a pile of shavings and scuttled away, leaving her to face the consequences. Grabbing her by the arms, he hauled her to her feet.

She tilted her head back to see his face, but wished she hadn't. If he hadn't held her in a firm grip, she would have collapsed. Her breath froze in her chest as she struggled to turn away from the disgust on his rugged face.

"Where were you earlier tonight?"

She blinked.

He shook her. "Tell me. Where were you?"

"I…I…" The words stuck in her throat. "I was…I…was with you. You know I was." How could he forget their passionate lovemaking?

His grip on her arms tightened, and he shook her again. "Where did you go after you left my house?"

"I…I came home. Why? What's going on?" He released her, and she staggered, regaining her balance by grabbing his arm. "Josh, what is this? Why are you so angry?"

His back was to her, his broad shoulders rigid. The muscles in his arm twitched and bunched beneath her hand.

"What's this all about? What does tonight have to do with what happened seventeen years ago?"

He spun to face her and she caught her breath at the

252

cold emptiness in his eyes.

"There was a fire at the mill."

"Tonight?" She reeled back on her heels and placed a hand over her chest, feeling as if the wind had been knocked out of her. "What are you saying?"

His hand shook and liquor slopped onto the cabinet when he poured himself another drink. "You heard me."

"The mill caught on fire? What happened? Was anybody hurt? How bad was the fire?" The questions, one after the other, spewed out as she struggled to take in the shocking news.

His bleak stare sent a chill coursing through her, but in the next breath, a fiery surge of anger overtook her. "You…you…" She fought to thrust out the words. The more she struggled, the more her fury grew. "You think I had something to do with the fire tonight? I burned the mill down seventeen years ago, and did the same thing tonight. That's what you think, isn't it?"

The accusing expression on his soot-blackened face was answer enough.

"I'd like you to leave." Her voice was wooden, devoid of the pain of her heart shattering.

"Sharla-Jean…I…" He grasped the thin fabric of the sleeve of her housecoat.

She shook him off and backed away unable to bear for him to touch her. She'd never been so furious in her life. She wanted to strike him, to hurt him like he'd wounded her. Raising her hand, she swung.

He grabbed her arm, halting the slap meant for his too-handsome face. Rubbing at the dark whiskers shadowing his cheeks, he dropped his head. "I had to ask. I had to know the truth."

"You *had* to ask?" Her rage flared. "After what happened between us tonight, you had to ask me if I'm crazy enough to burn down a mill I'm half-owner of?"

"It's because of what happened tonight I have to know." His eyes reflected his pain and outrage. "I have to be certain."

"Certain of what?" She yanked her arm free. "Certain I'm not an arsonist? Or worse?" The words spewed from her in an enraged torrent. "Do you really think I'd go to bed with you as a ruse to trick you into trusting me, just so I could sneak out of your bedroom and burn down the mill?"

A sheepish expression replaced his earlier fury. "Sounds ridiculous when you put it that way."

A visceral hurt mixed with anger burned through her. Tears welled in her eyes, but she blinked them away as she clung to her fury to give her strength. Ignoring her deep-seated fear, she'd jumped into his arms and into his bed. What a fool. She swiped at a traitorous tear on her cheek, unable to believe how wrong she'd been about him. If he believed her willing to set fire to the mill tonight, she might as well give him the pleasure of finding out she was also capable of other deceptions. She glared, but her fury faltered as she looked closely at him.

Deep in the dark depths of his eyes lurked a wounded sadness as if he regretted his outburst. He slumped down on the couch and covered his face with his hands. "Look, I'm sorry."

She hesitated, but his hurtful words rang in her ears, and she quelled any misplaced stirrings of empathy. "Just so you don't beat yourself up too much for your unfounded accusations, I have something of yours." Before she changed her mind, she marched over to the cupboard on the far side of the room and yanked open the door. Her hands shook as she retrieved the book she'd hidden two days ago. Facing him, she held out the black journal.

He lowered his gaze to the book in her hand, and his mouth tightened until the lines in his face looked as if they'd been carved in granite. "Why do you have my journal?" He shook his head. "No, never mind. I don't want to know."

"I found this in the desk drawer in your office."

He raised his eyebrows. "You *found* my journal in my private office in a locked desk drawer?"

"Okay, okay." She shrugged. "I pilfered your keys while you were sleeping at the cabin and searched your office and found this."

His face flushed and a vein throbbed in his neck. "Go on. This keeps getting better and better." He turned and stared out the window as if he couldn't look at her a second longer.

Sweat broke out under her arms and trickled down her sides. "When…I…I found the journal, I hoped you'd written something in there I could use against you." She shivered at the layer of ice freezing his features. Already she regretted her decision to confess. "You have to understand, things between us were different then. I—"

He whirled, his eyes stormy. "I hope your skulking was worth the effort."

She opened her mouth to tell him she hadn't read the journal, but swallowed her words. He already believed her an arsonist, what difference if he also assumed she'd read the private thoughts he'd written in his journal? It was just like with her father. He hadn't believed her either.

In the midst of her fury, a small voice of reason fought to intervene. Anyone would suspect her of starting the fire tonight if they listened to the rumors about her running rampant through town. After all, she'd been responsible for one fire, why not another? She silenced the niggling voice. Josh had no right to come here with his baseless suspicions, no right at all. Especially not after what had happened between them.

An image of Josh holding her in his arms and his tender caresses in the aftermath of passion rose before her. She thrust the memory aside, but her vision blurred as tears streamed down her face. Shoving the journal at him, she fled before she collapsed on the floor sobbing. The taunting silence of his condemnation pursued her as she ran up the stairs and into her room.

The knock on her bedroom door minutes later was light, a mere brushing of knuckles against wood. Her heart raced, half-fearing, half-hoping Josh had come to beg her forgiveness.

"Sharla-Jean, are you okay?"

A wave of disappointment washed over her. She wiped her face with the sleeve of her robe and hugged the pillow to her chest. "Everything's fine, Pauline. I'm sorry you were woken up. Go back to bed."

"Sharla-Jean?"

The door cracked open, and Pauline's anxious face peered around the half-open door. "Oh, my poor girl." She rushed into the room and swept Sharla-Jean into her slender arms. Her hands patted Sharla-Jean's back.

At first, Sharla-Jean held her body stiff, rejecting her old nanny's comfort. But then, with a convulsive sob, she dissolved into tears and allowed Pauline to soothe her as she had so often when Sharla-Jean was a child.

Later, much later, the tears eased and she straightened, shoving her tangled mass of hair off her face. She blew her nose with the tissue Pauline offered. "Thank you. I guess I needed some Pauline cuddling."

The old woman smiled, but her faded eyes were filled with concern. "Why don't I get some warm milk? A nice, warm drink will help both of us sleep." Without waiting for a reply, she got up and shuffled out of the room.

Sharla-Jean sat up against the pillows and wiped her damp cheeks. Her eyes burned with unshed tears, but she willed them away, refusing to waste any more tears over Josh Morgan. She'd never forgive him for accusing her of starting the fire tonight. He'd never forgive her for taking his journal. So be it. They'd reached a stalemate.

She flashed back to the previous night…the rapid beat of his heart, his familiar, earthy smell, his muscles rippling beneath her questing hands. And overall, the certainty she'd finally come home. After all these years of running from love, terrified she'd be hurt if she allowed herself to care, she'd overcome her terror and handed him her heart. She gulped and swiped at a fresh spate of tears. *Her heart? Love?* She shuddered. Had she fallen in love with Josh?

She jerked up and shoved back the covers, swinging her legs over the side of the bed. She knew what she had to do, what she always did when life was too painful. Nothing had changed. Nothing ever did.

Setting thought to action, she leaped from the bed

and ran over to the closet. Flinging open the door, she dragged out her empty suitcase and ripped clothes from the hangers and tossed them into the small, battered case, uncaring the clothes landed in a jumbled mess. *Leave.* The urgent command roared through her. *Leave now.*

"Going somewhere?" Pauline shuffled into the room, two steaming mugs in her hands.

Sharla-Jean didn't pause in her frantic packing.

"And here I imagined you'd grown up."

The disappointment in the old woman's voice struck her like a blow, but Sharla-Jean continued packing as if she hadn't heard her.

"You ran away when you were sixteen." Pauline blew out her cheeks. "Running away didn't solve anything then. You carried your pain with you and kept it as your sole companion all these years. Why do you think running will help now?"

Tears streamed down Sharla-Jean's face. She sat back on her heels, wiping her wet eyes. "I have to go. Don't you see? I have to."

"Are you telling me you're going to run away like a frightened mouse? I raised you better than that."

Sharla-Jean blinked through her tears. Fresh pain rippled through her at Pauline's censure. "I have to."

"Bullshit. You don't have to do a damn thing unless you choose to."

Sharla-Jean's eyes widened. Pauline never cursed.

The housekeeper stood with her feet planted apart, her hands resting on her narrow hips, her eyes blazing. "You're telling me you're going to leave town, run away with your tail between your legs, because someone accused you of something you didn't do?"

"You heard?"

Pauline nodded. "How could I not? The two of you were shouting to beat the band."

"Then you know why I'm leaving."

The old woman shook her head, her gray curls dancing around her wrinkled face. "No, I don't. So Josh asked you where you were tonight when the fire started. Can you blame him? He loves the mill. He's worked hard to make the place a success." Fire spit from her eyes. "No wonder he's trying to figure out who set the fire. Lord knows you're one likely suspect, especially after what happened seventeen years ago."

"But—"

"No buts. He shouldn't have had to ask you. He should have trusted you, but he was upset. He'd just watched his business burn to the ground." Pauline shrugged her narrow shoulders. "He made a mistake. Everyone makes mistakes. You, of all people, should understand how easy mistakes are to make; forgiving's what's hard."

Silence filled the room. Sharla-Jean sank against the side of the bed. "He hurt me." She placed her hand over her heart. "He hurt me here."

"I know, child. I know."

"You don't understand, I…I…we…" How could she tell the woman who'd raised her she'd made love with Josh? How to explain all the myriad emotions being with him evoked? How could she tell her she loved him? How could she tell her anything after the way he'd treated her tonight?

Pauline's faded blue depths filled with compassion and love. "It's okay, child. I understand." She set the cups of hot milk on the bureau and sat on the side of the bed and rested her hand on Sharla-Jean's shoulder.

Sharla-Jean relaxed under the warmth of Pauline's touch. She covered Pauline's veined hand with her own and squeezed. "I knew you would." Blowing out a breath, she rose to her feet and retrieved the steaming cups. She held one out to Pauline. "Here, better drink this before the milk gets cold."

As Sharla-Jean sipped, swirls of warmth flooded her throat, spreading through her belly, melting the block of ice. She nodded. "Okay, I'll stay. But only until I find who's responsible for tonight's fire."

Pauline beamed and raised her cup in the air. "That's my girl."

Chapter 21

Josh rubbed his hand over the rough bristles covering his cheeks. He hadn't shaved this morning or yesterday. He glanced down at his rumpled pants and stained shirt. Streaks of dirt and grease were smeared across the front of his shirt. His jeans were worse. The knees were black, and his thighs were covered with soot where he'd wiped his grimy hands. He lifted his arm, sniffed, and wrinkled his nose in disgust. He hadn't showered since yesterday, or was it the day before? Two hours spent crawling around on his hands and knees at the construction site hadn't helped.

He leaned back in his chair and closed his eyes against the brilliant sunshine streaming through the large office window. Exhaustion, his constant companion these days, settled deep into his bones. He'd hardly slept last night. After he'd drunk a few beers, well, more than a few, he'd crawled into bed, his body bent with exhaustion, desperate for the oblivion of sleep.

No sooner had his head hit the pillow and he closed his eyes, than he was assailed with images of Sharla-Jean. Even though he'd stripped the sheets from his bed and washed them a dozen times, her scent lingered, every toss and turn tantalizing him with images of her in this bed, naked.

If he dared close his eyes, their time together

replayed endlessly through his mind. The velvety softness of her skin, the little sounds she made when he caressed the soft undersides of her breasts, her flat stomach cupped between the sensual flare of her hips, the honey-sweet taste of her, all replayed in agonizing detail, hour after hour, night after night.

If, by some miracle, he managed to fall asleep, he'd awaken, sheets twisted around his legs, his body aching with need. No amount of cold showers helped. No sooner did he lie back down on the bed, than the longing for her rose again and once more, he was lost.

He rubbed his hands over his eyes, pressing until he saw spots. Why the hell couldn't he get her out of his mind? She wasn't the first woman he'd bedded. Hell, no. So why couldn't he forget her and get on with his life?

He cursed, the sound echoing throughout the plush, executive office. At least he didn't have to worry about anyone hearing. The office staff wouldn't begin to arrive for another hour.

He'd been here since dawn, had already put in a full day's work, but there still was so much to do. If only he could focus on the job, concentrate on what needed to be done. And forget that damn woman. He sprawled in the chair and scratched his beard.

A wrenching screech followed by a loud thump filtered through the window's thick glass. Ever since the fire and the destruction of a good portion of the mill, a construction crew worked twenty-four hours a day, seven days a week, on the rebuilding efforts. The noise and frenetic activity were constant.

He'd convinced the fire chief to allow the reconstruction to begin even though the investigation wasn't complete and they hadn't caught the culprit. Too many people depended on the mill.

The work was tedious and slow, but they were making progress. They had to. Families needed to be fed and mortgages paid. He didn't care about the cost. He wanted his people back at work. The sooner, the better. The mill wasn't up to full operation, wouldn't be for months, but if construction progressed as planned, basic production could begin in three weeks.

He pinched the bridge of his nose. Three weeks. That was if shit like this morning didn't happen. He'd no sooner stepped out of his truck than the night foreman had hailed him. The number-two saw housing was acting up, and he wanted Josh to check on the issue.

Josh had followed the foreman into the half-completed sawmill and studied the saw housing. He'd found the problem, but not before he'd climbed all over the damn frame and hammered the joists into place himself.

He yawned again and stretched, trying to ease the persistent ache in the back of his neck. Grabbing his coffee cup, desperate for the rush of caffeine, he gulped, grimacing at the cold, bitter taste. He wasn't a fool. He knew what his problem was. His guilt over accusing Sharla-Jean of starting the fire dragged at his soul. But, damn it all. Who could blame him? She'd admitted she set the fire and destroyed the mill seventeen years ago. After Nelson's sly insinuations, he'd had to ask.

He swore again. Why would she have set the fire? What would she gain from destroying the business? Sure she'd burned the mill years ago, but she'd been a kid. Kids did stupid things.

He'd realized his mistake the second the damning words were out of his mouth, and apologized, but then she'd showed him his journal and his fury went ballistic once again. She had no right to take his personal journal. A chill settled deep in his gut. Had she read it? Did she know his secret?

There was a brisk knock on the door, but before he could tell whomever it was to get lost, the door opened.

Perfectly groomed and looking every inch the rising executive, except for the multi-colored swelling around one eye and slightly crooked nose, Kevin Nelson strode into the room. Without asking permission, he settled on the chair facing Josh.

"What the hell?" Josh jumped to his feet. "Didn't you hear me when I told you what I'd do to you if you dared show your sorry ass around here again?" He pointed to the door. "Now get the hell out of here before I make good on my threat."

Nelson crossed one leg over the other and leaned back. "Yeah, I heard you. Loud and clear." He studied his nails and picked at a cuticle. "I want some answers, and then I'll get out of your hair. Believe me, I don't like spending time with you any more than you do with me."

"You're trespassing on private property, Nelson."

Nelson chuckled. "Sharla-Jean rehired me, remember?" He smirked and thrust out his chest. "So, unless you want to pay me a six-figure wrongful-dismissal settlement, I still work here. Until I decide not to, of course."

Josh's hands tightened on the arms of his chair as if trying to crush the metal. He reined in his anger. He'd damn well speak to Sharla-Jean about this. No way he could handle this smug bastard working at Bromley. But for now, he'd discover why Nelson was here looking as happy as a dog who'd rolled in cow shit. He made a point of studying his wristwatch. "You have thirty seconds."

"Has the fire investigator completed his report?"

Josh's jaw tightened at the gleam in Kevin's ice-blue eyes. The man was enjoying this. "Why are you so anxious to know?"

For a brief moment, Nelson seemed flustered, but he quickly covered with a tight smile. "I'm concerned. If Sharla-Jean's responsible, I'd like to know." He smoothed his hand over his gelled helmet of dark-blond hair. "I feel responsible. I'm the one who showed her all over the mill. I welcomed her with open arms." He sniggered. "Talk about letting the fox into the henhouse."

"We don't know she set the fire." Josh studied the other man, trying to figure out his reason for being here.

"Who else could have done it?"

"I thought you were her friend."

"I don't want to see her get hurt." Nelson shrugged. "If she has a problem, she needs help."

"A problem?"

"Arsonists are compelled to set fires. It's an illness. They can't help themselves."

"And you think Sharla-Jean's an arsonist?"

Nelson shrugged. "Someone is."

"Exactly. *Someone* is." Josh narrowed his eyes, trying to peer through Nelson's guile to the man beneath. Something in his attitude made the hair on the back of Josh's neck rise. Why was he so determined

Sharla-Jean be blamed for the fire? He blew out a breath. Who gave a shit about Nelson's devious schemes? He'd had more than enough of the creep. "Time's up. You've said what you came here to say. Now get the hell out."

Nelson didn't move. "There's something else."

Josh ground down on his back molars. "What?"

"I examined the mill accounts and found discrepancies in the figures."

"I know."

For a brief moment, Nelson was nonplused, but once again, he recovered quickly. "You have a thief working for you." He sat forward. "This company has already suffered a loss of revenue with the fire. We can't afford to lose any more money. What would the shareholders think?" He smirked. "They might lose faith in the current manager and decide to replace him." He gave a half shrug. "Who could blame them?"

So that was why the bastard was there. "Are you attempting to blackmail me? Did you come here thinking I'd pay you to keep quiet about the missing funds?"

Nelson paled. "Of course not."

"Good, because I'd have to call Sheriff Montgomery and tell him your plan. You'd be looking at hard time in federal prison." Josh's turn to smirk. "I'm sure those hardened felons in jail would take a real liking to a pretty boy like you."

Nelson gulped, his Adam's apple bobbing in his throat, but he met Josh's glare. "Don't you think it's odd that as soon as Sharla-Jean returns to town, a mysterious fire resulting in hundreds of thousands of dollars of damage to the mill occurs? Now we discover someone is stealing from the mill accounts. A coincidence?" He sat back, that damn smug smile back on his face. "I think not."

The pounding in Josh's head reached a crescendo. "What are you trying to say, Nelson?"

"Nothing really. Just thinking out loud."

"Well, don't bother. If I want your input on anything, I'll ask. Until then, I want you the hell out of here. Stay off Bromley mill property. The next time you show your face here, you'll regret it."

Nelson's face reddened, and he made a visible effort to control his rage, though his eyes flashed fiery sparks. "I guess I'll see you in court. When I'm done, you won't have a pot left to piss in." With a final scathing glare, the conniving bastard stormed out of the office.

Josh blew out a breath and gave in to the relief of rubbing his throbbing temples. He dug in his bottom desk drawer and grabbed the bottle of pills he kept for such an occasion. Before he opened the bottle, a tap sounded on the door. Cursing under his breath, he stuffed the pills back in his desk. He'd kill Nelson for sure this time. To hell with the consequences.

But the man who strode into the office wasn't Nelson.

Josh glared at J.D. "Doesn't anyone sleep? What are you doing here at the crack of dawn? This sure as hell isn't lawyer's hours."

"I have the report from the fire investigators."

The muscles in Josh's stomach clenched. "And? What did they find?"

The heavyset older man tugged a handkerchief from his suit coat pocket and dabbed at his gleaming brow. "The fire wasn't an accident."

Josh nodded. He'd known from the start someone had set the blaze. The fire had grown too quickly, burned too hot, destroyed too much, to be a result of faulty wiring or a carelessly tossed cigarette. "Any idea who's responsible?"

J.D. shook his head. "I'm afraid not. An accelerant was used. Someone poured gas on the buildings and torched the place. They meant business. A miracle no one was hurt and anything was saved at all."

Josh fought to think over the jackhammer pounding in his head. Arson. The word alone left an acrid taste in his mouth. Who stood to gain by the destruction of the mill? Bromley Forest Products was the town's main employer. He couldn't imagine any of the hundred-and-fifty employees wanting to destroy their livelihood. The culprit had to be someone else. But who and why? Was it the same person who'd vandalized the mill equipment? The one who'd attempted to start the fire in the storage room and hurt Sharla-Jean?

"This isn't the first time this mill was destroyed by a fire." J.D. refused to meet Josh's eyes, and his face flushed with obvious discomfort. Unlike Kevin Nelson, the lawyer didn't relish telling him. "If what people say is true, Sharla-Jean was involved in the first fire."

Josh rubbed his aching temples. "You're the second person this morning to point the finger of blame at her."

"I didn't—"

Josh cut him off. "Yes, you did." A heavy silence descended. "I want you to check into Kevin Nelson's background. Find out where he was and what he was up to before he showed here." He inhaled a breath. "I also want you to find out more about the fire seventeen years ago. Something tells me the two fires are connected."

"That's what I was trying to tell you." J.D. removed his glasses and polished the lenses.

"Sharla-Jean didn't start the fire."

"But—"

"She didn't." Josh pinned the other man with a determined look. "You know people. I want you to find out who did this."

J.D. blew out a breath. "I'll try."

"Do more than try."

J.D. nodded and wheeled around to leave, but Josh's next words drew him to a halt.

"Don't forget to check out Nelson. I don't care what it costs. I want to know where he grew up, where he attended school, what he eats for breakfast, even how often he pisses, every damn thing."

Again J.D. nodded and bustled out of the room.

Grim determination tightened Josh's muscles, increasing the ache in his head. The lawyer might be pompous and blustering, but he was skilled at what he did. If anyone could dig up dirt on Kevin Nelson, J.D. could. His gut told him Nelson was involved. How, he didn't know, but he always trusted his gut instincts.

Always.

Chapter 22

Sharla-Jean stared into the dark. The incessant chirping of crickets, and the croak of a bullfrog in the nearby marsh filled the night. The air was chilly, and an icy fog rose from the damp ground by the pond. She wrinkled her nose at the earthy stench of composting vegetation, mud, and murky water. Myriads of stars twinkled in the clear night sky. A full moon rose over the crest of the hill, illuminating every bush and rock with startling clarity.

She stamped her feet and rubbed her hands together. Shivering, she tightened the collar of her down jacket. The luminous dial of her wristwatch showed five minutes since she'd last checked. Where was he? Maybe he wouldn't show. A wave of relief washed over her. Maybe she didn't have to do this.

Even after seventeen years, the thought of confronting Tyler Maddox terrified her. His phone call earlier today had stunned her. He'd said he had information about the fire at the mill. If she was interested, she was to meet him at nine o'clock at the old gravel pit.

She shivered again, but this time the chill coursing through her wasn't from the penetrating cold. Meeting the man who'd raped her was perilous. But she wasn't stupid. She gripped the butt of the compact semi-automatic pistol weighing down her pocket. She'd found the gun in the top drawer of the old filing cabinet in her father's study. The weight of the handgun distorted the smooth line of her coat, but the nine bullets lodged in the firing chamber gave her confidence.

She'd never used a firearm, but how hard could it be? Release the safety catch, point, and pull the trigger. And shoot a man in cold blood? She gulped. Maybe not so easy, but she didn't plan to kill Maddox. The gun was for protection. He wouldn't dare try anything with a gun pointed at his chest.

After her conversation with Pauline, she'd realized running away wouldn't solve her problems. The only way to prove her innocence was to find the person responsible for the mill fire. Unfortunately, Tyler Maddox was the key. If what he'd said was true, he knew something about the fire.

The thought of facing him again knotted her stomach. She still struggled with the scars of his brutal attack. But she'd go through the very gates of Hell if it meant finding the person who set the fire. This was something she needed to do. For her. No one else. Just her. And then maybe, just maybe, she could move on.

She stuffed her hands in her pocket. One hand grazed the cold, metal gun barrel, adding to her confidence. She wasn't the frightened girl she'd been seventeen years ago. Not even close.

Glancing at her watch again, she grimaced. Where was he? She stamped her feet to keep the blood in her toes circulating. Her breath hung in a cloud in the frosty air. As she leaned against the hood of her car, her thoughts reverted to their constant theme: Josh. She hadn't seen him since the fire. Since that terrible night, she'd hid in her office like a coward, avoiding the snide comments and sidelong, suspicious glances of the mill employees, while he'd been busy organizing the rebuilding of the mill.

This morning she'd peered out her office window at the rubble and blackened timbers of the ruined mill and watched the furious pace of the construction crew. The scene changed every day as burned debris was hauled away and walls were erected to house the new planer mill and sawmill. As usual, Josh, ruggedly handsome in his faded denim jeans, tight black T-shirt, and white hard hat was in the yard directing the action. Did he ever rest? The scene from the morning played before her as if she were watching the events on television.

His tall, muscular form moved with an air of supreme confidence as he bounded from one massive piece of equipment to another amid the flurry of construction activity. As if sensing her watching him, he twisted in her direction, shoved his hard hat back on his head, and stared up at her.

She gulped and tried to back away from the window, but her feet wouldn't move, and she remained glued to the glass, devouring him like a starving dog salivating over a prime roast of beef. He'd lost weight, and his normally snug-fitting jeans hung on him. The sun lit his rugged face in bold relief, illuminating the dark circles under his eyes and the gauntness of his cheekbones.

Across the distance separating them, his gaze pinned her.

She staggered as if a laser beam blazed from his eyes across the hectic yard, through the glass window.

Time stood still. Nothing existed but the sizzling link between them.

One of his men approached and tugged on Josh's arm. Josh lifted his hand to his head in a mock salute to her that showed more than words exactly how much he detested her, and then he turned to the worker, severing the intense connection.

She yanked the blinds over the window, and like a puppet whose strings had been cut, fell to her knees in a heap on the floor. Tears filled her eyes and slipped down her face, dripping onto her blouse.

She shook off the painful memory and rubbed her freezing hands. The past days at the mill had been a nightmare. The fire investigation was finished, and the authorities had confirmed the fire was deliberately set. As a result, the local sheriff had called in the state arson investigators.

Of course, as far as everyone in town was concerned, they already knew who'd set the fire. No one, other than Josh, had said anything to her face, but she hadn't missed the scorn on the faces of the people she passed at the grocery store, or the deliberate avoidance of pedestrians on the sidewalk. The whole damn town thought she'd done it. Once the experts showed up, she'd be pointed out as the prime suspect.

That was why she was here tonight. The last place she wanted to be, but she'd promised Pauline she wouldn't leave until she'd cleared her name and found the arsonist. If meeting with Tyler was the price she had to pay to find answers, facing the monster from her nightmares would be worth it.

A branch snapped, and she peered into the darkness. "Who's there?" Her voice was shrill. "Tyler, is that you?" The crickets had ceased their cacophony, and only the rising wind in the trees broke the looming silence.

A footfall sounded, heavy and ominous, and Tyler Maddox broke through the trees and stepped into the clearing. He stopped several feet from her, his face lit by moonlight.

The years had been hard on him, and he appeared far older than his thirty-six years. His hair was no longer dark, but streaked with gray, the once handsome face, bloated and heavy. His coat strained over a substantial paunch, but his legs, encased in tight black jeans, were skinny and bowed. "Hey, Sharla-Jean." He inspected her, beginning with her knee-high, black, leather boots, and moving up over her jeans and thick down coat, settling on her face.

She shivered at the hungry smile curving his thick lips. A nightmare image of those fleshy lips mashing against her mouth, his tongue plunging, rose before her, followed by the sour taste of bile filling her mouth. She backed up until her hips bumped against the hood of her car. Fear blossomed, and her hand tightened on the gun in her pocket. *Don't be afraid. He can't hurt you. Not anymore.* The words ran through her like a soothing mantra. She inhaled a steadying breath. "I was beginning to think you weren't going to show up."

"I'm an important man in this town." He puffed out his chest. "I've got all sorts of business to see to."

"I hear you're married." Before she'd agreed to this meeting, she'd spent some time checking up on him.

"Got three kids." He rubbed the arms of his scuffed, black leather jacket and examined the tiny clearing. "Looks the same as the last time we were here, don't it?" He licked his lips. "You haven't changed either. Still as sweet as ever."

Her stomach clenched, but she schooled her expression to hide her revulsion. "Okay. I'm here like you asked." She blew out a breath. "You said you know something about the fire at the mill. What do you know?"

His snickering, a cruel cackling sound, lingered in the night air. He fished in his coat pocket and drew out a joint and a plastic lighter. Lighting the end of the rolled white paper, he inhaled a deep breath before blowing out the smoke in a billowing cloud. He strolled closer and held out the joint. "Want a toke?"

She shrank back. Her fingers tightened around the pistol grip.

"Still a tight ass, I see." Taking another drag, he watched her through narrowed eyes. "What's it worth?"

"What are you talking about?"

"My information. What'll you give me in exchange for what I know?"

She should have known he'd try something like this, should have been prepared to offer him some cash. "I don't have much money."

He sucked on the joint. "I'd be willing to accept payment in another form." He grinned, leering at her chest.

In spite of the frigid night, beads of sweat broke out on her brow. Taking a breath, she dug deep for courage. She couldn't afford to show fear, couldn't let him have the upper hand. Yanking out the gun, she fixed him with a hard look. "Lay one hand on me, and I'll blast that tiny appendage drooping between your legs to smithereens." She smirked, enjoying the fear on his bloated face. "I expect I'd be doing the women of this town a favor if I castrate you. The mayor might even give me a medal."

"You're gonna shoot me?" He snorted. "You don't have the balls. You never did."

"I don't think your wife would take kindly to the news her husband raped a young girl, and left her to burn to death."

He tossed down the joint. "Go ahead, tell anyone you want. That's ancient history. My old lady doesn't give a shit what I do, so long as I pay the rent and keep her supplied with plenty of booze and drugs." He advanced on her.

Her heart raced at the cruel intent in his icy eyes. She raised the gun. The barrel wavered as she fought to hold the gun steady, unused to the weight. She gripped the butt end with both hands, but her arms trembled. "I'll tell the police you were the one who started the fire at the mill seventeen years ago. I'll tell them you raped me while your buddy, Jack, watched."

He kept walking, drawing closer with each step. "Go ahead. No one will believe you. They didn't then; they sure as hell won't now. Besides, everyone thinks you started the fire." He giggled. "Didn't hurt none that Jack and me helped spread that bit of information."

She itched to jam the barrel in his face, jerk the trigger, and blow his brains all over the ground. Beneath his swagger, she sensed his wariness. He wasn't as fearless as he pretended. The realization gave her courage. "I hear you work at the mill. You're on the afternoon shift, aren't you?" She tossed her hair. "That makes me your boss." A smile tugged at the edges of her mouth. The power over him felt good. Damn good.

"One word from me, and you're fired. Are you willing to risk that paycheck your wife is so fond of?"

He stopped moving. His eyes were heavy-lidded, the pupils dilated and glassy.

She wanted to pump her fist in the air. He'd come to the meeting full of male arrogance, but he'd discovered she was no longer a child he could intimidate.

His expression changed to one of disgruntlement. He fished out another joint.

She lowered the gun to her side. "This is getting us nowhere. I didn't come here to rehash the past. Tell me what you know. Who started the fire?"

His fingers shook as he fumbled with his cigarette lighter. He looked up and met her gaze. His red-veined eyes zeroed in on her with surprising clarity. "I don't know."

She opened her mouth to protest, but he cut her off.

"I wasn't supposed to be working the night of the fire, but I traded shifts with another guy. I was out behind the drying shed when I heard somethin'." He dropped his lighter, cursed, and bent down and scrambled after it in the dark. Finding the lighter, he stood and flicked the tab with his thumb. A tiny flame flared to life, and he lit the end of his joint. He sucked in a long puff, held the smoke, and then expelled it in a rush of skunky air.

She motioned for him to continue. What difference if he wanted to smoke his brains out? As long as he told her what he knew.

He coughed and blew out another plume of acrid smoke. "As I said, I was out back taking a break, and I heard this noise, so I figured I oughtta check it out. As soon as I rounded the corner, I smelled gas. Two guys were pouring gas on the number-six dryer shed." He inhaled another drag. "Before I could ask what the hell they were doin', one of 'em lit a match and tossed it. The whole place went up with a whoosh. I got the hell out of there."

She didn't have to ask him why he hadn't reported the fire. He'd been stoned out of his mind. The last thing he would have wanted was for his supervisor to find out he was high on the job. The mill had a strict no-drugs policy. He would have been fired on the spot. "Did you recognize the men?"

He shook his head. "Too dark."

"You're sure you saw two men."

He staggered toward the car and sagged against the rear bumper. "Yep. I think."

Disappointment rippled through her. This was a waste of time. "Thanks for nothing." She shoved the gun back in her coat pocket and opened the driver's door of her car. She'd have to find answers somewhere else.

"I forgot one thing." His voice cut through the night.

She regarded him through the open door. "What?"

"One guy called the other a name."

"A name? What name?"

He eyed her blearily.

She ground her teeth in frustration. "What name, Tyler?"

"I dunno. Somethin' weird. Kale, Kade, maybe." He shrugged. "Whatever." His voice took on a singsong cadence as the drug coursed through him.

"Kade?" she asked.

"Kane." He beamed like a little boy who'd answered the teacher's math question correctly.

"Are you sure?"

He swayed back and forth, his complexion turning green. "Whoa, man. I'm wasted." He giggled and held up the remains of his joint. "This is powerful shit." He tossed the glowing joint to the ground. "I gotta go see a man about a horse, if you know what I mean." He giggled again and pushed off from the car and stumbled away, but then he paused and faced her. "Look, Sharla-Jean, I'm sorry for what happened. You know, at the mill with Jack and all?"

She remained silent.

He rubbed a hand over his face. "We were just kids, you know. Lookin' for fun. It didn't mean nothin'." He blinked. "I mean, it's not like anyone was hurt, right?"

Didn't mean nothin'. Was he serious? Raping a girl was nothing? She yanked out the pistol and pointed the black barrel. Her hands shook as her finger caressed the trigger.

He paled and staggered back, tripping over exposed roots, his arms flailing. Falling, he landed on his butt in the dirt. "Whoa!" He held up his hands in front of his face. "Easy, girl. You don't want to have no accident. That gun looks loaded."

"Sure is."

His throat worked as he swallowed. He wasn't laughing anymore. Sweat beaded his forehead. "Don't point that thing at me. You could hurt someone."

"Really? And why would I want to hurt you? You didn't do anything. Right? You raped me, but no big deal. You and Jack were just two good ol' boys havin' some fun. Right? Isn't that what you said?" She mimicked his voice, "*Didn't mean nothin'.*"

Tears filmed his eyes. "Okay, okay, I'm sorry. I was wrong. I hurt you. I'm sorry." His chin wobbled, and he started to sob. "Don't shoot. I'm a family man. I got kids." He scrabbled backward, using his hands and feet, moving like a crab across the uneven ground, blubbering and begging.

Disgusted, she lowered her arms. He wasn't worth killing.

Staggering to his feet, he ran, stumbling and tripping, weaving crookedly into the forest.

Hands shaking, she set the gun on the seat beside her and wiped her damp palms on her coat. Blowing out a breath, she shuddered. She'd almost shot him. Hell, she'd wanted to. More than anything. But she hadn't. That was the main thing…she hadn't pulled the trigger.

A weight lifted from her shoulders. She'd faced her worst nightmare and conquered the beast. She'd stood up to him. It hadn't been easy, but she'd confronted one of her attackers and won. Never again would she let a man use her. Never again would fear rule her life.

But she wasn't done. She had to find the two men Tyler had seen set the fire. If he was telling the truth, she had a name. The trick was to find the person. Was Kane a first name or a last name? No employee at the mill was called Kane. She'd studied the personnel files last week searching for likely suspects. An unusual name like Kane would have stuck in her mind.

She'd been away from Renton Falls for a long time. Kane could be living in town, and she wouldn't know. She could go to the police, but they wouldn't believe her. As far as they were concerned, she was the prime suspect in the mill fire. Why would they look for anyone else when they had her?

She started the car and cranked up the heat. Shifting into Drive, she drove out of the gravel pit onto the narrow lane leading to the highway. Suddenly, she jammed her foot on the brake. The car skidded to a stop. *Of course!*

Kevin Nelson had told her he was a private investigator. She'd rehired him at the mill so he could continue his investigation into the missing money. He'd help her find this man named Kane.

With renewed determination, she stepped on the gas. Kevin would locate Kane, and they'd find his partner, and turn the arsonists' names over to the authorities. But that wouldn't fix things between her and Josh. She might find the arsonists, but there was still the little matter of her taking Josh's journal. He'd never forgive her for that lapse in judgment.

Chapter 23

Josh shoved his chair back from his computer and rubbed his temples, trying to ease the ever-present pounding. He yawned and ran his palm over his hair, smoothing the tangled mop. A six-inch pile of file folders sat on the top of his desk beside the laptop. Contracts, union concerns, business correspondence, employee issues…all urgent, all demanding his attention. He'd been staring at the same pile since dawn, unable to focus.

His office door opened and J.D. strode in. He swept aside the pile of files and the laptop on Josh's desk and slapped a file folder in front of Josh.

"What's this?" Josh raised his eyebrows.

J.D.'s usual lawyerly demeanour was absent, replaced by bubbling excitement. "It's all in the file."

Josh rubbed his aching eyes. "I'd rather you told me."

"The state investigators still don't know who's responsible for the fire."

Josh scowled, though this news didn't surprise him. The evidence recovered from the fire was inconclusive. The fire had burned so intensely, any incriminating clues left by the perpetrator had been incinerated. All they had so far was certain knowledge the fire had started behind one of the drying sheds, and gasoline was the accelerant. Aside from chemical residue indicating gasoline, the investigators had uncovered the remnants of three five-gallon, plastic gas containers.

He'd met with the team of investigators yesterday morning, and told them about the red, plastic gas can found in the office storage room. They were aware of the fire seventeen years ago, and were considering some sort of connection between the two fires, but so far, nothing substantial had been uncovered.

"…and so the investigator I hired called in some favors and found this guy's phone number." J.D. rubbed his hands together. "He called him."

Josh blinked. "Phone number? What are you talking about?"

J.D.'s brow furrowed. "This isn't like you, Josh. You're not focusing these days. You're distracted all the time, and you're always tired. Something's wrong. Is there anything I can do to help?"

The concern in the lawyer's eyes made Josh smile. If he told J.D. a woman was the cause of his distraction, especially if he knew the woman in question was none other than Sharla-Jean Bromley, the staid lawyer would have a coronary. But J.D. was right on the money. Josh couldn't put two coherent thoughts together without thinking about her.

Even now, when the very existence of the mill was at stake, he couldn't concentrate. Visions of the silver lights in her green eyes when she smiled, the streaks of gold weaving through her long, auburn hair, the husky timbre of her voice, the satin softness of her skin intruded on his every thought.

Other than brief glimpses of her through her office window, or as she headed to her car at the end of the day, he hadn't seen her since the night weeks ago at her house on Marwood Street when he'd as good as accused her of setting fire to the mill. He should apologize, but every time he envisioned confronting her, he remembered she'd taken his journal and he changed his mind.

"Josh?"

Damn. He'd been thinking of her *again.* "What is it, J. D.?" He regretted his sharpness the second the words left his mouth. Even more when J.D.'s mouth tightened, and his round cheeks flushed. "Sorry, J.D., I'm just so damn beat." He blew out a breath. "What did you find?"

"It's what I didn't find that's interesting." J.D. settled on the chair in front of Josh's desk. "Kevin Nelson appeared out of nowhere. I haven't been able to find anyone who knew him where he supposedly worked before Bromley Forest Products. In fact, when I checked his resume, I found several discrepancies. The people he listed as references know a Kevin Nelson, but the man they know doesn't look anything like our Kevin Nelson."

Josh nodded. He'd had his suspicions. Nelson was as phony as a plastic cigar. "What do you think this means? What's he up to?"

"He knows the lumber business, that's for sure. Other than that, I don't know. He's told a pack of lies and was hired under false pretenses." He shook his head. "I don't know why Big Jim was so high on him, but right from the start, he was determined to hire Nelson."

Josh mulled over this information. Nelson had appeared out of nowhere. Josh had arrived at work one morning and found him ensconced in an office on the upper floor. His official job title was Comptroller of Operations, but his responsibilities were unclear. After hiring Nelson, Big Jim had been vague on the topic and refused to discuss Nelson or his assigned duties. One thing was certain; the incidents of petty vandalism began not long after Nelson started working at Bromley.

"There's something else."

Josh glanced up at J.D.'s somber tone. "What now?"

"My investigator tracked down a lowlife named Jack O' Malley, and ah"—he coughed—"*convinced* him to talk. O'Malley revealed some interesting information about the previous fire at the mill."

Josh sat forward. "And?" His body tensed. The old lawyer wasn't finished. Something else was stuck in his craw, something Josh knew he wasn't going to like.

"Sharla-Jean wasn't to blame."

Josh held his breath as he waited for J.D. to continue.

"The night of the fire, O'Malley, a friend of his, and Sharla-Jean drank a bunch of beer and snuck into the lumberyard. According to this Jack character, he and his friend planned to have some *fun* with her." He grimaced as if he'd ingested something rotten. "His words, not mine." He narrowed his eyes. "Anyway, she wasn't interested, but his buddy didn't take no for an answer. He forced himself on her." His mouth pursed. "Before the attack could turn into a gang rape, they noticed the fire and ran away like cowards. They left her there."

Josh sagged back in his chair feeling as if he'd been sucker punched. *Rape!* Sharla-Jean had been raped. He squeezed his eyes shut, trying to block out the shocking horror. Sixteen years old and raped by one man while another watched and waited his turn. Jamming his fist in his mouth, he fought to block the vicious reality. He couldn't imagine her physical and emotional anguish. No wonder she'd fled this damn town. No wonder she hadn't returned in all these years.

"Are you okay, Josh?"

He opened his eyes and stared hard at J.D. "How did you get this information? I can't imagine this jerk would confess to being an accomplice to rape."

J.D. smirked. "Once we had a name, my contact flew up to Alaska where Mr. O'Malley currently resides." He spread his hands on his lap. "After that, it was just a matter of persistence."

Josh's mouth tightened. He'd known J.D. for a long time. Despite his middle-aged, plump body and stodgy manner, the lawyer knew some rough individuals. He could only imagine the type of *persistence* his contact had used to convince Jack O'Malley to talk. "What's the name of the bastard who"—he swallowed—"who raped her?" The very words left a vile taste in his mouth.

"O'Malley refused to reveal his partner's name. Apparently, he's terrified of him, but he did indicate the man's still living in this area."

Josh ground his teeth in frustration. He didn't have the rapist's name yet, but he would. He sure as hell would. He'd find the bastard and cut off his balls, then stuff them in his mouth.

"Look, Josh, I didn't tell you this so you'd go off half-cocked and do something foolish."

The lawyer's sonorous voice was almost lost over

the furious pounding in Josh's head. "So why did you tell me?"

"O'Malley said the fire appeared out of nowhere. Within seconds of them noticing the smoke and flames, the fire was out of control."

"So how the hell did the fire start?"

"The two men were smoking marijuana. O'Malley thinks one of their discarded joints or a match might have started the blaze."

Josh sucked in a deep breath and unclenched his fists, rubbing at the marks his nails had gouged in his palms. "Sharla-Jean didn't set the fire. Not deliberately."

J.D. shook his head.

"But everyone thinks she did." Josh rubbed his temples. "Why? Why didn't she tell people the truth? Why let everyone assume the worst?"

Again J.D. shook his head. "You'll have to ask her. Some women are too embarrassed to go to the police after a rape. They believe the attack is somehow their fault. Or they think no one will believe them. I'm ashamed to say it, but that's sometimes the case. The legal system has a long history of blaming the woman for what happened…you know, the way she was dressed"—he shrugged—"if she was drinking alcohol, if she knew her attacker… That sort of thing."

Josh rubbed his temples harder, trying to drill holes in his head, anything to ease the agonizing pain stabbing through his brain. "That's bullshit! She was just a kid. Those men should have gone to jail. Hell, they should still be rotting in some dank and dark cell."

"True. But for whatever reason, she didn't tell anyone of the attack." J.D. removed his glasses and used his handkerchief to wipe the lenses. "What happened to Sharla-Jean was horrible, but what we need to focus on is the fact she didn't set the fire."

Josh blinked, trying to listen to J.D., but he couldn't get past his rising guilt. Everyone in town blamed her for setting the fire seventeen years ago. Even he'd accused her of the crime. Once again, his hands clenched as he recalled his angry accusations. Big Jim had always believed in her innocence, but he'd been alone in his defense of his daughter.

Did Big Jim know about the rape? Had Sharla-Jean told him? Did she go to her father after the attack, seeking his help? He slammed his fist on his thigh, barely registering the pain. If she'd told Big Jim, he would have done something. He wouldn't have let his daughter leave town, battered, beaten, and alone. Would he?

"Josh?"

J.D.'s sharp rebuke pierced his tormented thoughts. "I'm listening. Go on."

The lawyer blew out an aggrieved breath and continued. "If she didn't set the first fire, she probably didn't set this recent one." He lumbered to his feet and replaced his glasses on his face. "The authorities are looking at her as their prime suspect, but they're wrong. Someone else started those fires." He leaned over Josh's desk, placed his palms on the desktop, and fixed Josh with a scowl. "We need to find the guilty person. We need to clear Sharla-Jean's name once and for all."

"Don't worry about that. I'll find the bastard and when I do…" Josh let the words trail off.

J.D. nodded as if satisfied and marched out of the office.

Josh stared at the closed door. His earlier lethargy had vanished, replaced by a frantic urgency to act. He'd find the man who raped Sharla-Jean. Damn right, he would. But first he had to beg her forgiveness for his baseless insinuations. He'd made a mistake, one he prayed wasn't too late to rectify.

For the first time in days, he had a purpose, and his steps were lighter as he ran out of his office and down the hall. Leaping into his truck, he tore out of the mill, careened through town, raced down Marwood Street, and spun into Sharla-Jean's driveway. He jumped out of the truck almost before he cranked off the engine and sprinted up the walkway to the front door.

He fought to control the urge to kick down the door. Instead, he pounded his fist on the shiny wood. After an interminable wait, the door opened.

Pauline didn't blink at his sudden appearance. "Well, about time. I thought you were never going to get here."

"Where is she? Is she here?" He moved to brush past her, but froze at her next words.

"She's gone."

He staggered and grabbed the doorframe to steady himself. "What?" A chill rippled along his spine. "She's gone?" He sank on the front steps, all his energy drained. "Why?"

"Those fire inspectors showed up here early this morning."

He nodded. "They're talking to everyone who works at the mill."

The old woman's mouth tightened, and she placed her hands on her hips. "You and I both know they weren't here just to talk. Why, the questions they asked her were downright rude. They as much as accused her of starting the fire." Her eyes shot sparks. "They wanted to take her in for questioning, but I wouldn't let them. I told them she wasn't going anywhere with them without her lawyer."

He blew out a breath. "Is she at the sheriff's office?"

She shook her head. "They weren't pleased, but they left. What choice did they have? They didn't have an arrest warrant. Last I looked, this is still the good old US of A."

"They'll be back." The team of arson investigators were persistent in their quest for the truth. They were certain Sharla-Jean started the fire. They'd be back, and when they returned, they'd have the proper paperwork and take her to the sheriff's office for interrogation. But not if he talked to them first and told them what J.D. had discovered about the first fire. That information put a different spin on this latest fire, and took the spotlight off Sharla-Jean. He ran his fingers through his hair. "Why didn't she tell anyone about what happened? Why is she still keeping quiet?"

Pauline narrowed her eyes. "So you know."

He nodded. "I just found out."

She sank onto the step beside him. Silence settled over them. Birds chirped in the apple trees lining the driveway, a lone car cruised by on the street in front of the house, a neighbor's dog barked. She expelled a long breath. "I was away when the fire happened. My sister in Spokane broke her hip, and I'd gone to lend a hand. When I returned, everything was different. Sharla-Jean had run away, the mill was destroyed, and everyone accused Sharla-Jean of starting the fire. The most shocking change was Big Jim. He was stone-cold sober. He hadn't been sober in years, not since his wife died in that terrible accident. He never drank a drop of alcohol again."

"Did he know?" Josh asked. The question had hounded him since J.D. told him about the rape. "Did he know his daughter had been raped?"

Another silence descended. The throb of a jet flying high overhead was loud in the morning stillness.

"I believe he did."

Josh faced her, his anger building. "Why the hell didn't he do something? Why didn't he help her? Why let her leave? Why let everyone think she set the fire?"

"I wish I knew." She hung her head. Her heavily veined hands twisted the fabric of her skirt. "You have to understand. I loved him. He was like family to me, but what he did to that poor girl…" She shook her head. "I never forgave him. I stayed, but I didn't forgive."

Josh ran his fingers through his hair. Big Jim had taken him in when he needed help the most. The man had been more of a father to him than his own father. Everyone adored Big Jim. He was well respected in town. But he hadn't been happy, not in the slightest. There was an emptiness inside him, as if he carried the weight of the world on his stooped shoulders. Josh had always wondered why. Now he knew. Big Jim's guilt over his treatment of his daughter ate at him like a cancer from the inside out. The gossips were right. Big Jim died of a broken heart, not caused by Sharla-Jean's absence, but the poison of his own guilt.

"She left this for you." Pauline held out a business-size, white envelope.

He studied the envelope. His name was written in

Sharla-Jean's precise script across the front. "What's this?"

"Open it and see."

With shaking hands he tore open the envelope and withdrew a single, folded piece of paper. Unfolding the paper, he read what she'd written, and with each word, his heart sank more. When he finished, he groaned and buried his head in his hands.

Pauline's warm touch on his shoulder made him look up.

"You love her, don't you, son?"

Too upset to bother hiding the truth, he let out a discouraged breath. He'd wasted these last weeks when he should have talked to Sharla-Jean, begged her forgiveness, done everything in his power to make her feel what he felt. Now he was too late.

"She said she was going to stop at the cabin for a spell before she headed back to Portland." Pauline patted his knee. "If you're quick, you might be able to catch her."

As the full import of her words struck him, he let out a whoop and sprang to his feet. He gathered Pauline in his arms and swung her around in a circle.

She blushed like a young girl. Even though her mouth was turned down in a stern expression, pleasure gleamed in her eyes. "Set me down, you big oaf. You'll break one of my bones."

He did as she requested, and then bounded off the steps.

"Now, don't you go and break her heart, Josh. You hear me? She's been hurt enough."

Her words of warning followed him down the walkway and into the cab of his truck. Hurting Sharla-

Jean was the furthest thing from his mind, though he might strangle her for what she'd written in the letter.

The powerful engine revved and squealed as the truck surged ahead. He leaned forward, his hands gripping the steering wheel, as if by doing so he could make the vehicle go faster. He had to reach the cabin before she left. He steered the car around a tight corner and swung onto the highway.

Chapter 24

Sharla-Jean studied the glistening surface of the lake and the towering peaks beyond. A fresh layer of snow shrouded the mountains and sparkled under the midday sun. The willows lining the shore were in the midst of transforming from summer green to vibrant shades of red and orange. She inhaled, filling her lungs, relishing the earthy scent of warm, damp soil.

Leaning back on her elbows, she faced the sun, the warmth a gentle caress against her skin. The echoing cry of a loon floated over the lake. She closed her eyes.

Shore birds cheeped as they pecked the seeds of dried wildflowers, water lapped against the old wharf, the wind soughed through the evergreen branches, and a flock of Canada geese flying high overhead honked.

The tranquil peace soothed her jangled nerves. After the past tumultuous weeks, she needed this respite. She'd been in Renton Falls such a short time, but so much had happened. Only a few weeks ago, she'd read of her father's death, and bought the slutty red dress, and arrived in town determined to settle a score.

Revenge hadn't been at all what she'd imagined. Instead of feeling relief because her father was gone, she'd come to realize that in spite of his drinking, his catastrophic mistakes, his cold-hearted withdrawal, and his callous treatment of her after the nightmare of the rape, she loved him.

After her mother died, and her father withdrew behind a wall of grief and guilt, she'd tried to please him; tried to be the perfect child. When that hadn't worked, she'd acted out in ever more outrageous ways, doing everything she could think of to get his attention. Any attention, even his anger and disdain, was better than the icy wall of silence. After the rape, when she needed him the most, he'd scorned her, severing any hope of a loving relationship between them.

All these years, she'd lived with bitterness and anger; her one goal was to avenge the wrongs committed by her father. But then she'd met Josh and her world had been turned upside down. She'd erected barrier after barrier, but somehow he'd managed to break through and worm his way into her heart. In the process, he'd shown her she was able to forgive, and capable of love.

Time was running out. The arson inspectors had finished their investigation. It wouldn't be long before the authorities returned with an arrest warrant. She had to act now. She'd contacted Kevin Nelson days ago and given him the name Tyler Maddox had told her he'd heard the night of the fire. Kevin promised to check into the matter. He'd find whoever was responsible for starting the fire and turn him over to the police. She'd done what she'd promised Pauline. The perpetrators of the fire at the mill would be punished.

She imagined Josh's relief when he read her letter. The agreement she signed stated she'd return to Portland and leave the day-to-day running of the mill to him. She'd come back to Renton Falls when necessary to meet the conditions of her father's will. Once the twelve months were up, she'd hand him her half of the mill. He'd be the sole owner of Bromley Forest Products, something he desperately wanted.

The laboring roar of an engine broke the quiet, and she glanced toward the cabin as a dark blue, four-wheel drive truck sped around the bend and burst into the clearing. The heavy vehicle skidded to a stop in a spray of gravel and dust. As if conjured by her thoughts, Josh flung open the door and leaped from the cab of the truck. He ran toward the cabin and onto the porch, calling her name.

She remained still, hardly daring to breathe.

He was out of the cabin and back on the porch in seconds. Dark sunglasses covered his eyes, but the sudden stiffening of his shoulders and tightening of his mouth told her he'd spotted her.

Her heart beat a trip-hammer in her chest.

His dark hair gleamed like a raven's wing under the bright sunlight. Alternating streaks of shadow and light highlighted the rugged angles of his face. Black jeans revealed the lean muscles in his thighs. His red plaid, flannel work shirt was unbuttoned at the collar, exposing his tanned neck and a tuft of dark hair.

He stepped onto the rickety old dock and strolled toward her. Kneeling on the warped wooden planks, he faced her, inches separating them. He removed his sunglasses and placed them on the dock beside him.

The heat from his body burned her. The air between them pulsated in time to the throbbing of blood through her veins. She risked a peek at his face, and was caught by the power of his lethal gaze.

She was vaguely aware of distant sounds…a crow croaking in a nearby pine, the wind tangling in the branches of the willows, the gentle lap of water against the dock.

"What the hell is this?" He tossed an envelope on her lap.

"Isn't it what you wanted?"

He studied the lake. "At first, maybe, but not now, not like this."

"You've worked hard all these years. You're the reason the mill is doing so well."

He remained silent, staring into the distance.

"Take this." She pressed the envelope into his hand. "Please. I want you to have it."

He frowned, but stuffed the envelope in the back pocket of his jeans. "Pauline tells me you're leaving town."

She nodded.

"Why?"

She worried a cuticle. Didn't he realize she didn't have a choice?

"Why are you running away, Sharla-Jean? What are you afraid of?"

It was her turn to study the distant mountains. "I'm going back to Portland. I don't belong here."

"Your father figured you did. He left you half of his mill because he believed you'd do a good job. He wanted you here. He wanted us to run the mill together." He grasped her chin, turning her to face him. "I know you aren't responsible for the fire at the mill. Just like the one years ago wasn't your fault."

She stared, her throat working, fighting to swallow over the thick lump.

"I know the truth. I know what happened to you that night." Leaning closer, he trailed the callused pad of his thumb across her cheek. "I know about the rape."

"How—" She sucked in a breath.

"J.D. found out the truth. He tracked down a guy named Jack who told him what happened." He sat back on his heels, his gaze never leaving hers. "Why didn't you tell anyone?"

"I did."

His brow furrowed, and he threaded his fingers through his hair and nodded. "You told Big Jim, didn't you?"

Tears overflowed her eyes and slid down her cheeks. "He…he didn't believe me. He thought I made up the story so I wouldn't be blamed for starting the fire."

Josh's mouth tightened into a thin line. A pulse ticked in his rigid jaw. He reached in the front pocket of his jeans and withdrew a red-and-blue-checked, cotton handkerchief and dabbed gently at her cheeks, wiping the tears. "I'm so sorry." His voice was rough. "I can't imagine how that made you feel. He deserted you when you needed him the most."

"He…he was drunk like he…he always was." She massaged the back of her neck. "After…after I told him…" She gulped, fighting to spew out the hideous words. "After I…I told him I'd been…raped. He laughed at me and accused me of lying." She brushed her tears away. "All he cared about was his damn mill. He blamed me for the fire."

"Pauline told me Big Jim stopped drinking the night you were attacked." He wiped her cheeks again. "Don't you see? He spent the next seventeen years punishing himself for what he did. He died a broken man."

"Why didn't he contact me?" She pressed a hand to her throat. "Why did he ignore me all these years?"

"Maybe his guilt was too overwhelming, and he didn't think he deserved your forgiveness." He placed his thumb beneath her chin and urged her to face him. "He loved you, Sharla-Jean. Until the day he died, he waited, hoping you'd come back and forgive him."

"Too late now. He's dead."

"It's never too late. If you forgive in your heart, he'll know. Somehow, he'll know."

She blinked away her tears. "How do you know?"

"Because I know what it's like to live with guilt eating away at you, day in and day out. The weight of the shame destroys your soul." His face was pale, his eyes haunted.

"Tell me," she whispered. "Tell me what happened."

Once again, he stared into the distance, though she knew he wasn't seeing the vista of glistening, snow-capped mountains and crystalline lake.

"When I was fourteen, my sister was kidnapped and murdered. She was only ten years old. I was supposed to be watching her, but I was too busy playing my video games. I didn't notice she'd gone outside to play with the dog. Not until—" His voice broke and his broad shoulders heaved.

Her breath hitched in her throat.

He faced her, his eyes empty hollows. "Losing Kayti destroyed my family. Her death filled us with darkness. It was as if we'd died with her." He grimaced. "We might as well have. No one blamed me, at least, not to my face. But it was my fault. I'm the reason my sister died that day. If I hadn't—"

"No." She grasped his hand, desperate to comfort him, to somehow ease his guilt. "Don't say that. It was a mistake. A simple mistake. And you were just a kid." But even as she said the words, she saw how little effect they had. Nothing she said would free him from his remorse.

He continued speaking as if he hadn't heard her, his voice wooden. "Mom died of a broken heart a few months later. Dad drank himself to death two years after that. I ended up in one foster home after another. None of them worked out." He shrugged. "I was angry all the time, mad at the world, at God, and most of all, furious I was still alive and Kayti wasn't." He tugged his hand free and rubbed his hands over his face, as if trying to erase the memory of the horrible event.

"I skipped school, drank too much, used drugs, got into trouble with the police…" He shrugged. "Anything I could think of to show everyone what a piece of shit I was."

Tears stung her eyes at his tortured confession. "Did they find the person who hurt your sister?"

"They arrested one of our neighbors. After the trial, he was sent to prison. He's still in jail as far as I know."

"I'm so sorry, Josh." Tears welled in her eyes, but she blinked them back. Crying wouldn't help him.

"The day I turned eighteen, I hit the streets, going from bad to worse." He shook his head. "I don't know how I stayed out of jail all those years, let alone survived. Then I arrived in Renton Falls." Incredibly, a small smile teased about his mouth. "I was boosting a car when your father showed up. Turned out, the car I tried to steal was his. Instead of calling the cops, he offered me a job. He saved my life."

She frowned. Josh's moving description of a man willing to give another person a second chance didn't fit any memory she had of her father. "He helped you?"

"I told you that you didn't really know him. In spite of everything he did wrong, all his mistakes, he was a good man."

"He helped you." Each time she said the words, they chipped away at the wall she'd built around her heart. She pressed her fingers to her eyes to stem the flow of tears.

"Big Jim saved my life. I don't doubt that for one second. If he hadn't been there for me, who knows what trouble I'd have gotten into." He sank down beside her, his thigh brushing hers.

They sat in silence as another flock of geese soared overhead, their honking cries filling the air. A fish jumped at the end of the dock, creating a loud splash. A late-season fly buzzed past, circling and landing on her leg. She waved it away and it flew off.

When he spoke, his voice was a rough croak. "I'm sorry I didn't tell you the whole truth the other night." He cleared his throat. "I guess I didn't want you to think less of me. I should have told you how Big Jim took me in and saved my life. He didn't care what I'd done in the past, he cared for the man he believed I could be, the man I am now." His warm breath fanned her face. "Don't you see? Your father loved me. He loved you too."

"I'm so sorry about your sister. I can't imagine…" She swallowed and once again tears blurred her vision. "Thank you for telling me." He'd bared his soul and by doing so, gave her a precious gift, the gift of insight into the man who was her father.

"I believe my sister forgave me for not being there when she needed me. I know in my heart she did." His dark gaze pierced her. "If you forgive your father, believe me, he'll know."

She dipped her forehead to his chest. "Thank you."

His palm cupped the back of her head. "Big Jim didn't know all the details of my past. He knew something messed me up pretty bad and was still eating away at me because he suggested I get help. He even offered to pay. The therapist told me writing my thoughts down would help." He shrugged. "What do you know? He was right. I've been writing in a journal ever since."

The journal! She wet her lips nervously. "About that." Her face heated. "I shouldn't have taken your journal, but I didn't read it. Really, I didn't."

He let out a deep breath. "I was always afraid someone would read what I'd written in there. I mean, I described everything…all the stupid, dumbass things I did, all the trouble I caused, all the heartache. I thought that if anyone saw what I'd written, everyone would forget all the good I'd done and focus on the mistakes of the past."

"I'd…I'd never do that."

"Really?" He arched a dark brow. "Isn't that why you took my journal in the first place? You were hoping you'd find something in there to discredit me?"

Her cheeks burned as his remarks hit home.

He nodded. "I thought so." He gave a dismissive wave of his hand. "It doesn't matter anymore. I've come to realize my past is my past. What I did back then is old news. I'm not the same person as I was then. I've worked my ass off to make Bromley a success. I'm proud of what I've accomplished. Nothing can erase that."

She swallowed hard under her crushing weight of guilt. He was right. The past was the past. People change. Her father had changed. She'd changed. Whatever Josh had done in his youth didn't matter. The man who knelt before her was a good man. A man she admired. "Look, Josh"—she reached beneath the neckline of her blouse and grasped the gardenia locket in her fingers—"I'm sorry for taking your journal. I had no right." The gold warmed under her touch, giving her strength. "I'm sorry for doubting you. I was wrong."

Silence stretched between them.

She held steady under his penetrating gaze, desperate for him to forgive her.

The corners of his mouth twitched. "I would have done the same thing if I were in your shoes."

She raised her eyebrows. "What?"

"It's important to seek an advantage when dealing with an adversary."

"Adversary? *I* was your enemy?"

He shrugged. "You were for a while. I figured the only reason you'd returned to town was to take the mill from me."

"I never wanted the mill."

"I know that now." He smoothed the back of his hand along the curve of her cheek.

She closed her eyes against the tingle of heat his touch aroused.

"I'm sorry for the pain I've caused you." His callused fingers rasped across her skin as he traced her lower lip with his thumb. "I had no right to accuse you of starting the fire at the mill. I should have trusted you.

303

I hope someday you'll see fit to forgive me." His eyes were pleading.

Her lips trembled as she smiled through her tears. "I forgive you, Josh. For everything."

He reached for her and wrapped his arms around her, drawing her close.

She snuggled into the comfort of his solid body and cried for his sister's senseless death, and the years she'd wasted hating her father. His cotton shirt was damp when she inhaled a shaky breath and sat back. "Sorry." She used his handkerchief to wipe her face.

"Tell me who raped you." His eyes narrowed, and the lines in his face hardened.

"I've already taken care of him." The night she confronted Tyler Maddox, she'd overcome her fear and sent him slithering away like the worm he was. Standing up to him had felt damn good; it still felt good.

His dark brows rose. "He deserves to be in prison for what he did."

"If the police become involved, I'll have to testify in court." She shuddered. "I couldn't bear to relive the nightmare in front of everyone and have all the sordid details exposed. I just want to forget the whole incident."

"Everyone in town believes you burned the mill to the ground. We have to set the story straight."

She shook her head. "Why should I care what they think? I'm going back to Portland. Besides, I've taken care of the matter. The real culprits will be in custody soon."

He arched a brow. "You know who started the fire?"

She gulped. *Damn. She'd said too much.* Josh wouldn't like the fact she'd asked Kevin to help locate the arsonists. Much better if he didn't know. Besides, once the guilty parties were exposed, all he'd care about was justice had been served. Risking a glance at him, she winced.

He watched her like a hawk, his gaze fierce and unrelenting.

"Look, Josh, I'm sorry, but you're going to have to trust me on this."

"Who started the fire?" His voice was demanding. "Tell me what you know."

She toyed with a lock of her hair, studied her fingernails, flicked a spot of lint off her pants, anything to avoid looking at him. "I don't know for sure who's responsible. It's just a theory I'm working on. It may come to nothing." She wasn't lying. Not really. Tyler's information could be wrong.

A lengthy silence stretched between them. His hand on her thigh flexed and relaxed. "What if you didn't go back to Portland? What if you stayed?"

"Stay here? Why?" She laid her hand over his, stilling his nervous flexing. "You don't need to worry. You have the letter I signed. The mill's yours. I'll come back whenever you need me to make an appearance, just like you wanted, but I won't interfere."

"I don't recall accepting your terms." His eyes darkened. "I can't run the mill by myself. I need you." His lips brushed her cheek as he whispered. "Besides, I've kind of gotten used to having you around."

"But, I—" The rest of her words were lost in a muffled squeal as his mouth covered hers. She stopped thinking and gave in to the rush of desire blazing through her. Opening her mouth, she welcomed the thrust and parry of his tongue. She slid her hand under his shirt and caressed the flat plane of his stomach, slipped over his prominent hipbones, and traced the ridge of muscle above his narrow hips, thrilling at the contrasting play of hard muscle and soft skin.

"Let's go inside." His voice rumbled in her ear.

She barely heard him over the rush of blood and heat threatening to devour her.

With a groan, he stood and swept her into his arms as if she weighed nothing. He carried her across the old wooden wharf along the path to the cabin. Climbing the steps to the porch, he kicked open the door and strode across the main room to the bedroom and laid her on the bed.

She reached for him, wanting, needing his heat, his touch.

He towered above her, his eyes dark pools of longing. And then he joined her in a fervid embrace, his mouth seeking hers.

Desperate to feel his heated skin, she ripped at the buttons on his shirt as his tongue entered her mouth and she tasted him.

His body stiffened, and he tugged his mouth from hers and jerked up. "Someone's here."

She moaned in protest, but froze at the pounding of heavy feet on the wooden floor in the outer room of the cabin. She fought to clear her passion-fogged brain. "Who—"

The door to the bedroom burst open, and Kevin Nelson stood framed in the open doorway.

Chapter 25

Kevin's usually well-groomed hair was disheveled, his eyes wild. A black smear darkened one cheek. His shirt was wrinkled and stained, a ragged tear ripped along one sleeve.

"What the hell?" Josh snapped. "Get out of here, Nelson. Now!"

Kevin ignored Josh's order and lurched into the room. His gaze swung between Sharla-Jean and Josh. He smirked. "Well, well, well, isn't this just peachy? I should have known I'd find the two of you rutting like a pair of mangy dogs."

Heat flooded her face.

Josh's arm muscles bunched beneath her hand as he clenched his hands into fists. "You'd better have a damn good reason for being here, Nelson."

She shivered at the venom in his icy voice.

To her surprise, Kevin grinned. "I couldn't let Sharla-Jean leave town without a proper goodbye, now could I?"

A frisson of unease rippled along her spine at the hatred in his bloodshot eyes. A swirl of madness lurked in the pale blue depths. "You're crazy."

Josh's hand slid over hers, his fingers tightening, warning her with his touch to be cautious. "You've said goodbye, now get the hell out of here before I—"

Kevin cut him off. "Before you what?" His eyes

were cold and hard.

She bit off a shriek as Kevin jerked a gun out of his jacket pocket. He pointed the barrel at Josh. "Come on, Morgan, go ahead. Hit me. I know you want to. Why don't you try now?" he taunted.

Josh's body tightened, every muscle tensing to spring at the other man.

"Josh, no, don't." She grabbed his arm. He resisted, trying to shake off her grip, but she held firm, knowing that to let go meant his certain death. Finally, the ripped tautness in his muscles eased, and he sat back, his chest heaving.

Kevin chuckled. "You're one lucky man, Morgan. You have a woman protecting you from your own stupidity." The gun in his hand never wavered, the deadly barrel pointed at Josh's heart.

"You bastard." Josh's eyes blazed, and a muscle in his jaw ticked. "Why are you here? What do you want from us?"

"I hoped we'd have a chance to talk before—"

"Before what?" Josh shrugged off her hold on his arm and bounded to his feet. "Before what, you asshole?"

Kevin pointed the gun at her. "Don't try anything stupid or I'll shoot your girlfriend."

A moan escaped her lips at the maniacal gleam in his eyes. She stared at the gun and gulped. The polished metal glowed in the light shining through the window. Kevin's gun was bigger than the one she'd found in her father's filing cabinet. The pistol he pointed was at least ten inches long. The opening at the end of the long barrel was a dark tunnel to Hell through which death would come.

His hand holding the weapon shook, and his finger caressed the trigger with a nervous twitch.

She shrank back. Was this how her life would end? Shot in cold blood by a crazed maniac?

Josh squeezed her hand, and she slid a glance at him.

Matching fear stenciled across his rugged features, but his lips curved in a reassuring smile, lending her courage. Something indefinable shone in his eyes, something fine and pure in this terrible moment when they hovered on the brink of death. His lips moved, and even though he didn't make a sound, she read his words as clearly as if he'd shouted them. *I love you.*

Joy soared through her. *I love you. Josh Morgan loved her.* The refrain rang through her soul, and with each echo arose courage to face the madman threatening them.

"Get up!"

Caught in the thrill of discovering Josh loved her, she didn't react for a moment.

Kevin towered over her, the wavering gun inches from her head. "I said, get up."

Her breath hitched in her throat. With shaking legs, she rose to her feet. Their only hope was to do what he asked, at least for now.

He pointed the hand not holding the gun toward the bedroom door. "Move. We're going into the other room." He scowled as he studied the bed with its disheveled quilt and rumpled pillows.

She stumbled forward. The cold metal of the gun barrel jammed into her temple. She yelped at the sharp pain.

Kevin grabbed her around the shoulders and

yanked her against his body. "Try anything reckless, Morgan, and I'll blow her fucking brains all over the wall."

She cringed as the rank odor of sour sweat blanketed her. Craning her head back, she used her eyes to plead with Josh not to do anything foolish. The idea of losing him made her weak in the knees, and she sagged in Kevin's arms.

"What the hell?" Kevin's hand snaked out, and he grasped her hair. "Don't fuck with me, you bitch."

Tears stung her eyes as he twisted his fist in her hair and jerked.

"You bastard! I'll kill you if you hurt her."

Josh lunged toward them, but Kevin ground the barrel of the gun deeper into her temple.

She whimpered.

Josh froze, his chest heaving, his eyes ferocious.

"No, Josh," she pleaded, "don't. Please."

She read his agony in his dark eyes, but he slowly retraced his steps and sat down on the bed. His face was the hardness of granite, his fists clenched by his side.

She blew out a shaky breath.

"Atta boy." Kevin's thin lips curled in a smirk. "Now, listen carefully. We're moving into the other room, and you're going to follow. No sudden moves, or she dies."

Kevin released his grip on her hair and shoved her ahead of him.

She stumbled, grabbing the doorframe to keep from falling. In the cabin's main room, she glanced back.

Josh followed, keeping a safe distance, his eyes watchful as he waited for the chance to attack.

The biting stench of gasoline hung heavy in the air, and her blood congealed. A red, plastic gas container rested on its side beside the cold fireplace. Liquid leaked from the spout, seeping into the old, wooden floor.

Kevin grabbed her shoulder, his fingers digging into her tender flesh. He pointed to a coil of rope and a roll of duct tape on the table. "Pick up the rope."

Her eyes stung from the pungent fumes, and she shook her head, trying to think over the reek of gas. How had he hauled all this equipment into the cabin without them hearing? Of course. She and Josh had been so wrapped up in each other they wouldn't have heard an army march through the cabin, let alone a car drive up.

Kevin tightened his grip on her shoulder, his long fingers digging deep. "Do it."

She picked up the length of nylon rope.

Kevin nodded. "Now tell your lover boy to sit in the chair." He pointed at one of the hard-backed wooden chairs by the table.

Josh crossed the room and sat as ordered.

"Tie him up."

She shook her head. Once Josh was tied, Kevin would kill them. She opened her mouth to refuse, but Josh cut her off.

"Go ahead, Sharla-Jean. Do as he says."

"Better listen to him." Kevin waved the gun in the air. "Tie him up like a good girl."

She studied Josh's face, trying to read his expression, but his stony features gave no hint of what he planned.

She knelt before the chair, and with trembling

hands, wrapped the rope around his ankles, all too aware of the gun pointed to her head.

"You're the one, aren't you, Nelson?" asked Josh. "You're the one who's been causing all the trouble at the mill. You've been busy vandalizing equipment these past couple of months."

Kevin's self-satisfied smirk didn't falter.

"You left the gas can in the storage room in the office and started a fire. When Sharla-Jean interrupted you, you shoved her aside and ran out. Then you started the fire at the mill."

She gaped. Kevin had set the fire? But Tyler had told her someone named Kane was involved. Her breath whooshed out of her, and she staggered back on her heels. "You're Kane." She stared at Kevin. "You're the one Tyler Maddox witnessed pouring gas on the drying shed."

Kevin grinned, and the hairs on the back of her neck rose.

"So, you finally figured it out." His grin widened. "I couldn't believe when you asked me to try to find a man named Kane." He chuckled. "You were so damn gullible." His gleeful grin widened. "Oh, and thanks for telling me where you'd be today. You made my life so much easier."

The enormity of what he'd done was almost more than she could bear, but she had to keep him talking until she could figure a way out of this nightmare. "You weren't alone. Tyler Maddox told me two men set the fire. Who helped you?"

Kane simpered. "Good old Tyler. He's such a loser. He'll do anything for drugs."

She stared with a sickening realization. "Tyler

Maddox was the other man? He helped you set the fire?"

"Score one for the lady." He licked his pointer finger and drew an imaginary number one in the air.

"But why? What would he hope to gain?"

"Tyler got wasted one night, and we had a little chat. He told me how you two got it on one night." He licked his lips and eyed her up and down. His gaze lingered on her breasts. "Apparently, you like rough sex"—he winked—"a lot."

Vomit filled her mouth, but she swallowed back the acrid bile.

He sniggered. "He's worried you'll go to the cops and tell them all about it." He shrugged. "I guess he figures they'll believe you now. You're not a rebellious little girl trying to get back at daddy anymore." His hand holding the gun shook, and his arm wavered, and then lowered. He scowled and raised his arm again and leveled the gun at her. His wild-eyed gaze zeroed in. "Tyler hates you. He hates the power you hold over him. With a little convincing from me, he agreed to set the fire at the mill. I told him you'd be blamed and either go to jail, or be forced to leave town. At the very least, your accusations against him wouldn't hold water. No one would believe anything a convicted arsonist said."

She struggled to make sense of his wild ramblings. "But Tyler's the one who told me about you...about Kane, I mean."

He gave a half shrug. "What can I say? You can't trust a druggie."

"You've been stealing from the mill," Josh burst in.

Kane cackled. "Like taking candy from a baby." His arm shook. The strain of holding the gun pointed at Sharla-Jean was evidently wearing on him.

"You told me my father hired you to find out who was stealing." Her voice was shrill as the reality of how he'd played her for a fool sank in.

Kane shrugged. "I lied." His eyes narrowed to reptilian-like slits, and he motioned with the gun for her to continue tying the rope around Josh's ankles. "Make the knots good and tight."

Her fingers were clumsy as she fumbled with the rope.

"You can thank dear old dad." Venom laced Kane's voice. "He's the reason I'm doing this."

"My father?" Beneath the cover of her hands, Josh tugged at the ropes with his feet. She turned and faced Kane, using her body to block his view of Josh, hoping Josh could loosen the ropes enough he could escape. "What does my father have to do with this?"

"Big Jim killed my brother."

"I don't believe you. Who was your brother?" Behind her, Josh's foot bumped her back as he worked free of the bonds.

Kane's eyes were unfocused, and he stared off into the distance. "Kale was the smart one in our family. He graduated from high school at the top of his class, but he didn't want to go to college. He wanted to work and save money for travel. We were going to see the world, the two of us." A smile twisted the corners of his mouth, and his eyes softened with a faraway glow.

"Kale worked at Bromley?"

He pinned her with a look, and she flinched under the gleam of madness lurking in the blue depths. "Oh, yeah. Your old man hired him right off. Started Kale on the green chain. I was in college, and he wrote me all about his new job and how much money he was making." His mouth turned down at the corners, and a deep furrow grooved between his brows. "Kale was a good worker. Within a week he was assigned to the debarker." His frown deepened. "And then everything went to shit."

She hesitated, leery of provoking his anger, yet desperate to keep Kane distracted for a few more minutes. "What do you mean?"

The whites of his eyes were streaked with red, his pupils black pinpricks. "He fell into the debarker."

Blood drained from her face as a horrific image of the massive debarker rose before her. The razor-sharp, steel spikes meant to strip the bark from logs would rip a man to shreds. Death would be instantaneous. Or, at least she prayed so. "What a horrible accident. I'm so sorry."

"Accident, hell! The lock-down key was broken."

She wrinkled her brow. How could that be? All the major machinery in both the sawmill and the planer had lock-down keys. The keys were essential security devices. The only safe way an employee could complete repairs on the immense machines without the fear of them starting up while he was in the midst of them was to ensure the lock-down key was secured in the proper position.

"You must be mistaken." Regular, scheduled safety checks were conducted on each machine's lock-down key. Any defects or wear marks were recorded, and if necessary, replacements were ordered. A safety officer, whose sole job was to make sure the equipment was secure, reported weekly to the mill manager.

Her father used to boast about the mill's safety record and how many accident-free days the employees had achieved. Employee safety was a priority at Bromley Forest Products. As long as his precious mill was safe, that had been all Big Jim Bromley cared about.

She inhaled a deep breath and softened her voice, hoping to instill as much empathy as possible. "I'm sorry about your brother, but what happened to him was a terrible accident. If my father knew a part was defective, he'd have had the machine repaired."

"Bullshit!" Spittle flecked the corners of Kane's mouth. "I found the original safety report. Your father knew the part was broken. He couldn't be bothered to repair a simple device. He was too damned concerned about making a profit. My brother died because of your father's greed." His eyes bulged as he shouted, and his cheeks flushed red. "Big Jim Bromley was a murderer." He shoved the gun against her forehead.

Her blood froze, and a whimper slipped out. This was the end, the moment he jerked the trigger and fired the gun. Mouth dry, she struggled to swallow. She closed her eyes, waiting for the bullet to tear into her.

"If Big Jim made a mistake, you can't touch him." Josh's voice was loud and filled with authority, impossible to ignore. "He's dead. Hurting us won't do any good."

Sharla-Jean opened her eyes and peeked at Kane. His attention was fixed on Josh, but the lethal gun remained centered on her.

Kane chortled, a cruel, harsh sound. "Oh, I've hurt him all right. I've destroyed his precious mill."

Josh's gust of laughter thickened the tension in the cabin.

What the hell? Sharla-Jean swung back. *What was he doing?*

He laughed harder.

"Shut up!" Kane took a threatening step toward Josh. "Shut the fuck up."

Josh snickered. "You're hilarious, Kane, you know that? Your whole revenge plan is a failure." Another chuckle burst forth. "You may have set fire to the mill and caused some damage, but we're rebuilding. Haven't you noticed? The mill will be back up and running in a couple of weeks."

Kane's face tightened in a rictus of a smile. "You're the one who's a fool, Morgan. While we've been here chewing the fat, my good friend, Maddox is starting another fire." He nodded, his grin stretching wide. "Amazing what a few cans of gas and some matches can do. Especially to a mill under construction."

Sharla-Jean couldn't prevent her sudden intake of air.

Kane sniggered and checked his watch. "Yep, that's right. Your mill will be a pile of rubble in a few minutes." He swung the gun back and pointed at Sharla-Jean. "Now comes the best part. I'm going to kill Big Jim's daughter." He grinned at Josh. "You get to sit and watch."

Knowing time was running out, Sharla-Jean dropped to the floor and rolled behind the couch.

Kane lunged and grabbed her arm, dragging her out in the open.

She yelped and kicked.

He avoided her feet and tightened his grip, his nails gouging the tender skin of her upper arm.

His maniacal laughter grew louder. "I'm not going to shoot you, you stupid bitch. Shooting you would be too easy, and easy sure as hell isn't what I have in mind."

"Let her go, you bastard," Josh snarled.

Kane grinned, exposing sharp canine teeth, resembling a rabid wolf. "My plan's perfect. Everyone will think your deaths are just another unfortunate accident. These old log cabins are tinder dry. Chimney fires are common. Places burn. Shit happens." He giggled. "All they'll find will be the ashes of two unfortunate lovers." He faked a sad pout and wiped pretend tears. "Boohoo. So sad, so tragic. Yada, yada, yada."

Without any warning, Josh sprang up, toppling the chair as he threw his body at Kane.

Sharla-Jean scrambled out of Josh's way. She jumped to her feet and spun, ready to help him in his attack.

A deafening blast filled the air.

She screamed.

As if in slow motion, Josh stiffened and collapsed on top of Kane.

She screamed again, an anguished howl of protest.

Kane shoved Josh aside, and Josh's limp body hit the floor with a loud thud. Kane's eyes were wild as he climbed to his feet, his face chalk white.

She scrabbled across the floor to Josh's motionless body. Tears poured down her face, but she ignored them as she grabbed his arm and tugged, heaving him onto his back.

His eyes were closed, dark eyelashes sweeping his gray face.

Her hands flew over him as she searched for the bullet wound. His shirt was wet with blood. Scorch marks rimmed a small tear in the soft cotton. She tore the shirt aside, ripping and tearing to get at the wound beneath.

Her breath rushed out in a whoosh. Blood welled from a small, puffy hole on his right shoulder, pooling and spreading bright red across his white skin and dripping onto the floor. She glared at Kane. "What have you done?"

Kane rubbed his eyes, looking bewildered. The cloak of insanity dulled his eyes. With infinite slowness, he raised the gun toward her. "Move away from him."

Ignoring him, she concentrated on removing Josh's bloody shirt. How could so much blood leak from such a small wound?

"Get up!"

She wadded Josh's shirt in a ball and pressed the makeshift compress on the wound, trying to staunch the steady flow of blood. A flash of movement flickered in the corner of her eye, and she twisted toward Kane.

His hand was raised, the fist clenched. And then he swung.

Her head snapped back, and she fell, slamming against the floor. Blackness surrounded her, but she fought against the dark. A fiery pain throbbed in her cheek, and the salty taste of blood filled her mouth.

"I said, get up, bitch."

Dazed, fighting off waves of agonizing pain, she blinked, fighting to clear her vision.

A smile lifted the corners of his mouth.

She shuddered at the cold malevolence in his pale blue eyes. "What are you going to do to me?"

He studied her for a long moment, his gaze sweeping over her, lingering on her breasts and hips. He arched a brow. "What would you like me to do?"

Her stomach clenched. She couldn't breathe. She slid a glance at Josh lying so pale and still on the floor. Blood had soaked the cloth covering his wound.

Inhaling a shaky breath, she shoved her pain and fear away and faced Kane. "You'll never get away with this. The police will know the fire wasn't an accident. They'll find you."

He smirked. "I'll be long gone by then." Keeping the gun trained on her, he used his other hand to dig in his pants pocket and withdrew a cigarette lighter. He held it up for her to see. "These little gizmos sure come in handy." He flicked the lighter, and a tiny, blue flame sprang to life. "Such a little thing, and yet so powerful."

Chapter 26

"You don't want to do this, Kane. Killing us won't bring your brother back." Even as she said the words, she knew they were futile. He was determined to kill them, and nothing she said would stop him.

"True, but revenge will sure be sweet." He narrowed his gaze. "When the daughter of the man who murdered my brother is dead and his company destroyed, I'll have avenged Kale's death."

Josh moaned, and she let out a breath of relief. He was still alive, but he wouldn't be for long. He was losing a lot of blood. "Josh isn't part of this." She pointed at his unconscious, bloody body. "You can't blame him for what happened to your brother. He wasn't working at the mill then. Why don't you let him go? He needs a doctor." If she could make him think twice about killing Josh, maybe she could figure out a way to save them both. If not, at least Josh would be safe. "I'm the one you want."

Kane spit a gob of phlegm on Josh's leg. "I never much liked him." He grinned. "Call this a twofer. Both of you dead for the same effort as killing one." The grin widened and he cackled. "Win-win, as far as I can see."

Fury seethed through her at his callous words. She was damned if she'd let this madman murder them. She wouldn't go down without a fight. If he was going to kill them, she sure as hell wasn't going to make their deaths easy. Without pausing to think of the consequences, she let out a roar of rage and kicked at the gun in his hand. Her boot-clad foot connected with his arm with a resounding crack, and the gun clattered to the floor.

In an instant, Josh was at her side, standing tall and strong in spite of his injury. He punched Kane in the face, a sickening crunch of bone and gristle.

Kane screamed in pain and raised his fists and charged at Josh.

With an agile shuffle of feet, Josh evaded the wild blows. He slammed into Kane and smashed his fist into his face again and again.

Sharla-Jean jerked back from the two grappling men and scrambled across the floor on her hands and knees. *Where's the damn gun?* There, under the table. Bending low, she slithered under the table and grasped the barrel of the gun and dragged it toward her.

The handgun was heavy, but using two hands on the grip, she lifted the gun and turned back to the men.

Kane's face was red, and sweat dripped off his forehead into his eyes. He was puffing and fighting for breath. The glimmer of rabid insanity blazed in his eyes.

In spite of his oozing wound, Josh hardly seemed winded as he pummeled Kane in the face, the shoulders, and side of his head. Blood oozed from a small cut by Josh's left eye where Kane had landed a lucky blow. With a loud curse, Josh smacked a solid punch to Kane's stomach.

Kane groaned and slumped to the floor, retching. He slid the hand holding the lighter out from his side, flexed his thumb, and the lighter flared to life.

"No," she screamed.

The lighter slipped out of Kane's hand and fell to the gas-soaked floor. A whoosh of yellow heat seared the air.

For a timeless moment, she met Josh's gaze across the sheet of flames.

Matching horror filled his eyes, but then he leaped across the growing wall of fire and gathered her in his arms. "Come on. We have to get out of here." In the next breath, the light went out of his eyes, and he wobbled, staggered a few steps, and his body folded.

"Josh!" She clutched his arm, holding him, stopping him from falling.

His anguished gaze met hers. "Sorry, babe. I…I can't go any further." He swayed and fought to stay upright. Cupping her chin, he leaned close and pressed his lips to her forehead. He slid a trembling palm over her hair, and then gave her a gentle push toward the door. "Go. Get out of here." His face paled, and he stumbled, and sagged, his knees bending as if they couldn't support him anymore.

"No!" She braced one arm across his back, and gripped his arm with her other hand as she took his weight. "I'm not leaving you. We're getting out of here together." Supporting him, forcing him to take one slow, stumbling step after another, they fought through the searing heat of the crackling flames toward the cabin door. Smoke stung her eyes, and her lungs burned, but she held onto Josh as if to a life preserver.

After an eternity, they lurched through the door and onto the porch. The fire scorched the air behind them.

She gulped in great draughts of fresh air as she dragged Josh across the porch and down the steps, away from the inferno, before collapsing on the ground.

Josh fell back with a groan.

She swiped her streaming eyes and gaped at the flaming cabin. Fire soared inside the small building like a living creature, climbing the log walls. Smoke billowed through the open door.

An agonized scream echoed from within the inferno.

"Kane!" She had to help him. She couldn't let him burn to death. Not even he deserved to die like that. Scrambling to her feet, she started to return to the blazing cabin.

"Sharla-Jean, no." Josh struggled to sit. His hand clutched her arm, stopping her. "It's too late. You can't save him."

"I have to." She shook him off, and once again turned to the fire, but froze when the front window shattered, and shards of glass exploded onto the porch.

With the sudden influx of air, the fire flared with new life. A loud roar rent the air, and the cedar shake roof collapsed. Clouds of ash and cinders filled the air.

Her gut gave a sickening lurch. *Kane was gone.* No one could survive the firestorm.

Josh's moan reached her over the furious bellow of the raging inferno. She spun back.

The remaining color drained from his face. His eyes rolled back in his head, his face went slack, and he sank back onto the ground.

Crouching beside him, she fumbled for a pulse, faint, but steady. Her breath expelled in a loud whoosh. A stream of blood seeped from the wound in his shoulder. She placed her hands over the hole and applied pressure. She had to get him to a hospital.

As if in answer to her prayers, sirens rent the air, echoing off the surrounding hills. A fire truck sped into the clearing, followed by an ambulance. Men spilled out of the vehicles. Exhaustion overtook her, and she sagged beside Josh. Help was at hand. The nightmare was over.

****

Sharla-Jean shoved open the door and stepped into the gloomy hospital room. The blinds were drawn over a large window. A weak pool of light from a lamp on a table set against the far wall provided scant illumination. The steady beeping of the machine beside the bed broke the heavy silence. Her eyes adjusted to the dim light, and she studied the readings on the monitor. The reassuring hills and valleys of the green line indicated Josh's condition hadn't worsened in the time she'd taken to get a cup of coffee.

She resumed her seat in the hard-backed chair beside the bed and clasped Josh's hand. His skin was warm, but his fingers remained motionless. The doctors told her his body was healing, but he'd likely remain unconscious for several more hours.

Afraid to let him out of her sight, she'd traveled in the back of the ambulance from the smoldering ruins of the cabin. As soon as they arrived at the hospital, he was whisked away to surgery.

The bullet had passed through his shoulder, missing a major artery. He'd lost a great deal of blood, and they'd given him a blood transfusion. With rest and time his body would recover.

The gash by his left eye was stitched in a fine line. His right eye was puffy, the skin around the socket discolored. His chest, under the thin layer of hospital blankets, rose and fell with reassuring regularity.

The low light and absolute stillness of the room soothed her soul, taking away the jagged edges wrought by the events of the past hours. She leaned back in the chair and stretched out her legs.

Kane had been willing to stop at nothing to avenge his brother's death. The cabin's old log walls had been soaked with gas, and the police found several empty plastic gasoline containers stashed in the woods behind the cabin. She shuddered. No question Kane had planned to burn Josh and her alive.

Fortunately, Kane's plan to destroy the mill had also been thwarted. Fred Kowalski, the night security guard had spotted Tyler Maddox sneaking two cans of gasoline onto the mill site and called the police. Tyler was arrested on multiple arson charges, though she'd heard he was protesting his innocence.

She glanced up at a light tap on the door.

The door swung open and J.D. Webster appeared in the open doorway. He motioned for her to join him in the hall.

She hated to leave Josh. If something happened while she was gone, she'd never forgive herself. In the time he'd been in the hospital, she'd only left his side when Pauline forced her to eat something. She rubbed the grit from her tired eyes. She couldn't remember the last time she'd slept. She'd dozed a few times in the chair beside Josh's bed, but those brief periods of awkward rest were punctuated by dreams of fire and death, and she'd awakened with terror in her heart.

J.D. coughed, impatience stamped on his round face.

Taking one last look at the man lying so pale and

still on the bed, she rose and headed toward the door. Once in the hall, she blinked under the glare of the dazzling fluorescent lights.

J.D. patted her shoulder. Compassion filled his eyes behind his thick lenses. "How long since you've slept?"

She shrugged. What did sleep matter when Josh was lying injured in a hospital bed?

He tugged on her arm. "Come on, let's get you something to eat."

"I can't leave."

The doctor who'd operated on Josh strode down the hall toward them, white coat billowing behind him. He turned to Sharla-Jean. "How's our patient today?"

"He's still sleeping."

"That's good." He pushed open the door to Josh's room. "Wait out here while I examine him. I won't be long."

She hesitated, but the doctor's gentle tone belied the firmness in his eyes.

"She'll be in the cafeteria." J.D. steered her down the hall to the elevators.

She slumped at a table in the busy cafeteria while J.D. filled a plate from the buffet and set the steaming mound of food before her. To make him happy, she lifted her fork and pushed the French fried potatoes, peas, and mystery meat immersed in greasy gravy around on the plate.

He stole a fry from her plate and nibbled on it. "I checked into the story Kane told you about his brother."

She sat forward on her chair, her tiredness gone. "What did you find out?"

He sipped his coffee and dabbed at his lips with a

napkin. "His brother's name was Kale Nordstrom. He was employed at the mill for a few months, and he was killed in an accident…crushed in the debarker."

She released her breath in a burst of air. "So, Kane's story was true. How did the accident happen?"

"His death was a terrible tragedy, but neither the police nor the industrial safety investigators found a mechanical reason for the accident."

"The lock-down key? Kane said the key was broken."

He shook his head. "The equipment was in perfect working order. The mill, and your father were absolved of all blame."

"Then how—"

He cut her off. "The official report was accidental death, but I spoke to a few of our long-term employees. The scuttlebutt around the mill at the time was that Kale was a heavy marijuana user. He smoked at work during his breaks. Word is he was stoned out of his mind, lost his bearings, and fell into the debarker. No lock-down key was involved."

He sipped again from his steaming cup. "From what I heard, your father did Kale's family a favor. Had Big Jim written in the accident report Kale Nordstrom was high on drugs at the time of the mishap, his family wouldn't have received a penny from the insurance company. Big Jim hushed up Kale's drug use, and the boy's family was fully compensated." He dabbed his mouth with the paper napkin. "A terrible tragedy, but…" He shrugged.

An upsweep of relief washed over her. Her father hadn't been negligent. He hadn't caused the death of an innocent employee. Sadness swamped her at all the heartbreak resulting from Kane's misunderstanding. If he'd known the truth, he'd still be alive, and Josh wouldn't be lying in the room upstairs. Tears stung her eyes.

"Don't shed any tears for Kane Nordstrom." J.D. placed his hands on the table. "He was insane. All his destruction, all his deceit, was a result of his insanity. Nothing anyone could have done or said would have prevented what happened." He eyed her uneaten plate of food. "Are you going to eat those fries?"

"You eat French fries?" Somehow she couldn't picture the staid attorney munching on greasy fries.

His face reddened and he nodded. "My Achilles' heel, I'm afraid."

In spite of the terrible events of the past days, she chuckled and pushed the plate toward him. "Enjoy."

He slathered the mound of fries with ketchup and sprinkled vinegar over the top. Picking up a loaded fry, he popped it in his mouth. Closing his eyes, he chewed. Once he'd swallowed, he opened his eyes and met her gaze. "There's more you should know." He wiped his mouth with his napkin. "The forensic auditors we hired located the missing mill funds in a bank account in the Cayman Islands under Kane's name. I'm in the process of having the money transferred back to the States and returned to the mill accounts."

She sat back and clasped her hands in her lap. "So, it's over."

He nodded and munched another fry. "The best thing we can do is put this behind us."

J.D. was right, but she couldn't help regretting the terrible waste of a life. The thirst for revenge drove people to great lengths. But vengeance wasn't cheap. It destroyed a person's soul. Look at all the years she'd wasted hating her father.

A cafeteria worker, her gray curls covered by a blue hairnet, bustled over to their table. "Excuse me, Miss, Doctor Johannson sent me to get you. Mr. Morgan's awake."

Sharla-Jean leaped from her chair and hurried across the cafeteria toward the double doors leading to the corridor. Not bothering with the elevator, she flung open the door to the stairwell and sprinted up the stairs, taking two steps at a time. She wrenched open the third floor door and sped down the hall.

The doctor stood in the corridor outside Josh's room. He held up his hand and stopped her before she rushed inside. "I'm sorry, Miss Bromley, only one visitor is allowed to see the patient at a time."

Focused on seeing Josh, she stepped around the doctor and grasped the door handle. His next words stopped her cold.

"Mr. Morgan asked to speak with Mr. Webster first."

Sharla-Jean's heart sank. Josh preferred to see his lawyer before her? Her eyes burned with unshed tears as J.D., red-faced and puffing, hurried down the corridor. The doctor opened the door to Josh's room and ushered J.D. inside. The door closed behind the lawyer with a whoosh of air.

With a brisk nod, the doctor strode down the hall.

She stared at the closed door, and then she plodded away with leaden feet. She wanted to cry, but most of all, she wanted to sink to the floor and let oblivion drag her away. Her heart shattered into a thousand pieces.

Tears streaming down her face, she stumbled past

the floor nursing station.

A nurse glanced up from her paperwork and called out to her.

Sharla-Jean shook her head and staggered on. No one could help her. No medicine in the world could mend a broken heart.

She lost track of time as she paced the long hospital corridors, passing open-backed hospital gown-clad patients trailing IV stands; doctors rushing by, their white coats flapping; visitors carrying bouquets of tissue-wrapped flowers.

He doesn't love you. The words reverberated through her like a death knell. The man she loved didn't return her love. Finally, her tears dried, and unable to walk any longer, she wrapped her arms around herself and sagged against a wall, staring unseeingly at the gleaming tile floor. *He doesn't love you.*

But what about in the cabin when he'd mouthed those very words? Had that been a lie, a boon to give her strength to stand up to Kane? Her instinct was to flee, but she'd learned it was impossible to outrun a broken heart. Josh was a part of her, and no matter how far she travelled, the agony of losing him would remain with her. But what if she were wrong? What if he did love her? If she left without finding out the truth, without telling him how she felt, she was a coward, and she deserved to be alone.

Her next move was the hardest she'd ever made, but gaining strength with every breath, she shoved away from the wall and thrust her shoulders back. With a determined stride, she retraced her steps down the maze of long corridors and up the elevator to Josh's floor.

She hesitated a heartbeat before she shoved open the door and burst inside.

Josh was pale, and shadows underlined the hollows of his eyes, but he was sitting up. Best of all, he grinned when he saw her.

Her insides melted as a fresh spate of tears threatened. She wiped her eyes and pasted a matching smile on her face.

"Where have you been?" His grin vanished, and a frown took its place. "I have half the nurses in the hospital looking for you."

Their gazes met across the room, and she shivered. She wanted to touch him and feel the beat of his heart beneath the tanned skin of his chest, but she remained where she was.

"Come here." His voice was a rough croak.

Her legs jerked to life, and she lurched to the side of his bed.

He clasped her hand. "I've missed you."

"I'm glad you're okay."

His gaze traveled over her face. "You look tired. J.D. tells me you never left my side." He tightened his grip on her hand. "Why?"

What did he want her to say? She loved him, and she couldn't bear to leave his side? That she'd rather die than live without him? Well, wasn't that what she'd returned to say? She opened her mouth to confess, but halted when J.D. strode into the room.

The urbane lawyer was frazzled, his hair mussed, sweat beading his brow and upper lip. He carried a large, white, rectangular package, which he placed on the bed.

"Is that it?" Josh nodded at the box.

J.D. mopped his gleaming brow with a cloth handkerchief. "I had to run all over town, but it's exactly as you wanted."

"Thanks. I owe you, J.D."

The lawyer beamed, his stodgy face lighting up like a young boy who'd just hit a home run. "Be happy." He shook Josh's hand, nodded at Sharla-Jean, and beat a rapid retreat. The door swung closed behind him.

Sharla-Jean turned to Josh.

His grin widened, exposing a row of even, white teeth. A dimple danced in his lean cheek. The tiny lines at the outer corners of his eyes crinkled.

Her heartbeat kicked up a zillion notches, and her breath caught in her throat. "What…what was that all about?"

"I asked J.D. to pick something up for me." He patted the white box.

She clutched the blanket, fingers digging deep. Her head was spinning. What was he so happy about? Her heart was broken into tiny pieces, and he sprawled on the bed, a foolish grin wreathing his too-handsome face. Of all the unfeeling—

He held out the white box. "This is for you."

She eyed the package. "What is it?"

"Open it and see."

Still she hesitated. She didn't want a thank-you gift. She wanted only one thing: his heart.

"For once in your life will you stop being so stubborn and open the damn thing?" He thrust the box at her.

She sat on the chair beside his bed, and with shaking hands, set the box on her lap and lifted the lid.

She moved aside a mound of white tissue paper and froze. Something red was buried among the layers of tissue. Trembling, she lifted a dress from the box and held it before her.

Not just any dress, but the most gorgeous gown she'd ever seen. Red wasn't an adequate word to describe the color. The gown's vibrant scarlet glistened in the sunshine streaming through the window. Tiny diamonds were sewn into the silk bodice, other shiny jewels sparkled along the narrow skirt. A lump formed in her throat, and tears filmed her eyes.

"Do you like it?"

"Like it?" She blinked. "It's…it's incredible. But why—"

"I've always liked you in red." He raised her hand to his lips and kissed her knuckles. "I want you to wear the dress at our wedding."

"Our *wedding*?"

His smile faltered. "That is, if you'll marry me."

This time she let the tears fill her eyes and overflow onto her cheeks as his words sank in. She giggled, a giddy carefree sound as her heart soared. She glanced from him to the red dress and back again. This wonderful man wanted to spend the rest of his life with her. Or did he? "Are you just saying this so you won't lose the mill?"

His eyes narrowed, and the sharp planes of his face hardened. "Is that what you think of me?" He rustled through the mound of tissue paper in the box and found a white business envelope and held it out. "Open this."

She lifted the flap and peered inside the envelope. Frowning, she tilted the envelope upside down. Dozens of tiny, torn pieces of white paper fell onto the bed. "I don't understand. What is this?"

"The agreement you signed."

She frowned, still not understanding.

"I don't want the mill, not without you." He clasped her hand and drew her closer. "Your father wanted us to work together running Bromley Forest Products. The mill was his gift to you. If you won't stay and work with me, I'll have J.D. sign the whole works over to Remington River. They can have it."

She chewed on her bottom lip as wonder filled her. "You'd do that? You'd give up the mill…for me?"

He nodded. "Just watch me."

She ran her hand over the soft silk skirt of the red dress and studied the torn paper bits scattered across the bed, and then she peered at him through her tear-filled eyes.

"Well?" He released her hand and crossed his arms over his chest. "You haven't answered my question. Will you marry me?"

"I need to know one thing first."

His smile faltered. "What?"

"What does the C stand for in your initials?"

"My initials?"

"JCM. It's written on the cover of your journal."

Two patches of red bloomed on his cheeks. "Cornelius. I'm named after my grandfather."

"Cornelius, eh?" A smile tugged at the corners of her mouth.

He nodded. "Is that a deal breaker?"

"Depends."

"On what?"

"On whether you love me or not."

He leaned forward, wincing as he captured her face

between his hands. "I love you, Sharla-Jean Bromley. I've loved you from the moment you strutted into the church at Big Jim's funeral in that sexy red dress and mile-high heels." His warm breath washed over her. "I love you more than life itself."

The coldness, so much a part of her life dissolved in the rush of warmth engulfing her. "Then I do, Joshua Cornelius Morgan. I most definitely do!"

He grinned and drew her into his embrace. His lips descended on hers, sealing their love.

A word about the author…

C.B. Clark has always loved reading, especially romances, but it wasn't until she lost her voice for a year that she considered writing her own romantic suspense stories. She grew up in Canada's Northwest Territories and Yukon. Graduating with a degree in Anthropology and Archaeology, she has worked as an archaeologist and an educator, teaching students from the primary grades through the first year of college. She enjoys hiking, canoeing, and snowshoeing with her husband and dog near her home in the wilderness of central British Columbia.

Visit her on Facebook:
https://facebook.com/cbclarkauthor
And follow her on Twitter:
https://Twitter.com/cbclarauthor
Check out her Blog:
https://cbclarkauthor.wordpress.com

Thank you for purchasing
this publication of The Wild Rose Press, Inc.

If you enjoyed the story, we would appreciate your
letting others know by leaving a review.

For other wonderful stories,
please visit our on-line bookstore at
www.thewildrosepress.com.

For questions or more information
contact us at
info@thewildrosepress.com.

The Wild Rose Press, Inc.
www.thewildrosepress.com

Stay current with The Wild Rose Press, Inc.

Like us on Facebook

https://www.facebook.com/TheWildRosePress

And Follow us on Twitter
https://twitter.com/WildRosePress